Redemption in Time

By

William Clark

D1445455

PART ONE

Best Intentions

"Cast a cold eye on life, on death,
Horseman pass by!"

WB YEATS

Table of Contents

Chapter 1

Eastern Montana - Yesterday

The hand had kept its secret all this time. The bones, fragile, light and paper-white in color, had been there all along, underfoot for years, through countless rainstorms, wind and cold. It had survived holding the evidence literally in its grip, a small hand by today's standard. People over a hundred years ago were physically smaller. Nutrition was poor, medical care nonexistent, so to a Sioux Indian warrior a fifty-year-old man was ancient.

With the soft brush strokes of a Renaissance painter, Greg Gander gently whisked away a quarter-size piece of Montana clay from the hand. The sweat from the effect of the late June Montana sun ran past the bottom rim of his glasses and dripped on his arm as more and more of the hand saw the light of day.

To Gander this was the best part of his job, being in the field away from the lab. To his great surprise, he discovered that on the middle finger of the hand a large turquoise ring was now visible. A huge rush of excitement surged through his body as he brushed back more dirt, exposing the clay-encrusted treasure. The ring, from the preliminary look, was exactly appropriate for the middle to late 1860's. "Slow down," he whispered out loud. He had to control the adrenalin. He had seen other dig sites damaged or ruined altogether by the over exuberance of people finding one thing of value while trampling or missing something of even greater importance or value.

He sat back looking up into the bright Montana sky as the sun hammered onto his back. A warm, faint breeze blew past his face carrying the scent of wild sage; the smell stirred something in him, a physical reaction of excitement. It was the smell of open ground, places of quiet desolation where no houses or freeways or taco stands or anything else had been built that announced modern men had been there.

Looking back at the shallow hole, he waved a small pinpoint metal detector close to the hand. Its main purpose was for locating small coins after you had used the big eighteen-inch loop detector to find the dig site. Expecting to hear a steady but mild tone from the device, the detector surged with an electronic squeal, a tone far too strong for just a small metal ring. He waved the pin-pointer again and heard the same high-pitched sound. He sat back, studying the exposed bones. There was something else in the ground, something under or near the hand that was registering the heavy electronic hit.

The hand was positioned in the clay palm down, exposing only the dorsal hand, the fingers and thumb curled under, gripping something. Gently, brushing back more of the dirt, he saw an odd yet strangely familiar object emerge. Stunned, he sat back, still not believing what he was looking at. It could not be – impossible! "What the fuck?" he whispered, leaning back over the hole. He quickly pulled a small garden trowel from his belt pouch and carefully dug around the edges of the hand until all the fingers and thumb were exposed and the object was in clear view.

C'mon he thought, *this had to be some kind of joke, a gag someone was playing on him.* He looked over at the four University of Montana grad students he had brought with him from Missoula. They were a good sixty yards away, carefully digging, their heads bent close to the ground. If they had been involved in this prank, then they were not showing it. He looked back at the hand trying to comprehend the importance of the discovery. The sheer craziness of the thing is what confused and deeply disturbed him the most. He bent down close to the hand, brushing back more of the dirt. He now saw that the hand was still connected to a shattered wrist and then to a portion of the forearm bones that ran to an almost nonexistent elbow.

Back at the hand, he carefully brushed the last bit of clay away that was covering the fingers, totally exposing what he had only seen partially before. He took out his small digital camera from his shirt pocket and laid the trowel next to the hole for scale. He took six pictures from different heights and checked his handheld GPS, noting the exact coordinates. He stood up, looking across the heat waves of the wide-open prairie, knowing that he would have to tell somebody else about this. He would have to show them this was real, that he hadn't just staged the whole thing for publicity. He recognized his need to share what he had found; yet he instinctively knew he could not, not now, not until he could prove that what he had discovered was really there.

Kneeling carefully beside the hole, he used a small medical forceps from his tool bag to gently grip the end of the object that was firmly gripped by the fingers. He took a small penlight from his shirt and read out loud the numbers on the object -"7.62". The numbers were clearly stamped on the end of the casing. In itself finding a single modern-day shell casing in a skeleton hand on the site of the Little Bighorn Battlefield would cause shock waves through the archaeological community, but what he was now looking at, still unable to mentally digest the sight of, were ten unfired 7.62 caliber machine-gun rounds still linked together.

****

Bob Cullen had been the lead control room operator at the Kit Carson PNM station for twelve years now. He had worked his way up, kept his head down and finally got the management position he had wanted. Kids were almost grown, and just last night he told his wife Julie that she needed to start planning that Bahamas trip they had talked about for the last ten years. He had vacation time coming, and by God he was going to take it. He pulled into the empty parking lot right at 7:30, took his aluminum coffee mug out of the holder and headed across the lot. He liked getting to the station early. It was quiet which gave him time to catch up on the night-shift events and any problems.

He pushed his PROX card through the reader and heard the gate-lock click, allowing entry. Inside he spotted Mike Gomez, the night shift supervisor with his feet up on the main console desk reading the paper. "Morning Mickey, anything going on?"

Gomez checked his watch. "Jesus, Bob, you're a half hour early," he replied looking over the top of his glasses.

Cullen sat down next to Gomez while picking up the night log. "Yeah I know. I like being here early. Anyway you can take off, hombre. I got it. Steve will be here at 8. "

Gomez pushed himself out of his chair. "Okay, it was all quiet last night; the only call was from the crew boss working out of the Shady Brook area at 23:30. It's on the log. Said they were unable to trace that big drain we saw last week. Anyway they are going to be out again today trying to find it."

"Okay, take off; the A-team is now on duty."

Gomez pulled on his jacket and picked up his lunch box. "Oh, yeah, before I forget, Collins over at the Palo Verde station let me know yesterday that the NRC investigator dropped by their office asking about the big hit last week."

Cullen put his feet on the desk. "Yeah, not surprised," he replied. "A two-Gig surge throughout the entire grid is going to be noticed. I just hope the field crews find the source."

"You itching to get back out there, you know, get back in the truck for old-time sake?" asked Gomez.

"Not on your life, my friend; I am very content to be in the rear with the gear. Besides I am way too old to be climbing poles and dropping down into pits."

Before Gomez could reply, both grid-alarms went off and then the third. "Jesus," whispered Cullen, sitting up in his chair.

Gomez quickly rolled up a second chair as the station phone rang. "Yeah, Gomez here." He pointed at Cullen to pick up the other line, which was now ringing; in fact all four lines were activated.

"Yeah, we registered the same thing here." Covering the phone with his hand, "Palo Verde just registered a 2.5 Gig hit," he announced to Cullen. As suddenly as the alarms were activated, they went off. Both men sat stunned, watching as the gain needles on all three panels slowly started dropping to normal levels.

Cullen quickly reviewed the numbers now coming up on the display. "Jesus Christ," he whispered. "We just got hit across the board... I'm talking Farmington, Afton, Lordsburg, Palo Verde and us."

"What can possibly pull that kind of gain?" asked Gomez, quickly punching in data from his console.

Cullen thought for a moment. "We gotta call the NRC. The only things I can think of that can pull that kind of juice across the grid would be a nuclear generator or a freakin Particle Accelerator."

Gomez pulled the lot-map up on his computer. "I got a signature," he announced excitedly. "That flash came out of the Shady Brook area about 15 miles from here."

Cullen rolled his chair over looking at the map. "Get on the phone to the Feds right now, Mikey. The only things in Shady Brook are vacation homes and maybe somebody with a Goddamned nuclear reactor in their basement. We definitely have a problem."

****

Gander had been in the Miles City Community college lab since before dawn staring at the pictures he had up-loaded into his computer. The JC had graciously given him and his team lab space for the two weeks they were on the site. He still had not told anyone about what he had discovered. He had excavated the hand and the ammunition as discreetly as he could and was now waiting for the toxicology report on the residue soil that he had scraped off the bullets. Maybe erosion had somehow moved the linked ammo into the bone field. Maybe it was just one of those freakish anomalies that sometimes happen and he was making way too much of it -maybe.

Several minutes later, he pulled the read-out from the machine - samples were normal, nothing other than trace amounts of copper, zinc, carbon and iron, simple eastern Montana dirt. To get the answers he needed, he would have to go about it in a different way, a different direction. He opened the small sample drawer and used his forceps to lift out the small belt of linked ammunition. For the tenth time, he cross-checked the downloaded picture of 7.62 machine gun ammo with the sample he had found; they were identical. An idea suddenly flashed across his mind - if the bullets were modern, maybe there were modern fingerprints or DNA residue on the casings.

He found his cell phone and dialed the number to the Missoula County Sheriff's Department. "Yes, this is Dr. Gander from the University. I would like to speak to Rob Jamison in your lab please. Yes ma'am, I'll hold." Over the last several years he had worked with the department when they had come across human remains on other dig sites throughout the Missoula County area. Most of the time, the bones found were on old Indian burial grounds. On two occasions they had been the scenes of homicides. On both cases he had been called as an expert witness for the prosecution concerning what he had found. The Sheriff's department CSI team was one of the best in the state, led by Rob Jamison, who over the years of working together had become his friend. After a moment, Jamison came on the line. "Hey, Greg, how you doing? Still chasing those pretty grad students?"

"They are getting faster, and I am getting slower, my friend. Hey listen, I know you're real busy, Rob, but I think I need your help on something."

"Sure, wadda'ya got?"

"Well, I found some modern-day linked 7.62 machine gun ammunition on one of our dig sites and was wanting to see if there might be any prints on it. You guys still using the MXRF print machine?" He had used the same machine on other digs that had turned out to be crime scenes.

"Yeah, we do. You think this is connected with something illegal? If it is, it's way out of my jurisdiction. I mean you're clear over near Miles City and I am in Missoula, nearly five hundred miles away."

"No, this is not crime scene material; it's just an odd thing to find, and it would be a big favor to me if you could run this stuff through your magic machine. I need to know who has been running around our dig sites."

There was a long pause on the phone. Finally Jamison spoke up. "Yeah, no sweat, Greg. Send me what you have, and I'll run it through IAFIS if I get anything."

"Thanks, Rob. I'll be here for the next week, and then I'm heading back to Missoula. I owe you on this one."

"Better believe it, pal. This is at least a two-beer deal. I'll check in with you if we get something. Hey, I have to get to court. I will be looking for your bullets. Gotta go."

"Thanks, Rob." *Jesus,* he thought ending the call. He was already starting to lie to his friends, and he hadn't told any of the other members of the team what he had found. In his gut he knew he shouldn't, and that is what disturbed him most. His head was telling him one thing, but his gut was saying something else. No, he would have to tread lightly with this; something important was about to happen, something that he intuitively knew would change everything.

****

Taylor no longer fought the vibration nor the hundred-channel fear he felt during the process. He let it roll over and through his body, knowing now what would soon follow. The nausea and vomiting and the sustained motion sickness would be intense, sometimes lasting hours. On the Quantum side of the procedure it was getting easier; on the physical side the process was horrible.

As he fought to keep the tight fetal position that he had adopted, he took some comfort in knowing that his self-imposed workout routine was now providing measurable results. His core was stronger and he had much better cardio reserve although he knew that a major body transformation from a 59-year-old man who had done limited physical exercise was pretty much out of the question. Seconds later, he felt the now familiar massive gust of frigid air blow by and then the immediate deadness of sound. The uncontrollable feeling of panic soon followed as he fell, tumbling out of control the last few feet.

Aside from the motion sickness, this was the part of the process he hated the most, the sensation of being propelled through total darkness into or onto the unknown. It was like jumping off a cliff in the dark. He had been working on everything from body position to object reference points, trying to make his entry less violent, less painful. Nothing had worked so far, nor had he been able to calculate his arrival in daylight or darkness.

A specific geographic location was fairly easy to hit, usually within 10 to 12 feet. Residual emotional energy remained a constant giving him a straight-line vector. If the emotion had been particularly intense, such as a large battlefield or some natural disaster, the markers were easy to pick up. The one thing that was not a constant was if someone had built something since his last visit. A horse trough, a curb or even a building presented very real hazards on entry. Being dumped onto a paved or hard-packed dirt road tore his clothes and left him filthy, a condition that made things that much harder to explain. One of his biggest fears was that of getting injured or worse, knocked unconscious and then treated by local medical people. Trying to explain his arrival or worse, why he had to leave at a pre-designated time would be impossible.

Seconds later he caught the first flash of ambient light and then an unexpected sound of children's laughter. He thudded to the ground almost in a seated position. His speed was still high as his velocity slid him across the cobblestones and into the side of a large wooden trash box with a heavy thump. He sat for a moment desperately trying to control his breathing and slow his heart rate. *Christ,* he thought, *that was a violent transition.*

As his vision cleared, he could see that he had been dumped into a narrow alley illuminated by two dimly lit gas streetlights at the far end. As he wretched for the first of many times that would follow, he saw that he had an audience of children - children who were now staring wide-eyed and opened-mouth. They were standing in a small semicircle less than ten feet away, unable to speak.

Several awkward seconds passed until a little girl in pigtails spoke up, her voice barely a whisper. "Are you an angel?"

Taylor wiped his chin, still trying to catch his breath. "No, sweetheart, I just fell off the roof." He looked at the stunned faces of the children as they continued to stare. "Are you kids okay? I... I didn't hit anyone did I?"

The children shook their heads. "Momma said we could play out here till supper," announced one of the other girls quietly. Taylor guessed her age to be about nine or ten.

"Oh, that's fine," he replied, slowly getting to his feet and inspecting the small tear in the knees of his pants. *Just once*, he thought fighting the dizziness, *just once, I would like to arrive not looking like he had been mugged.*

In the distance he could hear the comforting sound of a slightly out-of-tune piano and of men laughing. He was near a tavern, maybe the one he was looking for. He vomited again not able to hold back, making the small circle of children back up. One of the little girls ran off calling for her mother; one of the older girls standing nearby stepped up. "My sister went to get my mother, mister. You look really sick."

Taylor waved off the girl's concern. "No, no, it's okay. I'm fine. Please don't bother your parents." He had to start moving or this was going to get complicated. Taking a deep breath, he steadied himself and started walking down the alley towards the street just as a heavy, wheeled, horse-drawn wagon stacked with beer barrels rumbled by.

A cool night breeze blew past his face as he stepped out into the street. The air was filled with the scent of fresh horse dung, stale beer and wood smoke. Across the street in the large tavern he could see people moving around in the orange glow of the gaslights.

As he walked closer, he could make out the garishly painted sign on the façade above the door. Amazed at how well he had done on his calculations, he read the name out loud - "Station Café and Tavern." He had found it, landed practically on the doorstep. A female voice from across the street startled him. "Sir, sir, are you injured?" Taylor turned. A short, middle-aged woman stood under the streetlight holding the hand of one of the girls he had seen in the alley. "My daughter said that you fell off a roof. Are you all right?"

This was exactly the kind of thing he had been trying to avoid. "Yes, madam, I'm fine. Just a stumble."

"But, momma, he was really sick. I saw it," announced the girl.

Taylor knew he had to end this conversation quickly. Surely a husband would soon show up or maybe even local law enforcement. "I can assure you, Madam, I am fine. Thank you for your concern," he replied, working hard at correct period English. "Good-evening, Madam," he turned and quickly walked away while doing everything he could to keep from retching where he stood. Mercifully he made it across the wide street and stepped into the shadows of the building before vomiting. After several minutes, the dizziness was almost gone and he collected himself in the darkness. The woman and child looked in his direction for a moment and left, hopefully satisfied with the answers he had given.

Stepping back into the dim streetlight, he checked his wallet, making sure the paper currency was still tucked inside. On several other trips he had brought the wrong kind of money and had been turned down for food and drink. Getting the correct currency for the period and the correct attire were proving to be some of the more difficult parts of his preparations. Some objects came through; some did not. Certain metals such as titanium and platinum never made it for some reason.

Taking in a deep breath of cool night-air, he walked up the steps of the tavern. He needed to sit down, relax, and blend into the scenery. He smiled to himself as he stepped inside the boisterous room letting the ambiance and the smells of cigar smoke and whisky wash over him. Yes, he told himself, Missoula, Montana, in 1901 had a definite smell. He was going to thoroughly enjoy the evening. By the time he reached the bar through the crowded room, he was feeling fine.

*****

Gander recognized the Missoula 406 prefix on his cell phone and answered it on the second ring. It had been four days since he had over-nighted the ammunition to Jamison at the Sheriff's department. "Hey, Rob, hope you got some good news."

"Howdy, Greg, yeah I do. Kind of a head scratcher though. Are you sure this stuff wasn't found at a crime scene?"

"Nope, just a dig my team and I are on. Why? What's the problem?"

"Well, how long did you say this was in the ground?"

"Not sure. Probably a good while. Years maybe," replied Greg.

Jamison paused. "I don't think so, pal. Prints degrade pretty quickly from mud, water, weather, and generally from being exposed to outdoor conditions. But on one of the shell casings, I was able to get a pretty good print, probably only a couple days old at most."

Greg was stunned. "I, ah, are you sure? This stuff was found in a very old grid."

"Yeah, I'm sure, pard. Got an ID hit on it from the IAFIS also. The prints come back to a guy named Bruce Edward Taylor. The Feds had it on file because of his government clearance. Ah, let's see here, okay here we go. I'm looking at the computer now. Anytime you contract on a Department of Defense job or anytime you need a government clearance, you get fingerprinted. This guy has a current Federal clearance, TS. I guess that stands for Top Secret. He has a completed SF-86 on file and because I asked for the info from a law enforcement organization, they sent me a copy. It lists his contact info, home of record, relatives, stuff like that."

"Can I get a copy of that?" asked Greg already knowing the answer.

"Ah, no-can-do, ol'buddy. This is private background stuff that really cannot be shared. But what I can tell you is that he lists a home-of-record residence in a town called Shady Brook, New Mexico. I think that's near Taos. I'll text you his address in a minute. That's about as much information as I can give you, my friend, other than the fact that he is not wanted and his place of employment was Sandia National Laboratory as of two years ago. I think that's why he needs a clearance. All kinds of hush, hush government shit going on there."

Greg sat down, trying to digest the information. "I, ah, thanks for the information, my friend. I'm going to check out a few things here and then I'll get back to you."

"All right, Greg. Let me know where this goes. Personally I think somebody is pulling your leg, either that, or you got people shooting a machine gun on your dig site, and by the looks of it, it's your Mister Taylor there."

"Thanks, Rob. Like I said, I am going to check on a few things and then I'll fill you in, all right?"

"Counting on it, my friend. Hey, I gotta go. Call me when you hit town. Looks like we have a lot to talk about."

"All right, I'll give you a shout when I get back," replied Greg. He ended the call and then read the address on the incoming text message - *Bruce Taylor, 165 Holston road, Shady Brook NM.* He wrote the name and address in his notebook feeling a deep unease flush through his body. This was at least a place to start - a name, an address, and an occupation. In a strange way, he was relieved that at least one other person knew a little bit about what he was looking into. Carrying this kind of discovery alone was getting wilder and heavier by the moment. If things got any more bizarre, he could not think of a better guy than Rob to be there when it did. Within the hour he had booked a flight to New Mexico and was headed to the airport.

Chapter 2

Taylor had been in the lab all morning trying to calibrate the Pellicle beam splitter on the laser table. The splitter itself was a circular anodized aluminum hoop two millimeters in diameter with an ultra thin nitro cellulose membrane stretched across. The purpose of the splitter was to split a beam into both infrared and green light.

The film would transmit ninety-two percent of the light while reflecting eight percent. He had been trying to build a crude, yet efficient signaling device or target indicator that would help in course calculations. When he had worked at Sandia, what seemed like a century ago, he had been one of the main innovators of the Multi Spatial Targeting System currently being used today on all United States Military fighter aircraft. The MTS was a laser so accurate it could put a thousand pound LGB into a twenty-four-inch square ten miles out.

He knew there had to be a way to shoot a vector from a fixed location to wherever he was physically standing on a pre-designated time. This signal or shot would be the highly calibrated return beacon. In the past he had only been able to return within several yards of his original entry, which had resulted in minor, but no less painful, collisions with fixed objects. He simply could not keep crashing into lawn furniture and outdoor yard ornaments on return.

He liked working in his lab alone, enjoyed the envelope of quiet concentration the work put him in. He would spend hours working an equation or an experiment, his mind oblivious to the trappings of everyday life. He found the social interactions of normal life - dinner out, movies, casual conversations of wives/husbands to be dull, silly. In fact he had used those same words to the only woman in his life that had put up with his aloof personality, his tepid emotions.

He had married Bonnie a year out of grad school, having met her in her senior year at Berkley. At first she found his brilliance endearing, interesting, but after 21 years of emotional neglect, dinners alone, and separate beds with no real hope of ever recapturing the spark they briefly once shared, she left.

Sometimes, at night after way too much Scotch, he would think about her, pick up the phone, and stare at the number he would never dial. He would remember how she came to him, her nervous smile, the smell of her hair, the softness of her skin; all the tender memories pushed the needle of pain deep in his heart, a pain no amount of Scotch could ever take away. He still loved her, always would.

For the hundredth time this week, he pushed the thoughts of Bonnie out of his mind and willed himself to focus on the problem at hand. Lately he had met several women who had reminded him of her. It seemed her ghost was everywhere. He slowly turned on the Argon gas valve and then off again, checking the needle. He made a mental note to himself to have more of the gas delivered; it was vital to his experiments. The vexing problem he now faced was the thermal relaxation rates of magnetic nano particles in the presence of magnetic fields. Not finding constant continuum navigation, a problem that if not corrected, could cause time differentials decades apart.

He powered up the generator and then checked the beam pulse duration, making sure he was within limits. He then slowly integrated the coaxial gas to prevent plasma oxidation and absorption. He checked the laptop feed as new data started to download. Just as the experiment was starting to provide some answers, the front doorbell, which had been wired into an amplifier to be heard in the basement lab, began to ring. The one thing he had learned over the last several years is that ignoring people who came to his door was not a very sound strategy for keeping the curious at bay. If they heard a noise in the house while knocking on the door, they would not go away but would become more persistent in talking to him.

He turned the power off, removed his safety goggles and apron, and tried to imagine who might be ringing his doorbell at ten o'clock on a Tuesday morning. "Yes, coming," he announced after locking the basement door. Looking out the living room window, he didn't recognize the white sedan parked in his driveway. He opened the door just wide enough to expose his face. "Yes, can I help you?"

"Hi, are you Bruce Taylor?"

Taylor had never seen the middle-aged man now standing on his doorstep before. "Ah yes, how can I help you?"

"Sir, my name is Greg Gander, and well, I don't know how to start explaining this, but I need to ask you a few questions."

"Are you a police officer, Mister Gander?" questioned Taylor.

"Ah, no sir, I'm an archaeologist."

"A what?"

"An archaeologist. I am a professor from the University of Montana in Missoula."

Greg quickly opened the manila folder he was carrying and pulled out one of the eight-by-ten photos of the linked ammunition. "Sir, I found this on one of my dig sites. Can you tell me why your fingerprints were found on this?"

Greg watched the color instantly drain out of Taylor's face as he looked at the photo. "I -ah-I- I think you need to come in," he replied, his voice nearly a whisper.

Greg stepped into the room, immediately noticing that there was barely any furniture or signs of anyone actually living in the house. The large living room had several cardboard boxes stacked neatly on the floor below the large picture window. Through the hallway, Greg could see a dining room with a table and one chair. There were no pictures on the walls or family knick-knacks anywhere to be seen.

"Ah, Mister Taylor, as I said I am not the police, nor am I conducting any kind of formal investigation," announced Greg. He could see that the photograph he had shown Taylor had upset him deeply. "In fact, the only way I found you was that your finger prints were on the shells. I had a law enforcement friend of mine run them through the Federal database, and because you have a government clearance, your identification came up."

"Oh, my God," groaned Taylor, looking as if he might pass out. "I really need to sit down, Mister Gander. I am feeling sick."

Greg quickly stepped into the bare dining room and retrieved the chair. "Here you go," he replied, allowing Taylor to sit down. Greg pulled up a small stool from the corner and sat. "Sir, I really did not come here with the intention of accusing you of anything or upsetting you. I just needed to find out for my own sanity how the objects I found on my dig site were connected to you. I'm sure there has to be a logical explanation."

Taylor thought for a moment. "You say that law enforcement has my fingerprints? Am I going to be charged with a crime?"

"No, not that I know of, Mister Taylor. I came here because I found modern day automatic weapons ammunition in the hand of an Indian who has been dead over a hundred years. That's why I am here."

Taylor stood up and slowly walked over to the picture window. "Well, I guess it was just a matter of time." He snorted a laugh while looking out into his yard. "Time" he whispered.

"What's that, Mr. Taylor?" questioned Greg, not able to hear what he was saying.

"Greg, may I call you Greg?" questioned Taylor turning back from the window.

"Of course."

Taylor sat back down, sighing heavily, "I guess the time has come for me to start trusting someone, anyone actually. You did say you were an archaeologist, correct? A scientist?"

"That's correct. I'm a tenured professor at the University of Montana in Missoula, have been for the last 12 years," replied Greg.

"Well, Greg, I have known you, what- about ten minutes - and I am about to tell you something that is probably the most extraordinary thing you have ever heard."

"Okay," replied Greg smiling, "I'm all ears."

Taylor knew he was up against the wall on this. He had been running from a truth about what he was really involved with. He had been getting away with something beyond the pale of human experience. He had been selfish, not allowing anyone to know of the achievement, chalking up the rationale to his or her possible misunderstanding of the complexity or the enormity of what he had accomplished.

He had studied the pathology and mental process of people confessing great and terrible secrets to complete strangers. The Catholic confessional was a prime example. A believer, who carries a huge burden of a terrible secret, a sin, and steps into a box and reveals the secret to a stranger, feels a release, a sense of absolution. He needed to tell someone, needed to have some kind of validation for his discovery.

Gander could see that Taylor was wrestling with some kind of emotional quandary. The weight of whatever he was carrying seemed to be immense. "Like I said, Mr. Taylor, I'm sure there is an explanation I can live with."

"Not one you would believe, Greg," replied Taylor looking at the floor. "Nobody would."

"Well, like I said, I'm all ea…"

"The ammunition is mine," interrupted Taylor. "I put it there."

"How were you able to put it there? That dig site has been off limits to the public for a year?" questioned Greg.

"You should have found more. I'm surprised you didn't find the weapon that fired it."

"Were you target shooting? Are you a gun guy or something?"

"Not really. It's very hard to explain. You see that ammunition was dropped 8 days ago."

"Impossible. I found that ammunition last week, dug it up myself," replied Greg, still not having a clue as to what Taylor was trying to say.

"Well, it really wasn't 8 days ago, well, not your 8 days ago, but my…. It was actu…."

"You know what, that's fine," interrupted Greg. "If you don't want to tell me, that's fine. As I said, I am not a police officer. I just found something unusual and needed to try and get some answers. That is all." He stood up pushing his stool back in the corner. "I really don't have a lot of time; I have a flight to catch in about two hours."

"You're going to miss your flight, I'm afraid," announced Taylor, standing, while leveling a steady gaze, "I need you to see what I have in my lab."

"That's kind of a creepy way of saying something. You haven't got a basement full of knives and meat hooks do you?" asked Greg smiling.

Taylor walked over to the heavy basement door and unlocked it. "Like I said, I think you're going to miss your flight." He then snapped on the light and headed down the stairs.

Greg stood in the empty living room battling with a sudden fear of what Taylor was getting to while at the same time wanting to know what was really going on. For a second, the thought of the bearded eccentric being some kind of dangerous reclusive killer flashed across his mind as he headed down the short flight of stairs. The sight at the bottom of the stairs stunned him. He was amazed at how big the basement was. It was at least 80 feet across and fifty or even sixty feet wide. The floor and walls were painted a spotless white in color, which was only amplified by the rows of large florescent lights hanging down. It was astonishing how bright the room really was.

Four eight-foot-high commercial grade generators stood against the far wall humming with power. A laser-table ran the length of the room, ending at a large eight-by-ten sheet of two-inch-thick plate steel. The rest of the room was filled with large black marble-topped tables stacked with blinking LED readout panels, relay switches, and hundreds of active circuit boards. In the center of the room was an eight-by-eight foot square taped on the floor with a small metal stool in the center. Two-inch thick conduit pipe ran the entire length of the walls packed full with high voltage wiring, all culminating into the sides of the large grey generators at the far end.

"My God," whispered Greg, trying to take it all in. "You must be pulling down massive amounts of power to run all this."

"Yes, I am," replied Taylor turning on several more lights and wall panels. "For what I am doing, I need every volt I can get."

"Okay, "announced Greg walking over to one of the larger circuit boards. "You have my attention. What's all this for?"

Taylor picked up a small green hardbound ledger from one of the tables and handed it to Greg. "How much do you know about Quantum Mechanics?"

"Not much," replied Greg, opening the book. "Is that what you're doing here, some kind of advanced electrical studies or something?"

"No, it's a little more complex than that. I've made a discovery that is probably the greatest in the history of Mankind."

Greg scanned through the book and saw that it held column after column of what appeared to be twelve-digit geographical grid coordinates. "Okay," replied Greg starting to get tired of the cryptic exchange, "why don't you just cut to the chase and tell me what's going on."

"The coordinates in that book represent all the places and spatial references I have physically been to. I'm a traveler."

"A what?"

"A traveler. I have discovered a way to bend the space time continuum and physically move through it."

"Okay, Bruce, listen I really don't know what you're doing down here, but I really do need to know how you were able to get into my dig site and contaminate it with this ammunition. I doubt any real law was broken, but I will probably turn what I know about this over to my friend at the Sheriff's department."

Taylor seemed genuinely alarmed at the threat. "No, really Greg, you have to listen to me when I tell you that what I have done is real."

"All right, Bruce, first of all, time travel is impossible, a myth, science fiction. Now, I know you are a scientist of some kind and have worked at Sandia in New Mexico, but c'mon. Do you really want me to believe that you're a time traveler, really?"

"Yes, I do, because I have, numerous times. I've gone to the past, walked around, met people, had a meal, spent money, and used the bathroom for God's sake. Yes, I want you to believe me."

Greg had no idea what to say. The only conclusion was that Taylor was a deeply disturbed individual who had somehow gotten onto his dig site and contaminated the ground. Owning belt-fed ammunition was not a crime, so going to the sheriff's department with what he found would accomplish nothing. "Okay, Bruce, I'm just going to go. Good luck with whatever you're doing."

"How can I prove to you that I am not fabricating this whole story? What do I need to do to convince you?"

"Why do you have the need to convince me of anything? I am not the police and I doubt you have committed any crime, so what difference does it make?" Greg handed the ledger back. "Here you go, Bruce, sorry I bothered you about this."

Taylor took the ledger. He had the look of a child that had been punished for something he didn't do. His feelings looked genuinely hurt. "I- ah -I understand." He set the ledger on one of the tables. "I have been working for a very long time on this, Greg. I've had many victories in the research and just as many challenges, and I have done it alone. I guess, on a basic human level, I just wanted to share my discovery with someone."

Greg checked his watch, "Tell you what, I have a few minutes. Why don't you tell me what you have been working on, and let's see if you can make me a believer."

Taylor smiled, "I can do better than that; I can take you there."

"Take me where?"

"Pretty much anywhere you would like to go."

"You mean, in the past?"

"Yes."

"Time travel?"

"Yes."

Greg was surprised at Taylor's conviction; he really seemed to believe what he was saying. "Okay, Bruce, what does a person have to do to be a time traveler?"

Taylor sat down and pulled a small notebook from his shirt pocket. "Well, first I have to tell you what I have learned. This is not an exercise to go back and kill Hitler or another paradox endeavor. My intention on traveling back is to make the smallest footprint presence possible. I am merely an observer. I dress like the locals, try and keep my speech to a minimum, use time-period currency, and generally try to blend into the environment."

"Where do you get your currency?" questioned Greg.

"Coin collectors, people who collect older money. It's amazing how much of the older stuff is still in the hands of collectors."

"And you said you try to dress in the period? How do you do that?"

"If I am going back to the middle 1900's, I get on the computer and research vintage clothing suppliers. I found a great company out of Los Angeles. I then buy it and have it Fed- Ex-ed."

"Anything else a seasoned time traveler needs to know?" questioned Greg, not trying to hide his smile.

Taylor shook his head. "You don't believe a word I say, do you?"

"No, Bruce, I don't." He checked his watch again. "Well, look, it's been nice meeting you and now I have a plane to catch. I still don't know how you got that ammunition into my dig-site, but hey, sometimes you just got to live with a mystery."

"How current are your inoculations?" asked Taylor while scribbling in his notebook.

"Why do you ask?" questioned Greg, standing to leave.

"Because when you go back, small pox, diphtheria, and a host of other pathogens are there. Things we fixed in the twentieth century have not been eradicated in the past. What I have found to be the worst in that time period is tuberculosis; I had no idea it was that pervasive."

Greg started heading to the stairs, "Well, I am good on my shots, Bruce, healthy as a horse. Anyway, it's been great talking to you and I wish you luck on your time-bending or traveling or whatever else you call it. I'll let myself out."

As he started up the stairs, he heard the heavy snap of a large laser being turned on. He turned and saw Taylor adjusting several mirrors around the beam. "Would you like to take a short trip?" he announced loudly over the whirl of the generators.

"And where would that be, Bruce?"

Taylor looked at Greg and smiled. "How about dinner at a nice steak-house I know of? My treat."

Chapter 3

Chris Abbott read the spot report again, still trying to figure out what he was looking at. Somebody from the SAC, Homeland Security office in DC named Todd Richardson had flagged the report from the New Mexico power company and forwarded it to his desk at the NRC. Homeland Special Investigations had an agent inbound and would be at his office by three that afternoon. Chris turned in his office chair and handed the memo to Joe Hollister, his deputy.

Both were assigned to the Albuquerque office, a decent posting, responsible for enforcement and compliance of NRC regulations at the Los Alamos Nuclear Laboratory. Within the administrative framework of nuclear fuels control, two different agencies were responsible for regulation oversight. The Department of Energy was primarily responsible for most security and compliance as it related to nuclear weapons. The NRC or Nuclear Regulatory Commission had the oversight responsibility for civilian nuclear power plants and research. Both organizations tended to cross-pollinate in duties and responsibilities. Los Alamos was a classic example where both military and civilian nuclear projects and experiments were conducted.

"What do you make of this?" questioned Joe, reading the memo again.

"Well, evidently the SAC in DC has a bug up their ass about the last three major drains that hit the area last month. I kind of figured we would be getting a call on this."

Abbot never really liked working with the WMD Anti-terror Task Force that had been set up in DC nine years ago. Way too gung-ho for his liking and tended to be reactive instead of proactive in a lot of the incidents they had worked together in the past. They seemed big on political damage control and short on any real long-range strategies of security enforcement. The organization was controlled and operated strictly by political appointees who as a rule had very little background in security investigations or law enforcement intervention relating to Nuclear Security. Hence the moniker "Homeland Insecurity" used by many in the Federal ranks.

Abbott's main responsibility over the last two years had been dealing with procedural safe guards of all nuclear fuel at Los Alamos. Everything from uranium dust to plutonium plates, all fell under his responsibility. He had received some of the PNM reports of several of the power grids in his area being hit by the semi-regular power spike. What concerned him most in the reports was the fact that the duration and volume of power had remained a constant and was noted with growing frequency.

He had checked with every government contracting agency and sub group working at Los Alamos to see if they were using anywhere near the kind of voltage that was showing up in the spikes and had come up empty. No one at the facility was drawing that kind of juice. On top of his already busy schedule, the facility was getting ready for a full-blown oversight inspection from DC within the next thirty days, a two-week ball-busting audit by an outside contracting agency that checked everything from compliance of the guards, gates, and guns of the facility to policy and procedures for nuclear safeguards. The inspection was a big deal and if it went bad, could end careers within the industry and close down facilities, not to mention the heavy fines that could be leveled at the lab for being out of regulation. Having a Homeland AT task-force guy running an investigation, probably out of his office, was something he really did not need right now.

"You know, Joe, you're probably going to have to take my meetings today while I deal with this investigator," announced Abbott, rummaging through his desk drawer looking for the half-empty bottle of Tums. He had been hitting the antacids pretty heavily over the last three weeks, a condition he chalked up to the increase in job stress and the crappy food he had been eating. He did not tell his wife about the bouts of jaw and shoulder pain that had kept him up several times last week. He simply did not have time to see a doctor, and if he said anything to his wife about it, she would ride him into the ground. His desk phone rang stopping the conversation.

"Abbott, NRC."

"Yes, morning, sir, this is Todd Richardson over at the SAC here in DC. How are you this morning?"

"Fine, Todd, how can I help you folks?" Abbott really did not have time for chitchat. He was hoping Richardson picked up his tone.

"Well, hopefully you folks received the spot-report concerning the power spikes that have been occurring in your area and particularly the information about one of our agents that's headed your way."

'Yep, got it this morning. We've kind of been looking into this from our side for awhile now," replied Abbott. "Nobody from the lab is drawing that kind of power."

"Yeah, I figured you guys were already on top of it as far as the lab was concerned," replied Richardson. "From our side of the house, we are always looking at the critical infrastructure angle. Anyway, I just wanted to make sure you folks got my notification about our guy touching base with your office."

"Yep, we are good. We will be looking for him. I'll make sure he gets through badging without too much aggravation. If you'll send me his ID information, I can send it over to Access Control and they can get him his badge."

"Very good. I will e-mail it to you right away and thanks again for the help on this. Let me know if you need anything else from my side."

"You got it. I will keep you posted if we come up with anything. Okay, take care."

"Thanks again," replied Richardson. "Good-bye."

Short and sweet, just the way Abbott liked it. Ten minutes later, the HIS agent's ID information came in on the computer. He would do his best to cooperate with the investigator and then get him back to DC as quickly as possible. He had more important things to worry about. He found the Tums and drank the last bit of his cold coffee. Maybe he would mention his growing discomfort to the wife. Hopefully his chest pain would not get any worse. It was getting harder and harder to ignore the pain.

****

Greg was feeling very self-conscious and was deeply regretting his decision to go along with Taylor's nonsense about time travel. He had put on the 1900's period-piece suit and shoes and was now sitting on the metal stool in the middle of the taped-off square. Taylor was also dressed in the same period and was currently in a fury of activity adjusting meters, checking power levels, and positioning several large metal screens near the square, their edges matching marks on the floor. "Hey Bruce, I know I rebooked on a later flight, but if this takes much longer, I'll miss that one too."

Taylor looked up from his checklist. "I think we are about ready. Now, when I reboot the proton accelerator, there will be a time lag of approximately ten seconds. You will experience fairly heavy nausea and extreme fatigue and then a frigid blast of cold air. I will explain the process later. This is the first time I have done this with another person, but if my calculations are correct and I believe they are, then it should work." He looked around the lab one last time and then squatted down beside Greg in the center of the square. He was holding what looked like a small garage door-opening device in his hand. He gave Greg a wink and then pushed the button.

Greg was now feeling beyond uncomfortable. His doubts about the whole crazy, make-believe game of being time travelers was now deeply embarrassing. Taylor, crouching down and then grabbing his hand was the limit. "All right, Bruce," he announced, starting to stand, "This is stupid. No more games. I really do need to get going. I don't have the time to.." Before he could finish his sentence, he buckled to the floor from a stunning blow to his lower back and then experienced an intense feeling of being pulled in every direction at once. He felt as if he was being torn apart.

There was an intense sense of movement, but he could not see any references that he was moving through or past a fixed landscape. He was sure that this is what it was like to die. He thought about his wife of fifteen years back in Missoula, his dog and his Norton Commando motorcycle that took him a year to restore. It all rushed back as he fought the helpless feeling of being hurled blindly through the darkness at incredible speeds. Brief flashes of light seemed to hang in the air like a flash bulb in slow motion. He felt a wave of nausea and then a total cessation of all sound, even his own breathing. Seconds later he was slammed to the ground on his back as if he had been pushed out of a pickup truck backwards. In agony of having his wind knocked out, he rolled to a stop on his side, grunting for air.

Grass - he was laying face down in a patch of tall grass. Its earthy smell filled his nostrils as his vision began to clear. He heard a distant voice, familiar, far off, and it carried a tone of concern. "Greg, are you all right? Greg, breathe my friend. I should have warned you not to stand up right away. Are you okay?"

Greg slowly sat up and let the cobwebs dissipate. "Jesus, what happened? Did the lab blow up?" he asked, feeling the sudden urge to vomit. "I'm going to be sick," he announced before throwing up for what seemed like five minutes. "Aghaa, what the fuck is,,,, aghaaa". Finally, he stopped and lay on his side, more exhausted than he had ever been in his life. "What is going on?" he mumbled, noticing for the first time that it was night outside.

With great effort, Taylor slowly helped him to his feet. "C'mon, you'll feel better if you stand up. What you're experiencing now is what I call jump sickness. It goes away quicker if you start moving around."

Greg struggled to stand as he looked around. He was shocked to see that he was standing on a hillside looking down on a large, yet dimly lit city. The streetlights were a deep orange yellowish color as were the lights in many of the buildings' windows giving the entire town a hazy dream-like appearance. The smell of wood smoke filled the air along with the distant sounds of wagons being pulled by horses somewhere down there in the dark.

"My God," whispered Greg, still not believing what he was looking at. "Am I dreaming? Is this real? Where are we?"

Taylor chuckled, still helping him stand. "It's not so much of where we are, but when. I would say by the look of things around 1905 or six, give or take a year or two."

Greg finally had the strength to stand on his own. He stood, staring down into the city, totally awestruck by what he was seeing. "Impossible," he announced, his voice barely a whisper. Taylor started moving down the hill. "C'mon, time to meet the locals," he said cheerfully.

Greg was having real trouble accepting the fact that he was actually awake and walking down some grass covered hillside in the dark. This simply could not be real, he told himself. There had to have been an accident in the lab. He had suffered some kind of serious injury and was in the hospital in a coma. Had to be. And yet as he continued to move down the hillside, he noticed that the shoes Taylor had given him pinched his feet, and he was starting to build up a sweat under the wool-frock coat he had been given to wear.

With every step, his head began to clear more and more, and he became aware of more sounds, sights, and smells of the world he now found himself in. The voices of children playing and running in the dark could be heard somewhere off to his right. The clop of hooves on cobblestone became clear as they moved down onto level ground. At street level, it was much brighter than Greg would have guessed.

The buildings in the area all appeared to be two or three stories high with a surprising number of people out on the sidewalks. The smell of warm peanuts and the familiar sound of an organ grinder could be heard somewhere up the street. This was no dream, no coma-induced hallucination - he was really here. As they continued to walk up the gas-lit avenue, Greg was suddenly self-conscious about how tall he was compared to the men and women around him. They were small. Most of the men averaged five-foot-six. The women were even smaller; he guessed that most appeared to be around four-eleven to five-foot.

As they walked, he was also struck by how quiet the general atmosphere was. No loud music from car stereos, no loud buses or trucks on the street, no sounds of mechanical construction. The only sounds were of horses pulling wagons and the occasional soft murmur of people talking as they walked. The quiet was incredible. He was now painfully aware of how noise-polluted the modern world was. Simply amazing!

"Isn't this something?" announced Taylor as they walked. "How are you feeling? Better I hope?"

"Bruce, this is the most incredible thing that has ever happened to me or will happen in my lifetime," replied Greg, stopping and gripping Taylor's elbow. "I cannot even express my gratitude in words for this mind-blowing opportunity. I ..I..."

"It's okay, Greg," replied Taylor interrupting. "There really aren't any words to describe this. It really is beyond the pale of human experience. I know just how you feel. C'mon let's get a beer. I have a lot to tell you."

*****

"Son-of-a-bitch!" shouted Cullen as he sat watching all three major metropolitan power grids on the control desk throughout the Albuquerque area spike, fade, and then slowly start to recover. He quickly dialed the phone to PNM Farmington. "Yeah, Jim, did you guys just register that spike? Jesus Christ, that was at least a 2 GIG flash! Looks like it took everything from Taos all the way out to Arizona and then some." He wrote down the information as he listened to the Farmington lead give him their data. "Okay, well look, go ahead and send me what you have. I'll upload time, date, duration, and levels on my report and send it up," he announced.

This was now more than just a ghost-in-the-wire kind of deal, he thought, *hanging up the phone. These were planned events, and whoever was drawing this kind of power had to be energizing something really off the charts. It was the kind of flash that would be like the combined cities of Taos, Santa Fe and Albuquerque, New Mexico, all turning off, then on every light and electric appliance at the same instant.* Little did he know that as he watched the gain indicators surge and then move back up to normal, the power behind the gauges would soon be the thing that would alter his life forever. He would be a witness to something extraordinary.

*****

Agent Carlos Ania had been an HIS criminal investigator just under three years before being transferred to the Fairfax, Virginia SAC office. The assignment of chasing down someone or some group who was stealing huge amounts of commercial power just was not the kind of investigation he really wanted to spend a whole lot of time on. The NRC OI guys were already on it, and his involvement seemed to be a case of 'way too many cooks in the kitchen'.

At the Los Alamos badging office he slid his ID card under the thick glass partition and his driver's license for a second form of ID. "Here you go, Mister Ania," announced the security officer behind the glass. He then slipped the visitor's badge and lanyard under the glass along with a form for him to sign. "If you would, sir, just sign the release form at the bottom. We keep your driver's license here. When you leave, return the badge, and we will give you your license back."

Ania signed the form and nodded to the guard. "Thank you, pard," he said, pushing the form under the partition. "Now, which way is the NRC office? I have a meeting with those folks."

"Sir, back out those doors. Take a left and it's two buildings down - building 200. You're headed to the second floor, room 18. I'll call and let them know you're on the way. Who's your POC?"

Ania checked the small notebook he always carried. "Ah, let's see, a Mister Abbott."

"Roger that, sir. I'll let him know you're on the way, and, Mister Ania, just a reminder- Your badge has to be visible at all times when you're on facility grounds."

"Thank you, officer," he nodded to the guard and then headed out the door. Moving to Washington DC was the one duty location he had wanted since he started with ICE. His first posting out of (FLETC), the sprawling Federal Law Enforcement-Training Center in Glynco, Georgia, was at the Detroit SAC office, a posting he could not stand from day one. He had hated the weather, the crappy housing, and the generally depressed atmosphere that seemed to hang over the entire area.

Detroit was a dying city, and anybody who lived there felt the vibe. It just was not his kind of town. Hell, he never really found a good gym there to workout in. If he didn't get in some heavy sets at least three days a week, it shot his whole routine to shit. He had been on top of his supplements and diet for the last sixty days and was really starting to show some results. He was now benching two-sixty without too much trouble, a weight he hadn't even come close to as a gym-rat in the Marines.

Now in DC, he was able to hit all the right clubs, flash the new caps and the big arms, and slay all the Georgetown pre-law-tail like ducks in a barrel. He was single, had a great condo in Crystal City, a new five hundred series Beemer in the garage, and life was good. The sooner he wrapped up this lame-ass power drain investigation, the sooner he could get back to his town.

He found the building and headed to the front entrance. To his delight, the large glass door was coated on the inside with Mylar, which gave the glass a mirror finish. He adjusted his tie and straightened his belt-line. *Damn I look good*, he thought, checking his hair while opening the door. The new hair gel he picked up was doing the job. Taking several stairs at a time just to check cardio, he found room eighteen at the end of the hall.

"Come in," announced Abbott hearing the knock.

Ania stepped into the small office where he found the two NRC inspectors. "Morning, Carlos Ania from ICE," he said, shaking hands with Abbott. "How you guys doing?"

"Pretty good," replied Abbott, "Did you get through badging all right? Sometimes those guys can get aggravating with access rules."

"No sweat, rent-a-cops are easy to handle," he said, pulling up one of the chairs by Abbott's desk.

It took about three seconds for Abbott to size up this ICE investigator and the conclusion was not positive. The dark suit that looked like it had been painted on, along with the designer shoes, topped off with the heavy hair gel, said more about the guy then the rent-a-cop crack. "Nice suit," he said, trying to hide the sarcasm.

Ania smiled. "Brooks Brothers, decent five-hundred-thread-count. I get my gear the same place Harry Reid does. I notice you guys don't wear suits out here in the wild west."

"Yeah, well, we go for comfort. Levis and polo shirts are pretty much the standard uniform. Anyway, let's get into what you're here for." The sooner he was shed of this man-scaped peacock the better. "As I told your boss, we've checked with every DOD contractor and all the civilian projects at the facility and none of them are using anywhere near the kind of power that has been spiking lately."

"Yeah, I kind of figured you guys were already on it," replied Ania taking notes. "Do you know if the power company has the area pinpointed yet?"

Abbott thumbed through the file. "Yeah, looks like from the preliminary trace, it's coming out of the Shady Brook area. That's a town about ten miles from Taos, nice area, not a whole lot of people up there."

"Got to be honest with you. I really don't think we have any kind of crime-deal involving national security," announced Ania closing his notebook. "I mean, how much power we talking about anyway?"

Abbott was shocked at how little the investigator knew about his own case. "Ah, well, we are talking about a two-Gigawatt spike that's happened three times in the last month."

"Yeah, how much power is that?" asked Ania smiling.

"It's enough to power up a particle accelerator or a small nuclear reactor."

The smiled slowly faded from the Agent's face. "You gotta be shitting me."

"Wish I was," replied Abbott, handing the PNM file to the Agent. "Looks like you're headed to the Shady Brook Area and, according to my boss, my partner and I have been assigned to your investigation. Looks like we are all going."

Ania thumbed through the file. "So you think we may have something here?" he asked, already seeing a quick turn around and his weekend back in DC fading in the New Mexico sunset.

Abbott smiled. "I'd bet them fancy shoes you got there, Agent, and, by the way, did you bring any boots? That's big time snake country, and this time of the year they are out."

"Snakes! You're shitting me, right?"

Abbott smiled, thinking that the agent was probably going to be saying that a lot in the next few days. Hell, just to see him walking around out there would be worth spending time with the guy. There hadn't been any big rattlers killed up that high in years; he would keep that to himself.

*****

Dillon Conroy from NEST had been told specifically not to make contact with any other government or non-government agency until after his initial sweep of the area was complete. The shot-callers at DOE and the NNSA did not want to spin up anyone as to the limited possibility of nuclear material in the area if there wasn't anything to report. The Shady Brook area of Taos, New Mexico seemed like the last place anyone would find even a low Rad count, much less any uncontrolled nuclear material.

His three-man team had been sent to the area last Thursday and had been slowly driving the specially equipped van that monitored radiation signatures around the outlying neighborhoods. It was a million-dollar rig that was part of the nuclear detection arsenal currently used by the United States Government. The NEST acronym stood for the Nuclear Emergency Support Team, a highly funded, closed access organization of scientists, nuclear physics experts and a host of other highly trained nuclear specialists.

Earlier in the week, one of the AMS, Aerial Measuring System birds picked up a hot read in the area during a routine flight on its way to Los Alamos, something that caught the attention of the folks who read the reports and make the calls. Every nuke site and laboratory working with nuclear material in the United States was subject to the over-sight and unannounced inspections of the NNSA. This flight was no different. "Hey Kelly," spoke Conroy, looking at his computerized Rad monitor, "take a left at the next block. Got a faint trace. Not sure what it is, maybe nothing." Conroy slowly dialed in the monitor as they turned the corner. It appeared to be a standard residential neighborhood with only several cars parked in front of the middle class homes. "You see a street sign, Kelly? I'm getting a stronger signal the further we go this way." The driver turned in his seat. "Ah, yeah, looks like we are on Holston, the one hundred block."

"Stop the van," announced Conroy, "my readings just went off the scale. It's coming from this brown house on my right."

He checked his readings again before dialing his cell phone. "Yeah, Mike, this is Conroy. I'm going to need the rest of the team on my location. I'm not sure what I have, but we are going to have to check it out. I'm getting some odd readings coming from a residence here in Shady Brook."

Mike Boaz had been with NEST for over three years. He had moved through the ranks of government service and had gotten his GS-15 rating last September, the high-water mark on pay and privilege. He knew he owed much of his success to guys like Conroy, pros who were seldom wrong and always cautious. "You got it. Where do you want the team to fly into?"

"Tell you what, Mike, let's have the team fly into Santa Fe. It's about an hour and twenty minute drive from Taos. I would like to run a scan from the airport all the way up here."

"What else do you need from my end?" questioned Boaz.

Conroy unfolded the state map of New Mexico. "Yeah, I also want a ground based scan from Albuquerque to here. The rest of the guys can fly into Albuquerque and run the highway up to my location. I am going to go ahead, get a hotel, and set up a CP."

"How many folks you need, Dillon?"

"Okay, let's see. I'm going to need Marshfield from Atmospherics, Collins for my IT hook-ups, ah, Clark from weather, Brenner, Cruse and let's use the new kid from MIT. What's his name?"

"Nemec, you sure you want a rookie on this, Dillon?" asked Boaz. "Sounds like you might have something out there."

"Hey, he's gotta get his feet wet sometime. This is as good a time as any. I will call you back later today and give you the details about where we are setting up. Make sure those guys bring the full kit on this, Mike. I really am not sure what I am dealing with."

Over the years Boaz had learned to trust any assessment that came from his senior scientist. "You got it, Dillon. Troops are on the way. I'll have Stacy call you when they are airborne."

"Thanks, Mike."

"Dillon, you think we need to notify the FBI on this?"

"Ah, not yet. I need to gather more data. I think that it would clutter things up. Give me a day or two. I should have some more answers."

"Okay, your call," replied Boaz. "Let me know where you're setting up, and I will start things moving from this end. Stay safe."

"Thanks, Mike."

Confident that the operational wheels of the machine had been set in motion, he handed the secure-line cell-phone back to Kelly. "All right, my friend," he announced, "let's go find a command post. Troops are on the way."

As they slowly made a u-turn in the middle of the block, Dillon wrote down the house address and a brief description of the nondescript house. Little did he know that his actions had moved the cosmic tumblers of fate and circumstance another click. In three days nothing would ever be the same - nothing.

Chapter 4

Greg followed Taylor into the warmly lit tavern, desperately trying to get his head around where he was and what he was seeing. These people were real; as they brushed past, he could smell the perfume on the women and the body odor of the men. The room was filled with the sounds of people talking and laughing. It was the sound of life in all its glorious color. The music from the piano played above the noise in the room, wrapping everything into a loud, pleasant cacophony of sensory input.

This was no dream. The floor he was walking on was solid, and the air carried the heavy familiar scent of cigar-smoke and beer. He estimated the room to be at least fifty, sixty feet across, illuminated by three large gas-burning chandeliers. The long, black marble-topped bar ran the length of the room, its sides filled shoulder to shoulder with men and women drinking and talking. The high ceiling was shrouded in a thin haze of cigar smoke, giving the entire room a dream-like appearance.

Taylor found a table near the back of the room and motioned for Greg to sit down. "Well, what do you think?" he questioned above the noise.

Greg moved his chair around so his back would be to the wall "I, I really don't know what to say. I mean, my God, did this really happen? Are we really here?"

Taylor patted Greg on the arm. "It's okay. I know how you feel. When you calm down a bit, all this will be a lot easier to take in. I promise."

"I sincerely doubt it. I mean, this is the greatest discovery in the history of Mankind and I am part of it. I find the ramifications of all this staggering."

Taylor smiled while motioning to one of the heavy-set barmaids by the bar. "Relax," he replied, holding up two fingers to the woman. "We are dealing with simple math."

The woman walked over and set two large mugs of beer on the table. "That will be six bits," she announced with her hands on her hips.

Greg sat staring at the woman. "I'I,,,"

"Here you go, Madam," interrupted Taylor, dropping some coins on the table, "and is the kitchen still open?"

The woman eyed Greg suspiciously. "What's wrong with him?" she asked picking up the coins.

Taylor smiled and dropped several more on the table. "Those are for you, madam, if you can get us a couple of steaks. Greg, how would you like yours cooked?" asked Taylor smiling.

"Ah, I am a Vega..." he choked off the words.

'What's a vega?" she asked, confusion clouding her face.

"You'll have to forgive my friend, Ma'am," interrupted Taylor. "He is very tired from our journey and probably needs sleep more than food. The one steak will be fine."

The woman studied Taylor for a moment. "All right, I'll see what we have left. A bunch of shit-kickers came in a while ago from Miles City and damn near ate everything we had."

"Thank you. That will be fine. Whatever you have," replied Taylor.

The woman seemed to accept the explanation and disappeared into the crowd on her way back to the kitchen. "God, she must think I'm an idiot," spoke Greg, taking a long drink of beer. "Ahgh! It's warm," he announced.

"Yeah, not much refrigeration in 1905," replied Taylor smiling. "But look at the bright side - no chemicals - probably the purest beer you can drink."

"I'm still in shock that we are really here," replied Greg. "I mean, why here? Why now? And how do we get back?"

Taylor thought for a moment, "Okay, bear with me a moment, and I will try to explain. First off, you have to forget or at least suspend your current notion of time. All human activity that has taken place on the planet can be converted into measurable energy. Energy residual, depending on the emotion that was expended, is still here, still presenting a pulse or beacon, if you will. Basically I have found a way to tap into that finite signal energy and get back to its source."

Greg shook his head. "I get the energy field stuff and the expenditure of human emotion, but I really do not understand how you, or we, are able to get back to its source."

Taylor leaned close. "I really don't expect you to understand Quantum Mechanics, Greg, but the simplest explanation is that I have discovered, that with enough generated energy, the space time continuum can be bent and somewhat manipulated. No voodoo here, my friend, just a bit of advanced math."

Just as Greg was about to speak, the same barmaid walked up carrying several large plates. "Here you go, gentlemen. The cook is drunk, so I can't guarantee you won't die from poison," she announced, setting the plates on the table. "And I brought one for our mister Vega here." She leaned across the table, "And if either one of you boys wants a pull, just let me know. Gotta couple rooms upstairs," she winked at Greg. "Just let me know; only cost you three dollars."

Greg nodded and smiled. "Thank you, Ma'am, I will be sure and let you know."

"My God," replied Greg, watching the woman head back to the bar, "did she say what I thought she said?"

Taylor could barely contain his laughter. "As you can see, there is nothing new under the sun. You just got propositioned by a hundred and thirty year old woman. Go ahead; try your steak. It was really good the last time I was here."

"How many times have you been here?" questioned Greg.

Taylor cut a bite size piece of the meat with his knife, "Enough times to know that just about all the females that work here have various degrees of venereal disease. Although on the bright side, it's a fairly young and unsophisticated pathogen that is quite easy to treat. Remember, it's a venereal disorder from a hundred years before our time, not the super modified strain we see in our reality."

Greg shook his head. "And how in God's name would you know all that?"

Taylor took the meat and smiled while chewing, "When in Rome my friend.... It was all done in the name of research." He downed the rest of his beer and motioned for another from the barmaid. "You have to look at this as a scientific experiment, Greg. We are supposed to observe and try and learn not to repeat the errors of the past. I am convinced in my heart that this is the purpose of this discovery."

Greg swallowed a second drink of beer; this one tasted just as bad as the first. "And how does getting the clap move the scientific world into enlightenment, Bruce?" asked Greg smiling. "That's really risky behavior, you know. What if she got pregnant? She could have had your grandfather or something worse."

Taylor laughed out loud. "Please, you give me far too much credit. I never had physical relations with any of these females. On several occasions I was able to take blood samples while posing as a Doctor," he continued to laugh, almost choking on his food.

Greg patted Taylor's back, trying to help him clear his throat. "Well, Bruce, you had me going there for a moment," he laughed. "I was just trying to picture you with our barmaid friend over there."

Taylor waved, still coughing. "Not a very flattering picture I can assure you," he replied catching his breath. "Anyway," he continued, "the reason we are here is that the instruments that I have been working on are only precise enough to vector in on an extremely strong emotional energy."

Greg tried a bit of the steak and was pleasantly surprised by the good flavor. "What event or action by a group of people makes 1889 Montana so strong?"

Taylor took a long drink of beer before answering. "Greg, you're an archaeologist, specializing in nineteenth century western dig sites, correct?"

"That's correct."

'Okay, what was the one seminal, fork-in-the-road event that happened in this region around 1870?"

Greg thought for a moment. "My God," he replied, "the Battle of the Little Bighorn. It was a pivotal event for the country. It changed the entire western migration process."

"Exactly," announced Taylor. "I have been a student of the Custer legend since I was a kid, fascinated by the things he and his brother Tom were involved with. Did you know that he was going to run for President the year he was killed out here? He was that popular in the country."

Greg was no longer picking at the food. The steak was delicious. "I did know that. I also know that President Grant hated him and his brother with a passion. The year he died, he was supposed to testify before Congress about Grants' brother, an Indian affairs agent, who was stealing hundreds of thousands of dollars from the government fund. Custer knew about it and was going to blow the whistle."

"And when Custer went down with the Seventh, June 25, 1876, it sent total emotional shock-waves throughout the entire country," replied Taylor. "People simply could not believe that someone of Custer's ability as a soldier could be killed by primitive Indians. It was simply inconceivable."

"And this is the emotional energy you were able to key in on?" asked Greg. "That was what, twenty-years ago from now? I assume this is 1889."

"Correct," replied Taylor. "It was a pivotal point in American history. With Custer being killed at the Little Bighorn, the action spelled the end of the American Indian, indigenous people who had been living in the area for hundreds of years."

"The country changed after Custer died," agreed Greg. He finished the warm beer. "So you were there? You were at the battle? My God, Bruce, you were at the Battle of the Little Bighorn!"

"Yes, I tried in a feeble, stupid way to change history. It was a mistake."

Greg could hardly contain himself. "Jesus Christ, Bruce, what happened? What did you do?"

Taylor sat back in his chair, collecting his thoughts. It was obvious the memory was painful and that he was struggling to put it into words. "In my foolish attempt to balance a scale, as it were, I may be responsible for the deaths of - I don't know how many people," he said staring at the table.

"What happened? Does this have anything to do with the ammunition I found at the battle site?"

"It has everything to do with what you found," replied Taylor. "I brought it there, and it's exactly what I did not want to happen when I started doing this. I had gone to extraordinary lengths to limit my carbon footprint into the past, knowing full well the possible catastrophic consequences of my actions."

Greg thought for a moment. "Okay, how many times have you gone into the past, and what do you think you have changed?"

"This is my ninth jump to this area," replied Taylor.

Before he could say anything else, a different barmaid stepped up to the table. "You gentlemen done with your plates?" she asked.

"Yes ma'am," replied Taylor, stacking and sliding the plates across to the woman. "Here ya go."

The woman picked up the dinnerware and then paused, "Say, aren't you that traveling doctor that was here about a month ago?" she asked smiling.

Shit, thought Taylor, he'd been recognized. "Ah, yes Ma'am. I am."

"I thought I recognized you. You back to tend someone who's sick?" she asked. "Are you a doctor too?" she asked, looking at Greg.

Greg looked over at Taylor and then back to the woman. "Yes ma'am, I am." His mind was swimming about the thousand possible ramifications of even talking to the woman.

'Well, now," she said smiling, "we got two doctors in town. That is really something."

"Molly, stop jawing. I need help at the bar," announced the fat bartender loudly from across the room.

"Nice meeting you, gentlemen. We don't get that many in here," she said frowning at the bartender. She picked up the plates and hurried back into the crowded room.

"Listen, we need to leave," announced Taylor, standing. "I don't want anymore encounters. It's too risky." Greg stood and slowly followed Taylor though the crowded room, being careful not to bump into any of the increasingly intoxicated men and women who filled the tavern. As he made his way behind Taylor, he spotted more then a few pistols tucked into waistbands and belts. Getting shot dead in 1889 in a drunken fight could have incredible consequences for his family and friends in the 2013 future.

The night-air felt clean and brisk as they stepped out onto the porch. Greg was surprised at how warm it had been inside. Taylor lit a cigar and motioned down the street. "Let's walk."

"So, how does this work?" questioned Greg as they walked down the wooden sidewalk. "How much time goes by from the time we leave 2013 and then return?"

"It depends how long we stay here," replied Taylor. "In real time, which I mean by measured time in 2013, I have found that only seconds go by."

"You mean you're only gone from 2013 for seconds?" asked Greg, trying to get his head around the statement.

"That's correct."

"Okay, Bruce, let me get this straight," replied Greg, stopping under one of the orange glowing streetlights. "We left the Lab in 2013 measured time, at what eleven, eleven thirty in the morning?"

"Eleven-forty-nine, to be exact," replied Taylor, blowing a perfect smoke ring into the air.

"Okay, eleven-forty-nine. So when we go back after what, two hours here, how much time will have gone by in 2013?"

"Approximately four minutes."

Greg was stunned. "Four Minutes! That's it? Four minutes?"

"Give or take a second or two."

"So, time is not a constant?" questioned Greg.

"That's correct. It shifts and can be manipulated. It's actually a very fluid medium, quite amazing really."

"I would say 'amazing' is the understatement of all time," replied Greg. "I mean, I'm a scientist and have seen some pretty amazing things, but this peaks the meter, Bruce. Do you fully understand what you have discovered? I mean, do you see how mind-blowingly incredible this is? And most importantly, what people will do to get it?"

"Yes"

"Yes, what?" questioned Greg. "You understand what you have discovered and that people, governments will kill you to get it?"

"I understand all of that, Greg. Remember, I have worked within the military industrial complex my entire life. I was a weapons designer at Sandia labs for years and am fully aware of the drive and motivation of governments for ever increasingly powerful weapons."

"I'm glad you see that this could be used as a weapon."

"Absolutely," replied Taylor, flicking the stub of his cigar into the street. "Which is why I plan on destroying my ability to do it."

Greg was stunned. "You're kidding!"

"I am deadly serious," replied Taylor, looking up into the night sky. "You are correct by saying governments would kill for this ability. I simply cannot allow people with evil or self-serving intent, the ability to change the history of the world."

Greg thought for a moment. "Why did you do it?"

Taylor smiled, "To prove to myself that it could be done. I worked on this for almost sixteen years, with no real thought about how the powers-that-be would handle the ability to move through time. You are correct when you said people would kill for this." Taylor pulled out his pocket-watch, "Speaking of time, we need to move. I need to initiate the beacon to get us back."

"We're leaving now? Right now?" questioned Greg, with more than a little fear in his voice.

"Yes, in about thirty seconds. I suggest we get to a quiet spot; don't want any of the locals being a witness to us vanishing right before their eyes."

"Right, right," replied Greg, trying to push the fear away. "We can head into the alley over there."

They quickly walked across the street and into the darkened alley that ran along the side of several run-down shacks and low-roofed buildings. In the dark, Taylor gripped Greg's arm. "We should lock arms. Don't stand up. Try and stay in a tuck position. We should land somewhere near my house. Are you ready?"

"Wait a minute," announced Greg, squatting in the hard-packed dirt of the alley. "What do you mean land near the house? Won't this take us back to the lab?"

"Not exactly," replied Taylor, pulling a small square device from his coat pocket. "I'm still working on accuracy."

"Wait!" shouted Greg, "I'm not red...."

Instantly he felt the incredible jolt of movement backwards. The punch of acceleration made it hard for him to breath. He desperately fought the intense vertigo, seeming to spin through and around him in the dark. As before, he caught brief flashes of light and color as the sensation of being propelled at high velocity continued. Just as he was about to pass out from the ordeal, he felt an icy blast of freezing air and then the oddly comforting drop onto a hard surface.

He tumbled several times on, what he now could see in the bright sunlight, sand and scrub brush of New Mexico. He thudded to a stop at the base of a wooden fence at the back of Taylor's house. Slowly, he rolled onto his knees and was surprised to see Taylor next to him. "You ever get used to that?" questioned Greg, just before he vomited his dinner onto the sand.

Taylor carefully got to his feet while dusting himself off. "No, not really," he replied, fighting his own bout of nausea. He reached down and slowly helped Greg to his feet. "Well, at least we hit the backyard. Let's get inside. I have to check some calculations."

*****

Five miles away at the Hotel Don Fernando, Dillon Conroy and the other two members of his team checked into their rooms. The rest of the unit would be flying in that evening; it would be one of the largest deployments of NEST assets since 9/11.

As he tossed his cell phone and room-key on the bed, Dillon had a feeling that this investigation had an importance far beyond anything he had encountered over the last three years. Nuclear terrorism was the one thing that kept the DC shot-callers up nights. Many times, he had been on the third-floor at DOE when they ran the worst-case tabletop scenarios concerning a small yield nuclear weapon. The heavy numbers were always bad; a hundred thousand dead in a big city like Chicago or Denver were pretty much the norm. If even a small-yield device got cooked off, the world would change at the speed of light.

Nice place, he thought, sitting on the commode. He had needed to go all day. The beef burrito he had for lunch had been rolling around in his gut all afternoon. The phone rang beside the toilet paper dispenser. *Yep nice place,* he thought, answering the phone. "Yeah, hello?"

"Hey, boss, Kelly. Just got off the phone. The other guys will all be getting in around eleven-thirty tonight. You want them to wake you up when they get to the hotel?"

"No, just have them check in, and we will all meet for breakfast at 6:30 in the lobby," replied Dillon. "I have a bunch of paper work to get to before we hit the road tomorrow."

"Cool, I'll tell the guys. You want to get a beer later?"

"Yeah, give me about an hour. I'm on the shitter right now and this might take some time."

"Roger that," replied Kelly. "I'll meet you downstairs in about an hour."

70

Hanging-up the phone, Dillon had no idea that the safe and moderated existence of his everyday life was quickly coming to a close. He had played the game right, gone to the best schools, ran in the right circles, hell, even married the right woman. Met Terri at a seminar in Savannah seventeen years ago and knew the minute they met that he was never going to let her go. She was with OA 10, a DOE policy and procedural organization working out of the Forrestal building in DC and, to her credit, had more then a few guys wanting to get close to the pretty girl from Tennessee.

They had dated and married, all within three months and never regretted a moment of the brief but intense courtship. His son would be a senior next year and there was no reason in the world why he could not follow the Conroy path to success. With his good grades and love of science like his dad, it looked like Brown University would have another Conroy in its 2018 graduating class. It really was a shame that Dillon wouldn't be there to see it. You want to make God laugh? Tell him your plans.

Chapter 5

On the drive up to Shady Brook, Abbott put in a call to the PNM office in Farmington, letting them know that they were headed up to look around. The main supervisor there told him that a line investigation team was already in the area and that they might want to hook up and compare notes. Ania hadn't said much since they had left Los Alamos, being content to fiddle with his IPAD in the back seat. "You know," he announced, "I still get internet way out here."

"You had many cases like this before, Agent?" asked Abbott, looking in his rear view mirror.

Ania closed his computer. "Naw, not really. Still not sure what I'm supposed to be looking at or for. Looks more like a power company deal. Hell, for all we know, whoever is using this much juice is running a big grow house. "

"Not likely," replied Abbott. "These power surges are just that, surges, like a switch is being pulled and then shut off. Guys who grow weed need power on twenty-four seven."

"You sound like an expert," laughed Ania from the back seat.

Abbott smiled. "Well, you know, I read a lot. Besides with that much power you would have a grow house the size of Yankee Stadium."

Ania thought for a moment. "Do you know if anybody else has been called in on this?"

"Nothing from my office," replied Abbott. "I think everybody is waiting to see what, if anything, we turn up."

Abbott let the conversation die as he tried to remember the last time he had been up in the Shady Brook area. It had been at least a year he thought. He had taken his wife and daughter up to the Angel Fire Resort to go skiing in 2012. His wife, Donna, had been an avid skier growing up in Vermont, and since his new posting at Los Alamos, she had been dying to hit the New Mexico big runs.

He smiled to himself remembering how turned-on she was physically after a full day of skiing. Because they were sharing a room with his ten-year-old daughter, they had made love like teenagers in the shower that first night, damn near running all the hot water out of the hotel. When he thought back to their time together that weekend, it had been almost perfect. The food had been great, Jenny his daughter had behaved, and the skiing had been perfect. He told himself that he would go back, find a sitter for Jenny, and reward himself with a good old-fashioned adult weekend. He had been turning in twelve and fourteen-hour days for the past year now. A weekend with Donna might be just what he needed.

*****

Having finally cleared his head, Greg sat heavily in the high-backed office chair near one of the long instrument-filled tables in Taylor's lab. He retrieved his cell phone from the basket and discovered that his wife had called six times. "Jesus, I better call the wife," he announced, watching Taylor move about the room, adjusting and positioning different instruments and equipment. He started to dial the phone and then stopped. "What the hell am I going to say?" he asked. "I mean, I just had the most incredible thing in my life happen and I can't tell anyone about it. No one would believe me; Jesus Christ, I still can't believe it."

"So, what's the next step?" asked Taylor, looking up from one of the instrument panels. "What do you want out of this? I would like to know what you're thinking."

Greg thought for a moment. "Bruce, to be perfectly honest, my whole life has been turned upside down by this experience, and I am having a really hard time trying to get my head around the fact that I just traveled back to 1889. I now have the opportunity to study the past, which is my field. It's, it's just an absolutely mind-blowing experience, and the ramifications of it all are staggering. My God, Bruce, we are talking about time travel!"

Taylor walked over and rolled up another office chair. "I have a suggestion," he said sighing deeply. "I think you should go home, see your family, and mentally digest what you have experienced."

"And then what?" questioned Greg. "My God, Bruce, this is the biggest discovery of all time and I know about it. My life cannot, will not, ever be the same. At this moment, this very second, I am seriously thinking about never going home again."

"You're not serious," replied Taylor. "You have a woman who loves you. That has to be more important than this."

"Bruce, I'm a scientist. You have fulfilled the dream of all scientists, and that is to travel to the past and watch history in the making. I, I cannot think of anything greater to do, I really can't. And yes, I love my wife deeply, but this is the greatest discovery of Mankind, and I know she would want me to be part of it, no matter where it leads me."

Taylor thought for a moment. "All right, I do need your help with this, and I am willing for you to be a contributing colleague. But I will not let you work on this project until you go home and talk to your wife. I have no idea what you could possibly tell her, but you owe her some kind of explanation of what you're getting involved with."

"And what are you going to do while I do that?" questioned Greg.

"I have some extensive recalibration work that needs to be done before we attempt another jump, which should take about a week. Does that give you enough time to talk to your wife?"

"Yes, that will be fine," replied Greg, running his hands through his hair. "I'm going to tell her that I am going on some kind of long-term sabbatical overseas, something remote."

"Will she believe it?"

"Yes, she will. I also have to figure out what I am going to tell the University. Shit! How am I going to pay my bills?"

Taylor smiled and rolled his chair over to one of the tall metal file cabinets along the wall. "Money is not a problem," he announced, reaching into one of the lower drawers. He pulled up a five-inch stack of bills wrapped in rubber bands and tossed it to Greg.

Greg caught the brick. "Good grief, how did you get all this?"

"Well, whenever I go back, I always try and pick up a few twenty-dollar gold pieces or other valuable coin from the time period. Do you have any idea what a mint-condition 1850 twenty-dollar gold piece is worth in 2013?"

"Not really," replied Greg, still shocked by the huge bundle of cash.

"You would be amazed. I pick up a few, bring them back and sell them on the Internet for incredible amounts. It's what has funded most of this," he announced, pointing to the large laser array. "Tell your wife that your sabbatical pay is double what you're getting now. Does that help the process?"

Greg smiled, tossing the block of money back. "Yeah, that will definitely help the process."

"Good, then from this moment on, consider yourself on the payroll. Here, take this with you," replied Taylor, tossing the block of money back. "You'll need to pay for a plane ticket, first class of course. As you can see, money is really not an issue. I have more then I will ever need."

"My God," replied Greg, shaking his head, "I really do not know what to say."

"Well, you better think up something real good. You have a phone call to make to your wife. I would advise that you do it sooner than later."

Greg stared at the money, desperately trying to think of a reason why he should not get involved with Taylor and his incredible machine. He had a wife, the home in Montana he had always wanted, and was well respected in his career. Now he was sitting in a basement in New Mexico with a man he barely knew and was a witness to the greatest discovery of all time. How in the world was he going to tell his wife Carol about this? How could he tell anyone about what he had seen?

Taylor checked his watch. "You feeling well enough to travel today?"

"Yeah, I guess," replied Greg slowly standing. "Hey, Bruce, I have to ask you something."

"By all means," replied Taylor studying Greg closely.

"Why me?"

"I'm not sure what you mean."

"You don't know me, Bruce. I'm sure you have colleagues that are far more knowledgeable about this kind of research than I am, men who would be of greater value."

Taylor thought for a moment. "Greg, when I retired from Sandia and government work in general, I had had enough of 'committee science' and all the stifling collaborative project-work I could stand. I don't know how I can say this without sounding terribly egotistical, but I grew to hate working with other people on projects that I wanted to do. I knew that time shifting within the parameters of Quantum Mechanics was possible. The theory had intrigued me for years. I simply could not work on the project while still working for the government."

Greg sat back down, his legs still a bit shaky, "So what happened?"

"I put in twenty years of government service, retired as a GS 15, got divorced, and retreated into this lab for sixteen years, working on something I knew I had to.

"So why me? You could have just told me to get lost, let me stew in the mystery of how that ammunition got into my dig site. You didn't have to tell me a thing."

Taylor got up from his chair and walked over to the small coffee-making machine on the counter. "To be perfectly honest, I guess I just got tired of being alone with my discovery. Secondly, I was more than a little afraid you would go to the authorities with what you found."

"No law against belt-fed ammunition," replied Greg.

Taylor smiled. "You seemed like a decent fellow, Greg, and more importantly, you're a scientist. I'm sorry I don't have a more complex answer for you."

Greg chuckled. "Well, you seem like a pretty decent guy yourself there, Bruce. Thank you for the trust."

"Does that answer some of your questions?" asked Taylor, pouring two cups of coffee.

"Yes, it does, and for me, probably the bigger question is, where does this go from here and what do you want to accomplish with this?"

Taylor sat back down and handed one of the cups to Greg. "Short term, I need to correct a wrong."

"What wrong is that?"

Taylor kept his gaze on the floor. "Greg, are you aware of the Ton Ta Tonka ceremony and myth practiced by the Lakota Sioux out in Montana?"

"As a matter of fact, I am. As I recall, Ton Ta Tonka means 'mighty wind' in the Sioux language, and the ceremony is a reenactment of the Great Spirit giving a powerful weapon to the Lakota Sioux, which helped defeat all of their enemies."

Greg thought for a moment. "A 'mighty wind' - you have got to be shitting me, Bruce. You had something to do with that legend?"

"I started it."

Greg could scarcely believe what he was hearing. "What..., I mean, how did you start the Ton Ta Tonka myth?"

Taylor sipped his coffee before answering, "You have to believe me when I tell you it was not intentional. In fact, the whole thing started with the best of intentions."

Greg could tell that Taylor was deeply bothered by what he was trying to say.

"The Ton Ta Tonka legend is a relatively new story that really caught fire around the mid 1870's," replied Greg, "which was also around the time of the Little Bighorn Battle."

"That's correct, and it was all caused by me and my stupid, ill-conceived plan to change history." Taylor was now visibly shaking as he talked. "I have always been a great admirer of the American Indian. I've always felt that they endured a great injustice by being removed from their lands, pushed aside in the name of progress. It was especially true for the Plains Indians. I really thought I could do something about it, change the outcome, how this country dealt with the Indians in general."

"What did you do, Bruce?" questioned Greg.

"I took an automatic weapon back to the Battle of the Little Bighorn."

Greg was stunned. "You did what?"

"I know, I know. It sounds more desperate and ridiculous every time I say it."

"Speaking as a scientist, Bruce, I would say that was an understatement," replied Greg. "Start from the beginning. Tell me what happened."

Taylor stood up and poured himself a second cup of coffee. "Okay, I thought that if I went back and demonstrated the fire power that would be brought to bear on the Sioux, that they would not stand and fight. I intended to even the odds."

"But the result would have been the same," replied Greg. "Were you trying to fight on the side of the Indians? That advantage would have made an even more decisive victory than the one they achieved."

"Absolutely not," announced Taylor, sitting back down. "In my misguided thinking, I guess I wanted to go there and be a sort of arbitrator, a referee of sorts."

"How, I mean how, would that even be possible?" questioned Greg.

"'What I was hoping to do was limit the Sioux victory and save Custer."

"I still don't see how that would have helped."

"Think about it for a moment," replied Taylor. "Remember how popular Custer was just before he was killed? He wasn't just popular throughout the country, he was a strong advocate for Indian rights. That is something most people do not know about the man. Secondly, he was going to run for President that January and would have probably beaten Grant."

"I still don't see your logic in this," replied Greg.

"If the Battle of the Little Bighorn had been just one more moderate skirmish and Custer had survived, the country would not have exploded with a collective rage against the Indian as it did when he was killed."

"You really think his death sparked the end of the free-ranging Indian, the virtual extermination of all indigenous people in the country?" asked Greg.

Taylor thought for a moment. "I think that if Custer had survived the battle, he would have run for President and in my heart, I believe he would have at least given the Plains Indian a voice at the political table. Instead, when he was killed, the whole country wanted revenge. It was over."

"So, what exactly did you do to start the Ton Ta Tonka myth?"

Taylor rolled his chair back to the large filing cabinet where the money had come from. He pulled out the bottom drawer and took out a newspaper. "Here," he said, handing the paper to Greg. "Look at the second page, near the bottom."

Greg noticed the date on the front. "This paper is fifteen years old, 1998!"

"Yep, read the story."

"Ah, let's see," replied Greg, reading aloud. "A Sandia National Laboratory over-site inspection team, responsible for policy and compliance matters, informed the Albuquerque Police Department that several weapons and an undetermined amount of ammunition were found to be missing from a guard-force supply container located on the premises. The inventory discrepancy was discovered during a facility audit. It should be noted that facility Senior Security management have denied that any weapons or ammunition are missing, blaming the report on a clerical error. No charges have been filed. Investigators from The Bureau of Alcohol, Tobacco, and Firearms have an open investigation into the matter but are still trying to determine if a crime or theft has been committed. Federal investigators have stated that they believe there is no present danger to the public and will continue to exhaust all leads concerning the possible theft of security equipment and weapons that are currently used at the facility."

"Jesus, Bruce, you had something to do with this?"

Taylor nodded. "Yes, I stole an M60 machine gun and a can of ammo. It was just so easy. I mean I had access to the entire facility. I saw where the stuff was unloaded and stored."

"So you broke into an arms-room and took this machine gun?" asked Greg, shaking his head.

"No, the security force was changing over from the Vietnam era weaponry. The M60 was an older machine gun from that time. The new security company brought in the new SAW, Squad Automatic Weapon. The old inventory was left in a locked connex-box for several days before being shipped back to wherever that stuff goes. I literally walked by one day, saw that the connex was unlocked and took what I needed."

"Why did you steal the weapon? Why didn't you just buy one yourself? I mean, if you had been caught, everything you worked for would have been flushed down the drain for nothing."

"First of all, I didn't want to leave a paper trail on any firearm I might have bought. Secondly. I would never have been a suspect - a long time Sandia scientist, highly respected by his peers. And thirdly, I needed a weapon that carried enough lethality to get my point across. The M60 fit all those requirements."

Greg was astonished. He simply could not imagine this grey-bearded, slightly overweight man in his sixties walking away with, much less firing an M60 machine gun. "So let me get this straight, you simply walked off with the stuff, brought them here, and then took it back to the Battle of the Little Bighorn?"

"That's correct."

"So what happened when you got there? Did you make contact? Did you shoot anybody?" questioned Greg, still amazed that he was even able to ask the question.

Taylor's face clouded over as he continued to stare at the floor. "I panicked," he replied softly. "I landed on the Indian encampment side of the river. I can still smell the water and the muddy bank. The cattail reeds were high, which mercifully hid my sudden appearance. I don't think you realize just how heavy an M60 machine gun really is, add to the fact that I was sloshing around in knee-deep mud and water." Taylor shook his head. "My movements were clumsy to say the least. God, what a sight I must have been."

Greg leaned back in his chair, trying to digest the gravity of what Taylor was trying to tell him. It was absolutely incredible that he was talking to someone who had actually been to the Battle of the Little Bighorn, the pivotal event in American Western history. "What happened next?" questioned Greg.

"Well, from what I could tell, I had arrived just as Major Reno was conducting his assault on the encampment, a good quarter-mile from my position. I could just make out the troops as they were attacking on horseback. The dust and the heat were incredible. It must have been at least a hundred and one in the shade."

"Could you see the intensity of the fighting?" asked Greg.

"Like I said, the dust was covering most of the action, but I could hear the shooting and that was amazing. Once I got out of the water, I made my way further downriver walking along the bank. I wanted to get across from the Medicine Tail ravine where Custer had come down to the river from his side. I was hoping to position myself right in the middle of where both forces met."

Greg shook his head, amazed. "My God, Bruce, what in the world were you going to do?"

Embarrassed, Taylor smiled. "To be totally honest with you, Greg, I was so pumped up with the fact that I was there that I really wasn't thinking very clearly. I could hear the fighting behind me, and up ahead, across the river I saw the advance party of Custer's unit already heading down the ravine. At that point things get kind of fuzzy."

"What do you mean, fuzzy?" questioned Greg, "Did you pass out? Get sick?"

"No, nothing like that," replied Taylor. "It's just that everything started happening at once. Something that shocked me out of my fog was that I started getting shot at from Custer's side of the river. Bullets were whizzing by all around me."

"Were you able to fire back?" questioned Greg, literally on the edge of his seat.

Taylor smiled sheepishly. "That's just it. My weapon was not loaded. When the bullets started buzzing by, I dropped on my belly behind the gun, pulled the trigger, and nothing happened. I could clearly see about thirty cavalry soldiers on horseback shooting in my direction on the other side of the river, with many more coming down behind them."

"According to some of the Indian accounts, Tom Custer was supposedly leading that group. Did you see him?" questioned Greg.

Taylor thought for a moment. "It's really hard to say one way or another. The dust was so thick, I had sweat in my eyes and at the same time was desperately trying to load the weapon. I really could not make out individual soldiers on the far bank. Frankly, I was just overwhelmed by it all."

"What happened next? I mean, did you ever load and fire?"

Taylor got up from his chair and walked over to one of the metal clothing lockers on the far side of the room. "I wanted to show you how I was dressed," he announced, opening one of the lockers. He pulled out a set of heavily mud-stained camouflaged fatigues along with a helmet and web gear. "This is what I was wearing when I made my appearance," he announced, laying the gear on the floor, "and yes, I was able to load and fire. I put a burst of, I think, about ten rounds across the river. Because the dust was so thick, I really did not see if I hit anyone."

Greg got up from his chair and knelt down beside the gear while picking up the helmet. "Geez Bruce, this looks like regular Army equipment. Did this come from Sandia?"

"Nope, ordered everything online. I went with the woodland cammo and the Vietnam era style helmet and steel pot because that is what I wore years ago when I did a short stint in the National Guard. It actually served me well, as you can see by the bullet crease on the left side."

Greg examined the helmet and noticed a two-inch long groove dug into the steel just above the left side edge. "Wow, Bruce, that was close! What happened after you opened up?"

"You know, it was the strangest thing," replied Taylor. "Just after I fired, it seemed like the entire battlefield went silent."

'Silent? No sound?" questioned Greg.

"No, there was sound. It was more like a sudden lull, as if the sound of that sixty going off shocked everybody anywhere near where I was shooting. They just stopped what they were doing and looked. Stared in stunned surprise would be a better description. It was incredible."

Before Taylor could say anything else, the house phone upstairs could be heard ringing. "I better get that," announced Taylor, walking towards the stairs.

Greg was on his feet, "What? Are you kidding me? You have to finish the story."

Taylor stopped before heading upstairs. "I really need to answer all calls. If I don't, neighbors and other folks start snooping around. I'll be right back. Besides, you need to make reservations to get home." He headed up the stairs, closing the door behind him at the landing.

Greg picked up his cell phone and speed-dialed the American Airlines reservation desk. As a platinum member he could make short-term bookings. Taylor was right; he really needed to get home and get his affairs in order with the wife and the University. He knew that at this moment in his life, the wheels of fate and circumstance had begun to turn. He felt the shift. Things were going to change, taking with it everything he thought he knew about the world.

There had only been a few times in his life when he felt propelled by circumstance, pushed into things and situations where reason and careful thought were absent. He hated feeling that way. He had made a successful career as a thoughtful, predictable team player. Now in one afternoon, he was about to walk away from everything he had worked for. As he punched in his Frequent Flyer number, he could barely contain his excitement. This was not a difficult decision.

Chapter 6

Heading northwest out of Bell Fouche, South Dakota, on the lonely and eerily desolate highway 212, the open ground started its slow roll to the Rockies. The knee-high Buffalo grass on both sides of the blacktop shifted and fell in the wind like waves on green water. The sunlight was different on the butte, its clarity and cast a treasure sought after by countless artists and seekers.

This was where myth and magic meet. Anyone who stood in the light, who in their heart was looking for truth, would be infected, changed in an instant from one who questions to one who believes. The Sioux, who rode this ground on horseback knew the power of the expanse, knew, just by being there that there was something greater than themselves. This was where the ceremony was held every year.

The round, nondescript stone-block hut two-miles off the highway, just past exit thirty-four, was where they gathered. Only those invited would attend. To be invited, one had to have a blood connection with the past, a flesh and blood descendent linked to that day. The Icon had been held by the descendants for over a hundred years, its shape now totally disguised by the countless wrappings of soft buckskin. The object was held in such high esteem that it was only taken from its secured location on the Nez Pierce reservation once a year, the 25th of July, and then only moved under armed tribal guards to the ceremony lodge.

By six-thirty in the morning, John American Horse and the twenty-eight other attendees of the ceremony were well on their way to the hut. The long line of headlights leaving the Res was the only traffic this time of the morning. The cycle would continue. The link to the past was still intact.

****

By ten-o'clock that morning, Abbott and Agent Ania were sitting just down the block from Taylor's house in Shady Brook, trying to figure out why their radio and cell phones, for that matter, were not working. "Agent, you have any signal on your phone?" Abbott asked Ania from the front seat.

"Nope, nothing. My lap-top is dead also, which is weird because I charged it up all night at the hotel."

On a hunch, Abbott started the car and slowly backed up till he was almost to the corner. Seconds later his cell phone pinged on as did Ania's in the back seat. "I'll be damned," he whispered. He looked at the agent in his rear-view mirror. "I think we have a bigger problem than we thought," he announced, slowly moving the car forward. Two houses down from Taylor's house the phones shut off again.

"Son-of-a-bitch," replied Ania. "What exactly does this mean?"

Abbott twisted in his seat. "What this means is that there is one hell of an energy field coming from that house, something strong enough to blank out cell-phone transmissions and radios."

Ania tried punching in numbers on his cell phone. "Okay, I need to call my boss and let him know what I have here. I am sure this will get his interest." Just as Abbott was about to agree, he noticed a large white van slowly turn on to the street and park several houses down. "Yeah, I need to call my guys on this also," he replied, studying the van. From the front, it was impossible to see through the darkened windows of the vehicle. Several large commercial antennas on the roof announced that this was something more than a vacation van.

'Hey, check that van," announced Abbott.

"What van?" questioned Ania from the back seat.

"That one up ahead, on the left," replied Abbott, fishing around in his coat pocket for an antacid. He had been having monstrous heart burn since he got up. "What does it look like to you?"

Ania leaned across the front seat, "Huh, looks like a surveillance van. You sure none of your folks are on this?"

Abbott quickly downed the tablets, "Nope, as far as I know only us and the power company guys know about this."

"Tell ya what," replied Ania. "Let's go over and see who these guys are."

"What are you going to say? You going to badge them? We still really don't know what we have."

Ania thought for a moment. "I have been doing this for a long time. Once I see what these guys look like, I'll be able to tell you if they are cops or Feds. If it's just someone waiting for their Aunt Tillie, I'll just say I thought they were someone else."

Abbott continued watching the vehicle for movement, looking for anything that would tell him that it was someone who belonged in the area. "Okay, you want me to drive over there or do you want to walk?"

Ania was already stepping out of the car. He leaned into Abbott's window. "Back in a sec," he said, smiling while adjusting his tie. Abbott watched as the agent made his way across the street. Talk about being out of place, Ania's shiny, dark suit shimmered in the sunlight giving him the appearance of some over-dressed hit man. Compared to the van, thought Abbott, Ania was the only thing that really looked out of place in this middle class neighborhood.

Dillon saw the man in the fancy suit walking in his direction and was surprised when he stopped and knocked on the driver's side window. "Something I can do for you?" he asked, after rolling the window down.

Ania smiled while looking inside. "That's what I thought; you guys are cops."

"Excuse me, sir, is there something I can do for you?" asked Dillon.

Ania pulled out his badge and credentials. "Agent Ania, Homeland Security. Who you guys with?"

Dillon smiled and pulled his ID out of his shirt pocket. "Dillon Conroy, NNSA." He shook hands with Ania through the window. "I think we may have something in common," he announced.

Ania smiled and then waved to Abbott who was still sitting a block away in his car. "Ah, yeah, I think you're right."

****

Greg had been able to book a non-stop flight to Billings and now, six hours later, sat in the airport lounge nursing a beer. His flight to Missoula didn't leave till seven which gave him time to think about what kind of lie he was going to tell his wife.

He was still trying to get his head around what he had experienced that last eight hours, and no matter how hard his rational mind accepted the notion that "it was all just a little advanced math," as Taylor had put it, it was still the most mind-blowing, off-the-scale life experience he had ever encountered. He also knew the incredible power Taylor's discovery carried. Governments and world powers would do absolutely anything to get their hands on it. Anybody associated with the project was a marked man, and in Greg's mind it was only a matter of time before his name came up.

He was also troubled by the fact that even though Taylor seemed to be somewhat aware of the incredible danger he had put himself in with this discovery, he was bothered by the fact that the man had been so easy to get involved with. Taylor had given up his secret and the most important discovery in the history of Mankind to a total stranger. If he was that readily compliant with him, just how much and how fast would he acquiesce if real government pressure came down? He drank down the last of his beer, trying to dampen the growing unease over the whole affair.

On the other hand, for all his talk about doing the greater good for the sake of science, he knew that he was now having real trouble backing it up. The shield of academia he had been hiding behind for years now, was being called into question. He had written the papers, followed the old adage of publish or perish, but what had he really done in ten years in his field?

He had received tenure, given the obligatory lectures, and gone to the right endowment parties, but what had he really gained? "Security," he whispered out loud. Now, today, at this moment, he was changing everything. He couldn't be fake anymore. A discovery of this incredible magnitude had to be taken as is. Whatever cost now being demanded, he knew he would have to pay. As he paid his bar tab and gathered his things, he still could not shake the feeling that he was involved in some sort of crime. He had crossed a line, a border that shouldn't have been crossed.

As he headed to the gate, a sudden strange fatigue rolled through his body. For a second, he felt the nausea rise and then fall, the same sensation he felt during the time-jump with Taylor. Attributing the feeling to the two beers on an empty stomach, he walked into the restroom hoping a good solid piss would fix the problem. As if he had been punched in the chest, he suddenly stopped in the middle of the brightly lit restroom and stared at his image in the large array of mirrors above the sinks.

He was 43 years old but now had the grey hair of a man in his sixties. Stunned, he slowly walked up to his reflection while gently touching the side of his face. "What the fuck," he announced, just as an older man in his seventies stepped up to the sink from the urinal to wash his hands. "Yeah, I know what you mean partner," the man replied pulling several paper towels from the dispenser. "I started going grey when I was thirty. Happens to all of us," he said, smiling. Greg continued to stare at his image, turning his head to the left and to the right. He instinctively realized that this had been caused by the jump. What was even more alarming was what if something else in his body had been adversely affected.

The older man patted him on the shoulder, "Times a real bitch, son," he announced, leaving the room. Greg shook his head, still looking at himself in the mirror. *Jesus*, he thought, *the price was getting higher by the second.*

Two hours later he watched the Billings airport roll by at a hundred miles an hour as his plane lifted off on its way to Missoula. Looking out the window, he still could not think of what he was going to tell his wife when he got home. No doubt she would notice the hair and probably smell the lie thirty seconds later. Oh yeah, the price was definitely getting high.

****

"So, guys, just what in your opinion do you think we are dealing with?" Abbott questioned Dillon and the other members of his NEST team. They had all driven to the parking lot of the Shady Brook Inn and Café and were now trying to decide a course of action. "Well, from my readings," replied Dillon, "the EMP signatures coming out of that house are well into the interference scale." Dillon handed his clipboard, with the data sheets attached, to Abbott. "As you can see on the sheet, we are getting a fairly wide band, a good indication of non-atmospheric slush, something man-made, controlled."

Abbott handed the data to Ania. "Your call, Agent," he announced. "I think Homeland has the jurisdictional lead on this."

"Ah, I'm not so sure on that," replied Dillon. "I think probably the FBI needs to be notified. I mean, I think these readings merit a possible national security review. I'm also getting a trace signature of Gamma ray anomalies that would indicate some sort of radiation source. I think this has got to go up the chain, no offense, Agent."

Ania handed the clipboard back to Dillon. "None taken. You guys are the experts here, and I am going to follow your lead on what you think we need to do next. But from a strictly law enforcement point of view, I think before we notify the FBI or any other agency on this, I need to make contact with whoever lives there and just see who we are dealing with."

Abbott nodded and looked at Dillon, "What do you need from the NRC?"

"Well, I think we will tee-off with whatever Agent Ania finds on his initial contact with the home owner. After that, I think we are probably going to be rolled up as SME's with the FBI if it goes that far."

"Probably right," agreed Abbott. "Well, Agent Ania, looks like you're on deck."

****

Two miles away, Taylor readjusted the last three centrifuge calculations before turning on the new machine. He had ordered it three weeks ago, and now it had arrived and was ready to be put to use. The gas centrifuge was essential for the separation of the isotope of u235 and u238. Uranium in its natural state was unusable for energy, and now, with the increased demand for a stronger, more reliable power source, the small bit of uranium-ore he had acquired had to be enriched. The new machine had cost him twelve thousand dollars, money he considered well spent. Besides, money really wasn't the issue.

With greater power came a better degree of target vectoring and special reference accuracy. The new energy sensor would now be able to dial into the jump destination a greater time away from when the event had taken place. He typed the new calculations on his desktop and then backed up the information on a disk. Through all his experiments, he had been meticulous with his notes and lab information. Copious data entry had been his strong point throughout his career.

In all the time he had labored in his lab alone in his quest, not once had he questioned his right or even his obligation to do what he was now doing. There had been no moral check, no filter, and no emotional reticence about the work. But now, he could not shake Greg's statements and palatable fear that governments and men of power would do anything to have control of the process. Killing would be justified for the greater good, and anybody that stood in the way would be eliminated. He sat back in his chair, tossing his reading glasses on the table while rubbing his eyes. He needed to sleep, having spent the last twenty-hours straight working.

Drinking down the last bit of cold coffee, he rechecked the centrifuge settings and then decided he'd sleep for a few hours on the small cot he kept in the lab. It was times like this when he missed her the most. It had always been a comforting thought to know that she was upstairs doing the things she did to make the house a home. Meals were prepared, the clothes washed, and the household run with a comforting hum, the white noise of stability that only a woman can generate. As he kicked off his shoes and snapped off the lab lights, he let the memories of her touch and smell dance just beyond his reach.

How long had it been since she left, five years, ten, a thousand? He lay back on the cot listening to the late afternoon wind blow against the house above while the truth of who he was as a husband crept in. He had failed her, led her into the dead-end of his life, and now he was alone.

At sixty-four, he should have grandchildren, golf games with friends, lodge meetings, and quiet walks with the woman that loved him for all that he was and for all that he wasn't. Regret chased him into his sleep. The crush of emotional failure hammered away, giving him neither comfort nor clarity. Even in his dreams, he was aware that a man could have the whole world and all of time in his possession, but if there was no one to share it with, it meant nothing.

As his fitful sleep continued, he was unaware that the science of his own making was expanding at a fast, yet unseen, rate. The dark energy bubble that had been amplified and used for the time continuum jump was now feeding on itself and had grown larger than the zero point he had designated in his lab. In fact, the invisible bubble was now four times the original size, which meant it could encompass and transport four times the target mass upon any viable energy ignition.

If he had been aware of the anomaly, he would have been able to calculate the expansion and would have come to the stunning realization that within the new mass and depth of dark matter available, he would easily be able to move not only himself and an assistant through the continuum, but probably the mass of his entire house. There was now a tear in the very fabric of time, a tear he had gone through without consequence until now.

Taylor heard a door bell ringing and then a heavy knock on the door as he looked at his wrist watch and noticed that he had been asleep a solid three hours. The doorbell rang again. He didn't move. The sleep had been wonderful and heavy, and whoever was at the door would just have to come back some other time. He rested in the fact that the doors were locked, the lights were off, and he was secure in his lab. No, sleep is what he needed now, not some mindless chatter from a nosey neighbor. Whoever was outside rang the doorbell again and then apparently left. Taylor was asleep a minute later.

Chapter 7

By eight, Greg had just gotten up after a fitful night's sleep. The argument with his wife Carol had gone long and badly. He had gotten into Missoula around ten last night, and she had met him at the airport. After her initial shock at seeing his grey hair, he could tell she was in no mood for bullshit. They had been married for six years and normally called each other several times a day. In fact the other faculty members at the university gave him a hard time about the numerous calls he received and made to Carol throughout the day.

They were crazy about each other, and it showed to any casual observer. On the ride home from the airport, he desperately tried to explain his behavior. "Leaving his grad-students on a dig, not phoning in for nearly a day, and what, in God's name happened to your hair." She had listened quietly while driving, deeply suspicious of the whole story. By the time they arrived home, she had heard enough. She was not going to bed and have welcome-home-sex until she had some straight answers.

"Listen, Sweetheart, I just need to sleep tonight and tomorrow I will fill you in on what is going on," he announced stepping out of the shower. She stood in the doorway with her arms crossed and her head cocked to the side, the way she always did when she was pissed or scared. "Are you having an affair?" she asked. "You know, I've seen that pretty grad student Suzy or Sissy or whatever her name is flirting with you, saw it at the faculty tea last month."

He tossed the damp towel in the sink. "What, no, you're kidding right? C'mon, baby, you know I wouldn't do that." He pulled her close. "I promise I will tell you everything. It's just that I am so Goddamned tired right now that I honestly think I am about to pass out. Something extraordinary has happened, and I really need to be rested when I tell you about it"

He pulled her close and kissed her just as she was about to speak. "I swear to God, Greg," she announced, "if this involves some perky little student of yours I'm gonna cut these off in your sleep." Her firm grip on his balls and the serious look in her eyes let him know that she was only half kidding. It would have been a turn-on if he hadn't been so exhausted. He held up a three-finger salute. "Promise ya, killer. It's going to knock your socks off. Just let me rest."

She kissed him quick.   "All right go to bed. You just remember what I said."

"You got it baby. God, you're sexy when you're jealous." He rolled into bed and was asleep in minutes.

This morning he shuffled into the kitchen following the smell of coffee, still not sure how he was going to explain what he had seen and done the last twenty-four hours. One thing he did know for sure was that he was going to tell her the truth. He just could not keep something this spectacular from her. His fear now was that she would laugh in his face and not believe a word he said. He found her sitting on the couch in her robe and pajamas, looking like she had been up for hours.

"Okay, let's hear it," she announced. He poured a cup of coffee and sat down beside her on the couch. "Oh, and before you start, Melissa, your department head called and wanted to know if you are coming in today. They said they needed to discuss some things about your trip."

"So what did you tell her?"

"I told her that you and I had some things to discuss." She pulled the thick stack of bundled bills out from under her robe and dropped it in his lap. "I think we have a lot to talk about."

He looked at the stack of money, having completely forgotten about it. "You went through my bag?" he asked, setting the money on the end table.

"You better believe it, Greg. I have six years of my life invested in this marriage, and I am not going to be left without answers. Finding that money scares me more than finding some grad student's panties. What are you involved with, Greg? Are you doing something illegal?"

He sipped his coffee trying to figure out where to start. "No baby, not yet."

An hour and a half later he stopped talking, letting the information settle in the room. Carol had said nothing as he told her everything. She now sat open-mouthed and visibly stunned by what she had just heard.

"C'mon baby, say something. I need to know what you think."

"Time travel - you have got to be shitting me!" Carol very rarely swore. Her strict religious upbringing and personal style just seemed out-of-sync with profanity. He had always found it amusing when she swore.

"All true, Sweetheart, every word. I am still having trouble believing it myself." The phone rang in the kitchen, stopping the conversation.

"That will be the school," she replied, getting up from the couch and answering the phone on the third ring. "Yes, just a minute. It's for you," she said holding the phone.

"Yes, Hi, Melissa. Ah, yes, I will stop by this afternoon. One o'clock would be fine. Okay, thank you."

Carol sat back down on the couch. "What are you going to tell them?" she asked. "Hopefully, not the same thing you told me."

"You don't believe me?"

"I don't know what to believe, Greg. Put yourself on my side. I mean, we just bought this house, my job is going great, you're established at school, and now you come home with this fantastic story and all this money. I mean, my God, Greg, how am I suppose to react?"

She was right and she deserved better, he thought, but he also knew that he would be going back to New Mexico as soon as he could book a flight. Now that he was rested and his head halfway clear, he knew he had to get back as soon as he could. This was far too important an event.

"Go with me."

"What, go with you? Where? How can I go anywhere? I have to be back at work tomorrow. For that matter, you have to be back at work tomorrow."

He sat down beside her, holding her hands, "Listen I am telling you the absolute truth and I really need you to believe me. We have plenty of money for me to do this. Nothing changes between you and me, but I need to see this thing through. This is the most incredible discovery ever made, and I am part of it, Babe. I have to do this."

She nodded, while looking at her lap, "Okay," she replied quietly. "Go do what you need to do, but I will be staying here."

He lifted her chin. "It's going to be okay, Sweetheart, promise." He kissed her as she brushed back a tear. "Please call me when you get this figured out," she whispered.

"I promise I will stay in touch on a daily basis." A second later, he knew in his gut that he would never be able to keep his promise. Instinctively he knew his world had changed. This was not a temporary parting. He was saying goodbye. By ten o' clock that morning, he was already on his way to the airport.

****

"So, I plan on going over to the house this afternoon. You guys are more then welcome to come along." Ania and the rest of the NEST and NRC group were seated around one of the large tables in the back of the Shady Brook coffee shop. They had all met in the morning for breakfast and were discussing their next move. Ania had been unsuccessful yesterday at contacting the homeowner. "If I don't make contact today, I am going to get a hold of the FEDs and get a search warrant," continued Ania. "I don't want to drag this thing out too long. We need to find out what's going on."

"Agreed," replied Dillon. "I am getting pressure from the higher-ups to get some answers."

"All right," announced Abbott. "What time we heading over there?"

Ania checked his watch. "I think we should head over about one o'clock. That gives me time to make a few calls. If you guys need to gather some more info, now would be a good time to do it."

Abbott drank down the last of his coffee. "I am going to go ahead and contact the local power crew that's here and see if they have anything new."

Dillon tossed several bills on the table. "Yeah, we have some things we need to nail down. We need a few more peripheral scans. We will meet you guys at the house at one."

****

Fourteen hundred miles to the west, Greg was settling into his seat just before takeoff. Carol was now a reluctant witness to the process. He had told her the truth, which gave him some comfort. As far as the University was concerned, he had ducked his meeting, citing health issues. He had over twenty-three sick days on the books, and now was as good a time as any to call them in. If they wanted more answers concerning his recent behavior, then they would have to get in line.

Just before leaving home, he had Carol count the money Taylor had given him. It was just under thirty thousand dollars, a fairly sizable sum to spread out on the kitchen table. He took five and told Carol to put the rest in their account. If anybody at the bank asked about such a large sum, just tell them it was savings we had kept around the house over the years. When she asked him how long he would be gone, he pulled a wild guess and said about two weeks. He asked her again if she wanted to go, and again she refused.

When she had kissed him goodbye at the airport, there had been an odd finality about the embrace. Something cold, brusque, and off-putting was now visible in her body language and general manner. She was taking this very hard, which only made his leaving that much more painful. As he sat looking out the plane's window at nothing, he knew the life he had before he met Taylor was gone forever.

When the plane lifted off, he felt an odd kind of relief, a sense of purpose he had never felt before. Even though he had no idea what was coming next, he knew he was doing the right thing. There wasn't a scientist alive that would not trade places with him in a second. It was a good rationalization, and it hung around for a good minute and a half.

If the truth were told, he was scared right down to his balls. He had just left the woman he loved and the job he had worked years to get. He was now making decisions of epic scale without having any real facts to back them up. He pushed his seat back and tried to rest. Maybe he would be more settled, more sure of his decision when he landed in Taos, and then again, from this moment on, maybe he would never be sure about anything ever again.

****

If Dillon had known who he wanted to talk to or even what the home owner looked like, he would have noticed Taylor driving past and turning at the corner after stopping at the stop sign. It was now five till one, and Dillon was anxious to see just what was going on at 165 Holston Drive. Abbott parked behind Dillon's van and then headed over to the front porch of the house. Ania pulled his identification from his coat pocket and knocked on the door. "Doesn't look like anybody is home," announced Abbott, looking in one of the living room windows.

Ania knocked again. "Looks like I'm getting a search warrant."

"Looks like the place is empty, not a whole lot of furniture in the living room or the kitchen from what I can see," replied Abbott, still looking in the window.

Dillon stepped off the porch and headed back over to his van. "Hey, Kelly, hand me that meter. I can hear some kind of hum coming from the house when I am standing on the porch." Kelly, the driver, handed Dillon the small Atmospheric signal-meter. "You think this place is hot?"

"Not sure. Go ahead and turn on the sniffer. Let's see if we get a Rad count."

Kelly turned out of his seat and disappeared into the back of the large van. "It's on."

"You getting anything?" he asked, turning on his own meter.

"Ah, hang on. Wow! I am getting all kinds of ambient fluctuations here. It's like a pulse. You might want to look at this, Dillon."

Dillon opened the van door and took a seat beside his tech. "Jesus, look at the peak," he said, leaning in close to the computer screen.

"You ever see anything like that?" asked Kelly.

"Nope, never on the street. These are lab readings. There is something going on in that house, and we need to find out what it is."

Just as Dillon was about to pick up his cell and call DC, Abbott stuck his head in the van window. "Hey, guys, the home owner is back. He just drove up."

Taylor felt a ball of fear start to roll in his stomach as he pulled into the driveway of his house. The three men standing on the porch had the look of government law enforcement and were now heading across the front yard.

"Can I help you, gentlemen?" he asked, stepping out of his car.

"Sir, do you live in this residence?" asked Ania, stepping forward.

"Ah, yes, and you are?"

"Sir, I'm Agent Ania from Homeland Security. We need to ask you some questions. Can we go inside?"

Taylor thought for a moment. He really had no choice. He knew that if he refused to talk to these men, they would be back. Then he really would have no choice." Sure, no problem."

As the group walked into the house, Dillon noticed the energy meter peak. "Sir, are you running some kind of large generator or alternative power source here?"

Taylor was desperately trying to stay as calm as possible. "Ah, why do you ask? And I did not get your name."

"Sir, my name is Dillon Conroy, and I am from the NNSA. And your name?"

"Bruce Taylor. Am I under arrest?"

"No, Mister Taylor," replied Ania. "This is just a preliminary inquiry. The reason for us contacting you is that we have received some information that there are some rather unusual power readings and power usage levels coming from this residence. Maybe you could explain this."

"Ah, well, I have a lab in my basement where I conduct some experiments. I'm a retired aeronautical engineer from Sandia Labs."

Dillon looked up from his meter smiling. "I knew that I knew you, Dr. Taylor," he said, extending his hand. "I read your book about alternative propulsion elements a couple years ago. Incredible work."

Relieved, Taylor shook hands smiling. "Gosh, I didn't think anyone would read that stuff. It was a lot of theory and a long time ago."

"Still, it was a great read, and I really picked up a lot of good information," replied Dillon.

"Dr. Taylor, we really do need to wrap this up," announced Ania. "Can we see this lab of yours?"

"Sure, yes, of course. It's in the basement."

"After you, sir," replied Ania, nodding.

As the men walked down the basement stairs, Taylor could not shake the feeling that something was not right about the lab. An odd, almost visible kinetic energy was in the air. Taylor turned on the lights and led the group into the middle of the large room.

"My God," announced Dillon, "this is some lab. What kind of work are you doing down here, Dr Taylor?"

"Laser calibration mostly, and some inert nano structure experiments."

Dillon surveyed the extensive amount of equipment carefully, while checking his meter.

"What are the fatigues and tactical gear for, Dr. Taylor?" questioned Ania, looking at the gear still lying on one of the tables.

"Ah, those, just some old stuff I picked up at a surplus store. I have an interest in military uniforms and equipment. I collect it."

"Dr. Taylor, my name is Abbott, and I am from the NRC," he announced, stepping down from the stairway. "I'm really not sure what we have here beyond the fact that you're using an incredible amount of power, which I think you're probably going to be charged for, by the way."

Taylor nodded. "Yes, I fully understand, and I will pay for what I have used."

"Sir, it could be in the hundreds of thousands of dollars," replied Abbott, "and this kind of power draw from this residence is going to have to stop."

"For what reason?"

"We are not here because we like the scenery. We are here to determine if what you're doing constitutes a threat to national security."

"National security? You're joking?"

"No sir," replied Dillon, "we are going to have to shut down all of this while we make an assessment as to the possible risk to the public. I also need you to address the fact that I am picking up a fairly high Rad count."

"Probably because I am enriching some uranium ore."

Alarmed, Ania spoke up. "Did you say, Dr. Taylor, that you're enriching Uranium ore?"

"Yes, I did, but it's only a very small amount. I am looking for a more reliable power source for my experiments."

Ania walked into the middle of the room. "All right, I have heard all that I need to hear. Mister Taylor, this lab is now shut down and you are going to have to leave the residence while I get a team in here. I need you to turn off and shut down any equipment that is currently running, and then we are all going to leave."

Dillon had been looking closely at one of the large metal circuit arrays near the activation zone. "Dr. Taylor, can you tell me what this station is for?"

Taylor could see where this was going. They were closing in with their questions. If possible, they were going to charge him with a crime. "Ah, I do harmonic resonance experiments between those panels, minor stuff really."

Dillon looked up from the large panel. "Really? Would it be possible to show us exactly what you're doing - a brief demonstration? I think it would go a long way in helping us determine the threat level we are dealing with, if any."

"Absolutely not," announced Ania, walking over to Dillon. "From the Homeland Security side of the house, I believe this place constitutes a very real danger to the city and possibly the country. I do not want to risk this place blowing up half the town."

"Listen, from the nuclear side of the house, I need to see with my own eyes what I am dealing with here. Whatever I observe from a science standpoint has to be in the record. Now, in order for me to determine the level of threat that may or may not exist, I need to see what he is doing."

Abbott walked over to where the men were standing. "Guys, I think Dillon is correct. I really think we need to see just what exactly is going on here before we start making heavy decisions. I personally would like to see what this is all about."

Ania thought for a moment. "All right, you guys are the experts. Let's see what he's doing."

Dillon nodded to Taylor. "Go ahead, Doctor. Please show us what you're working on."

Taylor could feel the panic start to rise. "Ah, well, okay, what I was working on last week was the main parabolic mirror adjustment of that laser over there." Taylor walked over and turned on the main switch that controlled all three power stations. A low hum filled the air as the machines came to life.

Less than a split second later, Taylor knew something was terribly wrong. As he turned, he saw the brilliant blue and white flash of light and then a thunderclap explosion that blew him off his feet and into the back wall with enough force to nearly knock him unconscious.

An odd, sulphur-smelling haze drifted around the room as he struggled to his feet. He found his glasses on the floor and stood slowly, surveying the lab. Glassware had been broken throughout the room along with several of the electrical panels that now lay in pieces on the floor. Still shaking the cobwebs from his head, he found the lab ventilator switch and turned it on. Instantly the haze began to clear, giving him a sharper picture of the damage. His ears were still ringing as he made his way over to where the three men had been standing seconds earlier. To his shock, the only thing left of the three was a single shoe. They had vanished.

****

Dillon opened his eyes, trying to comprehend what he could now see. He was on his back, outside, looking up into the night sky. Painfully, he sat up and noticed Agent Ania lying beside him. The air was cool and the unmistakable smell of fresh horse manure, strong and close. Still dazed, he slowly got to his feet as the sounds of the area rushed in. Horses were everywhere. In fact, he soon discovered that he was standing in the middle of a large circular horse stable with at least fifty or more horses milling about nervously.

Ania was now moving and moaning at his feet, trying to sit up. He knelt beside the agent. "You okay?" he asked, slowly pulling the man to his feet.

"What the fuck just happened?" he asked, shaking his head. "Were we in an explosion or what?"

116

Dillon looked around, trying to make some kind of sense out of this new reality. "I, ah, I'm not sure. The last thing I saw was Dr. Taylor turning on the power to the lab."

Ania dropped to his knees. "I'm going to get sic..aaaghh." He vomited on Dillon's shoes, his back arching in heavy heaves. A second later, Dillon felt the bile rise in his own throat as he stumbled back trying to hold it in. Both men were now side by side on their knees retching.

"You there, what's going on over there?"

Dillon cast a sideways glance and spotted a large dark shape standing on the other side of the corral fence. Feeling slightly better, he got to his feet and waved. "Hello, I could use some help."

"You boys better leave them horses alone. Now get out of there!" shouted the shape. "I won't tell you again."

Ania was now on his feet. "Listen, Asshole!" he shouted, wiping his chin. "We need some help."

The shape stood motionless. "What did you say, boy?" questioned the figure angrily.

Ania held up his badge. "I'm a Federal agent, pal, and we need some help. So lose the attitude before you find yourself in real trouble."

"Mister, I don't know what a Federal agent is, but you got about five seconds to get out of my corral before I plant ya."

Ania quickly drew his weapon, pointing it at the shape forty feet away. "Get on the ground, Asshole! I'm a Federal Agen....".

A thunderous blast from Dillon's right lifted Ania off his feet, dumping him onto his back six feet away. Dillon felt the heavy numbing sting of something hot shoot through his forearm. Dazed, he fell to the ground beside the agent.

"Goddamn, Ross, ya hit 'em both. What the hell is wrong with you?"

"Hell, John, the other one was standing too close. How was I supposed to get that fella who drew down on ya?"

Both men climbed over the corral and walked up to where the men lay. Dillon could not make out the shadowy faces but could tell that one of the men was older. The older man knelt down beside him. "Where'd you get hit, mister? My deputy isn't the best shot. I would count myself lucky if I were you."

Dillon held up his right arm, which was bleeding heavily. "Who are you people?" he gasped, still trying to comprehend what was going on. "Where am I, I, What happened?"

The man pulled Dillon to his feet. "Well, sir, you just got yourself shot by my deputy and your friend there just got himself killed. We're not real fond of armed horse thieves around here. I'm Sheriff John Coleman, and you are?"

Dillon felt his knees start to buckle as nausea nearly took him to the ground. Just before passing out, he felt strong hands and several more voices in the fog pick him up. He was flying again.

****

Stunned, and still not sure about what just happened, Taylor slowly sat in one of the lab chairs. The smoke had now cleared, revealing a room full of broken glass and overturned equipment. The once pristine lab now looked as if a hand grenade had gone off in the middle of the room.

Looking around the room, he picked up one of the laptops that had been knocked off the table by the blast. Hoping it still worked, he started punching in his pass code. If there had been a measurable increase within the space continuum he had been using or some other off-the-scale power fluctuation, it would have been recorded. Finally getting to the data, he was astounded by what he saw. Seeing the numbers and the scale of the expanse, he was surprised that the blast had not been greater.

"Keep your hands in sight! Don't move!" shouted the man, standing at the bottom of the stairs.

Shocked to see someone else in the room, Taylor rolled his chair back, his hands raised. "I, I was just trying to find out what happened. Who are you?"

"Sir, I heard the explosion outside. Are you injured?"

"No, No I am fine."

"Sir, I'm an agent with the NNSA and I need you to tell me where the other investigator is, right now."

Taylor lowered his hands. "There were three investigators here. Were you with them?"

"I have been outside in the van. Now, I need you to tell me what happened. Where is the investigator?"

"I'm really not sure what happened. They were standing over there. When I turned on the power, there was an explosion and then they were gone."

Kelly pulled out his cell phone and punched in the secure number.

"Your phone will not work down here, "announced Taylor. "The room is shielded."

"Shit," replied Kelly, backing up the stairs. "You, stay right there!" he shouted, pointing. "The police are on the way."

Taylor looked back at his computer as the investigator disappeared up the stairs still trying to use his phone. It could not end this way he thought, loading the thumb drive into the computer. He had worked too many years, sacrificed everything important in his life for this discovery. As if he were out of his body watching another person, he quickly crossed the room and grabbed the small 22-caliber pistol from the cabinet by the stairs. In the past he had used it for snakes. Now he was using it to change the course of his life.

Raw, pulse-pounding adrenaline flashed through his body as he bounded up the stairs to the empty living room. He spotted the investigator in the front yard still trying to make his cell phone work. In three strides, he was outside behind the man, his pistol raised. "Put the phone down," he announced, trying to stay calm. "I said, put it down."

Kelly turned, his eyes wide with fear. "Okay, Okay, just don't shoot."

Taylor lowered the gun. "Put your hands down, for God's sake, and get back into the house. Now."

Kelly quickly walked back up the sidewalk with Taylor at his back. "Did you make the call?" questioned Taylor, shutting the living room door behind him.

"What?"

"I said did you make the call?"

"No, there is some kind of interference. I wasn't able to reach anybody."

"Get back downstairs," commanded Taylor. "Move."

"Surely, you don't think you're going to get away with this?" protested Kelly, moving down the stairway. "Somebody had to have heard the explosion. They will call the police. They're probably on their way here now."

Taylor closed and locked the basement door behind him. "I doubt that anybody heard anything. There are only two families living on this block, and they all leave for work early. Mrs. Hollister, next door, is almost ninety; I doubt she heard or saw anything."

Kelly walked down into the middle of the lab. "You willing to take the risk that there is no witness to this?"

Taylor kicked one of the lab chairs in Kelly's direction. "Sit down."

"Listen," shouted Kelly, "you're really getting yourself in deep. Stop now while you still can."

Taylor stepped up to Kelly still pointing the pistol at his forehead. "If nobody heard the explosion, sir, I can guarantee you that they will not hear the shot. Now sit down." Taylor cocked the hammer. "I said, sit down."

In all the years he had been an analyst, Kelly had never had a weapon pointed at him, nor had he ever been threatened directly. "Listen, just calm down. Let's talk."

Taylor stepped closer. "Do I look like I'm not calm? You have no idea what's going on here, so sit down and be quiet."

"All right, all right, okay." He sat down feeling as if he had aged ten years. It was obvious that he was not going to get anywhere by arguing with the man. "Okay, just relax."

"Stop saying that," replied Taylor. "I am relaxed. Just sit in that chair and be quiet. I have a lot to tell you and I need your full attention."

"Okay, fine, I'm listening."

Taylor walked over to one of the cabinets and pulled out several large plastic zip ties. "I use these for cables and such, and I think they will be sufficient for you." He zip-tied both of Kelly's arms to the chair. "Is that too tight?" he asked.

"No, listen, you really need to stop before anybody else gets hurt."

"How do you know anyone was hurt?" questioned Taylor, sticking the pistol in his back pocket.

"My boss came in here. I heard an explosion and now he's gone. What else would you like me to think?"

Taylor sat down in one of the other lab chairs, already exhausted from the exchange. "Do I look like someone who intentionally hurts people? What is your name since we are talking? I assume you know mine."

"My name is Kelly, Mark Kelly."

"Okay Mark, now that we are all calm," replied Taylor, smiling, "I have a story to tell you. I think that you will see things differently when I'm finished, at least I hope so. Now, how much do you know about Quantum physics?"

Chapter 8

"Looks like you're feeling better. This is Doc William's office. You've been out since last night."

Dillon eased himself up on his elbow, wincing from the pain in his arm. "Jesus, that hurts."

"Yeah, well I'm sorry about that," replied the older man sitting at his bedside. "Like I said, my deputy isn't the best shot in the country. Doc said the buck shot went clear through - nothing broken."

Dillon focused on the man's face, "Who are you again?"

"Sheriff John Coleman," he replied, extending his hand. "Like I said, I'm sorry about you getting shot. You just got between my deputy and that Mexican."

"How is he? Where is he?"

Coleman looked surprised by the question. "Hell, son, he's laying over at Longfellow's funeral parlor. You wouldn't know where his next of kin resides would you?"

The memory of last night came rushing back as Dillon lay back on the bed. "My God, where the hell am I?"

Coleman got up from his chair and poured a glass of water from the pitcher on the nightstand. "You're in Deer Lodge, Montana, not the prettiest town in the country but not the worst either." He handed Dillon the glass. "Now that you're able to carry on a conversation, I have some questions I really need to ask about you and your friend."

Dillon could feel the barely suppressed panic roll in his stomach. "I am really confused. I, I, don't know how I got here. I mean, Deer Lodge, Montana? How the hell did this happen?"

Coleman sat back down and hung his hat over the footboard post of Dillon's bed. "That's the same question I need to ask you. Now, I don't want you to get offended, but I went through your billfold when you were unconscious and I found these." He reached into his coat pocket and dropped Dillon's driver's license and several credit cards on the bed. "Sure would like an explanation about those."

Dillon picked up the cards. "These are my driver's license and credit cards. What's the problem?"

Coleman smiled. "Well, for one thing, what's a drivers license and credit cards, and what are they made of? I've never seen anything like it, and I've been alive fifty-seven years."

"Ah, I, I don't know what to say. Is, is, this some kind of western theme park or what?"

Coleman laughed. "Theme park? Well, son, we are in the West, but I'm not sure what a theme park is."

Dillon looked around the room slowly realizing the stunning truth that this was no dream. His reality had changed.

"What year is this?" he asked, not really wanting to hear the answer.

"It's 1889, Nov 6th, Thursday." Coleman kept a steady gaze. "Where you from, Mister Conroy, and how did you get here?"

"Am I being charged with a crime, Sheriff?"

"No"

Dillon thought for a moment. "What if I told you I have no idea how I got here?"

"Okay, I don't find that hard to believe. The reason for my questions is that you and your friend are dressed like nobody I have ever seen before. Also, you're carrying property that I have never seen before."

Dillon slowly sat up and swung his feet onto the floor. "Sheriff, you would not believe me if I told you where I am from compared to where I now sit. I, I can hardly believe it myself."

Coleman was quiet, trying to spot any deception in Dillon, "I'll tell you what, Mister Conroy. You get yourself up and around, and get yourself something to eat. The county is going to bury your friend later on this afternoon. After that, if you feel like you want to talk, I'll be in my office."

"Sheriff, was there anybody else that was dressed like me and my friend found in the area?"

Coleman stood up to leave, "Not that I know of, but if he is dressed like you, I'm sure he'll turn up. This town isn't that big."

Dillon nodded. "Thank you, Sheriff, I think I need some air. I'll come by your office later on. Ah, Sheriff, I ah, I don't think I have any money. I mean, I have money but I doubt it's the correct ty…"

Coleman waved him off. "Don't worry about paying for your supper. The least my office can do is pay for your meal. After all, we did put a couple of holes in you. Head on down to the Clear Water Café. It's next door. Tell Melvin I sent you. He'll get you what you want. The food is pretty good." Coleman put on his hat and headed for the door. "O yeah, before I leave, you never did tell me what those cards with you name on them are made of. I know it's not paper, and it damn sure isn't wood."

"Plastic," replied Dillon. "The cards are made of plastic."

Coleman said the word to himself several times. "Plastic, huh, that Mexican fella was carrying some cards just like yours. I have his belongings in my office." Coleman smiled, "I hope you'll come by my office, Mister Conroy. I'd like to hear more about this plastic."

Dillon nodded. "Okay, Sheriff, I'm sure I am going to need to talk to someone later."

"Good-day, Mister Conroy." He left the room, closing the door behind him, leaving the smell of dirty wool, leather, and chewing tobacco.

****

127

Tug Dugan was down to his last bit of whisky, which only soured an already bad mood. He downed the last bit and threw the empty bottle in the weeds as he walked along the weed-choked path that ran along the river. The Little Blackfoot River was a muddy, meandering stream that ran just on the outskirts of town.

Whenever he found, stole, or earned enough money for a bottle, he would head to the river. It was a quiet place to go. It was also a good place to get away from his two crazy brothers while he drank. The last time he had shared a bottle, Pete, the oldest of the three, pulled a knife in a drunken rage and cut off the ear of his younger brother Mel.

As he stumbled through the high weeds on his way back home, he thought about the depressing fact that someday he would probably have to kill Pete in order to save his own life. All the folks in Deer Lodge knew the Dugan boys were drunks and general hell raisers, and whenever anything of value or even junk turned up missing, the Dugans were the first ones suspected.

All three had been in the Army and all three had been drummed out for being unfit. Pete, in a drunken fog, had beaten a young Lieutenant half to death up in Bozeman and ended up doing three years in Leavenworth. Mel stole four cavalry horses when he was stationed at Fort Keogh and was caught when he tried to sell them to a whorehouse owner in Miles City. That bought him twenty lashes and a year of military confinement at the fort.

Tug had just been released from service for stealing three rifles from the armory and selling them to a trapper who was also a part-time cavalry scout. That earned him a year in jail and a beating from the military prison guards that left him half-blind in his left eye and a permanent limp from the broken left leg that never healed properly. Several months earlier, he had protested the bad food one day by throwing his plate against the bars. The guards took it personal and relieved their anger by throwing him down several flights of metal stairs.

It was getting dark and the wind was starting to come up, its bite common for November weather in Montana. He pulled his collar tight as he stepped onto the wagon track road that led into town. He hadn't gone more than three steps when he suddenly stopped after catching sight of the strangest thing he had ever seen. Up ahead, ten feet off the ground hung a man by one leg in an old cottonwood tree. The man, his face blue black, appeared to have gotten his leg tangled in the branches leaving him suspended upside down, high off the ground.

Tug slowly walked up, studying the man from below. He had seen dead men before and could tell that this one was definitely dead. A thin stream of blood hung from the man's nose like a gutted deer, a good indication he had been there awhile. Not sure what to do, he looked around for something to stand on to get a better look. He found half of a small stump and propped it up at the base of the tree. "Hey mister." He touched the man's shoulder just to be sure.

Tug saw the gold wedding ring and the strange silver metal band on his wrist. He was able to get the bracelet, but the fingers were too swollen to pull the ring off. He reached up into the pockets of the man's pants and found a wallet. In the front pocket, he found a small ring of keys and a small bottle made out of the lightest glass he had ever seen. Inside were several large pink tablets. On the man's belt was a small black box, which he pulled off and put in his coat pocket. *This body has all kinds of treasures*, he thought, as he stepped down from the stump. "Who the hell are you, mister?" he whispered. As he thumbed through the man's wallet, he found the strange smooth cards with a small colored picture on the front. Fascinated, he studied the name typed out beside the picture.

"Chris Abbott," he said out-loud. He looked up at the body smiling, "Please to meet ya, Mister Abbott."

"What you do'in boy?"

Startled by the voice, Tug spun around in time to see both his brothers stepping through the weeds. "We knew you'd be down here, pecker-wood," announced Pete, stepping out onto the road. The sun was now only a faint orange glow on the horizon, taking what little warmth it carried through the day with it. "Hey, ol' man Walters said he'd pay..." Pete stopped in mid-sentence, suddenly noticing the body in the tree. "Goddamn! Who the hell is that?"

Mel also saw the body and started backing up, "Jesus, Tug, what'd you do?"

"I didn't do a Goddamned thing!" shouted Tug. "That son-of-a-bitch was hangin there when I walked up. Scared three colors of shit right out of me."

Pete walked up and jerked on one of Abbott's arms. "I'll be damned. He's stuck for sure."

"Is he dead?" questioned Mel from the gloom.

"About as dead as a Christian can get," announced Pete, tugging the arm again. "Get over here, Mel, and help me pull."

"The hell you say. I ain't touching no dead man, especially one hangin in a tree at night. Besides whoever put him there just might want him to stay there."

Pete turned and faced his brothers in the dark. "Listen son, you don't help me get him down, then you don't get nothing I find in his pockets. That goes for you too, Tug. I get him down, I'm keeping every Goddamned thing I find."

Minutes later, they had pulled the body down and stripped it. Pete rummaged through the empty pockets getting madder by the second. "Not a Goddamned thing." Tug remained quiet as Pete suddenly kicked the corpse in the side. "Shit, this son-of-a-bitch is worse off than we are."

Knowing that he would eventually be caught and then suffer a fairly decent beating, Tug spoke up. "I cleaned him out before you boys got here."

Even in the dark, Tug could tell his older brother was burning holes in him with his stare. "I swear to God, Tug. I oughta kick the teeth out of your head for holding out."

"I ain't holding out, Goddamnit. I just told ya. I cleaned him out," protested Tug.

"C'mon fellas, we gotta git. Somebody is gonna come by for sure and see us," announced Mel from the dark.

Pete thought for a moment. "All right, let's get him in the river. Ground's too hard to bury him." After a heavy effort, they were able to drag the body down the steep weed-filled bank and push it into the slow moving current. Tug stood in the now freezing darkness watching the black tide gently roll the body in the moonlight until it disappeared. He knew the Little Blackfoot never gave up its dead. Hard men in the past had used the brown water for much of the same. An hour later the body of Chris Abbott was a mile downstream. Might as well have been on the moon.

****

By four-thirty in the afternoon, Greg had already picked up his rental car and was now making his way to Shady Brook. Tuning the radio to the soft-rock station, he used the white noise to help him relax as he thought about every good and bad scenario concerning his involvement.

What would happen when the press found out about Taylor's discovery and the mega media blitz that would follow? In addition, he knew down to his core that the government would never let this discovery see the light of day once they became aware of it, a realization and suspicion he found deeply troubling. As he drove, he noticed that he was physically trembling from anticipation with the thought of actually being able to move through the time continuum, an ability that was staggering with its implications.

Another source of his angst was his discussion concerning the actual mechanics of the process. Taylor had been vague, probably rightfully so, when he talked about "The Process". His astonishing intellectual depth concerning his discovery was next to impossible to convey to the layman. On the other hand, he knew Taylor was keeping extremely detailed notes, and he was resolved to have him attempt to explain them. Ironically enough, he was now feeling a tremendous sense of urgency, a pervasive sense that time truly was running out.

An hour later he turned onto Taylor's street and was more than a little alarmed to see a van and a second strange car parked in front. Before getting out of his own car, he sat for a solid ten minutes surveying the street for anything that might indicate a trap.

Confident he was alone, he left his car and walked up to the front door of Taylor's house. Just in front of the short flight of stairs that led onto the small porch, Greg spotted a cell phone in the grass. He froze in mid-step, instinctively knowing that this was a bad omen. He looked around while bending down to pick it up.

"That's my phone." Greg nearly had a heart attack. Startled and not sure if he should start running, he backed away from the man standing on the porch who was now studying him intently.

"Who the hell are you?" questioned Greg, still backing up.

"My name is Kelly. I'm with NEST, Nuclear Emergency supp..."

'Yeah, I know what NEST is," interrupted Greg. "Where's Dr. Taylor?"

"Downstairs. C'mon, I'm part of this now."

Greg looked up and down the deserted street, shocked, scared, and tremendously confused as to what was going on. "Part of what?" he asked cautiously.

Kelly stepped down from the porch. "Can I have my phone back?"

Greg tossed the phone over. "What's going on here? Am I under arrest or what?"

Kelly closed the phone before putting it in his pocket, "No, you're not under arrest unless you committed a crime I don't know about. Besides, I have no arrest powers. I'm not a cop."

"Then what are you? I thought the Feds always call the shots on things like this."

"Mister Gander, I am a scientist just like you, and I have just been told the most amazing, absolutely mind-boggling story. I really think we need to go back inside and try to find out if it's true or not." He turned and headed back up the steps to the house. "C'mon, Dr. Taylor is in the lab."

Still not sure what was really going on or what major event had taken place since he left, Greg was stunned to see the damage to the lab as he slowly walked down the basement stairs. Glass had been broken, and several metal wiring panels and circuit boards lay strewn around the room. "What happened?" he asked, trying to stay as calm as he could.

Taylor was busy typing on a laptop. "Not sure," he replied without looking up. "But from my initial readings, the continuum aperture appears to have grown in size."

Greg pulled up one of the lab chairs, "Ah, Bruce, you want to introduce me to our visitor here?"

"Yes, yes, I'm sorry. Greg, this is Mark Kelly. He works for NEST. Are you familiar with that organization?"

"And he's here why?" questioned Greg cautiously.

"We were in the first stages of an investigation. We picked up the readings from the lab on a routine flyover last month," replied Kelly.

'Jesus, so the government knows all about this? So, so, what's next?"

An awkward silence filled the room until Taylor spoke up. "Ah, well, as I said, from my preliminary readings, the continuum aperture has grown and due to an accidental power fluctuation, I may have killed his supervisor."

Greg's mind went blank with shock. He wasn't sure if it was the actual news of a possible death that knocked him senseless or the casual, matter-of-fact way Taylor delivered it. "What the fuck happened?"

"They were standing over by the array panels, and when I turned the main power back on, they were pulled into the continuum aperture. In essence, far too much power was used to initiate the jump."

"I heard the explosion from outside," announced Kelley nodding.

"So why haven't you called your superiors about this?" questioned Greg. "I mean, my God, somebody has possibly gotten killed. They now have to be called."

Kelly sat down in one of the other chairs. "Well, as it stands right now, Dr. Taylor has explained to me what he has been doing here and told me what he thinks happened."

"And you're fine with the idea that someone you know has been killed by this machine?" To Greg, the reality of what had just happened was starting to sink in. "I mean, this has gotten extremely serious now; this has got to be reported."

"Hold on," replied Kelly, "you didn't let me finish. Dr. Taylor thinks he can reverse the process, and in theory bring the men back. Considering the off-the-chart magnitude of this kind of discovery, I personally thought he should have that chance."

"And if he can't, if he can't bring them back, what then?"

Kelly thought for a moment. "If he cannot, then I will do everything I can to see that he is prosecuted to the fullest extent of the law." Kelly turned to Taylor. "You've got two hours. After that, I start making phone calls."

Taylor nodded while looking at Greg. "Well then, looks like we have some work to do."

Chapter 9

It took the two older men all morning to dig the grave. The nearly frozen Montana clay grudgingly gave up the 6-foot depth. Dillon stood beside the mound of black earth still trying to comprehend the enormity of his situation. The nausea had stopped hours ago only to be replaced by the dull, throbbing pain in his arm. It hurt to move his fingers, and the cold wind that was now whipping around the dreary graveyard was not helping.

He checked his watch as Ania's crude pine box was lowered into the hole. The watch was brand new, a birthday gift from his wife two weeks ago. The frozen hands read one-forty-five, the exact time he was blown, or flew, or was transported from the lab.

'If you want to say something, it would be all right," announced Coleman quietly.

Dillon looked at the other men who stood around the sad grave. This was real. He could smell the fresh dirt, feel the cold wind on his face and ears. The two gravediggers and the Sheriff were hard men, raw-boned from the weather, aged beyond their years by the daily hardships of their lives.

"I didn't know him very well," replied Dillon, looking down at the box. "In fact, I did not even know his first name."

Coleman dropped a handful of dirt onto the box. "Dust to dust." He looked across the hole at the two gravediggers, "All right boys, fill it in. Nothing more to do. We don't have a proper head stone. The funeral home said they would carve his name on a wooden cross. That Jenkins boy should have it done by this afternoon."

Dillon dropped a handful of dirt onto the box, not knowing what else to do. "Thank you, Sheriff. Ah, if you have some time, I think we need to talk."

Coleman nodded while taking two large coins out of a small coin purse. "Here ya go fellas," he said, handing the silver to the men. "Much obliged for your help." He nodded to Dillon. "C'mon, let's get out of this wind. I'm about to freeze to death out here. I could use some coffee."

Dillon pulled his collar tight and followed Coleman without looking back. The only thing left of Homeland Security Agent Carlos Ania was the sound of Montana clay hitting his coffin. The men walked back into town without talking. Dillon was still trying to figure out just what and how he was going to explain himself to the Sheriff. He could sense something in the older man, wariness, and a tangible fear that colored their conversation.

They crossed the wide dirt street and then up the short flight of wooden stairs that led into Coleman's office. "Just have a seat over there," announced Coleman, pointing to one of the wooden chairs along the wall. "You drink coffee?"

Dillon sat down, shivering from the long cold walk. "Yes, that would be fine." Dillon surveyed the room looking for anything that might be familiar, anything that might help him get in touch with his new reality. The room was bigger than it looked from the outside, as wide as a good size modern living room and twice as deep. A gun rack was nailed to the wall above a small table that appeared to be a catchall desk for papers and ledgers. The floor had a thin layer of sawdust while the room smelled like old leather and gun oil. A small potbelly stove in the back far corner snapped and popped from a hot fire of green wood. In the opposite back corner sat a flat metal bar cell about ten-foot square. The cell was empty, which gave Dillon a strange kind of relief. There was something about the heavy punitive vibe of the bars that was unsettling. Again, to Dillon the reality of the place was like a punch in the chest. Nothing was familiar, nothing told him that this was a bad dream, that when he woke up, he would be home with his wife and son.

"Here you go," announced Coleman, handing him a thick white mug of black coffee. "I made this today, so it should be okay, maybe a bit strong." Coleman pulled up a chair by the table. "Okay, son, I am all ears," he said, lighting his pipe.

Dillon took a sip of the brew and immediately regretted it. "Well, I'm not sure where I should start."

"Why don't you start at the beginning, like how you got to Deer Lodge in the first place? Hell, the only thing between here and the North Pole is a barbed wire fence. I can't see you traveling in clothes or shoes like you're wearing." He blew a perfect smoke ring and then looked at Dillon quietly, waiting for his response.

Dillon thought for a moment, working on the internal dilemma of coming clean with what he knew and who he was. This was something he had imagined before, going back into the past and talking to people who lived full lives, had dreams, fears, and aspirations just like him. "I'm still having a hard time adjusting to the fact that I am really here and most importantly how I got here."

"Why is that?"

Dillon took another sip of the bitter tasting coffee, "I am not from this time. Somehow I was put here."

Coleman leaned his chair back smiling. "What time do you think you're from?"

"2013. I have a wife and family. This is the past. This is not supposed to be possible."

"Feels possible to me," replied Coleman. "What's the future like, Mister Conroy? I have a little bit of time. Indulge me."

Dillon thought for a moment. "All right, see this?" He pulled his cell phone out of his pocket. "This is a cell phone. Everybody in the world in the future uses one of these." He flipped it open as the Verizon tone came on.

Amazed, Coleman stared at the phone. "It's some kind of music box?"

"No, it's for talking to people - a communication device."

"Like a telegraph?"

"Not exactly. It uses the airwaves to transmit a signal and then picks up those airwave signals so people can talk." Dillon handed him the phone. "If you push the number 9 and then the number 2 and hold it up to your ear, you will hear a message my wife left me. Go ahead. Try it."

As if holding a fragile eggshell, Coleman cautiously tapped the keypad and slowly put the phone to his ear. *"Hi sweetie, just wanted to say hel..."* Coleman jerked the phone away from his ear in stunned surprise. "I'll be damned," he announced, looking around the room. "How, I mean, where is she talking from? And how is her voice in this box?"

"I really can't explain how the phone works, Sheriff. It has to do with really advanced electrical information, and frankly I would have real trouble passing what little I know about it on to you. Suffice it to say, in 2013 this kind of device is extremely common. Even children use it."

"Can I see that again?"

"Sure," replied Dillon handing him the phone.

"And you say this is your wife leaving you a message?"

"That's right."

Coleman leaned back in his chair and listened to the message three more times before handing the phone back. Dillon was now aware of the fact that he may be having a negative influence on the future by even showing Coleman the phone in the first place. But he needed help. Most importantly, he needed someone to listen.

Coleman handed the phone back. "That box is truly a wonder. You could make a fortune just by showing it to folks."

Dillon smiled. "I'm afraid the battery would run down. I'm actually surprised it works at all."

"What's a battery?"

Dillon smiled at the question. *There was no way he was going to be able to explain 2013 technology to a man in 1889 and not come off sounding like a lunatic.* "It's the power source that allows the phone to work. Energy is stored in this tiny cube." He took the phone apart and pulled out the battery. "That's what allows the phone to work." He handed the small battery to Coleman.

"So what is in this little box?"

"Small circuits, electrical wiring, that's about the best way to explain it."

Coleman handed the battery back. "Okay, Mister Conroy, you have my attention." He tapped out his pipe. "Now I'm not saying I fully believe your story, but just for the sake of argument, let's say I did. What do you want from me?"

"Sheriff, I still have no idea how I ended up here - in this place - this time. I also believe that whoever sent me here will hopefully try and get me back. I guess what I need from you is a place to stay until whoever is responsible for sending me here comes back. I need to stay here and wait."

Coleman thought for a moment. "How long you fixing to wait?"

"For the rest of my life," replied Dillon softly. "I don't think I have much of a choice."

Coleman got up from his chair and stood, looking out the large window at the grey overcast sky outside. "I'll tell you what, Mister Conroy, there's a shed and a bunk out back. You can stay there. I take my meals next door at the café. You're welcome to eat with me. It's a lot of back strap and red beans, but it's not bad."

"I can't thank you enough for your help," announced Dillon. "I don't want charity. I'm willing to work for the room and board."

Coleman turned from the window, scratching his chin thinking. "Well if you are able, I have a need for a deputy. The one that put those holes in your arm ran off with old man Miller's wife last night. The old fool bought and paid for her all the way from San Francisco. I warned him about them Chinamen women - can't be trusted."

"You're kidding! You want me to be a deputy? A deputy Marshal?"

"Mister Conroy, I don't think you realize how hard it is to find good help. If they're not drunks and uneducated riff raff, they're wanted in some other jurisdiction. I don't think you're a drunk, and I can tell you're a whole lot smarter than anybody I have ever met."

"Yes, but I am not a formally trained law enforcement officer. I don't think I'm qualified."

Coleman sat back in his chair with a heavy sigh, "You ever fired a gun, Mister Conroy? Rifle, shotgun, pistol?"

"Well, yes, I was an officer in the Army National Guard for a short time back home."

Coleman slapped his knee. "Well, all right then. I was with the Union during the last part of the war, so you see, we have something in common. And being in the Army is qualification enough for the county. The County Commissioner has been wanting me to find some decent help for some time now, and the best part is that the job pays twenty-eight dollars a month."

Dillon thought for a moment. For the first time since his arrival, he smiled. "Sheriff, did you know my first name is Dillon?"

"Yes, I saw that on that card you have in your billfold. I have been calling you by your last name to be proper."

"If I took the job, I would be addressed by people as Marshal Dillon?"

"Is there a problem with people calling you by your name?"

"No, sheriff," he replied still smiling. "Marshal Dillon will be fine."

Chapter 10

Taylor punched in the third group of calculations that hour and then copied all the information to a thumb drive. He had assigned Greg the important task of monitoring all the power fluctuation numbers that were now being transmitted from both the small makeshift reactor and the direct current coming from all of the collectors in the lab. Kelly was busy calibrating the main laser and adjusting micrometer settings on the array panels that had been moved by the explosion.

"Ah, guys, I need you to come take a look at this," announced Taylor looking up from his laptop. A very real ball of fear rolled up from his stomach as he checked the information a third time. "I was looking at the recovery data from the explosion. Luckily the program was on, and it was able to capture most, if not all, of the data as far as bio reads and possible destination codes."

"So you know what happened, and where they went?" questioned Greg.

"Well, not exactly. You see here, here is the unmistakable heat and bio signal of them passing through the continuum."

"Where did they go?" asked Kelly, leaning closer to the screen.

Taylor punched in several more computer commands. "Ah, let's see. It's not so much where, but when. I am not one hundred percent sure with the information I have now, but under the default coordinates, I would say they landed somewhere in Montana territory between 1888 and 1889 - give or take a month or two."

"That's over a hundred years ago!" replied Kelly. "They're all dead by now, my God!"

Taylor studied the screen carefully. "They are in this specific time continuum but are very much alive in the past. At least I think so."

"The good news is," continued Taylor, "is that I think we can get them back. We have the coordinates and the time frame which will help in pinpointing the exact geographical location and, more importantly, the correct time."

"Jesus Christ," replied Kelly, "1889? Montana? Hell, they could be in the Rocky Mountains or out on the prairie where there isn't a living soul for five hundred miles in any direction."

"Not likely," replied Taylor, not looking up from his computer. "The array is set for carbon-based emotional readings -informational energy that is only emitted by human beings. Wherever they were sent, it will be around people."

"Why Montana?" asked Kelly, trying very hard to maintain his composure.

Taylor punched in the last bit of data before answering, "It's where the array has been set, and it's where I have been going for the last two months."

Greg pulled up one of the lab chairs and sat down. "Why that particular time frame? What was going on in Montana in 1889?"

Kelly quickly punched in MONTANA and 1889 on his computer. "Ah, here it is," he announced reading. "*Statehood, Montana became the 48th state on Nov. 6, 1889.* That's just the kind of high level of emotional energy the array would have picked up if positioned in that general direction," announced Taylor, reading the screen. "Everybody in the state would have been very emotional about becoming part of the union."

"Can you pinpoint the area or the town they landed in?" asked Kelly. "Let's get this thing fired up and go get them."

Taylor walked over to a second computer. "Well, it's not that simple. I'm still getting readings that the power source is not stable enough for a jump. I'm also looking at this data that, not only tells me that our people were pulled in, but that something of considerable mass came back."

Greg slowly rose from his chair. "What do you mean came back?" he asked cautiously. "There's nobody here but us."

Taylor thought for a moment. "Has anybody checked the back yard?"

****

Bob Cullen knew the head lineman who had been trying to hook up with the Feds that were supposed to be in the Shady Brook area. Terry Holland had been working out of the Palo Verde station for the last nine years now and was just the kind of guy the company needed to find the drain and do something about it. He and Cullen had started together and had become good friends over the years. PND had decided to go ahead and send Cullen out to Shady Brook and coordinate the effort.

Cullen pulled his cell off his belt and punched in Holland's number as he drove. "Hey, Terry, Bob here. How's it going?"

"Hey, Bobby, I heard you were headed my way. How far out are you?"

Cullen checked his GPS. "Ah, I'm about an hour away. Where can we meet up? Got some things I want to go over."

"That's good. I'll tell ya what. I'll meet you at the Shady Brook Cafe, you know, the one right off 68."

"Yep, I know where it's at. They got great pie there. Been there a couple of times," replied Cullen.

"Okay, see you in about an hour, and, by the way, since you're the big-time honcho, you're buying."

Driving through the early afternoon New Mexico landscape was something Cullen always enjoyed and getting a chance to see and catch up with his old friend, Holland would make for a pretty good trip. Besides, he had wanted to get out of the office for some time now, and when the call came down, he jumped at it.

The easy thing about this particular task was that he carried a signed and authorized shut-off notice, a power company work-order to the homeowner that power was going to be turned off immediately and would not be turned back on until a hearing was convened to ascertain penalties if any. Once they pinpointed the residence in question, something he knew Holland was well on his way to finding, the paperwork would be dropped off and that would be that.

In most of the shut-off notice cases the homes were either abandoned or squatters were on the premises, which is why they usually contacted local law enforcement to go along. It was an easy way to kill a couple of days in the sunshine.

****

Unsure of just exactly what he was looking for, Greg slowly made his way up the basement steps with Kelly close behind. They stepped into the living room cautiously looking around. "What are we suppose to be looking for?" questioned Greg.

Kelly walked over to the sliding glass door that looked out onto the large back yard. "Ah, you might want to take a look at this," he announced, looking out into the yard.

Slowly Greg walked up beside him. "Shit, what the hell is that?" He opened the door, stepped out onto the concrete patio, and was immediately bombarded by the oppressive, nauseating smell of dead livestock.

"Look's like dead horses. I'd guess three of them or at least what's left of them," replied Kelly covering his nose. From the barbed wire fence on the backside of the yard all the way to the edge of the small patio, lay the bloody gore of three full-grown horses. Gut, hooves, and heads lay scattered across the yard as if they had been ripped apart by a huge buzz saw and then thrown with great velocity onto the ground.

"I don't understand what this means," replied Greg quietly. "I mean, do you think anything human is rolled up in that mess?"

Kelly walked out into the yard, gently nudging the piles of gore with his boot. "Naw, I think this is all horse. You think the neighbors might notice this?" he asked smiling.

"This is getting more bizarre by the second," replied Greg.

"My God, what is this?"

Greg turned to see Taylor in shocked surprise at the back door.

"You tell us, Bruce. What does this mean?"

Taylor slowly stepped out into the back yard. "I ah, the only thing I can think of is that these animals were at the other end of the continuum when it opened up and they were pulled back through."

"How come they are all torn up like this?" asked Kelly.

"Not sure. Maybe their mass was too large. Maybe the speed of coming back through was too much. I, I just don't know."

152

"Well, here's how it's going to go, guys," announced Kelly heading back into the house, "Dr. Taylor, you had better do what you need to do within the next half hour or I am shutting this whole thing down. Right now, we could probably categorize this thing as some kind of freak accident, but if we cannot undo what's been done, then this will turn into a criminal case, which will be punishable by law. I have stuck my neck out long enough for this."

"I am not sure I can stabilize the power settings within the next half hour," replied Taylor.

Kelly walked back out to where Taylor was standing, visibly angry. "Sir, I believe you are responsible for the death of three men. I also believe there is a slim chance that you can save them, which is the only reason the FBI is not here now. Do not test my patience!" he shouted. "Do what you need to do, but in thirty minutes, I am calling the Feds and this will be over. Do we understand each other?"

"Yes, I understand," replied Taylor.

"And another thing, you pull a gun on me again, you better be ready to use it. You understand me, Dr. Taylor?"

"You pulled a gun on him?" questioned Greg stepping up. "What the hell were you thinking? My God, Bruce!"

"Okay, Okay, I get it. Everybody is upset, and I did what I had to do," replied Taylor, heading back to the house. "Please let's get back to work."

"Guys, what do we do about this?" questioned Greg, pointing to the yard.

"Nothing we can do," replied Kelly. "If and when the neighbors call, this will be over. Greg, if you're smart, you'll get as far away from this as you can."

"Are you saying that as an investigator or a scientist? There is a difference."

"Listen, I have known you about, what, two hours, and I am personally in so deep right now that Taylor and I will probably be sharing the same jail cell. You need to understand that this machine and Taylor's actions have probably resulted in the death of my supervisor and two other Federal Agents. That's how serious this is, Greg."

"Then why are you still here?"

Kelly thought for a moment. "Because three men vanished after they went into that house and I need to know what happened. Simple as that."

Greg nodded while looking back at the carnage in the yard. "I think I'm going to stick around. I want to be here if he pulls it off, something to tell my grand kids. And just so you know, I have gone back in time with Taylor. His process does work."

Kelly stepped up close. "Look me in the eye, Greg, and tell me that you really did travel back in time. You have no idea how much is riding on what you say."

"I'm telling you the truth. What he has accomplished is the most important discovery ever made."

Kelly thought, for a moment. "You know, I'm going to have to call this in. This is far too important and way above my pay grade to handle. And if you're right, this will change the world."

"I agree. So what now? Where do I fit in?"

"I'll need you to stay here. I'm sure you'll be required to fill out a statement. The FBI is going to want to talk to you. This could be a long couple of days."

"Okay," replied Greg nodding. "Do what you have to do. I'm going back in."

Kelly left the backyard and was walking to his van when he noticed a Taos County Sheriff unit pull up along with another unmarked car. Feeling his stomach tighten, he walked over to where the men were getting out of their vehicles.

"Afternoon deputy," he announced walking up to the young officer. "I assume you're here concerning this residence."

The deputy eyed him suspiciously. "Ah, yes sir, and you are?"

Kelly pulled his credential out of his back pocket, "I'm sorry, I am a Federal Investigator from the NNSA, and we currently have an investigation going on that involves the people who live at this residence."

Bob Cullen walked up as the deputy inspected Kelly's identification. "What's the problem?" he asked.

The deputy handed Kelly his ID. "Looks like there's a Federal investigation involving your house, Mister Cullen.

"Hello, Mark Kelly. NNSA," he announced shaking hands, "and you are?"

"Ah, Bob Cullen from PND Power. I just came up from Albuquerque to serve a shut-off notice. Didn't know you folks were even here. What's going on?"

Kelly noticed Greg looking through the picture window of the house. "Well we have a current investigation in progress. I assume that's why you're here, Deputy?"

"Ah, no sir, I'm just here as a courtesy, whenever a shut-off notice is served, in case there are squatters, or things get out of hand when the homeowner is told that their power is about to be shut off. Besides your office probably notified my superiors about your investigation and the word just didn't get passed down to the field. Happens all the time."

The deputy noticed Greg standing in the window and waved, thinking he was another investigator. "Well, Agent Kelly, if you don't need any help, we'll get out of your hair. Mister Cullen, you want to give him your shut-off notice? You can notify the homeowner since you folks are already working a case."

Cullen handed Kelly the pink form. "That's fine with me. If you don't mind, just let the home owner know that the power is being pulled as soon as I make the call in about 30 minutes."

Kelly put the paper in his back pocket. "I'll let him know. Is there anything else I need to pass on?"

"Just that our office is starting their own investigation concerning the massive amounts of power they have been using. I assume that's why you're here?"

"That's part of it," replied Kelly. "The rest is classified, and I would appreciate your discretion concerning our conversation."

The deputy held up both hands. "Hey, no problem. I got rolled up in a DEA case last year, thought I would never stop going to Federal Court, and I swear, every time I got called to testify, it was my day off."

Kelly laughed and shook hands with both men. "Okay guys, thanks for your cooperation. If you would, Deputy, go ahead and notify your dispatch that you made contact with us. Have to keep everybody in the loop."

"Roger that," he replied, getting back into his car. "Mister Cullen, are you good with him dropping the notice off?"

"That's fine with me," replied Cullen. "As long as they get notified, I'm good." The deputy nodded and then slowly drove away.

Cullen extended his hand to Kelly. "Thanks again for your help on this. I'm sure my boss is going to want to talk to you sometime soon. If you don't mind me asking, how long have you folks been looking into this deal?"

"Well, we are kind of getting into a sensitive area," replied Kelly, "but what I can say is that it's been awhile. There will probably be an official briefing for you folks sometime soon."

Cullen took his wallet out of his back pocket. "Great, here is my card. If you need anything from my end, just give me a call."

Kelly looked at the card and then stuffed it into his back pocket. "I'll do that. Well, I'd better get back inside. Pleasure meeting you, Bob," he announced, shaking hands. *It was amazing how much weight and credibility a Federal credential carried,* he thought, walking back to the house. Even though he had run off the local heat he knew Taylor's time was up.

Now came the crushing scrutiny and lethal second-guessing that seemed to be the lifeblood of any government agency. Careers were built on the bodies of those who made mistakes. Investigators from numerous agencies would soon be crawling all over this, and heavy questions would be asked.

Instinctively, he knew his career was over. As he walked into the house and down the basement stairs he immediately noticed Taylor sitting in the middle of the room between the array panels. What alarmed him most was not where he was sitting but what he was wearing. He slowly stepped down onto the lab floor. "What's going on? Why the fatigues?"

"What did they want?" questioned Greg on the other side of the room.

Before Kelly could answer, the lights went out.

Chapter 11

It took Dillon three tries to get the oil lamp lit. The small box of matches he found beside the lamp on the table had five matches left and he had used them all.

The golden glow illuminated the small room revealing a well-worn cot, two wicker chairs, and a potbelly stove in the corner. Three shelves were nailed to the far wall, the bottom shelf holding what appeared to be a half-burnt candle and a Bible. The room carried the strong odor of cigar smoke and wet dirt, its walls stained dark from ceiling to floor.

There were no linens or blankets on the thin mattress, which added a heavy touch of melancholy to an already depressing room. The overwhelming reality of his situation was now starting to hammer home it's deeply disturbing message. This was now his life - his new reality. He fought back tears as he thought about his wife and son. Did they know what had happened? Did anyone know what had happened?

He brushed back the tears while taking a deep breath. No, don't panic he told himself. He would get through this; he would survive. He had found shelter; he had found a place to eat and strangely enough, had found a job. He would tough it out, and whatever was going to happen, he would meet it head on. A knock on the door pulled him from his thoughts. "Yes, come in."

"Well, I see you're settling in. It isn't much, but it'll keep you out of the rain. How's the arm?" asked Coleman stepping in.

"Still bleeding a little bit, not much pain but I'm going to need a clean bandage. I can't thank you enough, Sheriff, for helping me out."

"Doc is pretty good at patching people up. By the way, my name is John. You can call me John."

"Okay, John, you can call me Dillon."

Coleman lit his pipe. "Well, Dillon, I was about to go get some supper. You hungry?"

"You know, John, I really am. Let's go."

As they walked down the muddy street, the sun was just beginning to set in the west, casting a purple-blue light in the cold November sky. The wind had died down, leaving a damp coldness that made Dillon shiver as they walked. Coleman seemed to pick up the response, "Let's stop by Miller's store. You're gonna freeze to death in them fancy clothes. You're going to need a good buffalo coat for the winter, and I don't think them shoes are going to last. What do you call those any way?"

"Ah, those are called Doc Martins."

"You know a doctor that makes shoes?"

"Dillon laughed. "No, he's not a real doctor. It's just a brand name for the manufacturer."

Coleman thought for a moment. "Funny name for a shoemaker."

"You do know, John, that I don't have any money to buy clothes or anything else."

"Well, you need some things. I can't have one of my deputies wearing out his doctor shoes and freezing to death. Consider this an advance on your first bit of pay."

They crossed the street and stepped into the dimly lit store at the far end of the road. Inside, the heavy smell of tanned hides and old apples filled the air. The room was large, illuminated by three oil lamp fixtures hanging by chains from the ceiling. Several glass and wood display cases ran along the back wall, while rolls of barbwire, pick axes, and shovels lay stacked in neat rows on the floor. "Hey Miller, where you at?" shouted Coleman. "I have a customer here."

An old man, well into his seventies, suddenly appeared from behind the counter, his pink complexion and bushy snow-white sideburns giving him a benevolent elfish look. He limped out from behind the counter adjusting his small spectacles. "Stop your yelling; I see ya."

Coleman laughed. "What are you doing back there, Miller? You got a jug you're hiding?"

The little elf stepped closer. "I'm pullin my pud, you damn fool. What do you want?"

So much for a benevolent elf, thought Dillon, laughing. The old man snapped Dillon a quick penetrating look, "What are you laughing at, pecker-wood?"

"Nothing, sir, "chuckled Dillon. "No offense."

The old man held his gaze while stepping closer. "Where you from, Mister? I haven't seen your like around here before."

"He's my new deputy," announced Coleman, smiling, "and he needs some things."

"Deputy, huh? Well, that reminds me, Sheriff. I'm going to shoot the nuts off your other deputy if he shows up for running off with my woman. Paid good money for that bitch, and she goes and runs off with your man."

Coleman chuckled. "I told you before you sent for that China-woman that she was bound to run off. Besides, you start shooting people old man, I'm gonna have to hang ya."

Miller waved him off. "Naw bull-shit, what do you want?"

Coleman walked over to the large display case. "He's gonna need one of them buffalo coats, a couple blankets, one of those shirts over there, and a pair of them boots you have on the shelf. I got cash money, so let's get a moving. My supper is waiting."

"John, you really shouldn't spend your money on my gear. I can wait. I just need some clean bandages."

"And he's going to need a hat. Go over there and pick one out that fits you," announced Coleman. "We'll stop by Doc's on the way to supper."

Dillon could see that Coleman was determined to make sure he was outfitted properly. "Thank you, John. I appreciate it." Evidently Coleman was feeling some level of guilt about the shooting and was doing his best to make amends.

Walking over to the hat-rack, Dillon picked up a dark brown, wide-brimmed hat that fit his head almost perfectly.

"That's a three-dollar hat, Sheriff," announced Miller, quickly taking out his pad and scribbling, "all the way from Denver."

Dillon walked up to the long mirror. "Never wore a cowboy hat before," he said to his own reflection.

"What's a cowboy hat?" asked Coleman, relighting his pipe.

*****

Seconds after the room was plunged into darkness, the emergency-generator hummed to life and the lab lights blinked on. To Kelly's shock, he saw that Taylor was still seated in between the array panels but was now holding a pistol, the same gun he had been threatened with earlier. "Everybody just stay where you are," announced Taylor.

"Bruce, what are you doing?" asked Greg. "This has gone too far; you have to stop."

"He's right," added Kelly. "The power's been cut; it's over."

Taylor shifted in his chair. "Gentlemen, please stop the dramatics and listen carefully. I am leaving but before I do, I need you to know how deeply sorry I am for the loss of those men. It was never my intention to hurt anyone."

"Bruce, you don't have enough power to start the process. Put the gun down before anyone else gets hurt. We can work through this; it was an accident. It does not have to end this way."

"Greg, I appreciate your concern, as misguided as it is. You need to know that, with the widening continuum gap, less power is needed. I won't bore you with the details, but there is enough power for one more jump. It's a one-way ticket, and it's something I have to do." He held up what looked like a small garage door opener, "When I activate this, you will have seven minutes to leave the lab and get as far away as you can."

Kelly took a step in Taylor's direction. Immediately, Taylor raised the pistol and fired a shot. The bullet buzzed inches from Kelly's left ear. "Jesus Christ!" he shouted, crouching low. "You damn-near hit me, you son-of-a-bitch."

"I told you to stay where you are. Now, please pay attention. As I said, you will have seven minutes to leave the lab. There will be a small fire and then an explosion that will blow this lab and house into splinters. That's why it is imperative for you to be as far away as possible."

"Please, Bruce," pled Greg, "there has got to be a better way. This discovery is too important to throw away, I mean, look at all the work and cost that has been put into this thing."

"Thank you, Greg, for your support, but I have to try and salvage something out of this. I have to try and fix something that never should have happened in the first place." He raised his hand above his head and clicked the button. "You now have six minutes and fifty-nine seconds to leave."

Taylor dropped the device on the floor and slowly held up his hand to Greg. It was an odd gesture, but one that Greg instantly knew had stunning importance. Just before Taylor vanished, Greg recognized the large blue stone turquoise ring on Taylor's left hand.

A blinding blue-white flash exploded throughout the room and then total silence - Taylor was gone.

"Jesus Christ!" shouted Kelly, slowly standing. "We've got to get out of here." Greg quickly followed Kelly up the stairs and out into the living room where the nearly over-powering smell of natural gas permeated the room. Taylor had rigged some type of device that released the gas into the house when he activated the jump. Evidently he was taking no chances with the lab being discovered and possibly used. Both men ran out through the front door and into the yard. Greg got to his rental car and was moving down the street in seconds. Looking in his rear-view mirror, he spotted Kelly on his bumper driving the large white government van.

Both vehicles were doing fifty miles an hour when they came to the end of the road intersecting the main highway. Greg slammed on his brakes and spun the wheel, broad sliding around the turn and into the main road. Kelly executed the same maneuver and fell in behind Greg's' car. Feeling he was far enough away, Greg pulled the sedan to the shoulder and turned on his emergency blinkers. Kelly pulled up behind him and did the same. One minute later, as both men were stepping out of the vehicles, a tremendous blue-white explosion illuminated the dark horizon. They could feel the shock wave where they stood two miles away.

"My God," whispered Greg, watching the illumination. "That's incredible!"

After a moment, Greg spoke up. "What now?"

"I have no idea," replied Kelly, from the dark. "I have no idea how I am going to explain this. I don't know who's dead or who's alive. Hell, how am I going to tell anybody what I witnessed without sounding completely crazy?"

Greg shielded his eyes from the dust, as a large eighteen-wheeler roared by. "I think that explosion may have given you an answer," he announced above the traffic noise. "They walked in, the house blew up, and they were vaporized."

Kelly thought for a moment as the sound of emergency vehicle sirens could be heard in the distance. "Even in the worst of fires and explosions, there is always some DNA left. You know as well as I do, the forensic team isn't going to find a thing."

"That's the best I got at the moment," replied Greg. Turning to Kelly, he asked, "Am I under arrest?"

Kelly shook his head. "No, like I said, I'm not a cop. I'm just someone who gathers facts about nuclear material."

Greg continued to watch the orange glow on the horizon. "What are you going to do now?"

Kelly pulled his cell phone out of his pocket. "What I should have done two days ago," he replied, punching in the numbers. "Yes, this is Kelly. We are going to need all the remaining teams in the area to converge on the Shady Brook residence. There's been an explosion, and we have people down. Agent Conroy is one of them. Please notify the FBI that they need to mobilize an investigation team. ATF is also going to have to be notified." Still holding the phone to his ear, he sat down on the low guardrail as early evening traffic continued to roll by. "No, I am not injured. My vehicle will be the command center until an official EEC is set up near the scene." He ended the conversation as a fire truck drove by with flashing lights and siren, obviously heading to the blaze.

"I have to go, Greg. I need to be at the scene when everybody gets there."

"You want me to go with you? I can back up your statement, whatever that's going to be."

Kelly turned and started walking back to his van. "Go home, Greg. There's nothing you can do that's going to help the situation," he shouted over his shoulder.

"Are you sure about that, Agent? We both saw things, things we can't explain."

"I am doing you a huge favor, Greg," shouted Kelly above the traffic noise. He quickly opened the door to the van and stepped up onto the running board. "You do not want to get rolled up in this. Go live your life; forget about all of this."

"Wait!" shouted Greg, walking towards the van. Kelly turned on the headlights, dropped the van in gear and roared past, only inches away. He merged into traffic and then executed a tire screeching u-turn among a flurry of blaring horns and locked up brakes.

Greg stood in the muted darkness of the highway shoulder, watching as three more fire trucks flashed by. The horizon was still aglow from the explosion, a clear indication that whatever device Taylor had rigged to destroy his lab and life's work had been extremely thorough. Nothing would be left but ashes.

Later that night as Greg drove on his way to the airport, he tried to put in perspective and in some kind of logical order the last twelve hours. Was this really the end of the adventure he wondered? Did he really see what he thought he saw or did he witness a suicide, a calculated act of self-destruction?

Taylor had rigged up enough power in his lab to vaporize any organic material. Maybe that's what it all really was - some lucid dream brought on by a massive jolt of unregulated energy. At this moment, alone in his car with the windows rolled down and soft frosty jazz playing on the radio, a fugue state of mind brought on by a blast of energy made a whole lot more sense than time travel back to the 1880's.

An hour later, he pulled into the Albuquerque Airport rental car return without even a clue of how he was going to explain this to his wife. He had burned up a tremendous amount of emotional currency between them by coming here, and now all he wanted to do was go home and try and forget the last two days. As he walked to the terminal, the large red and yellow sign above the entrance made him stop and reflect - NEW MEXICO, THE LAND OF ENCHANTMENT. He moved through the automatic doors and into the terminal, smiling to himself, *Yeah, that fit, definitely!*

****

Dillon followed Coleman outside, pleasantly surprised how comfortable the knee-high boots felt on his feet. He turned and looked at his reflection in the window of Miller's store and laughed. To himself, he looked like a bit-player in some B western movie. The oversized, extremely heavy buffalo-hide coat coupled with the large wide-brimmed hat made him feel totally ridiculous. As he stood looking at himself, Coleman stepped up. "By God, now you look like a local. Don't think you could get a better fit."

Not wanting to sound ungrateful, Dillon nodded. "Never wore this kind of hat before."

Coleman relit his pipe. "So, people in the future don't wear hats?"

"Well, some do. You think I'll pass for a cowboy now?"

Coleman looked at him curiously. "That's about the third time you have used that term - cowboy."

"I didn't mean to offend," replied Dillon.

"No offense taken. It's just that no sane man calls himself a cowboy if he doesn't have to." Coleman motioned that he wanted to move. "Herding cattle is the one thing a man does when he can't do anything else."

As they walked down the now-empty street to dinner, Dillon was struck by how thoroughly quiet it was outside. Absent was the modern hum of an over-industrialized city. No generators ran; no cars or trucks rumbled away in the distance; no thumping mega car stereos polluted the air. The only sounds were the distant ping of a blacksmith's hammer and the soft thud of their boots on the hard ground.

"You know, John, where I'm from there is a very romantic notion about the old West and cowboys."

"Nothing romantic about eating dust and cow shit for a living," replied Coleman. "Hell, there's not a man alive with any sense that wouldn't trade all that for a warm bed, a decent meal, and a dry roof anytime." They stepped up onto the wide porch of the café; the soft golden light from inside painted the frosty ground. "Out there," continued Coleman motioning with his pipe, "you could drown crossing rivers, get shot at by renegade Indians, have your stock rustled by thieves and malcontents, and that's just the beginning. I'm not even going to bring up the fact that you could get snake bit, struck by lighting, or get thrown from your horse and break something you need to stay alive." He opened the door to the café. "No, Dillon, nobody wants to be a cowboy."

As Dillon stepped in, the warmth of the room and smell of hot coffee and grilled meat cooking suddenly reminded him of how hungry he really was. Coleman nodded to an elderly couple seated at a table by the window. "Evening folks."

"Evening, Sheriff," replied the old man. "They got good cobbler tonight."

Coleman hung his coat and hat on the nearby hat-rack and sat down. "That sounds real good. I do believe I will try some."

Dillon pulled up a chair, while the elderly couple went back to eating their meal, not pushing any more conversation, content with their own company.

Coleman tapped out his pipe as a heavyset woman stepped out from the small kitchen. "Evening, John," she announced, wiping her hands on her apron.

"Evening, May. I hear you got cobbler."

"I do. Made a batch this afternoon. I also have some fresh venison. You boys going to have supper?"

Coleman took her hand. "And after supper maybe we can go walk by the river."

Blushing, she softly slapped him on the shoulder. "Ah, John, you're nothin but a rounder. You talk sweet but everybody knows it's all talk."

"I've been trying to take her on a walk by the river for years. Turns me down every time," said Coleman smiling.

Dillon extended his hand. "Evening, Madam. I'm Dillon, Dillon Conroy. Pleasure to meet you."

The woman shook hands while leveling a steady gaze, "This is a small town, Dillon. I don't recall ever seeing you before. Where you from?"

"I ah, ah, I'm from…"

"He's from Missoula, May. He's my new deputy. Got in yesterday," interrupted Coleman.

"Missoula, big city man. Why in the world would you want to come to Deer Lodge for God's sake? And what happened to your arm?"

"You know, May, for a pretty woman, you sure ask a lot of questions," replied Coleman. "Now how about two plates of that fine venison you have back there. And tell that half-breed, Clayton, not to burn it."

"I heard that, Sheriff," came a voice from the kitchen. "You'll eat what I fix or go hungry."

Coleman leaned over to Dillon. "Indians get kinda defensive about their cookin," he whispered, smiling. "I like to poke at him."

The woman playfully slapped Coleman on the shoulder again. "Stop picking at Clayton. He's the only cook I have. You're doing a fine job, Clayton," she announced loudly over her shoulder.

"Pleasure to meet you, Dillon. I'll go get your supper." The woman winked at Coleman and then headed off to the kitchen.

"Fine woman - May," announced Coleman, relighting his pipe. "Always serves a fine meal."

172

Dillon sat back in his chair trying to get his head around how normal everything felt. The smells, the sounds, the light all felt familiar and in an odd way, comforting.

His whole life he had lived in the reality of cars, television, cell phones, and airplanes - a world he navigated through everyday with an unconscious ease and awareness. Now, everything was foreign, minimized down to its basic form. Food was hunted and brought to the table; warmth was provided by wood and burned; personal actions, good or bad, had immediate consequences. People conversed, communicated, and listened to each other without distraction.

In the modern world, face-to-face verbal communication grew more and more limited every year. Email, Twitter, Skype, texting, electronic devices captured time and human contact, making it a world where a person could actually live and work without physically ever having any real human interaction.

As much as his heart ached to see his family, as much as he missed the modern comforts of an over-industrialized modern life, he could see himself living this way. He liked the idea of owning only a few, yet important possessions - things like a decent meal, a warm coat and somebody who honestly listened to you without interference. Yet he knew that to fully adapt to the current "now", it would take a monumental effort on his part. He would have to learn all the basics that the modern man had long forgotten - saddling a horse, driving a wagon, hunting for food, fighting. He knew the last one would be the toughest of all. He could not remember when he had actually been in a fight. Here, men fought with guns, most often with lethal consequences.

He was flattered that Coleman had offered him the job of deputy, but really? Could he really carry that role and be the man that kind of title demanded in this present time? Men, in the present reality, carried an unmistakable and pervasive toughness, honed by the hardships of everyday life. Here, you were judged by your word - followed by your actions. Here, you could not hide behind scheduling conflicts, dropped cell phone calls, and insulating social media. You were taken at your word until your actions proved otherwise.

No, this would not be an easy task or transition. It would demand everything he had, both emotionally and physically. His will to survive would be tested daily along with the constant reminder that he had a wife and family that were not even born yet.

My God, he thought to himself. *If he did not get back, then his son would never be conceived, never have a life of his own.* As he ate his meal, the final heart-splitting realization of not bringing his boy into existence hurt him the most. On the outside, it took every bit of emotional strength he had to hold it together and not to let the tears fall. On the inside, he was already in a million pieces. *So much for being a cowboy.*

Chapter 12

Taylor stood on the windswept ridge looking east, trying to get his bearings. He had been walking for hours and was almost positive he was on the opposite side of the river that he wanted to be on. As he trotted down the small hill, he knew his sore knees would not let him go much further without a decent rest.

Finally climbing to the top, his suspicions were confirmed. Down below, at least a mile away, the far west end of the Indian village was clearly in view. He knew that he was only able to see a small portion of the massive six-mile long settlement. He also knew that if any of the three thousand Indians living there saw him, he would be run down and killed on the spot. In the wind he caught the smell of countless cooking-fires being lit for the evening meal. It was also an indication that it would be dark in several hours, which would cover his movement down to the river.

Exhausted, he stretched out on his stomach in the tall grass, his camouflage fatigues blending in perfectly with the surroundings. The only way he could be seen was if someone were within feet of where he now lay. At least he got that right, he thought, feeling the warm early evening wind cool the sweat on his neck. He was early, maybe a day, maybe two. Because of all the activity and general commotion in the lab prior to the jump, he had not been able to refine his calculations. Added to the fact that the power had been shut off just before activation, it was a miracle that he made it this close.

It had all seemed very noble back in the lab, his safe haven from all the sharp edges the world could generate - high and lofty pronouncements about putting things right, correcting a lie. Now here alone, he had doubts about the whole affair, doubts about his own resolve to do it all again.

The first time had been different. He really had no idea what to expect, no inkling of how terrified he really would be. But now, he knew the horror of what was ahead. Real death was only hours, maybe days away - his death. This time there was no way out, no magic button to push that would make it all go away.

Just before he nodded off in exhausted sleep, he thought about his wife. What would she think about this? What would she say? A small dung beetle quickly crawled over his hand and then disappeared in the grass. He let the questions hang as he drifted off to sleep - *what would she say indeed.*

Hours later, he woke with a start as he felt and heard the heavy vibration of hoof beats near by. He had no idea how long he had slept and quickly dug the small pistol out of his pocket. Whatever was moving around in the dark was headed his way. He cocked the hammer on the gun and slowly raised his head just in time to see three Indian riders gallop by, horsemen so close that he could smell the sweat of the animals. There were three of them. To his great relief, he realized his camouflage had saved him.

The riders disappeared into the darkness, their hoof beats fading in the night breeze. He slowly rolled onto his back, working hard at slowing his heart rate and breathing. Looking up into the night sky, he was struck by how brilliantly bright the stars were. He could easily see how travelers were able to use them as a navigation tool - the Montana night sky was simply amazing. Regaining his composure, he slowly stood up and stared in awe at the sight of a thousand individual campfires burning along the Bighorn River. They looked like brilliant orange, red jewels spread out over a black blanket.

He de-cocked his pistol, still trying to figure out what he was really going to do next. It was all a guessing game now. As far as he knew, he could be days ahead of the battle, maybe even a week. He had no food, no water, no shelter, and worst of all, he was exposed. He stood in the dark wrestling with his emotions, slowly feeling his resolve fade. Feeding oneself into the teeth of history did not seem nearly as attractive as it did before. For a moment, he thought about shooting himself where he stood, a quick end to the emotional turmoil he now felt.

His poor preparation and haste to leave the lab was now costing him dearly. Even if he somehow survived, he had no money or anything else to bargain with for his continued existence. Totally demoralized by the crushing realization, he sat back on the ground, fighting back the tears. They were not tears of sadness or regret but tears of rage and frustration. He was not a brave man but one who calculated the odds, measured the risk and then negated much of it through meticulous planning and thought. He had violated all of the tenants that had served him well in the past. He had panicked, and in that rush of emotional energy, he had sealed his fate.

Suddenly, a sound to his left made his heart stop. He turned and to his shock saw an Indian wearing a cavalry uniform jacket pointing a large pistol directly at his forehead. It was as if he had materialized out of thin air.

The man silently stepped forward. "White Man," he whispered, cocking the hammer.

Taylor was only able to reply with a gasp and a nod before he was knocked into unconsciousness from behind. Within minutes, he had been bound hand and foot by a leather cord, thrown over a saddle and taken away. His choices and his life were now in the hands of others.

****

Dillon woke up with a start when he heard the knock. Trying to focus on his surroundings, he sat up, leaning on his left elbow. Immediately, the pain of his wound shot through his shoulder and into his neck, driving him back on the bed. "Hey, Dillon, you awake?"

Dillon recognized Coleman's voice from outside the shack. "Yeah, I'm up. C'mon in."

The shack was freezing inside, and when Coleman stepped in, a frigid blast from outside made it even worse. "Jesus, it's cold," announced Dillon, pulling his blankets tight. He had bought two at Miller's store and now realized he would need more.

"You let your fire go out," replied Coleman, stepping over to the small stove. He loaded some kindling from the pile and within a minute had a fire going. "You feel up to breakfast?"

Dillon carefully sat up this time, "Yeah, that would be good. What time is it?"

Coleman pulled out his pocket watch. "Ah, about 7:15. I think we're gonna get some snow today."

Dillon carefully pulled on his pants, his arm throbbing from the effort. "This thing is still bleeding a bit," he said, gently picking at the dried blood on the bandage.

"Hurt much?" questioned Coleman, sitting down in one of the small chairs by the stove.

"Dillon laughed. "Only when I lay down, roll over, or move. Other than that it's fine."

Coleman lit his pipe, filling the room with the smell. "Well, you're lucky it's your left arm. If it had been your right, you'd have to hire someone to wipe your ass."

Dillon chuckled while pulling on his shirt, "Yeah, I guess you're right, John. I guess I got lucky." As they walked through the early morning chill, Dillon began to realize that it was the small things in life that made the difference in the quality of life you lived. Little things like being able to keep a wood-fire going in the stove, having the right clothes for the environment - things he had taken for granted his whole life.

He was seeing everything in a different light now. It was no longer possible to fake it here. You just could not slide by without being held accountable for your actions or lack of action. After they were seated at their now customary table, hot coffee was poured and eggs were ordered. Coleman had been carrying a flour sack that morning, and as Dillon savored the coffee, he slid it across the table. "I figure you can use that better than I can."

"What's this?" Dillon asked, opening the sack.

"It's that gun and extra bullets your friend was carrying. I have no idea how the thing works, but I'm guessing you do."

Dillon pulled the pistol out of the bag.

"I like that fancy holster it's in," announced Coleman. "Can you tell me what it's made out of?"

Dillon pulled the pistol from the holster. "It's called KYDEX. It's a plastic composite."

"There's that plastic word again. Looks like a lot of things are made out of that stuff where you come from," replied Coleman. "What kind of gun is that? Never seen one like it."

Dillon ejected the magazine and put it on the table. "It's called a SIG SAUR, 45-caliber, made in Austria." He racked the slide, ejecting a round. "Very common law enforcement weapon; a lot of cops carry them."

Coleman picked the loose round off the floor. "Well, I don't know what a cop is, but by the looks of it, you're an expert with that piece. I think you should carry it. I like how you can just slip that holster on your belt. Real handy."

"John, I'm flattered that you would think that I had the real ability to be a deputy sheriff, but I have had no law enforcement training. Hell, I might end up getting someone hurt."

Coleman sat back in his chair thinking. "Dillon, I'm not an educated man. I don't have much formal education. But the one thing I do know is firearms. Shot em all, had em all, but that gun you're holding there is far and above anything that is being made now. It's the most advanced pistol I have ever seen."

"What are you saying, John?"

Coleman leaned forward, not wanting to be heard by the other diners. "What I'm saying is that I really am beginning to believe that you ain't, you know, from around here."

Dillon put the gun and holster back in the sack. "Thank you, John. Thank you for believing me. I did not want you thinking that I was some lunatic that you felt you had to take care of."

"Well, if you're done, let's head over to my office. I have some things I need to talk about. Too many ears here."

After Coleman had paid for breakfast, Dillon followed him out into the early morning sun. Before heading over to Coleman's office, they stopped by Doc Tillman's office to get the wound looked at and fresh bandages.

As they walked up the muddy street, Dillon thought about what his family would be doing now. His son would already be on his way to school; his wife would be doing her make-up in her pink robe and slippers; the dogs would be out in the yard barking. Life, his life would be spinning in greased grooves. Hopefully, people in his reality knew what had happened and were now working on ways to get him back. The only real ledge of hope he stood on was that men much smarter than himself were doing all they could to reverse what had happened. His faith was all he had.

****

Taylor could not stop staring at the young man sitting by the early morning campfire. He had seen his picture in history books and read about him and his brothers, but seeing him in the flesh, not ten feet away was an incredible experience. Boston Custer had been hired by the Army as a forager and mule-team driver. Even though he was never in the Army, being the youngest sibling of his famous brother George carried weight and constant employment opportunities wherever he went.

The man left the others by the fire and walked over to where Taylor was sitting on the back of a wagon. "How's your head?" he asked, handing Taylor a tin plate of beans and bacon.

"Ah, I guess I'm okay," he replied, taking the plate. "Can you tell me why I was attacked?"

The man laughed. "Mister, you're lucky White Swan found you and not the Sioux. A thump on the head would have been the least of it."

"White Swan -'The' White Swan, the Crow scout?" questioned Taylor.

A confused look clouded Boston's face. "You know who White Swan is?"

"Yes, I do, and I think your name is Boston Custer. Am I right?"

By now several of the soldiers who were sitting around the campfire walked up and stood beside Boston. "What's your name, mister?" asked one of the men from the group. "And how in the hell did you get out here?"

The history books had been right, thought Taylor. The man's Irish brogue was unmistakable. Modern historians had reported that eighty-percent of Custer's unit at the Little Bighorn were Irish immigrants.

"My name is Bruce Taylor and ah, how I got here is, well, kind of complex. Maybe I should talk to the General about the particulars."

None of the men from the group made a move. "How do you know my name? I don't believe we have ever met," questioned Boston, his tone just on the verge of angry.

Taylor knew he had to be very careful. "Like I said, I probably need to talk to your brother about why I am here and..."

"Hey, Tom, c'mon over here," shouted Boston past Taylor.

'Goddamn Boss, I have things to do this morning. What do you want?" A short thin officer walked up beside Boston, obviously irritated about being summoned. "I got to meet the General in five minutes."

"This is the man the scout's ran across last night," announced Boston.

The officer shook his head. "So, what do I care if some pecker-wood settler or miner is brought in by the Goddamned scouts?"

Taylor extended his hand. "You must be Tom Custer," he said smiling. "I recognize you from your picture...." He lowered his hand knowing immediately he had made a mistake.

The young officer studied him closely. "Who in God's hell are you, and what picture are you talking about?" he asked angrily.

"Look at those clothes he's wearing," announced one of the men from the growing group of soldiers, "and them shoes. Never seen anything like em."

Tom Custer was now staring intently at Taylor's boots and uniform. "Okay, mister, what kind of clothes are those?" he asked, more confused than angry.

Taylor, in a flash, had decided that he was tired of hiding who and what he was. No matter what story he concocted to this group of soldiers, they wouldn't believe him, so why not float the truth just to see what would happen.

"My name is Doctor Bruce Taylor. I'm a scientist from the year 2013. In my lab in New Mexico, I have developed a way to bend the space-time continuum and transport myself into pivotal events in world history, vectoring in on residual human emotion, which is just highly condensed measurable energy. That is how and why I am here." You could have heard a pin drop before the group suddenly burst into spontaneous laughter. "And if this is June 24th 1876," shouted Taylor above the noise, "You're all going to be dead by two o'clock tomorrow afternoon!"

The laughter died just as quickly as it started. "Is that right?" replied Tom, wiping tears of laughter from his face. "And just how is that going to happen?"

Taylor thought for a moment, realizing he could not turn back now. "You're going to be wiped out by over two thousand Indians that are camped out along the Bighorn River. The battle is going to take less than two hours and then it will be over. It's going to be recorded as one of the greatest battles in American history, one that you will lose."

Again the group broke into laughter until Tom spoke up. "Well, Mister, I'll tell you what. That's the best wild-ass yarn I have ever heard, and you have a real talent for telling it. But I will tell you and anybody else that will listen that there isn't an Indian alive that's gonna kill me. We've been chasing those dung heels for the last two years now, and not once did they stand up and fight. Hell, they couldn't run away fast enough."

"Tomorrow will be different," replied Taylor. "There are too many of them and they will not run."

"I ain't got time for crazy people," announced Custer. "I don't know how you got here, Mister, but if you're smart, you need to head back to wherever you came from before you get yourself scalped." With a dismissive wave, he walked away as did most of the soldiers who had gathered.

"Well, Mister, like Tom said, that's the wildest story I've ever heard," said Boston, dumping the remnants of the large coffee pot on the fire. "We're getting ready to move out."

Taylor
Dillon had to at least make an attempt to see the General. "Boston, could you at least tell the General that I am here and that I would like to talk to him for just five minutes. Just five minutes, that's all I ask, and then I'll leave, please."

"Tell you what, his tent is right over there. You want to see him, go right on."

Dillon hopped down from the wagon and shook hands with the younger Custer. "Thank you, Boston. Thank you very much. It's been a fantastic pleasure meeting you."

Custer nodded. "You're welcome. Oh, before I forget, the scouts that picked you up last night have some of your property. I think White Swan said you had a pistol. They have their camp just over by those wagons. If I were you, I'd go get it back. You might need that gun later. They give you any guff, you tell them I told them to give it back."

Dillon could see a real concern for him in Boston's eyes. "Take care of yourself, Mister Taylor. I don't think this is a very safe place for someone like you."

Taylor shook hands again and then headed off in the direction of the General's tent. He was amazed at the fact that he had announced who he was and how he arrived there, and the only response from the soldiers and frankly everyone else was that he was a lunatic. Couldn't they see how he was dressed? How else could they explain how a single white man could be found alive in the middle of Indian country with no shelter, no horse, and wearing the oddest clothing any of them had ever seen? They did not seem to be even mildly interested in his story.

As he walked up to one of the larger tents in among a group of four, which had been set up in a semicircle, he noticed a man in white buckskin sitting by the smoldering breakfast fire. He appeared to be deep in thought while smoking a short clay pipe. All around him were younger soldiers in a fury of activity, taking down tents, loading wagons, and saddling horses. Taylor immediately recognized the profile. Sitting no less then ten feet away was the famous General George Armstrong Custer, the epic figure of countless stories of western myth and legend, a man who defined American Western history. Tentatively, Taylor stepped closer. "Ah, sir, General, General Custer, can I speak to you for a moment?"

Custer turned in his chair. "Do I know you?"

"Ah, no, sir, but I feel like I know you very well. I know that sounds odd, but if I could have just five minutes of your time, I think I could explain."

Custer leveled a steady gaze as he continued to puff on his pipe. "You're the man my scouts found last night. Is that correct?"

"Yes, sir, it is."

"What is your name, sir?"

"General, my name is Bruce Taylor."

"Well, Mister Taylor, how in God's name did you get here? You have no horse, no supplies, this is Lakota Sioux country - very dangerous for a white man alone."

Out of the corner of his eye, Taylor saw the same Indian he saw last night step out from behind one of the tents. He was carrying a rifle across his arms and looked every bit as fierce in the daylight as he did in the dark. Custer looked over and nodded to the Indian. "That's White Swan. I believe you two met last night. He's a Crow, one of my best," announced Custer. The Indian walked past Taylor and handed the General a small leather-wrapped bundle. He carefully opened the pouch and pulled out Taylor's .22-caliber pistol.

"Ah, that's the weapon I was carrying last night," replied Taylor, still not sure what he was going to say next.

Custer examined the pistol closely. "This is a very fine weapon Mister Taylor. I am impressed with the workmanship. Where did you get it?"

Taylor knew he did not have a lot of time to say what he needed to say. He also recognized that this was an incredible chance to make a real difference in history. "General, I know about your work gathering mineral and floral samples for the Smithsonian in the Black Hills and your efforts to give a detailed historical chronology about the industrial expansion into the west, which is why I think you will be receptive to what I have to tell you."

Custer slowly stood while tapping out his pipe. Taylor was surprised by how really short he was, maybe five-foot-nine. His deep-set eyes and general manner gave one the impression that he was easily distracted or just bored with whatever or whoever he was involved with. He stepped up close, looking Taylor in the eyes. "Who are you, Mister Taylor, and why are you in my theater of operation?"

Taylor's mind went blank, being caught totally off guard by Custer's directness and barely-controlled hostility. "Ah, I, am not from this time. I, I am a scientist. I, I know things about the future. I.." He was babbling and could see the amused confusion cross Custer's face.

"Mister Taylor, here is your fine pistol. I would suggest that you stay with my pack train. My brother Boston will make that accommodation."

"General, I really do need you to listen to me - you will not survive this expedition."

Custer straightened his red silk scarf and smiled. "Mister Taylor, you sound like an educated man, and as such, I know you are aware of a thing called manifest destiny, are you not?"

"Yes, sir, I am very well aware of manifest destiny, which is why I need to tell you what I know about that destiny - your destiny."

Custer turned and motioned for the three Crow scouts, who were now standing quietly nearby to follow. A young aid handed Custer the reins to his horse. "I really do not have the time for your prognostications. Perhaps this evening we can discuss the mysteries of the future." He swung into the saddle, "so if you'll excuse me, Mister Taylor, I have a campaign to run." He reined his horse around and then around again, trotting up beside Taylor. "And before I forget, you owe my scout a small reward for saving your life last night. It is their custom. Please honor it by giving White Swan something."

'Sir, I really, sir, you should not go down to the river. You will not survive the day."

Custer sat back in the saddle, the leather creaking under his weight. "It's a beautiful day, Mister Taylor. Thank you for your concern." He pulled the reins sharply. "Good morning, sir."

As he rode off, the Indian whom Custer called White Swan slowly rode up and sat staring at Taylor. The horse sidestepped, making him move out of the way as the Indian held his gaze. Suddenly, realizing that he owed the man something, he pulled the large silver and turquoise stone ring off his finger and handed it to the scout. The Indian took the ring and nodded, the stern, vacant stare never leaving his face. He quickly rode off, as did several others who were mounted nearby, leaving Taylor in a cloud of thick alkali dust. It was the last he saw of the General and his scouts.

Chapter 13

Greg had gotten home that Wednesday and without saying much to Carol, decided to head into the office on campus to get things patched up with the head of the Anthropology Department. After a lengthy apology session all was forgiven, and he taught his first lab and lecture that afternoon. It felt good to get back into the classroom; the normality and routine of academia brought an odd kind of comfort and control to his life that he needed and thrived in.

And yet, he was deeply troubled by his experiences over the last week. He had traveled back, back in time. He had seen it with his own eyes, and whether he admitted it or not, was hungry for more. By three-thirty that afternoon, he had finished all the classes he was going to teach for the day and decided to head over to his office to catch up on correspondence and let his secretary know he was still alive.

After the obligatory "hello's" and '"how are you's", he finally got to his office and was surprised at the stack of mail that had been collected and heaped onto the middle of the table he used as a desk.

The large copy-paper box caught his attention first. He slid the rest of the mail stacked on top off it and read the Fed-Ex return name on the address label. His heart skipped a beat as he read the name. It was from Bruce Taylor, Shady Brook, NM, 87557. It had been mailed last week between the time he had left Taylor's lab and the time he returned. Not sure what he should do, he quickly locked his office door and then sat in his chair, staring at the box for a solid five minutes. Instinctively he knew that whatever was inside would change his life again.

He cut the tape and carefully unwrapped the package, fighting every emotional queue and feeling that he should put the box in a locked closet and forget he even had it. Carefully lifting the lid, he was shocked to see that it was stacked to the top with banded stacks of hundred dollar bills. A manila envelope lay on top of the money. Inside, Greg found the handwritten note and three thumb drives that had been numbered 1 through 3. His heart pounding with excitement, he read the note.

"Dear Greg, I know that this past week has been very difficult for you. You have had to believe in someone you barely knew, staking your personal and pubic reputation on a discovery that will change the world. I fully understand the stress and emotional price you have and will pay.

I have sent you all the money that was in the lab cabinet. I did not want it burned up in the fire and I thought you could use it. It is close to $350,000, which should help with your expenses. Concerning the numbered thumb drives, they contain ALL of my lab and PROCESS notes.

194

With this information, any top-level science research center will be able to duplicate my work. As you know from first hand experience, the process works. So you are now holding in your hands the greatest discovery known to Mankind; what you do with it is up to you. I am sorry for laying this heavy burden on you but I have no one else to give it to.

Maybe we will meet again, maybe not, but it has been my pleasure. .... Taylor.........

Greg sat in stunned silence as he read the letter two more times. He put the lid back on the box and tried to think of a safe place to secure the thumb drives. Men and governments would do anything to get their hands on the process, killing anyone to control it. He lifted the lid on the box just to make sure the money was really in there. "My God," he whispered out loud, his head spinning with possibilities.

Remembering that he had Kelly's card, he dug out his wallet. Finding it, he dialed the number and then immediately hung up. *What in God's name was he going to say,* he thought staring at the phone. It was a good chance the phones at the NNSA were monitored. Any word of this would bring the full weight of the United States Government right to his doorstep. *Even email could be intercepted; no, there had to be a better way to contact Kelly.* The instant he thought of what he needed to do, the now familiar ball of tension began to rise in his stomach. He would have to go in person, leaving his wife, and job and everything stable in his life all over again.

That evening, he started the discussion with his wife by walking in from the garage and setting the box full of money in the middle of the dining-room table. "I need to show you some thing," he said, tossing his coat on the couch. But before that, you need to read this. "He handed her the letter Taylor had written, visibly apprehensive about how this was all going to play out.

"What's in the box, Greg?" she asked nervously.

"Sweetheart, just read the letter. All the answers to your questions are there."

After reading the note, she looked up at Greg in astonishment. "You have got to be shitting me!" she announced. Whenever Greg heard Carol use profanity, it always made him laugh. This time was no exception.

"All true, sweetie; kind of takes your breath away, doesn't it?"

She read the letter again. This time Greg noticed that her hands were shaking. Overwhelmed, she took a deep breath and laid the letter on the table. "What do we do now?" she asked with tears in her eyes. Greg could see that she was hanging on by a thread. Dropping this kind of thing on anybody was enough to bend the head for days.

"It's okay, Sweetheart," he replied, pulling her close. "I wanted you to see what I was dealing with this last week. Now I need to know what you think." He could feel her heart pounding through her chest as she held him tight.

"What does 350,000 dollars look like?" she whispered, looking at the box.

196

Greg reached over and flipped the lid. "Like that."

She gently touched the bundled bills as if they were made of fragile glass. "This is incredible. I, I mean- where did all this come from?"

"It's money Taylor got when he sold the gold coins he picked up when he made the jumps. That's how he financed all of the research."

"You know, there is still a lot of the money left over from what you brought home last week. That was strange enough, but this is off the charts, Greg."

He sat down, pulling her onto his lap. "Listen, sweetheart, the money is not the problem. What I am wrestling with is what am I going to do about the thumb drives - Taylor's process."

"You're kidding, right?" She stood up with her hands on her hips. "You're going to destroy that stuff and not look back."

"What are you talking about? Destroy the greatest discovery in the history of the world? Are you crazy?"

He could see her anger starting to rise. "Greg, honest to God, are you seriously considering keeping this information? Do you really think you could control what happens once the government finds out you have it? Really?"

"Well yes I think I..."

"No, Greg, you couldn't," she interrupted angrily. "They will take this information away from you and then lock you up or worse. You should count yourself lucky that you got away from this the first time. Now you want to get right back into it?"

He thought for a moment, knowing deep down that she was right. Yet, he also knew that he would not be able to just walk away. "So, you really want me to destroy the information?"

"Yes, I do. There is nobody on earth that would not abuse this information if they got a hold of it. You know that as well as I do." She sat down as if she had been punched in the stomach. "My God, Greg, the government will kill you for this. This is way over your head. Please get rid of those drives and forget this ever happened."

"What about the money?"

"I couldn't care less about the money, Greg. Honestly it would help with the bills but it is not worth getting you killed over. Throw it away, burn it, bury it, I don't care. Just get rid of those drives."

"You know, I thought you might have been a little more supportive about this thing. I mean we are talking about time travel here."

"You have got to be joking, Greg. You are a tenured professor at a university, not some first-year grad-student looking for some left-field project to write a paper on. You need to grow up."

"Oh, okay, this is more about us than what I am getting involved with. Why don't you say what's really on your mind, Carol."

"You really want to go there, Greg?"

"Yes, I really want to go there, and what's with all the hostility?" he asked, trying hard to keep his voice down.

"Okay, let's get to the facts of the matter. At the drop of a hat, you run off to New Mexico without telling me or your employer anything. You come home with a bundle of money from someone you barely know and then go back without telling the school or me when you'll return."

"And how did that hurt you, Carol?"

"You really don't see how irresponsible you've been, do you? We had a plan Greg. We bought a house for God's sake. We put down roots. You just got tenure, and on a whim, you're ready to throw it all away. My God, you cannot be that stupid."

"Carol, I think this is important, probably the most important thing I have ever done."

She got up from the table, trembling with anger. "You know what, Greg, do what you want. I'm done with this. You want to throw your life away, go right ahead. I thought I meant more to you than this." She brushed past, slamming the bedroom door behind her.

"Carol, c'mon, open the door. Let's talk this out."

"I'm done talking!" she shouted from inside the room. "Leave me alone."

Greg knew her well enough to know that whenever she left an argument, it was best to let her cool off and not push the issue. He knew she was scared. Too much had come down too fast. "I love you," he said to the door. "Sorry for all of this." He left the house, feeling angry with himself for not handling the situation better.

She was right. Once the government caught wind of the fact that he had Taylor's process in his possession, he was a dead man. He should just take the money, buy a few toys, pay off some bills, and forget the whole Goddamned thing. He dug his cell phone out of his pocket and punched in Carol's number. She answered on the third ring. "It's me; you're right. I'm going to get rid of the drives. I'll be home in a little bit....Okay, I love you too."

He turned off his phone and immediately felt terrible about lying. He had no intention of destroying the drives, at least not until he could think about the ramifications and consequences of his actions a little more. This was too important a decision to be made quickly. No, he would bide his time and then make a move. For now the only thing he wanted to think about was where to secure them. *Where does one put the most important discovery of all time?*

He walked through the cold gloom, confident that he was doing the right thing. His favorite coffee shop further down on Higgins Avenue was just turning on the outside lights. It would be a good place to sit for a moment and think. He smiled to himself, remembering what his father had told him about making important choices in life – "In all things, deciding the correct path required that one demand a certain level of honest introspection. Never say 'yes' or 'no' right away." Besides, it felt good knowing that he had the power to change the world tucked away in his pocket - real good.

****

It had been a full week since Dillon had been dumped into Deer Lodge, and as the days continued to unfold, he felt himself sinking deeper and deeper into a heavy funk. He had a growing sense that this was permanent, something he would have to live with the rest of his life.

His arm was feeling better, and he now had full use of his hand. He had also worked at making his living accommodations more hospitable by adding two more blankets to his cot, another oil lamp, and an old, but clean, buffalo-hide Coleman had given him for a rug. All things considered, it was quite comfortable. He had learned how to stoke a fire so that the stove remained warm all night, had learned the names of most of the shopkeepers in town, and had started to wear his badge and gun under his coat, at least showing Coleman he was making an effort to be a deputy. One of the things he found most difficult about being there was figuring out what to do with his time. There was no TV, no radio, no internet, few books, none of the modern day time drains that had filled his day in modern life.

Now, he spent great blocks of time talking to Coleman about his life in 2013, covering everything from the current ridiculous political climate to the countless entertainment diversions that were so readily available. He talked about music, cars, airplanes, and the many wars and police actions the United States had been involved with. He was amazed at how much information he could expound upon as Coleman sat with his feet up on his desk, smoking his pipe, quietly listening to every word. He talked about computers, going as far as drawing pictures and explaining how just about everyone on the planet was connected through cyberspace - a concept Coleman found astonishing. Sometimes they would talk through the night and be surprised by the dawn. Occasionally Coleman would ask questions but mostly he would sit and listen in total amazement, lost in the thoughts of how he would fit into the fantastic world Dillon was describing.

A new fact that Dillon found somewhat distressing was his capacity to now drink hard-liquor. During his life in modern time, he could count on one hand the number of occasions he drank whisky or any other hard spirits. Things had definitely changed; he and Coleman were easily finishing off a bottle a night. He was starting to notice more subtle changes. His hearing was better, clearer, sharper; his knee pain from a skiing accident years ago no longer hurt when he woke up and took his first steps in the morning. The only thing he could think of that could have brought on these changes was the lack of pollution in the air.

It was eight o'clock in the morning on the sixth day, and Dillon headed over to the Café for breakfast. Coleman had gone out of town the previous day on business, leaving Dillon the keys to the office and a warning to be careful. He would be back the next day. Everyone in town knew Dillon was the new deputy and treated him with the respect that came with the title, even though Dillon felt he was as much a law enforcement officer as he was a beagle. He knew that Coleman was depending on him to at least make an effort, so in that vein, he played the role and did the best he could.

He sat at his usual table as the waitress brought him his coffee and eggs. Sitting in the far corner, were three men Dillon had not seen in town before. They talked in low tones, casting hard glances in his direction. It was not a look of challenge that some men are capable of, but looks of suspicion, colored with an edge of fear. Dillon smiled and nodded. "Good morning," he announced, as one of the men looked over.

The man turned back to his friends and spoke just loud enough for Dillon to hear. "What's so Goddamned good about it?" The other two chuckled without humor. Dillon could feel a ball of apprehension start to rise in his stomach. Something was wrong; the hostility from the men hung heavy in the air.

"Is there some kind of problem?" asked Dillon from his table. He was shocked that he had actually spoken up. In his reality, he went to great lengths not to have conflict with anyone. When someone cut him off in traffic, he smiled and waved. When he took his wife to the movies last year and the loud mouth punk would not stop kicking his seat behind him, he did nothing. Now, he felt an odd unfamiliar sense of righteous anger boil up, and the words just kept coming out. "I said, is there a problem?" he asked louder.

The heavy-set, bearded man, who appeared to be the leader of the three, turned in his seat. "Why don't you just eat your eggs there, Deputy, and mind your own business before you get hurt."

A sudden, unexpected bolt of angry excitement shot through Dillon's body as he deftly reached and held the pistol under his coat. His mind was now locked into some kind of violent drama that was escalating by the second. It was as if he was watching someone else using his body and his voice. Something raw, something primal, had taken over. He wanted the man to say something else, do something. He had this kind of ALL SENSORY RAGE. Under his coat, he snapped the safety off his weapon still in the holster. "Hey, asshole, what the fuck is your problem?" he shouted to the man. There it was again, that uncontrolled, yet focused aggression he had never exhibited before in his life.

Several of the other diners quickly got up out of their chairs and left the room.

One by one, all three of the men slowly stood up and turned facing Dillon, who kept his seat, his weapon firmly in hand under the table.

"Who you calling an Asshole?" challenged the leader. "That badge doesn't mean a Goddamned thing to me." He brushed back his coat, exposing the butt of a pistol. As if time slowed to half speed, Dillon saw the man slowly grab for the gun. Before the long barreled pistol cleared his belt, Dillon brought his weapon up and fired two quick shots, striking the man in his left eye and throat. The 45-caliber slugs blasted a pink spray of blood and bone in a high arch behind the man's head as he flipped back on to the table.

Dillon jumped to his feet and aimed the weapon at the second man as he was drawing his pistol. Two more quick shots sent the gunman spinning to the floor. The third man, much younger then the other two, was able to draw his weapon and fire. His shot went wide, nicking the bottom of Dillon's left ear. Dillon reacted as if he had done this a thousand times by firing the four remaining rounds of his weapon into the face and chest of the last attacker.

The gunfight was over in seconds, leaving the room filled with wafting clouds of gun smoke and the heavy, sweet smell of blood and bowel. Dillon stood transfixed at the sight of three dead men lying in their own blood. He slowly lowered his weapon, desperately trying to get his head around what had just happened. In a daze, he ejected the empty magazine in his pistol and reloaded a full one. The heavyset waitress was suddenly at his side. "Are you okay, Deputy? Your ear is bleeding. Clayton, go get Doc Tillman. Hurry!" she shouted over her shoulder.

Dillon suddenly felt light headed and weak in the knees. "I, I need to sit down," he whispered, finding his chair. "I didn't want this to happen. I, I, my God, I shot all three. I mean, what happened?"

The waitress knelt down beside him, dabbing the blood off his neck with a towel. "I saw the whole thing, Deputy. They drew first and if you hadn't shot 'em, they would have killed you on the spot. Them Dugans are bad to the bone. Frankly you did the world a favor."

"You know these men?" questioned Dillon, fighting back the nausea.

"They're the Dugan brothers. The big one is Pete; that one over there in the corner is Mel, and the younger one is Tug. They live down by the river in some rat hole. They come into town about once a month raising hell. Been nothing but trouble for years."

Doc Tillman and several other men walked in and quickly picked up off the floor the guns that had been dropped during the gunfight. Tillman checked the neck of each man, looking for a pulse. "I'll be damned, Deputy, you got all three," he announced, stepping over the bodies. "Virgil, go get the wagon that's over in front of Miller's. We'll use that to load these boys up."

Dillon had no idea what he needed to do or say and was stunned at the apparent nonchalance of Tillman and the others in the room. He had just killed three men, and the enormity of that fact was now starting to hammer in. "Doctor, I don't think we should move the bodies."

Confused, Tillman looked up from searching the pockets of one of the men. "Why's that, Deputy?"

"Well, there has to be an investigation by law enforcement. I mean this is a triple homicide."

Tillman wiped his bloody hands on the jacket of the first man shot. "May, did you see what happened here?" he asked, searching the man's pockets.

"Sure did, Doc. Pete stood up, drew his gun first, and then the deputy shot em, just like he did the other two."

"You willing to sign a statement concerning what you saw, May?"

"Sure am, Doc."

"They came in this morning raising hell," announced Clayton, the café cook. "I saw the big man there stand up and draw first. The deputy did what he had to do."

"How about you, Clayton? You willing to sign a statement about what you saw?"

"Well, Doc, I can't write, but I can sign my name...sure can."

Tillman walked over with all the contents he found in the men's pockets. "Well, Deputy, look's like self-defense to me. Aside from the guns, that's all they had." He dumped the items on the table. "Huh, never seen anything like this," he said, sorting through the men's things. Dillon nearly fainted from the shock. Tillman was holding up a cell phone.

Chapter 14

Sitting in his fourth floor office in the Forrestal building in DC, Kelly reread the after-action report from the FBI forensics team. Their findings raised more questions than answers concerning the disappearance of NNSA inspector Dillon Conroy. According to the AFT sub-report, the fire was caused by a buildup of natural gas, fueled by an unknown substance that literally burned the entire structure down to a fine powder.

At the bottom of the report, in the observation and conclusions section, one of the lead FBI investigators noted that even after the fire was out and the embers were cool, the air remained hot, unusual to say the least. Kelly closed the report, fairly confident that his version of the incident was not being questioned, at least not in official circles.

He had been absolutely honest with investigators about what he knew, carefully avoiding the actual account of watching Conroy vanish. He also left out the fact that Gander was even there. Preliminary Reports were going to indicate that Conroy made initial contact with the homeowner and then was incinerated when the house exploded. It was going to be classified as a murder-suicide by the FBI.

He sat back in his chair, watching the DC traffic crawl by outside, fully aware of the crushing reality of lying to the FBI. If all the facts, as fantastic and unbelievable as they were, ever came out, he would be on the sharp end of the investigation. Lying to Federal investigators or omitting information concerning a homicide, or any case for that matter, pretty much guaranteed a lengthy prison sentence.

He shook away the mental image of being handcuffed, telling himself that he had done the right thing. He also knew that, if he hadn't lied, he would probably be in jail right now. His delay in reporting the initial disappearance of Conroy and the omission concerning Gander's involvement had already put him way beyond the very real and harsh boundaries of culpability.

Before closing up his office and heading home for the day, he locked the investigation report in his desk and snapped off the lights. Lately he had been purposely leaving the office late, well after most of the other government employees on the floor. Since the apparent death of Conroy and his involvement in the case, the investigation had put a cold chill throughout his group of friends and coworkers. Now, he had his coffee alone in the mornings, ate his lunch alone and, by his own design, left the office alone.

Finding his car in the underground stall, he found himself thinking again about the possibility of quitting the NNSA. He knew that no matter the final disposition of the case, his involvement would forever mark him as someone not "viable" in government-speak for any kind of high-level leadership opportunity. He would never advance any further up the food chain. No one in the GS-rating category was ever fired from his position. Barring a criminal complaint, they just minimized your input, basically ignoring you to the point that you became irrelevant. Government supervisors never burned the dead wood. They just left it to rot on the ground.

By six o'clock that evening, he was home in his tiny condo in Fredericksburg, trying to heat up a TV dinner and catch the last bit of evening news. His girlfriend had called and left a message, but considering how he felt at the moment, the last thing he wanted to do was talk about his feelings, Frankly, all he wanted was to sit down, have a few beers, and look at his new SCUBA magazine that had come in the mail. A dive-trip to Costa Rica for about three weeks was something he was now seriously starting to think about.

Just as he sat down in his chair, his cell phone rang. He didn't recognize the number but decided to answer it anyway. "Hello?"

"Hey Kelly, it's Greg, Greg Gander."

A sudden feeling of dread shot through his body, "Hey, Greg, how you doing? What's going on?"

"Well, I wanted to talk to you about something that has come up."

"I don't know, Greg. I'm still knee-deep in the middle of an investigation and really don't want to complicate things."

"Listen. The last thing I would want to do is give you grief about anything Mark. It's just that this is really important and I just need about five minutes."

Kelly thought for a moment. "All right, five minutes - go ahead."

"Ah, I'm actually here."

"What do you mean, here?" questioned Kelly, getting out of his chair. "Where are you?"

"I'm outside your building in my rental car. What's your condo number?"

"How did you find my address?"

"You would be surprised how easy it is to look someone up on the computer, Mark. I flew in about an hour ago, picked up a car, and here I am."

"Jesus, okay, ah, I'm in number 307. C'mon up."

Several minutes later, Kelly heard Greg knocking on his door. "Hey, c'mon in," he said, shaking hands. "This is a shock."

Greg stepped in, "Yeah, well, I really needed to see you in person, kind of afraid of the phones and email."

Kelly led him into the living room. "Well, you came all the way from Montana. Have a seat and tell me what's so important that you flew clear across the country to talk to me about it."

Greg unzipped his coat and sat down. "My wife thinks I'm at a conference here in DC. If I told her what I was really up to, I'd be divorced. I'm really bothered by how easy it is to lie to her about this."

"Okay," replied Kelly smiling. "Seems like both of us have been finding it easy. Tell me what's on your mind."

Greg reached into his pocket and pulled out a small zip-lock bag. "A week ago, I received a box in the mail from Taylor. It had about three hundred and fifty thousand dollars in it and these." He dropped the baggie on the coffee table.

Kelly reached over and picked it up. "What is it?"

Greg took a deep breath. "Those thumb-drives contain the process Taylor discovered for moving through the space-time continuum. It's a set of blue prints for a time machine - a time machine that we both know works."

"You gotta be shitting me," replied Kelly. "When did this get mailed to you?"

"Sometime between the day I left the lab and just before you guys made contact with him."

Kelly studied the drives. "You do understand how powerful this information is, don't you?"

"Why do you think I'm here, Mark? I had to tell you about this. Jesus, it's been eating me up ever since I got that stuff last week."

Kelly left his chair and walked into the kitchen. "You want a beer?" he asked.

"Yeah, that would be great. So what do you think?"

Kelly walked back into the living room and handed Greg a bottle. "Well, the way I see it, we have two choices: You can take those drives, get back in your rental car and drive to the Potomac which is only about 20 minutes away, throw them in the river, then go home and never lie to your wife again."

"Okay, what's the second option?"

Kelly sat back in his chair while looking at the ceiling. "My career is over because of this thing," he announced. "This condo, this cheap beer, and twenty more years of more of the same is all I have to look forward to because of this case."

"Sorry, Mark. I didn't know it was that rough on you here," replied Greg. "Are you in any criminal trouble?"

Kelly laughed after taking a long drink of his beer. "Well, aside from lying to the FBI, ATF and my boss, I'm in pretty good shape."

"I thought everything was all right as far as the investigation was going?" replied Greg.

"Yeah, well, there's nothing official as far as charges go, but the Feds are really stumped as to how and why the place burnt down so completely. And don't worry, I left you out of the report altogether."

Greg thought for a moment, already sensing what Kelly's answer was going to be to his next question. "Okay then, what's our second option?"

Kelly dropped the baggie on the coffee table. "As it stands right now, I have little to no bargaining power with the Feds or the government in general, nothing to offer if this case goes sideways and they start looking for someone to hang this on. As you know, the government eats its own on something like this."

"So, what's your plan?"

Kelly smiled. "My plan is to get a knowledgeable guy that I can trust to go over this data and tell me if it's real and not some porn Taylor downloaded. Then I think we need to think very seriously about going into the time-machine business."

"You really think that's what we should do?"

"I don't think we have a choice," replied Kelly, sitting back in his chair.

"There's always a choice, Mark; we could just walk away."

"Greg, you and I are both scientists; I think that choice was made for us the second we saw what we saw in Taylor's lab. If we can duplicate the process, my God, Greg, can you imagine the value of that? Yeah, I think I am going to run with this thing and see where it leads."

"You're serious, aren't you?" asked Greg.

"As serious as eye cancer. Twenty minutes ago I was looking at a brick wall, Greg. Now you show up, and a way around the wall has opened up. Yeah, I'm serious. Besides Conroy went somewhere, and I owe it to him to try and get him back."

"You think he's still alive?" questioned Greg.

Kelly laughed, "Knowing Conroy, he's probably the mayor of some town by now. Hell, the guy has the luck of the Irish. If anybody can survive and thrive, it would be Dillon. Besides, how much trouble could you possibly get into in a week during the 1800's?"

Greg raised his bottle. "So, we are doing this? I've got the seed money."

Kelly raised his bottle. "We are doing it."

They clicked bottles, both instinctively knowing that they were now on a dangerous course, a direction that had the very real ability to end their lives. This was no game and both men knew it.

"So, what's next?" questioned Greg.

"Were you serious about using the money that Taylor sent you to get us started?"

"Absolutely, I even brought it with me," announced Greg, smiling.

"You brought three hundred thousand dollars with you from Montana?" asked Kelly. "How in the hell did you do that?"

"Just wrapped it up and put it through with my checked luggage."

Kelly shook his head in disbelief. "Took a hell of a chance, Greg. One nosey TSA dingbat, and it's all over."

"Ah, there's where another lie has crept into the equation," replied Greg. "Told the wife I was going to get rid of it, so, I got rid of it. It's in the trunk of the car."

Down on the dark street, sitting under the broken streetlight, the dark green van with the blacked out windows had gone unnoticed by the residents of Kelly's condo complex all day. It had arrived well before dark and now sat less then a hundred yards away from condo 307. The men inside were surrounded by the latest in audio surveillance equipment and sat motionless in their headsets listening to every word that was being said. A dangerous course had been chosen by all involved, all with the best of intentions - a dangerous course, indeed.

****

Feeling as if he were about to pass out, Dillon stepped up beside Tillman who was examining the cell phone. He handed it to him. "What do you think this is? I think it opens up - has a lid on it or something."

Dillon slowly opened the flip phone cover, praying that the power was off. It was going to be hard enough trying to explain the phone by itself, even harder if the power came on. To his great relief, the power was off. "Look's like some kind of adding machine," he announced, doing his best to look confused.

Tillman leaned close. "Samsung." He said the name two more times while looking at the phone. "What do you suppose that means?" he asked, taking it back.

Wanting to control the situation, Dillon quickly took the phone from Tillman along with the rest of the items on the table. He scooped all of it into his hat and picked up his coat. "Doc, I'm going to have to lock all this up for safe-keeping, just in case a relative shows up. Till then, it will be in Sheriff Coleman's safe".

"Good idea, Deputy," replied Tillman, "although, I doubt those three had anybody who gave a red piss about them."

Dillon nodded and headed towards the door. He had to get some air. "All right, Doc," he said over his shoulder. "I'm not feeling so well. I'll be in my office." He closed the café door behind him, cutting off any further conversation. Outside, a small crowd had gathered, all eager to see the carnage inside. He said nothing as he moved through the group. Apprehension mixed with fear hung over the crowd like a fog. He willed himself to take deep breaths and relax; now was not the time to fall apart. He walked across the street and into his office, slamming the door behind him as the nausea blasted his breakfast on the floor.

****

Heading south on highway 270 in DC, on the way to the town of Annandale, there is a nondescript three-story building. It can be seen from the freeway on the left hand side, right before 270 turns into highway 495. There is nothing especially notable about the structure. It carries the standard opaque glass and steel appearance that a thousand other Washington DC buildings carry. The façade of success, it is filled with young believers who drive too far, spend too much, and live in a virtual frenzy of misguided normalcy. In this building, there is no clique of young professionals right out of Georgetown who are determined to bend the world into a shape they desire; there are no expense account commandos or wanna-be spooks that spread their half-truths and bullshit to any happy-hour pretty face that desperately wants to believe. *If you have the gift of gab and have a job in some obscure office in DC that nobody has ever heard of, then you must be from the dark side.* The reality is that most of the people who work in the town are doing mind-numbingly, boring jobs. They sell copy machines and insurance, advocate for non-profits, or struggle under the heavy-handed bureaucracies of government employment such as the Department of Agriculture or the EPA.

This "building", the one just off Highway 270, has a different name, a name that only the highest in the DC food chain talk about, and even then, they are careful with their words. It is called "The Kingdom." Its staff consists of three, a slightly attractive, middle-aged female at the reception desk and the two men in their late forties who sit behind bullet-resistant desks at each end of the lobby. A single bank of elevator doors is the only way to access the vast set of underground offices. Everything above ground level is a façade.

Jason Chalks walked up to the reception desk and looked into the retinal scanner. The receptionist verified the reading. "Good morning, Mister Chalks. You're clear." She touched the small floor button that transmitted a green light to both of the men who sat behind their desks at each end of the lobby.

"Thank you, Edie." He then walked to the elevator and nodded to the stern-faced guard, "Morning."

"Morning, sir."

Three floors down, Chalks knocked on the door of Mason Braid.

His immediate supervisor, Braid, closed a file on his desk as Chalks walked in and took a seat by the desk. "Sir, I have the transcript and the audio from our team last night," announced Chalks, handing him the file.

"Give me the crib-notes; I've got to be on a plane in twenty minutes," replied the supervisor.

"Sir, it seems that Doctor Taylor was able to send the plans and schematics for the process to Mister Gander, along with three hundred and fifty thousand dollars. They plan on finding an outside source for data verification, and if this proves viable, they plan on building the process."

The supervisor sat back in his chair. "All right, make sure our man 'is' this outside source they are looking for."

"Yes, sir."

"If the information is valid, get it, all of it, and then dispose of all parties concerned. Are my instructions clear?"

"Yes, sir, perfectly."

"Anybody, and I mean anybody, even remotely associated with this case will be going away - wives, girlfriends, parents, friends, everyone. I want our best people on this, understand?"

"Yes, sir. Will you need any Presidential back-briefs from my end?"

"Absolutely not," replied Braid. "The President is not cleared on any of this, never has been. We don't deal with politicians."

"Sir, are there any other instructions?" questioned Chalks.

Mason handed the file back. "Jason, I just want you to be aware and to keep in mind how important this case is. We need to keep total control on every aspect of this thing."

"Sir, if I may ask, why don't we just close it down now?"

"Honestly, that was my suggestion to higher," replied Braid, "but the orders I received were to let them build the Goddamned thing. So that's what we are going to do."

"Yes sir, I understand."

"Okay, Jason, I think we are done here. You are sanctioned under written protocol to do whatever is necessary to control and close this case. The operation has been designated as "Stone Gate" - love the names these people come up with. So, are we clear?"

"Yes, sir, clear."

The Supervisor pushed out from behind his desk. "Now, if you'll excuse me, I have a plane to catch."

"Yes, sir," replied Chalks. "Sir, who is my POC on this?"

Braid stepped out into the wide, brightly lit hallway. "Only me," he said, locking his office door. "Take care of this, Jason. This is a big one."

An hour later, Chalks had already contacted all the team members he would need for the Stone Gate operation. SEAL Team Six immediately released four members from active duty in Afghanistan, tip of the spear assets that would be needed at the end of the case.

Lives would be changed, futures altered, and the status quo would continue. "The Kingdom" would handle the Stone Gate operation, just like they had handled all the other things that nobody talked about. There would be no loose ends; no one would be walking out of this - no one.

SECTION TWO

STONE GATE

Chapter 15

He had been in the wagon a good part of the morning, sitting on a barrel of hard tack crackers as the wagon bumped and thudded over the rutted ground. It was just past ten in the morning and it was already ninety degrees, the sun pounding down from a cloudless sky. He still found it odd that the surrounding men paid little attention to his presence. After all, his clothes were wrong. His shoes were wrong. Everything about him was a walking inconsistency. Apparently, to them he was just some lunatic who had wandered into Indian country. It was only through grace, that they had saved his life.

He had tried to convince them that he was not from their time, practically begging them to listen to his story. But they had responded with laughter and relegated him to the back of a supply wagon, giving him no more importance than a barrel of crackers.

He looked past the wagon driver at the growing dust cloud kicked up by a number of mounted cavalry that had stopped in a large group. Taylor could see that all of the Crow scouts were dismounted, their mood somber, almost sad.

General Custer, in his white buckskin coat, was walking among them shouting a stream of obscenities and Crow insults aimed at the scouts who were now beginning to sit down on the sunbaked ground. Even from his distance, Taylor could tell the General was clearly on the edge of self-control. Moving among the seated Indians, he leaned toward each man grabbing his chin, shouting directly into the stoic faces.

Taylor jumped down from the back of the wagon, wanting to get closer to the drama that was now taking place. Riders were riding back and forth along the long line of mounted cavalry and supply wagons shouting orders as thick clouds of chalk-white alkali dust drifted in the hot breeze.

Boston, who had been driving the wagon, breathlessly walked up beside him, his face streaked with sweaty dust. "Looks like George is giving em hell," he said smiling. "Wouldn't be the first time."

Taylor stopped walking, grabbing him by the arm. "Boston, stop and listen to me for a minute. This is the beginning of the end for you and everyone here."

Boston jerked his arm away. "Mister, I don't know what you're up to, but you need to mind your own business. We've been doing this a long time."

"Boston, I swear to you on my mother's grave that if you go down to the river, you will be dead in two hours." Boston turned to walk away. Desperate, Taylor grabbed his arm. "Boston your lives..." a swift blow from his rifle barrel knocked him to his knees."

"Goddamn it! Don't ever grab me like that, mister!" shouted Boston, standing over him. "Next time, I'll just shoot you." A sharp knee to the chest sent Taylor to the dirt. "Now, stay out of this!" he shouted, walking away. Hurried commands were now being given as horses and riders thudded by.

Through the choking dust and pain in his head, Taylor struggled to his feet watching men prepare for battle. Taylor could see the fear and apprehension etched deep in their faces as they passed. The thick dust coated their horses, their uniforms and their beards in a grayish white layer giving each the appropriate appearance of a shroud.

As the last soldiers rode past and the dust began to clear, Taylor could see the mounted scouts leading Custer along the ridge parallel to the Bighorn River. Down below on the far bank lay the endless camp of the Lakota Sioux. He now had a ringside seat to one of the most pivotal events in Western American History.

He exchanged a nod as he stumbled behind the last young trooper. This was going to happen. The 7th cavalry was riding into the pages of history and he was a witness.

He suddenly felt like a thief. He did not belong here. This wasn't his time or his destiny. The men he watched ride off into the dust had been appointed to be here. The great power that moved men through history had predetermined the fate of each. All their hopes, all their dreams would end today just as it was supposed to, and there was nothing he could do to change that fate.

227

Exhausted, he pulled off his fatigue shirt and sat down trying to figure out what he should do next. The rest of the supply train was a good ten miles behind while certain death lay ahead.

Through the heat shimmer he watched a large red tail hawk swoop down through the coolies and then up into the brilliant blue sky, oblivious to the drama unfolding down below. It was the little things he was now beginning to notice - how warm the ground felt under his legs, how the hot, dusty wind in his face made his eyes tear, the deep ache of the splinter in his palm from when he jumped down off the wagon. These were all feelings and sensations of a reality that should not be his. How long had it been since he took that violent jump from the lab to this world? A day? A week?

Alone with only the fading sound of horses and the jingle of harnesses, he got to his feet. If he started walking now, he would find the supply train by dark. There would be no heroic attempt on his part to change the events that were about to unfold, no misguided running to the guns, only a long dusty walk in the scorching Montana sun. For any man, to finally realize that strength and power of will is never a constant nor dependable in all of life's circumstances, can be a sobering, crushing realization. He closed his eyes and breathed deep the sage-scented air, pushing the sharp edges of fear and doubt out of his mind. His intellect, his research had made all of this possible. For sixteen years he had labored alone in the lab. Countless experiments and equations had produced a process that worked. Good or bad, it had worked and he had done it alone. His only task now was to try to live with what he had done. His father was right when he said, "Be careful what you ask for, son. You just might get it." No truer words were ever spoken.

***

It had been three days since the shootout in the café. Sheriff Coleman had returned the night of the incident and been told by several prominent townspeople and witnesses that the new deputy had done his duty in an admirable fashion. The Dugan brothers were dead. 'Good riddance' seemed to be the general consensus.

The townspeople's overwhelming approval of his actions did little to soothe Dillon's growing unease about his changing personality. He had killed three men, men who had done nothing to him other than show a level of animosity towards his authority. In fact, he had provoked the action that he knew the men would take. He wanted the fight, and even more disturbing, he had enjoyed it.

Over the last several days he had kept to himself, spending most of his time in his shack out behind the sheriff's office. He had begun to keep a journal, documenting the time and events that described his days living in the 1890's. He had been in Deer Lodge almost two weeks now, and in that time it seemed as if a lifetime of drama and discovery had taken place.

By lamplight, he read the chronology of events in the journal. Taylor's lab had been where it all started. He along with Agent Ania and Chris Abbott from the NRC had been caught in the lab's array and blasted back in time to Deer Lodge, Montana, circa 1890. Ania had been shot and killed within minutes of landing in a horse corral. There had been no sign of Abbott. He himself had been wounded in the arm when Ania was shot and had since nearly fully recovered.

A sudden knock on the door pulled him away from his reading. "C'mon in. It's open!" he announced. A cold blast of winter wind followed Sheriff Coleman into the room. "Goddamn, it's cold out there," he said, stamping his feet while slamming the door shut. Dillon slid a chair over from the table. "Jesus, John, have a seat. What are you doing out on a night like this?"

Coleman rubbed his hands together while standing next to the small stove in the corner. "I brought you your pay. Had it in my office for a day or so and since you didn't come by, I thought I would drop it off." He tossed Dillon a small cloth sack of coins. "There's a little extra in there, you know, on account of the shooting."

"You didn't have to do that, John. It's not something I'm proud of."

Coleman sat down and started lighting his pipe. "Well, maybe you're not proud but I am. The county commissioner is. Putting a few extra dollars in that poke is his way of expressing it." He lit his pipe, filling the room with the sweet smell of cherry blend. He sat back in his chair, his deep-set eyes hidden in the orange-yellow lantern light. "How you holding up?" he asked, blowing a perfect smoke-ring.

Dillon let the question sink in a moment before answering. If the truth were told, he felt terrible since the shooting. He couldn't sleep, couldn't eat, and worst of all, he had a difficult time looking into the faces of the townspeople. They were polite, cordial but between moments, Dillon could see the fear in their eyes, that unmistakable edge of concern that couldn't be hidden no matter how hard they tried. He had changed in their minds, changed into something dangerous, something they admired on the surface but feared within themselves. He had become a killer, someone who had crossed that life-changing, emotional boundary. "I'm fine John," he replied letting the lie hang in the air. "I just wanted to keep a low profile this last week."

Coleman continued to puff on his pipe. "Nothing to be ashamed of," he said slowly. "If there was ever a group of reprobate low-lifes that needed killing, the Dugans shore enough fit the bill. Hell, I damn near shot the older one, Pete, last year for stealing all those shovels out of Miller's store." He leaned over pointing his pipe at Dillon. "And I know them three son-of-a-bitches killed old man Collins last year up on the bluffs. Never could prove it, but I know they did it. You did the world a favor."

Dillon walked over and shoved another small log into the stove. "I don't know, John. I still feel bad about what happened. And the people in town look at me different now. I think they are afraid of me."

Coleman tapped his pipe out on the stove. "Well, I'll tell you what, Dillon. It was just a matter of time till I had a run in with those boys, and I doubt I could have got all three. That fancy gun of yours probably saved your life."

Dillon thought for a moment. He was appreciative of Coleman's support, yet it did little to relieve the emotional heaviness he felt about the incident. "Thanks, John. Sorry for all the trouble. I really mean that."

"Ain't no trouble," replied Coleman getting out of his chair. "Some folks are just born to be shot. You just had the high misfortune of running across three of them." He buttoned his heavy coat and adjusted his hat. "I'm going to bed. Will I see you for breakfast?"

Dillon nodded. "About eight?"

"Eight it is. Go to bed, Dillon. What's done is done. See you in the morning." He quickly opened the door and stepped out in to the dark.

Dillon could hear his footsteps fade away on the frozen snow outside. Before rolling into his cot and blankets, Dillon stoked the fire in the wood stove and turned down the lamp, making a mental note to work on his journal in the morning. He couldn't just live the hours and days in this alternate reality. He had to document every part of his existence here.

He had no idea how the killing of the Dugan brothers would affect the future. It was just too terrible to think that killing the three might have instantly ended the lives of hundreds of other possible descendants. As he lay in the dark listening to the wind blowing the snow outside, he let his mind touch the memories of his family. Would he ever see them again? The question danced in the dark as he drifted off to sleep.

****

It had been a week since Jason had spoken to the Deputy Director in the "Kingdom" office. His explicit orders were to control every aspect of the Stone gate operation. There were to be no loose ends whatsoever. Nor were there to be any surprises. Video surveillance along with phone taps and life-style dossiers were already producing results. The most recent phone tap had indicated that Kelly had contacted a physics professor and friend at the University of Notre Dame. They had set up a time to meet in South Bend this coming Friday. Jason, along with two SEAL team members, were now headed up the steps to the Professor's apartment.

Jason checked the name on the sheet before knocking. "I'll do all the talking. Is that understood?"

Both men nodded. "Yes, sir."

Confident that he had been understood, he turned and knocked. Several minutes later a short heavyset man in his middle forties wearing glasses answered the door. "Yes? Can I help you?"

Jason stepped into the threshold of the open door. "Professor Baker? Professor Edward Baker?"

"Yes, that's right. And you are?"

Jason held up an official looking credential. "Mister Baker, I need a moment of your time." He stepped closer as the two SEALS moved into the doorway, pushing Baker back. They were in the room with the door closed behind them before Baker was able to protest.

"Now hold on. Who are you people? Get out of my house right now." He made a move to push Jason back only to be chopped down by a stunning blow to his side, dropping him to his knees. A quick kick to the chest knocked him flat on his back before he found himself quickly jerked to his feet and shoved into the overstuffed easy chair in the small living room.

Gasping for air, he clutched his chest. "I, I can't breathe. I, I can't breathe."

"Shh, shh, shh, relax," replied Jason sitting down on the couch "You're all right." He pulled out a small notebook and pen. "Okay, Mister Baker, let's get this started."

"You broke my ribs, you son-of-a-bitch!" shouted Baker.

"Hey, look at me," replied Jason. "LOOK at me. I needed to get your attention, Professor. Now, are you going to calm down, or do I need to let these two gentlemen get your attention a little more? I have all day."

Baker nodded. "Okay, I'm listening," he gasped. "What do you want? I don't have any money. Take my car. You can have..."

"Hush, Professor," he interrupted. "I am not here to rob you. In fact, I am here to give you money - lots of it. A little cooperation is all that I am asking."

"What, I, I don't understand," replied Baker, catching his breath.

Jason opened his notebook. "Okay, now that we have all calmed down, I am going to tell you a story. It's about these two people who live in Saint Joseph, Michigan, not far from here really. Their address is 167 Ottumwa Avenue, and they go by the names of Ralph and Irene Baker." Jason looked up and smiled. "Now there's the names of two all American Mid-westerners, by God. Ralph is 68-years-old and has a mild heart condition that is currently under control. Irene is 66 and is in good health. Both attend the Lutheran church in Saint Joseph and are considered pillars of the community. How am I doing so far, Professor?"

The color had drained out of Baker's face. "Wha...., what does this have to do with my parents?"

"You see, Mister Baker, 'this thing' has nothing to do with Ralph and Irene. It has everything to do with you. You are going to see a Mister Chris Kelly this coming Friday. Am I correct?"

"Yes, but what,... wha?"

"A simple 'yes' or 'no' is all I want to hear, Mister Baker," interrupted Jason. "Yes or no?"

"Yes."

"Very good, Mister Baker. Now, when Chris Kelly arrives day after tomorrow he is going to show you some disks or thumb drives."

"You want me to take these thumb drives and give them to you?"

Jason leaned even closer. "Mister Baker," he said softly, "if you interrupt me again, I am going to have my associates dislocate both of your shoulders. Is that clear?"

"Yes," whispered Baker.

"Very good, Professor. Now, here is what you are going to do. You are going to help Mister Kelly in any way he sees fit. There is some extremely important information on those thumb-drives, and you are going to validate it.

You will have no need to contact me. All of your phones and computers are being monitored. You are being watched twenty-four hours a day. So you see, I know everything you do and everything you say. Nod your head that you understand what I am saying."

Baker nodded, the fear etched deep on his face.

"Now," continued Jason, opening his notebook, "this is the good stuff for you. You will be paid thirty thousand dollars a week for as long as you are working on the project with Mister Kelly. This will be paid to you in cash. You are free to do what you will with the money. I warn you to not go to the police because we are the police. Do not call any government law-enforcement agency because we are the government. If you ignore my warnings, your father will die from his heart attack. Your mother will be audited every year. You will also be visited by some of my associates and beaten within an inch of your life. Nod your head 'yes' if you understand."

Baker nodded, fighting the urge to vomit.

237

Jason closed his notebook and pulled a small yet thick envelope from his overcoat and dropped it on the coffee table. "Just to show you our good faith in the agreement, here is the first thirty-thousand in advance." He motioned both SEALS towards the door. "Now remember what I said, Professor," announced Jason standing. "All you have to do is coöperate with Mister Kelly. Validate the information and work with him as long as he needs you to. Understand?"

Baker nodded. "I understand."

"Good, good," replied Jason. "Oh, as a little incentive for your cooperation, we filmed and recorded your little romantic interlude last week with ah... just a minute," he pulled his notebook from his coat, "ah, here it is. A Mrs. Ross, Debra Ross. A member of your faculty, correct?"

Baker nodded, "Yes."

Jason smiled. "You know, Professor, Mrs. Ross is married. Now I know you're divorced and live alone, but I think that Mister Ross might not like the idea of his wife taking long showers with you on a regular basis. What do you think?"

Baker couldn't hold back any more and leaned forward vomiting on the floor. Jason stepped back. "I'll take that as a 'yes', Professor. As I said, I doubt Mister Ross would like to see the video tape of his wife doing what she was doing to you."

Jason knelt down close. "She is a very attractive woman. You have good taste. I would hate to see anything happen to her."

"I will do whatever you say," replied Baker, wiping his chin. "Just don't hurt my family or my friends."

Jason patted Baker on the shoulder. "Very good, Professor. I am glad we came to an agreement. You have made a wise choice. We'll talk again soon." On a silent cue, all three men walked out of the apartment as quickly as they had come, closing the door softly behind them.

Baker sat back in his chair desperately trying to get his head around what had just happened. His life had changed dramatically in a short ten minutes. He picked up the envelope and dumped the cash into his lap. "My God," he whispered. "My God."

****

As Taylor walked through the dusty rolling landscape of eastern Montana, he tried to figure out his role in this new reality. He now realized that he did not have the nerve for suicide nor the verbal horsepower to make a convincing argument that he was truly from the future. His confession had failed miserably. They had laughed at his pronouncements, ridiculed his mission, and defined his ravings that of a madman. If anyone was ever going to take him seriously, he would have to present a more calm and coherent voice of reason.

He had gone into this current realm of events carrying the modern day sense of "Self importance". He carried the false idea that he was smarter, more aware, and more intuitive than anybody around because he had gone to college, understood principles that had yet to be discovered, worked with technology from the future, and knew the destiny of the country. He realized that the computer and cell phone, along with a hundred other electronic devices that played a part in his modern life had stolen his time and isolated him from his world, from daily human contact.

Here, there were no computers, no Smart phones, no ATMs with overdraft protection, nothing that removed the raw edge of daily survival. You stayed alive in this present reality by thinking through problems, cooperating with others, and working hard. Here you earned your success or you withered and died.

As harsh and unforgiving as it all appeared through the dusty windows of time, to Taylor the realization that his modern life had woefully unprepared him for his current situation was staggering. He had read about the past, studying the daily lives of people from the era in-depth, yet was clueless how to put the knowledge he had gained to use in this new raw reality. He was not familiar with livestock. He had no idea how to saddle a horse or drive a wagon. Taking care of personal hygiene and attending to bodily functions were now presenting ridiculously awkward but very real problems.

Where and how does one take a crap in the middle of the Montana prairie without toilet paper? He laughed to himself at the last thought, realizing that he had a PHD in Quantum Physics and couldn't figure out how to take a shit on the prairie.

Thirst and overwhelming fatigue was now becoming a factor as he stumbled along in the blazing heat. He stopped and looked up into the mid afternoon sun knowing full well that a person without water could literally walk himself to death in this unforgiving landscape. To the east, the sun-bleached hills shimmered in the heat waves as gusts of hot wind whipped up patches of chalk white alkali.

He stood, slowly surveying this magnificent desolation. Three hundred and sixty degrees, for as far as the eye could see, not a fence post, not a tree, not a building or any other object that would indicate a human presence was visible. And then in the distance, there was the faint unmistakable sound of muted, muffled gunfire, like the sound of hundreds of car doors being slammed shut miles away. The sound sent a shudder through him as he realized he was hearing the echoes of history. Transfixed, he stood in the blazing sun and listened as the gunfire peaked and ebbed over the hours and then died out all together.

For the second time in his life, he had been a willing witness to the Battle of the Little Bighorn, and each time his effort to change the outcome had failed.

Exhausted from the heat, he turned away from the battle and started walking only to stop in stunned surprise moments later. He wiped the sweat from his eyes trying to clear his vision while focusing on the two mounted cavalry soldiers standing less then thirty yards away. Still not sure he wasn't looking at a cruel mirage, he raised his hands and waved. The horsemen stood stock-still for a long moment and then one of the men waved back.

My God, they were real, he thought, breaking into a stumbling trot. *They are real.* Minutes later he walked up to the riders in breathless excitement. "Gosh, I am so glad to see you fellas!" he announced stepping close. Both men stared at him as if he had risen out of the ground on fire. As Taylor drew close he realized that both men had their pistols drawn and were at the ready.

"Who the hell are you, mister?" demanded one of the men, his horse side stepping nervously away from Taylor.

"I'm a traveler," replied Taylor. "I've just come from the river," he said pointing over his shoulder.

The second soldier, a much younger man than the other, drew his horse close. "My name is Captain Weir. I need to know if you have seen any other soldiers."

To Taylor, there was no easy way to say what he needed to say, nor would he gain anything by announcing who he really was. The truth with all its terrible reality needed to be told.

"I know who you are, Captain Weir," replied Taylor, gesturing to the area around them. "Some time from now this place will be called Weir's Point. You will be famously known as someone who was loyal to General Custer."

The officer slowly stepped down from his horse and handed the reins to the other man. His Colt pistol hung loose in his hand as he stepped up. Taylor guessed his age to be in the middle to late twenties. His face was streaked with sweat and alkali, the eyes set deep with confusion. "What did you just say, mister? Have you seen the General?"

Taylor slowly nodded. "Yes I have, Captain. Several hours ago, I…."

"How in the hell?" interrupted the mounted soldier.

The Captain held up his hand. "Quiet Sergeant!" he shouted. "I need to hear what this man has to say. Continue, sir. You said you saw the General?"

Taylor looked in the direction of the battle and then to Weir. "Captain, General Custer along with his entire command has been wiped out by a massive number of Indians that have been camped along the Little Bighorn River. They are all gone."

"And you know this how?" questioned Weir.

Taylor thought for a moment, feeling as if he had aged ten years. "Because, Captain, I have been there – twice and each time there wasn't a damn thing I could do to keep him and his men alive." He let his statement hang in the warm air as a heavy gust kicked up, the dust partially obscuring the soldiers less than ten feet away, a fitting natural emphasis on a totally unnatural encounter. For Taylor, this was becoming the norm.

Chapter 16

It was the hardest phone call he had ever made. Calling his wife Carol from Kelly's apartment in D.C. and telling her that he was going to be there for awhile had not gone well. When he repeatedly tried to explain how important he felt it all was, the argument landed on deaf ears. She ended the call abruptly telling him that he would need to choose between what he was doing in D.C. and their marriage in Montana. He could not have both.

He knew the phone call would be easier than seeing her in person. It was never a fair fight when he faced things in her presence. As soon as he looked into her blue eyes she could see through all his bull shit. She knew him better than he knew himself. Even at this distance, she had been right on all counts.

Earlier in the day he had called the University and told them he would be taking a leave of absence, a move that did not go over well with the administration. They told him that he would only be allowed two more weeks of leave. After that, his position would be filled. A second phone call to the Chancellor confirmed the information. His professorship was hanging by a thread.

"Well, what did your wife say?" questioned Kelly.

Greg downed the last of his third beer that morning. "Not much. Said she was one hundred percent behind anything I decided and to get out there and kick ass."

Kelly smiled. "She said you were full of shit and to get your ass back to Montana or you're divorced. Right?"

"Yeah, that's pretty close."

"What are you going to do?"

Greg pushed himself off the couch. "Gonna take a piss and try to clear my head before your guy shows up. Man, you have to start buying better beer. Geez, that stuff is foul."

"What about your wife?" shouted Kelly hearing the bathroom door close.

"Don't worry about it," replied Greg, stepping out of the bathroom. "I'll get her on board once we get this end sorted out. What time did you say your guy was going to be here?"

"Said he would stop by around noon." Kelly checked his watch, "Which, ah, should be anytime now."

****

Two blocks away Baker sat in his car trying to calm down. For months now he had expected some kind of cosmic retribution for his actions of late. The affair and his false documentation in his most recent published paper provided for heavy karma payment on his part. But this was way over the line. His parents were being threatened; his own safety was now in question.

246

After being in the presence of these men, he had no doubt that they would do exactly what they said they would do if he did not cooperate. He would play the game and hope for the best. In his mind, he really had no choice.

Baker punched in Kelly's phone number while nervously looking around for signs of the surveillance. "Yeah, Chris? This is Ed."

"Hey Ed," replied Kelly. "You on your way?"

"Yeah. Be there in a few minutes. Ah.. just parking the car."

"All right. C'mon up."

"Okay. Bye."

As he locked his car door and slowly headed towards Kelly's condo, he was still unsure if he could pull this off. He had known Chris since college. They'd played racquetball together, knew each other's girlfriends and ex-wives, and been to each other's homes countless times. Now he was going to have to pretend that everything was normal between them when he knew it wasn't. It might be an act of deception that his friend would see through in a second.

Just before he knocked on Kelly's door, he looked down the street and noticed a dark green van. The sight of the van sent an involuntary shiver down his back at the thought that it might be there in surveillance of the activity at Chris's condo. If the goal, however, was to intimidate him, it was working.

Kelly answered on the second knock. "Hey, Ed. C'mon in. How you been?"

"Good. How about you?" he replied, stepping into the room.

"Ed, this is Greg Gander from Montana," announced Kelly. Greg shook hands with Baker immediately noticing that he seemed distracted and nervous.

"So, Chris, what's this 'thing' you want me to look at."

Kelly seemed genuinely surprised by the comment. "Wow, dude! You got a bus to catch or what? Jesus, sit down and have a beer."

"Naw, I can't. I'm busy; that's all. I have a lot of stuff I have to take care of today."

Kelly walked in from the kitchen and handed Baker a beer. "What is wrong with you, Ed? I haven't seen your sorry ass in a week, and you're trying to run off. Here, take the beer. Geez."

"Okay, okay," he replied, sitting down. "It's just been a tough week. Sorry."

"No sweat, Pard. Anyway since you're hurting for time, this is what I wanted you to look at." He handed Baker his laptop with one of the thumb drives already loaded. "Just open the drive and tell me what you think."

Baker typed in the open disk code and began to read the documents and mathematical equations.

"What the hell is this, Chris?"

"You tell me."

"Ah, this is really, and I mean really, advanced Quantum Physics. Where did this come from?"

"Does it really matter where it came from?"

Baker nodded. "Ah, yeah. It does matter, Chris. I can probably count on one hand the number of people in the world who can turn out this kind of work. I mean this is VERY high speed."

"So it's viable information?"

"I'm not sure what you mean by 'Viable', Chris," replied Baker, looking back to the computer.

"I mean, can you duplicate the results?"

Baker looked at the ceiling and then closed the laptop. "What is this about, Chris? Why is this data so important?"

"The information contained in the thumb drives includes detailed plans on a method of bending the space time continuum."

Baker chuckled. "Time travel! You brought me here to look at a time machine? You have got to be shitting me, Chris."

"It's real," stated Greg softly.

Baker shook his head smiling. "Ah, with all due respect, and no offense, Greg, unless you're the one who did this work I really doubt you could judge the merits of this information."

249

"No offense taken. And no, I did not produce the work. But I did go back in time with the guy who did, so I guess that gives me a little credibility."

Baker held up his hand laughing. "Okay, guys, you got me! The joke's on me. Chris, I'm not sure what's going on and I can take a joke, but, c'mon, you really don't expect me to believe that you traveled back in time, do you?"

"I'll give you ten grand if you'll read all of it and tell me if you can make the device laid out on the drives," announced Greg sharply. "This is no joke, Pard. We really need your help on this. It's a big deal."

Baker thought for a moment. "Let me get this straight. You are going to give me ten thousand dollars just to read this stuff and tell you if we can build a time machine from the data?"

"Cash money," replied Greg.

"No bullshit," added Kelly dropping a bundle of money on the coffee table. "And we need to get started right away."

Baker sat open-mouthed looking at the bundles of hundred dollar bills. "You do know, guys, that time travel is impossible." He looked at Greg adding, "No offense."

Greg took the last swallow of his beer and then set the empty bottle on the table. "No offense taken. I really don't care if you believe me or not. What I need is your expertise regarding the data, and then I need to know if you can build this machine. We are willing to invest ten thousand dollars to get your opinion."

"Guys, listen, I..."

"Twenty thousand," interrupted Greg.

"Chris, listen to me, okay? You're a friend of mine. I've known you since college. I don't want your money to look at this thing. I just don't want you to be chasing stuff that does not exist."

Kelly thought for a moment. "All right, I'll approach this another way. Aren't you just a little curious about the data?"

"Sure, it looks interesting on the surface. A lot of stuff does."

"Okay, that's good enough. So you'll look at it?"

Baker studied the face of his friend. "So this is that important?"

"Yes, that important, Ed. It's not my intention to waste your time. ...Please."

Baker picked up the laptop. "All right," he sighed. "Since you asked nice. You can get me another beer. And put that Goddamned money away. With the way my luck's been going lately, somebody'll bust in and rob us."

Kelly smiled, extending his hand. "Thanks, Pard. I think your luck is about to change."

****

Three and a half hours later Ed was still trying to comprehend the importance of the material he had just read as he made his way down the stairs. He found his car and slid in behind the wheel more excited than he had been in years. If what he had read was even remotely possible, the world as he knew it could be changed forever. The ramifications were staggering. Little wonder the government or whomever Chalks was working for wanted this information.

As he pulled away from the curb and into the late afternoon traffic, he came to the sobering realization that no matter how much he cooperated with Chalks, the second he was of no use to him he would be killed. This information was far too important. No, powerful men and organizations would control this project with little tolerance for people who did not run in their closely guarded circles. He knew he was only an asset as long as he produced results.

As if on cue, the black Mercedes was suddenly at his side as he prepared to turn at the light. The darkened back window came down, and Chalks waved him to the curb.

"Very good, Ed," announced Chalks, getting into the passenger side of Baker's car. "You are really getting the hang of this. Just pull into that spot over there, and we'll have a chat."

"So I guess you heard everything?" asked Ed pulling into the parking spot and turning off the ignition.

Chalks patted him on the shoulder a little harder than was friendly. "Yes we did. And I have to tell you that you were very good. You got real quiet there for a few hours but I assumed you were reading the information."

"That's correct."

"Well, Ed, my good friend, what did you think of the information? Did you find it interesting?"

"Interesting doesn't even come close and you know it. This could be the most important discovery of all Mankind."

"You know, I think you're right," replied Chalks smiling. "I am impressed with you, Professor." He took out a small notebook. "We did a little checking up on you. You really are one of the top physicists in the country according to your colleagues."

"There are a lot of good people out there doing very good work. I am nothing special."

"Oh, I beg to differ, Professor. According to our records, you worked on the God particle experiments at the CERN last summer. The guys who headed the team went on to win the Nobel Prize for that work. Very impressive. And the summer before that, you did a fellowship at MIT in the same kind of research."

"What's your point?"

Chalk's slapped him hard on the shoulder smiling, again, just beyond the range of friendly. "My point is, we now know that you're a really smart guy and that we could not have a better egg-head looking over this material. You are the man, Professor!"

Baker gripped the wheel until his knuckles went white, trying to control himself. "What do you want me to do now?" he said, flexing the muscles in his jaw.

"Well, you can tell me what you think of the data. Is it possible that this thing can be built?"

Baker shook his head. "It's too early to tell. I need more time to go over the data. Even if it can be done, I would need a state of the art lab and a nearly unlimited power source."

Chalks slapped him on the shoulder a third time. "Well, now we are getting somewhere. It's like we have this mental connection, you know? Wow, this is giving me the chills, Professor."

"Stop playing games, Chalks. Just tell me what you want done!" he shouted. "I don't have time for this."

Chalks suddenly whipped out a small leather wrapped lead sap and struck him over the right eye. The blow sent Baker's head thudding into the driver's side window. "Now, Ed, see what you made me do? You really need to learn to control yourself."

Baker held his hands to his face, feeling the blood run through his fingers.

"Now, do I have your full attention?"

"Jesus Christ. You broke my glasses," he moaned, slowly taking his bloody fingers away from his face.

"Ed, pay attention. It's just a scratch. Now listen to me. Because you are the main guy we need on this and I know it is going to take a lot of your time, you're going to put in for a six month leave of absence from your job."

"I, I can't do that, I...."

Chalks delivered a second blow to the side of Ed's face nearly knocking him unconscious. "Now, there you go again, Professor. This is not a negotiation. Don't you pass out on me!" He grabbed Baker by the back of his neck. "Don't pass out, pal. Now, listen, you're going to take a leave of absence and get on our little project full time, all right? Nod that you understand. Good. Now as you get more information, you start getting a list together of the things you will need - lab space, equipment, anything you need, and I will get it for you. Okay? Nod your head, Professor, if you understand. Very good."

Chalks pulled out a handkerchief. "Here, put this on you eye. Like I said, Ed, you have to learn that when I ask you to do something, I am not negotiating. Understand?"

Ed dabbed the blood off his brow, "Yes, yes, I understand."

"Good, that's good, Professor. Put your paperwork in tomorrow. Get your list together on what you're going to need. Okay?"

Ed nodded. "Okay."

255

"All right. I think we are done here. Go home. Clean up. We will be in touch." He gripped the back of his neck again. "Do not mistake my kindness for weakness, Ed. Understand?"

"I understand."

"Good man." Chalks opened the door and stepped out. "I'll tell you what, Ed," he said leaning back in, "why don't you give your girlfriend a call? I think her husband is out of town at some conference. Good-looking woman…nice ass. It would make you feel a whole lot better." He slammed the door smiling and walked back to the waiting black Mercedes.

As Baker sat behind the wheel of his car watching the Mercedes drive away, he tossed the bloody handkerchief out the window determined that he would never let anyone hit him again…ever. He was going to turn this around somehow. He would put the odds in his favor. He was smarter than his tormenter, of that he was sure. He just had to figure out how to use his intellect as a weapon. He would get his life back by targeting one thing at a time. His first target would be Mister Chalks. Driving away from the curb he felt an odd sense of power. He now understood the phrase "There is nothing more dangerous than a man with nothing to lose." Absolutely, Goddamn right.

Chapter 17

It had been four days since Taylor met the young Captain Weir on the dusty wind-swept hill that would later bear his name. They had escorted him back to the main body of General Miles' 5th Infantry command near the Tongue River, an outpost that would later be called Fort Keogh in honor of Captain Keogh, who was killed with Custer at the Little Bighorn. Taylor had kept to himself during the past few days, sleeping in one of the stables and eating the left over beans and bacon provided by a befriended camp-cook.

He had requested an audience with the General the day he arrived but had been denied for various reasons. He knew that the soldiers considered him nothing more than a strangely dressed vagabond. The fact that he had apparently survived alone in hostile Indian country and through sheer dumb luck wandered into their camp seemed to elude their good senses. They were simply too busy with the hardships of everyday life to listen to the ravings of a madman or consider another prospect.

The shattered remains of Custer's command had been found and the grim task of identifying and burying the dead was now in full swing. An air of stunned disbelief hung over the camp as the troops made trips back and forth to the expansive battle site. The massive Sioux village was now deserted except for the beheaded remains of two soldiers who had been captured during the fight.

Taylor was eating his breakfast on the wooden steps of the crudely built mess tent on the morning of the fifth day when a young sergeant walked up. "Morning, sir" greeted the young sergeant.

"Morning, Sergeant"

"Sir, the General said that he had some time this morning. If you still want to talk to him, I can escort you there."

Taylor set his plate down on the steps. "That would be fine, Sergeant. I am ready whenever you are."

The soldier led him through the rows of tents and crudely built lean-tos without speaking. Taylor guessed his age to be in his middle twenties though it was hard to tell. The uniforms, general scruffy appearance, and slight stature of the men made it difficult to guess their ages. Most were short, 5' 8" to 5'9", and weighed no more than 150 pounds. All appeared thin and wiry. Many, like the young sergeant, wore a large moustache or beard, disguising a normally youthful face.

Taylor had noticed that many of the men spoke Gallic among themselves. The ancient, native tongue of Ireland could be heard in curses, commands and daily conversation. The history books had been right, most of the troops currently in the units were right off the boat Irishmen.

After walking through most of the camp, the Sergeant stopped at the front of a large tent and motioned for Taylor to step inside. A thin older officer, seated at a small table writing in a large ledger book, looked up as Taylor stepped through the opening. "Ah, come in, sir," he said standing. "I assume you're the mystery man everyone is talking about."

"Yes, sir, my name is Bruce Taylor. It's my pleasure to meet you, General." As he shook hands, he was amazed at the strength of the man's grip. The General motioned for them to step outside. "If you don't mind, Mister Taylor, it's dark in this tent, and I like to see whom I am talking to."

Outside, Taylor could see the full six-foot stature of the great General. He wore a thick moustache and goatee streaked with grey. His close fitting, dark blue uniform jacket shoulders were tinged with the fine white alkali that covered everything in the area. As they walked over the fine dust covered earth, Taylor noticed the General's limp.

"Now, sir, what would you like to talk to me about?" questioned the General taking a seat in one of the outside chairs.

"May I sit, General?"

"By all means."

"Well, General, as I said, it is truly a great honor meeting you. Thank you again for taking the time to see me, especially since you are dealing with the Custer matter."

259

The General nodded. "Yes, I still cannot believe it," he paused. Looking up from his folded hands, "Now, Mister Taylor, how in God's name did you end up out here alone and without provisions? This is an extremely dangerous territory."

Taylor found himself in the same precarious situation he has been in when he tried to explain himself to Custer. He decided to try the truth again to see if it was received differently. "Sir, I am going to tell you a quick story because I know you are extremely busy with the Custer investigation. You see, sir, I am not from this time."

A slight smile creased the General's face, "Okay, Mister Taylor, I'll play along for a moment. What time are you from?"

"2013. I am a retired aeronautical engineer from Albuquerque, New Mexico. I worked for 16 years and discovered a process for bending the space time continuum." There, he had said it. He sat back and waited for the laughter.

The General kept his composure, studying him closely. "I am not familiar with the term Aeronautical."

Taylor leaned in. "Sir, it refers to the study of flight, the flight characteristics of airplanes."

A look of bemused curiosity crossed the General's face. "So you're telling me you can fly, Mister Taylor? I sincerely doubt that ability."

"Ah, no, sir, I cannot fly. Aeronautics is the study of flight. Ah, I am getting off track here. Sir, it will be almost impossible for me to explain the advancement in technology in the next century. But what I can tell you are some facts, things about the future."

The General took out his pocket watch. "I have a few minutes, Mister Taylor. Tell me some of these things."

"Well, General, I know quite a bit about you. I've been a student of the Civil war and of the Indian campaigns for years."

"Really?" replied the General, lighting a short cigar. "Continue."

"Yes, sir. To begin with, you were born in Westminster, Massachusetts, August 8, 1839."

"All information that could be gleaned from any newspaper, Mister Taylor. Go on."

Taylor could see where this was going. The General was right. He could have gotten any of those facts from the newspaper. "Sir, you married a Miss Mary Hoyt Sherman, the niece of General William Tecumseh Sherman."

"Again, sir, all a matter of public record. Now, if you'll excuse me, my time is limited and I can see that the scouts have come back from the Big Horn River. I have a briefing to attend to." The General stood up and tossed the cigar butt into the dirt.

"General, I also know when you are going to die," announced Taylor, seeing he was getting nowhere. "Your death is recorded as taking place in the early spring of 1925. You will attend a circus with your grandson and suffer a massive heart attack. You will be 85 years old at the time of your death."

Two Crow scouts rode up and dismounted near the General's tent. He waved to the men and looked back at Taylor, "I am not sure what your motivation is for telling me these things, Mister Taylor, but I have gone soft on the game. Now if you'll excuse me."

"Yes, sir. Thank you for your time," Taylor spoke softly, feeling defeated.

Several aides and other officers standing nearby listening quickly surrounded the General. The small entourage walked toward a tall stand of cottonwood trees, the obvious location of his meeting with the scouts.

The early afternoon sun was already starting to hammer down as he made his way back to the stable. Taylor had gotten nowhere with telling the truth. They had sized him up and had decided he was just another crazy wanderer with the dumb luck to still be alive in a rough part of the country.

Depressed and tired of being hot and filthy, he asked the cook at the mess tent for some soap. The cook threw him a large bar and a dirty towel along with a warning that if he left his dirty plate on the mess hall steps again, he would not get supper that night.

Apologizing, he headed down to the river for a cool swim and a much needed bath. The low sandbar that stretched to the middle of the shallow tide had become the bathing spot for the troops. He stripped his clothes and slowly stepped into the cool green water. He leaned back allowing the water to fold over him, silencing the sounds of the camp. He could not remember when a swim had been so refreshing. He stood waist-deep in the slow moving stream, and he scrubbed his hair into a thick lather washing five days of grit and grime from his body.

As he dove to the stream's bottom to rinse away the soap, his mind cleared. This was just the kind of relaxing diversion he had needed to strip away his frustration and point him in a new direction.

Taylor now knew he would have to use his intellect to better his position. Fortunetellers and soothsayers were as common now as they were in 2013 and the only way for him to lose that moniker was to present himself as an educated individual. He needed to find a way to improve something in his present day - to provide something of value.

Renewed in spirit and body, he gingerly stepped out of the water and found a sunny spot on the sandbar to sit and dry. He had failed miserably to change the outcome of Custer's death, a mission that had motivated and encouraged his work over the years. Now, lying in the hot Montana sun, he realized that he could do more than affect the outcome of a single battle. He could affect things of greater importance. He could change everything.

He realized that more than a few of the brilliant innovators of the twentieth century - Henry Ford, Thomas Edison, the Wright brothers - were alive right now. He could find them and offer his assistance. As he gathered his clothes, this new direction continued to crystalize in his mind. With his knowledge of aeronautics and propulsion alone, he could advance the study of flight nearly sixty years.

Pulling on his damp uniform, he thought of all the ways that he could literally change the world with what he knew. This was his new mission. If he had been more observant, more aware of his surroundings, he might have known that fate had other things in store for him. The natural order has a strange way of taking care of itself.

It's a tricky thing to change the world; he would find this out soon enough.

****

Kelly fumbled around on his nightstand trying to find the ringing cell phone in the dark. He answered it on the third ring. "Yeah, hello?"

"Hey, did I wake you up?" Kelly recognized Baker's voice.

"Shit, what time is it?" he replied turning on the table light.

"Ah, about five am. Go wake up your partner. Let's get some coffee. Greg is still staying at your place, right?"

"Yeah, he's in the other room. What's up?"

"Well, as you know, I have been going over the material for the last several days. I think we have something. I don't want to talk on the phone so get your ass out of bed and let's go get some breakfast."

Kelly was already pulling on his pants. "Where do you want to meet?"

"That new place down on William Street. I'm about ten minutes out."

"Okay. We're on the way."

Twenty minutes later all three were sitting at a table near the back of the sparsely populated dining room. The normal rush of D.C. commuters would not start heading in on their way to the trains for a good hour yet.

"So, wadda ya got?" questioned Kelly, sipping his coffee.

Baker opened a large notebook moving the coffee cups and water glasses out of the way. "I've been going over the information on the disks, and I wanted you guys to see this." He turned the book around so Kelly could read it. The scribbled equations and complicated math symbols meant nothing to the half-awake Greg who had crashed on Kelly's couch after a long 'discussion' with Carol.

"And as you can see here," continued Baker excitedly, "your Mister Taylor was spot on when he laid out this formula and this algorithm. It's simply amazing! I don't know why somebody didn't think of it before." He sat back smiling. "You guys have no idea what I'm talking about do you?"

"Plain English, Ed" announced Greg fighting back an early morning headache. "We're not advanced physics people. Is this information viable?"

Baker shook his head. "How in the hell did you guys ever get through college? Yes, it's viable! Hell, we can start building this thing tomorrow."

"Well, what's the next step?" questioned Kelly. "Hey, did the cops ever find the guy that beat you up and stole your wallet? Your eye looks better by the way."

Baker brushed off the question, "Naw, the cops said it was probably just some junkie needing money. That's eighty bucks and a nice wallet I'll never see again." He hated lying, but how else was he going to explain the injury to his face.

"Anyway, I've already contacted the folks at the University of Maryland. I have a contact there that will let us use the MTECH facility for six grand a month. Is that within the budget?"

"What else do we need to get started?" questioned Greg. "When I was in Doctor Taylor's lab, I saw that he was using a tremendous amount of power and lasers. Do we have access to that?"

Baker flipped through several pages in the notebook. "Yeah, here it is. Most of the stuff we need is already there. I ran some numbers on what we need as far as special equipment goes. We are looking at around two hundred thousand dollars. We are going to need some very high priced gear. There's no way around it."

Kelly sat back in the booth sipping his coffee. "Well guys, I think we just got in the time machine business."

Greg nodded, "Tell the people at that lab we will take it for three months and then start getting the gear you need. I'll give you the cash later on this afternoon."

Baker reached into his coat and dropped a pile of receipts on the table. "I am now officially on a leave of absence and I booked the lab two days ago. Just to show you how much I believe in this, I have all ready spent a shit load of credit card money for the gear." He smiled at Greg. "Gonna need about fifty thousand today. Time travel is expensive, my friend."

Smiling, Greg reached across the table and shook hands. "Time to rock and roll."

Chapter 18

Chalks passed the stack of folders to the man on his right, allowing the ten men in the room to take one in turn. "Okay, as you can see, there are three primaries listed," he announced as the men opened the folders. "Greg Gander, Professor at the University of Montana - married, no children, currently lives in Missoula. The second is Chris Kelly, NNSA field agent and NEST advisor, not married, and lives in Fredericksburg. The third subject is our guy Edward Baker, Professor at George Town, not married and lives in George Town."

"I want a complete medical and social work up on all of these people. I also want a third-ring workup on parents, ex-wives, girlfriends, brothers, and sisters. Anybody who is related to these individuals will not be living upon termination of this operation. Stone gate is a clean sweep. Are there any questions so far?" Chalks looked around the room at the impassive faces of the team. Every one of the men in attendance had been here before. They knew the drill.

"I want these people out of the gene pool by natural causes if possible. For the parents, it should be a slam-dunk. Heart attacks seem to be the best way to go, clean, easily explained. The others should involve car accidents and home related fatalities. Find out if any of the targets have chronic health problems. Diabetic shock is also very clean. Let's keep it warm and fuzzy if we can. Within twenty-four hours of take over, all of the players need to be eliminated. That's our window. Are there any questions on the time frame? It is not negotiable."

"Sir, can we start thinning the herd early?" questioned one of the men.

"That will be decided as some of the deliverables are achieved. You will be advised at that time when you can start the process. Okay, I need preliminary target packages in forty-eight hours. Team leaders, you can go ahead and start breaking down areas of responsibility. I will need to see a "Go" order in seventy-two hours. Let's get this done, folks. I want this as tight as a frog's ass, and that's water proof."

The systematic elimination of all possible witnesses and individuals who may have had only a limited access to potentially high-level information was standard procedure. The organization or "Kingdom" had been established prior to the Truman administration and only exerted its sizable power and influence in major world events or pressing national security issues. The reach of the organization extended across all geographic borders, totally unconstrained by third-string political influences and petty government bureaucracies. Presidents, Kings, and Prime Ministers were all willing or unwilling subjects to the rock-solid and deeply penetrating authority of the Kingdom. Just after the Kennedy assassination, European assets were allowed into the fold, making the Kingdom a force with no equal.

The organization had its roots and initial funding with the Truman mandate of NSC 68, a bare knuckle, fifty-eight-page document that spelled out in classified print, the road map for running the Cold War and defeating the Communists. Even though it was officially approved in 1950, it wasn't fully declassified until the seventies. It was the open secret that no one talked about. People were trained, standards and procedures were established, and the organization went into the shadow-war business.

With each passing year, the administration and the Kingdom grew in strength and influence, used by all sides for the heavy action that needed to be done in the back allies, the dark streets, and the guarded bedrooms of the power elite. DIA, CIA, IRS, and all the rest of the three-letter boys' clubs fed the Kingdom whatever it wanted whenever it asked. Dark side operators, the crazy brave, and enough political horsepower to change the course of any government in the world all found a home in the steamy, lethal shadow-lands of the Kingdom.

Even its yearly appropriation budget hearings were off the books, not open for scrutiny or debate. In the late eighties a fire-breathing freshman Senator from Nevada attempted to aggressively pry the lid open on some of the organization's "sensitive" operations. Three days after his closed door meeting with the leading House Chairman on the issue, he was found dead in his car on the hardedge side of D.C. The autopsy reveled a brain aneurism yet nobody could explain why both of his front teeth were missing or why there were needle injection sites on the bottom of both feet. The Kingdom had sent a message. The shot-callers and all the rest of the Brooks Brother suit crowd in the United States and abroad got the word. There are some doors that need to stay locked.

Chalks turned on the overhead projector. "This is MTECH at the University of Maryland where the project is going into operation. I want the lab and the surrounding perimeter under CCTV and audio at all times. I also want physical onsite surveillance. Pick up student IDs and establish roving teams to keep a ground truth baseline of who is coming and going. I want to know if any new players enter the game. Is that clear?"

The men in attendance nodded. "Okay, this thing is moving very quickly. I want all the moving parts accounted for. Team leaders take charge of your people." He turned off the projector, leaving the men in the dark. "That's all I have at this time."

****

Eighteen hundred miles to the west, Special Agent Dave Clark of the Albuquerque, New Mexico FBI office walked through what was the back yard of the destroyed house kicking up small black cinder-dust clouds. In his twenty years as a forensic fire and arson investigator, he had never seen a home so thoroughly destroyed by fire.

It had been three weeks since the catastrophic blaze, and the air around the site still exuded a strange kind of heat. Not only had the house burned to a fine powder, but the copper pipes, the concrete foundation, and even the scrub grass within 60 yards had been incinerated. All that was left of the 1,900 square foot home was a hole in the ground full of fine black ash.

He took a small glass vial from his shirt pocket and scooped a sample of the soot. He was still deeply bothered that the tox report had come back inconclusive for the direct cause of the blaze. Initially a natural gas build-up and subsequent explosion had been reported, but not even the largest natural gas detonation could account for this. No, this was something different. The heat ranges and combustion rates had to be off the scale in order to do this.

Kneeling beside the hole, he looked to where the front door would have been and was suddenly surprised by a nearly imperceptible shimmer, as if he were looking through the heat waves on a dry lakebed, an effect that distorts distance and light. He stood up and then knelt again, seeing the same anomaly. It was early morning with high desert temperatures only in the forties, far too cool for this kind of visual effect, he thought, changing positions.

He walked around the large hole that had once been the foundation boundaries of the house trying to see if the visual distortion was constant from all angles. The effect seemed to be located predominately over and around the main part of the house, maybe the living room/basement area. This also seemed to be the area of the greatest concentration of heat.

Intrigued more then ever, he stood up, looking for a stick or piece of pipe with which he could probe the fine deep ash that filled the hole. Across the street he noticed a long yellow-handled shovel leaning against a neighboring house. As he walked over, he noticed an elderly woman stepping onto her porch with a dustpan and broom. "Morning Ma'am," he announced stepping into her yard. Startled, she looked up. "Who are you? I ain't buying nothin."

"Yes Ma'am, I understand. My name is Agent Clark. I'm from the FBI." He pulled his ID and credential from his back pocket. "I was wondering if I could borrow your shovel?"

"What shovel? I don't have a shovel," she replied confused.

Clark walked to the side of her house. "This shovel here. I just need to borrow it for a minute." He held it up, moving closer.

"You put that back. That's my dead husband's shovel. I don't want you stealing any of his things. Now git, or I will call the police."

"Ma'am, I am the police. I just want to borrow this for a minute. I promise I'll bring it right back. Promise."

The old woman dropped her broom and dustpan and stepped back into the house slamming the door behind her. "I'm calling the police for you stealing my shovel!" she shouted from inside the house.

"It's okay, Ma'am. I will bring it right back!" He walked across the street as the woman continued to rant.

Standing beside the hole he knelt down where the air and the ground felt the warmest. A strange sense of nausea rolled through his gut as he leaned down close to the ground, prodding the ash with the shovel. To his surprise the soot was dry, in spite of the fact the Fire Department had sprayed water on the flames for hours in an attempt to put it out.

Shoveling back at least a foot of ash, he started to see a faint blue light deep within the hole. At first, he thought it might be a still smoldering ember. Looking closer, he saw that it was a long strip of light, similar to the effect of light shining under a closed door.

The queasiness grew stronger as he dug deeper into the soot. He was holding the shovel with one hand as he knelt beside the hole, having reached as far as he could, when the spade was suddenly jerked from his hand so violently that it almost pulled him in. He jumped back in stunned surprise, drawing his weapon. "Jesus!" he shouted aiming his weapon at the ground. "FBI, come out of there right now!"

Nothing stirred under the ash. "I said come out!" he shouted, keeping his weapon pointed at the ground.

The old woman was now standing on her porch. "You bring that shovel back right now!" she yelled. "I called the police, and they're coming."

He slowly and cautiously stepped to the edge of the hole. The strange blue light was no longer visible. The wispy black ash had filled in the hole. He checked his cell phone but found that he had no signal. In fact, the phone was completely dead. Sensing real danger, he backed away from the hole just as a Taos County Sheriff Department unit pulled onto the site. Clark holstered his weapon, pulling his badge and credential from his pocket. "FBI, Deputy," he announced. "I'm glad you're here. I think we have a situation."

****

Dillon lay in his bunk under the heavy buffalo hide listening to the early December wind whistle and moan through the cracks of the small shed he now called home. He had been awake for an hour, dreading getting out from under the warm blankets to light the stove that had grown cold during the night.

It had been a month since the explosion in Taylor's lab that had sent him and Agent Ania here. He and Sheriff Coleman drank far too much last night, leaving him with a stunning early morning headache and a deep melancholy as he lay missing his family, a family who had no idea that he was still alive.

The heavy footfalls on crusted snow announced that someone was approaching the shed. "Dillon, you up?"

Dillon recognized Coleman's voice. "C'mon in, John. It's open."

Coleman stepped inside, stamping the snow off his boots. "Judas Priest, Dillon, you let your fire go out. It's freezing in here." He walked over to the stove and began the process of breaking up kindling and relighting the wood. "Some morning I'm gonna find you frozen stiff."

"I have to quit drinking so much, John; makes it hard to get up the next day." The small stove came alive as the wood popped and snapped. He was always surprised at how fast Coleman could get a fire going. "What time is it?"

Coleman pulled up a chair and lit his pipe. "It's ten minutes after eight," he replied, checking his pocket watch. "I let you sleep in. You feel like taking a ride today?"

Dillon pulled himself up on one elbow. "You want me to ride a horse?"

Coleman smiled. "Yeah, well, I figured a real pistolero like you needs to know how to ride a horse."

"You know, John, I am not real proud of the fact that I had to shoot those guys, feel downright terrible about it if the truth were known."

Coleman leaned back in his chair and blew a smoke ring to the ceiling. "Did what you had to do, Dillon. Them Dugan boys were bad to the bone. They'd a killed you for sure. Fair fight, straight up. They lost."

Dillon rolled out from under the blankets and pulled on his pants and boots. "I don't know, John. I've gone over that day a million times in my head, and I really can't explain why I acted the way I did. It's just not my nature to shoot people."

Colman tapped out his pipe. "Well, water under the bridge now. Anyway, thought you might want to ride out to the Crawford ranch with me this morning."

"What's going on out there?" questioned Dillon, pulling on his shirt.

Coleman shoved another small log into the stove. "Earl Crawford has a small ranch about two miles east of town. He's a widower. Lost his wife from blood poisoning last year."

"Jesus, what happened?"

Coleman slammed the door shut on the stove. "Believe it or not, she was hitching up a wagon, dropped the king bolt on her foot. It caused a wound, got infected, and killed her three weeks later."

Dillon pulled on his heavy Buffalo coat. "You gotta be kidding me! She died from a foot infection?"

Coleman stuffed his pipe into his coat pocket. "Buried her last spring. Damn shame. She was a gentle soul. Anyway, she left Earl with five kids to feed. I know they been living off back strap and beans and not much else."

"Taking in more strays?" asked Dillon, smiling.

Coleman pushed himself out of the chair. "Well, not really. I just like to head out there once in awhile and say hello to Earl. See how he's getting on. I'll take him some coffee, maybe a little tobacco."

Dillon followed Coleman into the cold sunlight. "You have a good heart, John. People in this town are lucky to have you as Sheriff."

Coleman stuffed his hands deep in his coat pockets as they walked. Even though the sun was out, a frigid wind whipped at the men's ears and noses, turning them a bright red in seconds. "Don't know about that" replied Coleman. "But let's stop off at Miller's place and pick up a poke of peppermints. Them kids don't get much during the year."

"Sounds good. By the way, what the hell is a king bolt?"

****

An hour later, Dillon could see the small ranch house come into view as they crested the snow-covered bluff. Mercifully, Coleman had picked a very docile horse for Dillon. He had patiently shown him how to saddle the animal inside one of the large stables near the corrals, protecting him from prying eyes. He was grateful that no one could see just how inept he was around horseflesh.

"So you're telling me that very few folks ride horses in the future?" questioned Coleman riding close to Dillon's horse.

279

Dillon thought for a moment. "Nobody back home that I know of rides a horse. They are generally considered an expensive luxury, a hobby." Even though it was bitingly cold outside, Dillon was thoroughly enjoying the ride. The horse moved at a steady, even gait that made him feel both secure and off balance at the same time.

"Not sure I would like the place you're from, Dillon. Seems like it's awfully fast," announced Coleman lighting his pipe.

"That's actually a pretty good way of putting it. I miss parts of it, my family of course, but a lot of it I don't miss a bit." He looked up to the sky, struck by the sheer expanse. "You know what they call Montana in the future, John?"

"What, you folks changed the name of the states?"

Dillon laughed, adjusting his seat in the saddle. "No, it's still Montana. They just call it *Big Sky Country*."

Coleman thought for a moment, puffing his pipe. "Sounds like something a politician would come up with."

"You know, I think you're right. But you have to admit it really is something to see."

Suddenly Coleman held up his hand, pulling his horse up short. Alarmed, Dillon stopped his mount, trying to see what had stopped Coleman in his tracks.

Coleman eased out of his saddle, pulling his rifle from the saddle scabbard. He pointed off to Dillon's right while taking a kneeling position just under his horse's neck.

Less than sixty yards away stood a large Mule deer. Its short black and white tail flicked back and forth. Its eyes were firmly locked in Dillon's direction. Coleman crept forward, slowly handing the reins of his horse up to Dillon, who sat transfixed on the drama that was unfolding.

Just as Dillon wrapped the leather reins around his hands, Coleman fired. BOOM! Both horses jumped sideways at the sound, but not enough to throw Dillon from the saddle. The deer crumpled to the ground, the heavy 45/70 slug killing it instantly.

Nonchalantly, Coleman took his reins back from Dillon. "Looks like them kids will eat a little better tonight," he said, shoving the rifle back into the saddle scabbard.

"Goddamn, you're a hell of a shot!"

Coleman pulled himself into his saddle. "Not bad for an old 'cowboy' huh, Deputy?" he said smiling.

"Not bad at all, John. Not bad at all."

As they slowly rode to the carcass, Dillon felt a peacefulness he never had before. Experiencing the light and the sky from horseback stirred something deep within him; an awareness of something found that had been lost.

As Coleman showed him how to gut and clean the deer, he allowed himself to let the smell of the fresh kill wash over him and take him to a place he had never been before. He instinctively knew it as familiar, correct.

There was a balance here, a tempo of life that did not chaff at his spirit as it did in his modern reality. The meat of the deer would not be wasted but appreciated, savored. Horse and man had a purpose in their relationship. Neighbor cared for neighbor. He realized that if the time ever came for him to leave this time, this place, it would be difficult. In fact it was becoming more difficult by the day. *Big Sky Country indeed.*

Chapter 19

It had been two days since Taylor had met with General Miles. How he was going to leave Montana and start making the rounds of the great and powerful minds of the nineteenth century was still a mystery. He still had no money, no transportation, and no idea how he was going to get either. He was literally being kept alive by the good graces of the United States Army. He received beans, bread, and coffee twice a day. A worn out cot in a horse stable continued to serve as his lodgings. He was living like a vagrant.

He was quickly discovering that life in the "Old West" was in reality a fairly dull, hard-edged existence. Everything took an amazing amount of effort. From cooking to staying warm at night, it all required cooperation and time. Staying physically clean was a never-ending effort and seemed nearly impossible due to the ankle-high alkali dust that was everywhere. He woke up grimy and went to sleep smelling of his own sweat. Missing were the "essentials" of electric toothbrushes, mouthwash and deodorant, a fact that challenged even the toughest of olfactory sensitivities. Bottom line, the entire camp and everyone in it reeked of body odor and hot horseflesh.

As he made his way down to the river in the late morning for his daily bath, he spotted General Miles and several of his staff watering their horses near the sand bar used for bathing. The men seemed relaxed, even casual, as their horses drank long and deep. Taylor, now deeply self-conscience of his dirty clothes and generally disheveled appearance, approached the group. He had no intention of talking to the men, having been dismissed by the General in an earlier conversation. He nodded to the men as he stepped to the water's edge.

"Morning, General."

The officer looked over at Taylor, trying to fix a memory. "Ah yes, Mister Taylor, how are you this fine morning?"

"Fine, sir."

The General stepped over to Taylor. "You know, I was thinking about our conversation several days ago. Maybe I was a tad abrupt concerning your prognostications."

Taylor smiled. "I really do understand your hesitancy to believe what I say, sir. It is a lot to take in."

"You sound like an educated man, Mister Taylor. Where did you get your education, if I may ask?"

"Did my undergrad work at University of Southern California and my post grad studies at the University of Norte Dame."

The General handed the reins of his horse to his aide. "General, we need to be going," his aide announced.

"Just a moment, Captain. Mister Taylor, would you be available to join me for dinner tonight? Shall we say seven o'clock?"

"Yes, sir, it would be an honor. Ah, General, before you leave, I wanted to show you something." He had to somehow convince the officer that he was not some wandering lunatic with a tall story to tell. "This is my identification," he handed him his New Mexico driver's license.

The General studied the card intently. "My God, what is this made of? Is that a color portrait card of you? This is amazing."

"The card is made of plastic and it's my State of New Mexico authorization to drive a car, or as people in this era say, a horseless carriage. And, if I may be so bold, General, please read the dates on the card."

The General drew the card close. "Issued 2013, expires 2016, Date of birth 1/17/1953. My God! This has to be some kind of joke."

No, sir, it's no joke. That really is my identification. New Mexico doesn't become a state till 1912, roughly twenty-two years from now."

The General seemed to consider this and handed the card back smiling. "Mister Taylor, I think we are going to have a very interesting conversation at dinner. I will see you at seven."

"Yes, sir. It will be my pleasure." As he watched the General and his staff ride away, he felt a total sense of relief wash over him, a relief that finally someone might take him seriously, listen to what he has to say, and hopefully, gain some insight from the exchange. This had been his objective all along. What good was knowing the future if there was no one to benefit from the knowledge.

He sat down in the sand pulling off his boots and socks, letting the cool, slow-moving river water roll over his feet. It was only ten o'clock in the morning and already the sun beat down hard on his back. The air along the river was filled with the scent of sage and wild onion.

His mind drifted back to his home, his realty. It had taken him sixteen years to build his lab. It had been sixteen years of single-minded scientific labor, and in an instant of panic he had destroyed it all. Now he was marooned here. Here he was a man with a towering intellect, four university degrees, the honor of being published in all of the major scientific magazines, and the respect of the academic community, yet he now sat shoeless in filthy clothes on the banks of the Tongue River, trying to convince the people around him that he was not insane.

Tossing a pebble in the stream, he looked up and was startled to see an Indian staring at him intently from the opposite bank. The man was wearing a dusty blue Union Army waistcoat and dark brown leather pants. His hair was long and blew in the morning breeze, partially obscuring his face. Most alarming, he was slowly bringing up his rifle, pointing it in his direction.

There was no place to run, no cover to hide behind. If the man wanted him dead, it would happen. Taylor slowly stood, expecting to feel the impact of being shot at any second. Still, nothing happened. To his surprise, the Indian motioned with the barrel of his rifle for him to come across the water. Taylor slowly lowered his hands and picked up his boots, desperately trying to hide the panic that was just under the surface.

As he waded into the thigh, then waist-deep water, the heavy current pushed him further downstream. His Indian captor slowly walked along the bank, his weapon raised. With considerable effort he was able to get across the stream and fight his way through the weeds on the opposite bank. Now facing the Indian, Taylor was struck that the man was a good deal shorter than he at first appeared. The height he projected came from an air of confidence the man carried, a demeanor that announced that he was more than a match for most men.

His eyes were close set, emotionless. A deep scar on the left side of his face that started at the corner of his eye and crossed both his lips just under his nose said more about the man than anything verbal. It must have been a terrible wound, thought Taylor as he pulled on his socks and boots. An injury like that did more than mark a man on the outside.

As they stood less then ten feet apart staring at each other, Taylor could sense that this was less a kidnapping but more a brusque invitation, a summons of sort. The man lowered his rifle and held out his hand. Taylor was unsure what to do, not having seen many Indians shake hands in the past.

287

Taylor nodded and then stood in shocked surprise as the man dropped five-linked machine-gun bullets at his feet. At that instant Taylor knew that life, in all its terrible, wonderful complexity, had just shifted, changing the past and bending the future. Something incredible was about to start.

****

The ride back from the Crawford ranch started just after two o'clock in the afternoon, and for Dillon the visit with the family had been wonderful. The whitetail that Coleman had shot had been butchered, prepared and served as part of the lunch they all shared. It was clear that it had been a welcome change for the family. The children, ranging in ages from six to seventeen, were the center of the universe for their father, Ed, and it was obvious that the two older boys, Nat and Robert, idolized their father. The three younger girls carried the poise and modesty appropriate for young ladies of the day, their mother's influence still coloring their young lives.

Coleman stayed quiet, not at all his usual talkative self as they rode back. He smoked his pipe, keeping his eyes on the cold early afternoon horizon.

"Is everything okay, John?" Dillon asked, moving his horse up beside him.

Coleman spit before answering. "Yeah, I'm fine. Just worry about them kids. That's all. That little Becky melts your heart, don't she?"

Dillon smiled, remembering how the six-year-old had proudly pointed out her pet rabbit, telling him that the rabbit's name was Mister Twitch because his nose twitched all the time.

288

"Yeah, sweet kids. Ed is doing a good job raising them, and with you as mother, I know they're gonna be okay."

Coleman smiled. "Is it that obvious?"

"Nothing to be ashamed of, John. It's a great family. You have a soft heart."

Coleman tapped out his pipe on the saddle-horn. "Well, don't be spreading that notion around. Montana Sheriffs have a reputation as hard men. I kind of like to keep it that way."

"Your secret is safe with me, John. Promise."

Dillon's perception of these people had changed. The "Old West" as portrayed by modern historians was proving to be a gross distortion, a blanket caricature of real people living real lives. They loved, worried and cared about their children, their jobs, their reputations and all the other things responsible people cared about. They were not entertainment. Their lives meant something, and they strived everyday to make it all work. From raising five kids alone on some windswept butte to being the vanguard of law and order in a place where the laws were still being written, these were lives of honor.

"You know, John, you haven't asked me about the future lately," announced Dillon, slowing his horse's walk.

"I know. I was kind of thinking that you were really starting to miss your family. Didn't want to upset you. Besides I'm never going to see it. Makes me feel peculiar talking about it, like I'm doing something wrong."

Dillon was about to answer when he caught sight of something in his peripheral vision, something that made him stop his horse and stare in stunned amazement. Thirty yards off to his left, stuck in the ground was a yellow, fiberglass handled shovel.

Dillon slowly stepped down from his saddle and stood staring at the tool as if it were about to explode.

"John, do you see what I see?"

"Never seen a shovel handle painted yellow," replied Coleman stepping down from his horse. "How in the hell did it get out here? I didn't see it when we rode out and we're going back to town the same way we came."

Dillon walked up to the tool feeling an icy shiver run up his spine as he read the words on the handle. "It's not from here, John," he said pulling the spade from the ground. He turned and handed it to Coleman.

Coleman studied the printing. "What does True/value mean?"

"It's from my world, John, from a store that won't be selling this kind of thing for over a hundred years yet. It's from the future, and I have no idea why it's here."

Coleman handed the shovel back. "You know what this means, don't you?"

Dillon looked around as if trying to hear a familiar sound. "I have an idea what it means."

"It means, Dillon, that if this can get through, then things can go back. You can get back. You can go home."

Dillon felt an unexpected pang of sadness as he read the printing. "Maybe I am home, John," he replied softly. "Maybe I'm supposed to be here." A sudden icy gust of wind blew past the men making Coleman grab his hat to keep if from blowing off.

"What do you want to do, Dillon? We really should be heading back to town. It'll be dark in a few hours."

Dillon nodded, walking back to his horse. "Yeah, you're right. Let's get back. I'm freezing." He handed the shovel to Coleman. "Here, a gift from 2013."

If he had stayed a moment longer and looked due west, he would have seen the shimmer, less than ten yards away, that clear, almost imperceptible distortion of light that danced in the open prairie.

It might have all ended then and there, the recognition of a portal, the elation of escape, the reunion with loved ones. And yet, as the two rode away under the fading afternoon light of late November, Dillon sensed a missed opportunity. He now felt as if he were being watched, observed by the cold indifferent power that had brought him here in the first place.

291

By the time they reached the outskirts of town, a deep unease had settled in his heart. Things were changing and, in his mind, not for the better. Because of him, people he now cared about were going to suffer. He now recognized himself for what he really was, an intruder, an unwilling voyeur who was about to change the lives of people who were already on a solid course in life. No matter how much he wanted to be where he was, he knew he did not belong.

****

Later that night, as Dillon lay in his bunk with the small wood stove warming the room and the cold wind blowing outside, he let the tears fall for all the wrong reasons. If he were truthful with himself, he would have to admit that his present reality had put the hook deep in his soul. He had found peace yet knew in his heart that he had to give it back. And then again, maybe, just maybe, there was something he could do. The idea made him smile. Within minutes he drifted off to sleep.

****

In no less then three hours after Clark made the call, seven Federal agencies and three State and local organizations were staged near Taylor's burnt down home in Shady Brook, New Mexico. Every group from ATF to the EPA to the DIA had arrived on the scene, all straining at the bit to know what was going on and struggling to be in charge. The Command Center, set up by the FBI inside the Shady Brook Café parking lot, was already jam-packed with operational trailers, gas powered generators, and massive portable Klieg lights. Clark was in the process of briefing his immediate supervisor when four black Suburbans pulled up in front of the ECC.

A HRT agent, in full combat kit, stopped the two men getting out of the first car. "Whoa, hold on guys. Need to see some identification," he announced blocking their path to the short flight of stairs.

Chalks held up a badge the agent had never seen before. "Stand aside, Agent, this is my scene."

"Who the hell are you people? Let me see that badge again." Chalks turned and motioned to the second SUV. "I believe you recognize this individual."

The Agent looked past Chalks and immediately recognized the Deputy Director of the FBI. "Ah, yes, sir, good afternoon, sir."

"Good afternoon, Agent. You're doing a fine job. You will be staying." The Director stepped up and shook the agent's hand. "No one, and I mean no one, is allowed inside this building. Understand?"

"Yes, sir," replied the Agent.

The Director turned and nodded in the direction of the vehicles. Immediately six men in full military gear with weapons exited the Suburbans, taking up positions in a rough perimeter of the parking lot. The HRT agent recognized none of the heavily armed operators. To his further surprise, all of the men were carrying military SAW, 5.56 belt fed automatic weapons, extremely heavy firepower for any law enforcement agency, even for the FBI. The Director and Chalks walked past the Agent and disappeared inside the ECC.

Clark looked up from his briefing table as the two men walked into the crowded trailer. "Agent Clark?" announced Chalks looking around the room.

"Right here. What can I do for you?"

Chalks and the Director stepped up to the table. "Agent Clark, I presume you know the Deputy Director of your Agency."

Surprised, he nodded and then shook hands. "Ah, yes, I do. Pleasure to meet you, sir. I was starting to brief the others."

"The briefing is over," interrupted Chalks. "Gentlemen, please clear the room."

"Ah, excuse me," replied Clark. "This is the FBI's ECC. I say who leaves the room."

The Director handed Clark a letter. "Not any more, Agent. That's a Presidential Directive to relinquish the command and control of this incident and turn it over to Mister Chalks and his organization."

Clark read the short directive a second time. "Sir, I really don't understand."

Chalks snatched the letter from Clark's hand. "Agent Clark, it really isn't my concern that you understand anything. You have just been given a Presidential Order. Now unless you want to end up in a Federal prison, I would strongly suggest that you clear this room."

The senior EPA supervisor stepped up. "Ah, I am not really sure what is going on here, but we may have a very serious environmental situation up the road, and I think...."

Chalks pulled a small radio from the inside of his suit coat pocket. "Shut it down, everything, all roads, all communications, nothing out, nothing in." He walked up to the EPA supervisor. "You've been asked to leave the room, sir, as have all of you," he stated looking to the men in the room. "Now if this Directive is not followed immediately, I have the authority to have you all arrested for obstruction of a National Security Mandate and a Presidential Order. Have I made myself perfectly clear? We are not debating anything."

"Time to leave, folks," announced the Deputy Director. "This is no game. Clear the room."

The unmistakable roar of a Black Hawk helicopter could be heard over the trailer. It sounded as if it were going to land on the roof. "That, gentlemen, is the sound of a Presidential Order!" shouted Chalks above the noise. "I would suggest you obey it!"

Slowly the men filed out of the trailer, each receiving a sheet of paper as they came to the bottom of the metal steps. An unmarked military helicopter hovered thirty feet over the tops of the trees, its six-barrel mini-gun pointed in their direction.

Clark looked up at the menacing Black Hawk and then read the sheet.

This is a classified military matter

All reference to this incident is STRICTLY prohibited.

Your agency command structure has been notified and will expect your full compliance.

ALL cell phones will be turned into the Agent on scene, no exceptions.

Leave the area immediately in the vehicle you arrived in.

You will be reimbursed for ALL property confiscated at a later date.

This area is now OFF LIMITS until further notice.

Drive with caution. Checkpoints have been posted at all entrances and egress highways. Identification WILL be checked.

Sign and return this document to the attending Agent.

_____

In his fifteen plus years with the Bureau he had never seen anything like this. Hell, he had never even heard of anything like this. Whoever was now running the show had the kind of power only a few men in the world control. Whatever was in the ground in that burned-out basement had gotten the attention of the real shakers and movers.

"Gentlemen, can I have your attention please!" commanded the Agent passing out the forms. "Please, drop your cell phone and the signed document in the box in the back of this vehicle."

"You really expect me to drop my phone in that box?" asked the ATF chief out of Albuquerque. "Who the hell are you people? This is bullshit!"

Suddenly, two of the camouflaged Agents who had been standing on the perimeter of the parking lot made their way through the small crowd of law enforcement supervisors and high-level government officials. Clark could feel the intense mood of the men even from where he stood. Their body language exhibited every bit of intimidation and menace possible as they approached the ATF administrator. One of the men leaned close, speaking inches from the man's ear. The intense, one-way conversation only lasted seconds. Whatever was said immediately prompted the senior ATF administer to sign the form and drop his cell phone in the box. He quickly walked across the parking lot without looking back.

Observing the drama, the rest of the men apparently decided that they would need no further persuasion. Clark was the last to turn in his form and phone. Even though he had signed the sheet, there was no way in hell he was just going to walk away from this. No way.

Chapter 20

Kelly went over the list of expenditures for the lab a second time, trying to figure out how they had acquired so much equipment and yet had paid very little out of the three hundred dollars in cash they had available. Several times he asked Baker how much money he needed and had been told that MTECH was willing to let them use equipment that was already on site. The timer went off on the microwave oven. "Yo, Greg, your pizza is done!" he announced from the kitchen.

They had just returned from the lab after watching Ed set-up and calibrate the laser table and filter blocks, an arduous task demanding meticulous measurements and adjustments. They had arrived at MTECH just after seven in the morning for the last three days and returned home nearly twelve to thirteen hours later after a long day of work. Today was no different.

Greg walked into the kitchen, talking on his cell phone. He had been gone from his job, his wife, and everything else he had worked for in Montana for almost two weeks now, and the pressure to go home and try to repair the damage was building by the hour. "Well, my leave of absence time from work is just about up," he announced turning off his phone. "And the wife has just about had it. I gotta get home and smooth some feathers."

"How long are you going to be gone? I think the next couple of days are going to get us pretty close." He opened a beer and slid it across the table.

Greg took a long drink before answering, "Ah, let's see. Today is Tuesday. If I leave tomorrow, I should be back by Sunday."

"You know, Greg, you could bring her back here. She could see the city. Might make her feel better. It would be one concern off your back." A heavy knock at the door stopped the conversation.

"Hey, Chris, it's me, Ed. Open up."

Surprised that Baker had shown up at his apartment after a full twelve hours in the lab, Kelly quickly unlocked the door. "Jesus, Ed, don't you ever..." Standing in the open door was not only Baker but also four other men Chris had never seen before in his life. "Whoa! What's going on Ed? Who are these guys?"

Chalks stepped into the room. "My name is Jason Chalks, and I am your employer." The three other men stepped into the room, two of them carrying pistols.

Chalks unbuttoned his overcoat and sat into one of the overstuffed chairs. "C'mon and sit down, gentlemen. We have a lot to discuss, a plane to catch, and not a lot of time." One of the men holding a weapon motioned for Greg to move into the living room from the kitchen.

"Are we under arrest?" questioned Kelly, trying to control his fear.

Chalks took out his notebook and then looked up at Kelly and Greg. "Sit down, fellas. I won't ask you again." As Greg took a seat beside Kelly and Baker on the couch, he felt the control he had so desperately tried to keep in his life, silently slip away.

"All right, guys, let me fill you in. You have all been under constant surveillance since the lab at the Taylor residence burned down. You are now in my custody and will cooperate to the fullest of your capacity, or I will end your lives and drop you in a hole that no one knows about. Do I have your attention?"

All three nodded. "Why us? What possible value do we have?" asked Kelly.

Chalks smiled without humor. "Okay, I guess you deserve an explanation." Pointing to Greg, "You, Mister Gander, have actually traveled back in time and lived to tell about it. Incredible! So you're part of the team. You, Mister Kelly, actually worked with Doctor Taylor prior to the lab burning down, so that's why you're part of the family. And last but not least, Mister Baker, you are probably one of the brightest and most capable physicists in the United States, maybe even the world today, so you are definitely on the team. Does everybody feel better now?"

"We are very close to getting the MTECH lab up and running," announced Baker. "You can let them go. I can take it from here."

"Goddamn, Ed!" shouted Chalks. "That is soooo noble of you. You fellas hear that? Ol Ed here is telling me that he can do this on his own. But there is something you two need to know. Ol Ed here has been working with me, what, for two weeks now?"

"What's he talking about, Ed?" questioned Greg.

"Tell you what, Greg... Can I call you Greg?" interrupted Chalks. "You see, he really had no choice. I kind of insisted he cooperate, so don't be too hard on the good Professor, okay? Now, I have spent a lot of valuable time explaining myself, so we really need to get going."

"Why the heavy-handed approach with us?" asked Kelly. "We would have been part of this without the intimidation. Just what crime did we commit?"

Chalks leaned forward in his chair. "Chris, do you really think the powers that control the world we live in want to be your friend?"

"I, I don't know what you mean, I..."

"Do you think for one minute that these powers would trust you with the most powerful discovery in all of history? It's all about who controls this discovery. The United States Government intends to keep it. As far as criminal activity goes, time travel is classified as a National Security risk and you, fellas, are up to your neck in it. Understand?"

"How am I going to explain to my wife that I am in custody? I have a job to get back to in Montana," replied Greg. "You just can't kidnap people under the front of National Security."

Chalks thought for a moment. "You know what, Greg? I can pretty much do as I like. I can have you held indefinitely. I can have your family held for complicity after the fact. How long do you think your parents would hold up in a Federal prison? I would suggest that you cooperate. I would really hate to see Carol get rolled up in this. Pretty woman, by the way. You're a lucky guy."

Chalks could see that he hit a nerve mentioning Carol's name. "Oh, did you really think we didn't know your spouses, girlfriends, parents?" He looked over at Baker. "Mistresses?"

"So, what's next?" questioned Baker wanting to end this part of the conversation. It was obvious Chalks enjoyed the taunts and barely veiled threats. It was even more reason to end his life the second the opportunity arose.

Chalks stood up buttoning his overcoat. "Pack a bag, gentlemen. We are headed to New Mexico."

****

The long shadows of early evening were falling on the trail as the Indian gestured that he wanted Taylor to get back on the horse. Taylor could count on one hand the number of times he had ever ridden a horse, and that evening the pain in his hips and back from the ride made it easier to walk than sit. They had ridden all day at a moderate but steady pace, stopping only to water the horses.

Mercifully, just after dark his guide stopped at a small stand of cottonwood trees. Taylor slumped to the ground, more tired then he had been in years.

He had been trying to estimate their distance. Assuming that the horses were traveling at an average of three miles an hour, he estimated they were a good twenty to twenty-five miles from the river. He knew he was now well out of the reach of any possible help, totally at the mercy of circumstance.

As he watched the Indian tend to the horses and light a small fire, he was struck at how natural the man seemed in his surroundings. He moved with a quiet ease of someone used to living outdoors, someone who adjusted to the seasons and the elements as if they were part of him.

A warm gust of wind blew through the trees, carrying the heavy scent of wild sage through the night air, stirring something deep in Taylor's heart. It was the smell of the West, the scent of wide-open spaces, and the place where dreams are born.

The Indian handed him a piece of dried meat and a small canteen of water, then sat back, his dark eyes reflecting the dancing orange glow of the fire. They ate in silence, letting the fatigue of the day push them both into sleep. As Taylor drifted into his dreams, he let the fear go, opened his hands, dropping the nagging trepidation of the day. He intuitively knew that he would never be safer then he was at this moment. He lay in the Montana sweet grass, rolling the smell of the earth into his visions. He was home, and his soul knew it.

****

He had been standing by the corral gate for over an hour now, trying to see if there was any sign of the anomaly that had allowed the shovel to get through, anything that might indicate that he had a chance to find his way back. Coleman walked up smoking his customary pipe. "Find what you're looking for?"

"I don't know, John. Even though I can't see it, I think the answer is here where it all started."

"Well, I counted every head a third time, and you were right. Three are missing. Damndest thing, them disappearing like that. You really think those horses are connected with you showing up here?"

Dillon shoved his hands deep in his coat pockets as a biting gust of wind whipped its way around the corral. "Yeah, I do, John. I really do." Somewhere in the distance a murder of crows could be heard, their caws dropping and rising with the wind. "I should be able to figure this out. I'm just not looking at this thing right yet."

Coleman leaned on the fence tapping out his pipe, "Maybe you're trying too hard, Dillon."

"What do you mean?"

"Well, I don't know if this will help, but whenever I go hunting for deer or turkey or anything else, I don't think about shooting the game."

"I don't think I'm following you, John."

"What I'm saying is that I don't go out to hunt. I just go out, and whatever I run across, I shoot."

"Okay, I think I know what you're getting at."

"What I'm getting at, Dillon, is that you're hunting in one spot, looking for one thing. I think you need to go out where you know the game has been and see what you run across. Right now, you damn sure know where it ain't."

"How did you get so smart, John, out here in the middle of nowhere?"

Coleman pulled his collar tight while stuffing his pipe into his pocket. "You know, Dillon, even a blind pig finds an acorn once in awhile. Sometimes I get lucky."

Before Dillon could answer, a rifle shot split the air, blowing a fist size chunk of wood off the corral post Coleman had been leaning on. Both men dove to the ground as a second shot hit the post just above Dillon's head. Coleman quickly crawled behind a horse trough pulling his pistol. "Goddamn, Dillon, you all right?"

"I'm okay. How about you?" he shouted as a third shot hit the horse trough sending a spray of water in the air. "Where's that coming from?" he shouted as a fourth shot hit the frozen ground inches from his elbow.

Boom! Boom! Dillon could hear Coleman's 44 thunder from behind the trough. "He's over by Miller's! Looks like Chet Dugan!"

"Who the hell is Chet Dugan?" shouted Dillon, quickly checking to see if he had a full magazine in the Sig.

"He's a cousin of Pete Dugan! Hell, I thought he got himself killed out in Idaho last year."

Dillon jumped up from his position and ran into the large barn as a fifth and sixth shot zipped past his head.

He could hear Coleman firing back three more times. "Goddammit, Chet! You put that rifle down and quit shooting! Gonna get yourself killed if you keep it up!" shouted Coleman from behind the trough.

"Only people gonna get killed is you and that no-count deputy!" shouted the man from across the street.

Dillon carefully looked through the cracks in the wall of the barn for the man.

"I didn't know you were a bushwhacker, Chet!" shouted Coleman reloading his pistol.

Another rifle shot blasted into the water above Coleman's head. "You just keep running your mouth, Sheriff!" shouted Dugan. "You killed my kin. Now you're gonna pay for it!"

"Them boys went down hard in a square fight, Chet. It was three on one and your kin lost. Pete drew first!" shouted Coleman trying to see around the corner of the trough.

"I plan on killing you, Sheriff, and then I'm gonna plant that deputy! My course is set!" shouted Dugan, reloading his rifle.

As he knelt to pick up several rounds he had dropped in the cold, a voice behind him jolted him as if he had been shot. "Drop the rifle," commanded Dillon less than ten feet away. "I won't say it again."

Dugan slowly stood, his rifle hanging loosely at his side. As he turned, Dillon could see the striking resemblance to the first man he shot in the café, the one they called Pete. "Put the rifle down," he repeated, meeting the icy stare of the man.

"You must be that red-hot gunman everybody is talking about," sneered Dugan. "You don't seem like much to me."

"Over here, John, behind the store!" shouted Dillon raising his pistol. "Drop the rifle you son-of-a-bitch or I am going to blow your brains out."

"Do as he says, Chet," announced Coleman, walking around the building. "You got no cards to play."

The same slow motion dance of lethal action began again as Dugan raised his rifle. Instantly Dillon and Coleman fired their pistols. Dugan was lifted off his feet as both rounds blasted through his chest, spraying the back of Miller's store with blood and bone.

"Goddamn it, Chet!" shouted Coleman walking up and kicking the rifle further from the body. "It didn't have to end this way."

Dillon lowered his pistol. "Jesus, when is this going to stop?" he whispered.

Coleman knelt down and closed the man's lifeless eyes while holstering his pistol. "Well, you're sure earning that twenty dollars a month there, Dillon." He began going through the man's pockets, coming up with a silver pocket watch and a few coins. "Ain't much on him. Goddamn Dugans. Gonna end up kill'in the whole clan."

Dillon walked up holstering his pistol. "You think this is going to continue?"

Coleman stood up as Doc Tillman and several others rounded the corner of the store. "Jesus, John, you boys all right?"

"We're fine, Doc. Chet Dugan here has looked better."

Tillman walked over to the body. "You fellas do know that there are two more Dugans."

Coleman lit his pipe and tossed the spent match at the corpse. "He's right. There's the old man and then there's Mac."

"I thought Mac was down in Texas working for the Spurlin outfit," replied Tillman, kneeling down beside the body. "The old man lives out on the buttes with that Indian woman. Hell, if he's still alive, he's gotta be about eighty. I don't think he's gonna show up looking for blood."

Coleman looked up at the grey sky. "Looks like snow. Doc, you need anything from us?"

Tillman stood up, pulling his collar tight. "Nope, saw the bushwhack from my office. You fellas are lucky to be alive. I'll get the Thompson boys to help me plant Chet here. The ground is hard but they'll get him under."

"Thanks, Doc," replied Coleman. "I'll make sure the County pays you for your time and trouble. Also, you decide which one of the Thompson boys gets Chet's rifle. C'mon, Dillon. I need some coffee. I'm about to freeze solid."

309

As they walked away from the scene, Dillon was surprised by what he didn't feel, which was any kind of debilitating remorse for just having killed a man. In fact, the only thing he felt was cold. Coleman shot him a quick sideways glance as if had been thinking the same thing. "Trying to get a handle on the moment?" he asked, lighting his pipe.

"I was just thinking that this is getting easier, and that is really starting to worry me."

Coleman opened the door to his office. "You do what you have to do in this job, my friend."

Dillon walked over to the stove rubbing his hands over the heat. "I think maybe I'm the cause of this. I mean I've had a hand in killing four men."

Coleman sat down in his chair. "Four men that would have killed you at the drop of a hat and walked off laughing about it," he replied, taking off his heavy coat. "The Dugans were a bad bunch. If you hadn't done it, somebody else would've."

Dillon walked over to the window and watched as Doc Tillman and the Thompson boys loaded up the body of Chet Dugan, a man Dillon had never met until he killed him. Outside, in the steely grayness, a light snow began to fall, a fitting end to an encounter he would never forget.

God, he missed home, and at that moment, he missed the man he used to be.

Chapter 21

"So, you're saying we are not going to use the lab at MTECH?"

Chalks turned in his seat in the big Suburban. They had arrived in Albuquerque an hour earlier having flown in the government G4 from Dulles. "We don't need it," replied Chalks. "I think you're going to find what we do have very interesting."

During the flight Chalks had made it very clear again that their family members were indeed in jeopardy for some kind of federal prosecution if the men failed to cooperate with the project. In Greg's mind it was no more than government blackmail and barely concealed extortion for cooperation. When pressed about what specific crime they had committed, Chalks fell back into the National Security excuse for an answer. In Kelly's mind he was convinced that the minute the project was deemed "Viable" as Chalks had said, they would all be executed, probably by the man himself.

Baker had never been to New Mexico, and as he watched the high desert landscape roll by his window, he was struck by just how beautiful the stark openness really was. In the early afternoon sunlight he could see the muted pinks and reds of the colored sandstone, the images that were captured on countless guide books and commercial photographs taken from the area. If it weren't for the fact that they were now virtual prisoners of the government, this would be a pleasant drive through some amazing countryside.

Just outside of Shady Brook, Greg could see that the traffic was diverted at a police checkpoint manned by both Taos County Sheriff Department SWAT vehicles and what appeared to be military MPs. As they drove past the long set of concrete jersey bouncers, Greg was struck by the amount of control being used in containing the situation. Whatever had been found in town was something off the scale of importance. Chalks showed his ID at the final gate allowing them to proceed. They were the only car on the road.

Turning onto Holston Street, Greg hardly recognized the place where Taylor's house and neighborhood once stood. Every home on both sides of the road had been removed, right down to the dirt.

Taylor's house and lot had a huge steel building nearly the length and width of a football field built over the top. It was windowless except for a large set of sliding double doors at the end. A ten-foot high chainlink fence topped with four strands of razor wire surrounded the building. A small guard shack occupied by two military guards in full combat gear stood at the fence gate. It was clear that Taylor's lot was now a heavily guarded military complex.

"As you can see, gentlemen, a lot has changed since you were here last," announced Chalks as the Suburban pulled up to the guard shack. "Let's go. We're home."

The gate guard nodded to Chalks as the group passed. A second officer joined them on the other side of the fence. "Gentlemen, I need each of you to take a retinal scan before I allow you access into the facility. Please put on these Rad count badges."

"Jesus, Chalks, is all this necessary?" questioned Kelly, looking into the retinal meter.

"My game, my rules, tough guy," replied Chalks, showing the guard his credentials.

"All right, gentlemen, you're cleared for access," announced the guard pushing a set of buttons beside the large set of doors. A loud buzz alarm followed by a heavy thwack sounded as the door unlocked from the inside.

Greg was struck by how quiet it was inside as they stepped through the doors. Extremely powerful floodlights illuminated the interior of the building as bright as any indoor football stadium. A thick metal tarmac covered the entire floor over what once was the yard. A white, four-rail metal fence surrounded what appeared to be the basement area of Taylor's house. Several men in blue Hazmat suits stood near the railing taking measurements.

Baker walked over to a group of lab tables and electronic equipment. "This is the equipment that we had set up at MTECH?"

"Not exactly," replied Chalks pulling up one of the chairs. "We just duplicated everything you had. We have your living quarters over there including kitchen, bathroom, beds - all the comforts of home."

Greg sat down in one of the chairs. "What exactly are we here for, Agent?"

Smiling, Chalks pointed to the railing. "Take a look, Professor. You're gonna love it."

****

Taylor slowly eased himself into the saddle. Even though his back and hips hurt, he wasn't nearly as sore as he had expected. Despite everything that had been happening to him, Taylor couldn't remember when he had slept better. They had risen just after dawn and eaten more of the dried meat with water.

The prairie Bobwhites could be heard singing their song somewhere in the tall grass as they rode in the early morning light. Taylor guessed it to be only seven o'clock, and the air was warming fast. It was going to be another hot day.

His guide stopped his horse, allowing Taylor's mount to draw up beside him. He appeared to be looking for someone or something as he sniffed the breeze and listened in the quiet while their horses stood. The Indian suddenly appeared satisfied, tapping Taylor on the shoulder as he pointed straight ahead. "Nonpa Wicasa" he announced nodding. As if materializing out of the ground, two Indians on horseback appeared a hundred yards ahead.

As they drew closer, Taylor could see that these Indians appeared older, maybe in their late thirties, and carried the same air of absolute physical confidence he had observed in his guide. They stopped several yards apart. As Taylor's horse pawed the ground, his guide nudged his horse forward out of earshot. Taylor watched as the men spoke, sensing the intensity of their conversation. Something of great importance was being discussed, and it obviously involved him. Soon something appeared to be settled, and his guide motioned for him to follow them.

Taylor could see that his two new riding companions were wearing a mixed assortment of US Cavalry pistol belts and holsters along with their normal native Indian beads and mussel shell necklaces. A chill ran up his spine as he noticed the brass number "7" on one of the black leather cartridge cases hanging on one of the saddle horns. In fact, as Taylor inspected more closely, he realized that all of them were sitting on McClellan saddles, the saddles currently being used by the United States Army. He was shocked that he hadn't noticed it before.

It was late afternoon when they came to an expansive grouping of high bluffs. They followed a winding narrow path, the riders forced into a single file as they made their way deeper and deeper into the bluffs. The brilliant blue sky stood in stark contrast to the stony, sunbaked ravines. The narrowness of the trail seemed to focus and amplify the late day heat. When they finally came to a fork in the path, instead of taking the well-trodden trail to the right, the riders took a left onto a stony narrow rut that appeared to disappear further into the canyons.

The walls alongside the trail were now so close that Taylor's knees brushed the rock as they moved. He had to keep reminding himself that he was really here. Moving through the Montana Bad Lands on horseback, surrounded by Lakota Sioux warriors to a fate unknown, felt absolutely surreal. As they came around the last turn in the trail, the walls fell away and an expansive meadow at least three miles wide and three miles deep opened up before them.

The trail crossed the meadow and disappeared into a second set of rocky bluffs and broken ground that served as a natural fort. A slow meandering stream ran down the middle, and high bluff walls on three sides blocked the prairie wind and prying eyes. Taylor was surprised to see hundreds of teepees filling the meadow.

Women and children and small corrals of horses spread across the area, all going about the normal chores of everyday life. Few villagers even acknowledged his presence as the group slowly rode through the massive camp. A small group of children that began to follow were quickly stopped and pulled away by mothers and grandparents. Coming to a halt in front of a large teepee, the men dismounted and motioned for Taylor to do the same.

An Indian held open the doorway flap and motioned for him to step inside. Pulling up all the composure and courage that remained, he nodded to the impassive face of his guide and stepped through the door. It took a second or two for his eyes to adjust to the subdued light as he felt several more people come in behind him. Slowly he was able to make out the shapes and then the faces of two men who were seated on the far side of the tent. He moved closer to the center where a small cooking fire that had long since gone out sent a delicate streamer of wispy smoke up into a single shaft of sunlight coming through the apex of the tent.

317

As he looked around, he was surprised to see that he was the only one standing, as those who had come in after him had quietly taken seats. After a long awkward pause, someone spoke up in halting English. "I saw you on the river, before we killed Yellow Hair. You are Ton Ta Tonka."

Taylor could not see the man who had spoken. "I, I'm sorry, who is talking please?"

A man stepped forward from the gloom of the tent. His hair was long and pulled back at the sides of his head, held in a topknot of leather string and a single eagle feather. His eyes, set deep under a heavy brow, gave nothing away. Taylor noticed that the man was as tall as he, with a thick neck and broad shoulders that announced a natural strength. He would be a formidable, if not fierce, enemy.

"I am Cha Ho A," announced the Indian stepping closer.

Taylor's mind was spinning. In modern times, no photograph of this tribal leader even existed, yet here he stood, the Holy man, warrior, and leader of the war party of Dog soldiers that had killed George Armstrong Custer. "Cha Ho A" was the name his mother had given him. His father had given him the name of Crazy Horse.

Unable to remember any of the Lakota words he knew, he pointed to his chest. "Taylor, my name is Taylor."

Crazy Horse said nothing but continued to stare at him intently. "Ton Ta Tonka," he whispered finally. A wide grin slowly grew as he held out his hand and handed Taylor five rounds of linked machine gun ammunition. "Ton Ta Tonka."

Stunned, Taylor sat down, holding the bullets as if they were about to explode. *My God*, he thought, *just how much of this stuff did I leave behind that day?*

"You have much power, Ton Ta Tonka. I saw you at the river, and then I saw you disappear."

Taylor had to be very careful. What he said and did within the next few minutes could mean life or death. If he admitted to Crazy Horse that he did have great power, he would be asked to show it. If he admitted that he was just some ordinary white man, then he would probably be killed as quickly as they could pull their knives and axes. He was still alive because Crazy Horse thought he was something special. He needed to trade on that for as long as he could. Remembering the motto "Fortune favors the bold", he handed the ammunition back. "My gift to you, Cha Ho A. Now, where is my rifle?"

****

After donning bulky Hazmat suits and respirators, Greg, Baker, and Kelly cautiously made their way to the railing surrounding the expanse that had been Taylor's lab. As they stepped closer, they could hear a low, roaring sound much like the sound of waves rushing through a sea cave. "My God," Greg gasped, astounded by the sight. "What the hell is that?"

319

Kelly shook his head, totally transfixed. "I, I, don't kn…"

"It's a tear in space," interrupted Baker. "It's a gap in the continuum." He looked over at Kelly. "And it's incredibly dangerous."

Chalks walked up wearing the same Hazmat gear as the others. "Well, Professor Baker, what's your assessment?"

Trying to control himself, Baker turned to the agent. "My assessment? We have a possible world-ending event here, Chalks. Whatever political gain you hope to hold by keeping this a secret is totally misguided. The scientific world needs to know about this before it's too late. That's my assessment."

"You afraid of this thing, Professor?"

Baker stepped up to within inches of the agent, shaking with fury. "Are you fucking insane?!" he shouted. "Look at that anomaly, Chalks. Look at it very closely. It looks exactly like what it is, a tear, a wound. If you look into that blackness, you can see stars, real stars. Don't you know what that means?"

Chalks pushed Baker back. "Get a hold of yourself, Professor. This is why you're here. This is what you need to work on. Right now it's the one thing that's keeping you alive."

Kelly stepped up between the men. "Enough!" he shouted, pushing the men apart. "Enough of your threats, Chalks. You want cooperation? You got it. But drop the bullshit, and let us do what we came here to do."

Chalks stepped back laughing. "Now that's the spirit, guys. About time you grew some balls. Nothing like the threat of total world annihilation to get the ol' blood pumping." He stepped close to Kelly. "You keep everybody cool and calm there, Pard. Can't have anybody coming unhinged now, can we?"

"Unbelievable," replied Baker watching Chalks walk away. "He has no idea what he's fooling with here."

"He knows exactly what he has here," replied Kelly, turning back to the pit. "He just doesn't care." He motioned Greg closer. "Listen, guys, I think we all know where this is going."

"Yeah, a bullet in the head when we get this process up and running," announced Greg. "No way anybody is getting out of here alive."

It was the first time the three had talked about their situation since Chalks had picked them up. Greg turned to the railing, transfixed by the anomaly. "I'm still trying to figure out why all the intimidation and threats. You would think this kind of discovery would be joined by researchers and scientists from all over the world."

Kelly stepped up beside him. "They're going to use this as a weapon. It is the most powerful weapon ever known to man. That's why the secrecy. We are standing next to the world's greatest discovery, and only about twenty people know about it. Whoever is running this show is going to keep it that way."

"So how do we play this?" questioned Greg. "How do we stop them, whoever they are, and not get ourselves killed in the process?"

"It's still going to take us weeks to get the lab up and running," replied Kelly. "Until then, we play the game, play it safe, and wait for our shot."

"You think Chalks will really go through with all his threats?" questioned Baker. "I've personally seen how ruthless that son-of-a-bitch can be. He's the one that knocked the shit out of me last week."

"Don't worry, guys" announced Kelly looking to the far end of the building where Chalks was taking off his Hazmat gear. "There's a lot of moving parts in this operation, and we have time; our chance will come."

Greg couldn't take his eyes off the anomaly. "Ed, what am I looking at? This thing is incredible."

Baker seemed to collect himself, falling back into the physicist's mode. "Well, it appears to be an active fissure in the space-time continuum, a tear in the fabric of our three dimensional world. It's something I'm still trying to get my head around."

"How big do you think this is?" asked Kelly. Stepping close to the rail, he could feel the vibration through the steel.

Baker thought for a moment. "Well, in this dimension, the fissure looks to be fifteen to twenty feet in length and maybe four feet wide."

"The middle of it looks like the night sky. Why are we able to see stars?" questioned Greg.

Baker shook his head in amazement. "Because that's what infinity looks like. You're looking at God's front door."

Chapter 22

"So, you're telling me that I do not have access to public property in the state of New Mexico even though I am a bona fide FBI agent? Is that what you're telling me, Clay?" Clark had placed the call to the General Counsel Office at FBI Headquarters in D.C. that morning to get some kind of explanation for why he and the rest of the investigative agencies had been removed from the Shady Brook incident and, more importantly, why he was not even allowed back in the area.

Clay Roberts had been the senior counsel agent at the OGC for four years now and had never been exposed to this kind of internal control of information in all that time. The word had come from the top that Shady Brook, New Mexico, might as well be a black hole on the map as far as future investigations were concerned. Nothing was coming out, and nobody was going in - period.

Clay respected Clark as both an agent and friend and could hear the frustration and deep confusion in his voice after being taken off the case. "Listen, Dave, this shut-down is right out of the ADIC's office. If ignored, it could be the third rail for a career. You really need to let this go and forget about it. That's my advice as a friend and as General Counsel."

"Clay, this is happening just up the road, thirty miles from my Albuquerque office. How am I supposed to ignore this? I mean, who the hell are these people anyway?"

"They are people you need to stay away from, Dave. If you value your career and maybe even your freedom, you will stay as far away from this as you can. It's just not worth the grief."

Clark thought for a moment. It was obvious that he was getting nowhere with this. "All right, but I want you to know that I am not settled at all about this, Clay. I will be keeping an eye on what's going on up there."

"I've given you my advice, Dave. Tread carefully, my friend. You have zero, and I mean zero backup on this. Let it go. Anyway, I've got to get to a meeting. Take care, tough guy."

"Okay, you too."

The second Clark hung up the phone he knew he had made a mistake, maybe even a fatal one. He could hear the fear in his friend's voice. Clay was one of those bare-knuckle lawyers who hadn't had the grades or the money as an undergraduate for any of the fancy east-coast law schools. He had slugged it out in Boston, working nights as a school janitor on the tough west side, going to law school during the day. After getting his law degree, he had applied at the FBI testing three times before he was accepted. If this thing could put the yips in a guy like Clay Roberts, then it had teeth and the very real ability to draw blood.

On a hunch, he ran the name Jason Chalks on the NCIC. Not only was his name not found in the extensive FBI database, but there was no military record, no driver's license and no government identification. The NSB (National Security Bureau) had never issued an ID for a Jason Chalks. It appeared, as far as the United States Government was concerned, Jason Chalks did not exist. It would take an unheard of amount of power to keep someone out of every important database in the country. In all of his time as an FBI agent, Clark had never seen it done.

Just for kicks, he even checked Facebook, Twitter, Skype accounts and every other lightweight social media site he could think of. Again, there was nothing - no credit reports, no Social Security number, no IRS records or tax identification numbers found under the name of Jason Chalks. Incredible.

Two thousand miles to the east, in a non-descript office building six blocks from the D.C. Dulles airport, the information trip alarm from a computer search sounded. The operator immediately checked the source and confirmed the mainframe identification number and location. He punched the desk officer's number. "Yeah, got a flash from a confirmed source. Ah, let's see, it's the FBI office in Albuquerque. Someone called NCIC, their main database plus a bunch of social media stuff along with NSB.... Okay, that's all I got. Are you going to contact the ADIC?.... Sounds good, thanks."

Mark Twain once wrote that two people could keep a secret if one of them is dead. The Kingdom took that saying a bit further, making sure everyone connected with a sensitive secret didn't stay alive long. A liability was a liability - even a curious FBI agent.

****

Taylor was gambling big that his bluster would hide his insecurity and fear. Crazy Horse held his gaze briefly and then turned back into the shadows of the tent returning moments later carrying a mud splattered M-60 machine gun in his arms.

Taylor took the weapon, surprised by the twenty-three pounds of weight. He could see that only three rounds of the twenty-round belt still hung from the gun. "Thank you for protecting my rifle," he announced in his most confident voice. "It is good to have it back." Crazy Horse nodded, seemingly pleased with being able to give it to him.

Taylor considered that he was now stuck with the burden of carrying the weapon everywhere he went, not an easy task, especially for a sixty-one-year-old man with bad knees and a sore back. He looked at the gun carefully, praying that it had not been damaged. With the three or four rounds left in the gun and the few rounds he had received from both his river guide and Crazy Horse, he had maybe fifteen rounds total, not a whole lot of ammunition if he needed to demonstrate his "omnipotent power" in order to stay alive.

Taking a risk, he unsnapped the bipod legs on the gun, set it on the ground and turned to Crazy Horse. "There was a box, a metal box, that was left with my rifle. I would like to have it back."

Crazy Horse nodded, speaking a short command. A moment later one of the Dog soldiers emerged from the shadows holding the OD green ammunition can. Breathing a sigh of relief, Taylor took the can and opened it to be sure the ammunition was still inside. It would buy him some time and hopefully some distance. He had no way of knowing how long his vulnerabilities could stay hidden.

He nodded to Crazy Horse. "Thank you. I can now fight again." He realized that he was talking like some B-movie character, but could not think of a better way to communicate. He knew he was in over his head.

Crazy Horse motioned for him to sit down between the two elders. It was obvious that they were an integral part of this formal inquiry. He recognized that Crazy Horse was trying to understand the things he saw during the fight with Custer.

"Ton Ta Tonka, I speak the white man tongue. I will tell the Chiefs what you say."

Taylor nodded that he understood.

Crazy Horse looked at him closely. "Why are you here?"

Taylor's stomach started to roll. *This is exactly the kind of over the top, game changing scenario he had been trying to avoid since he started. Nothing he could say would make any sense to these serious minded but primitive men.*

328

The concept of incremental time was as foreign to the Sioux as Latin. References to spatial and measurable time displacement would mean nothing here. The Sioux made sense of their world by the things they saw, as opposed to theory and conjecture.

Their lives and the concept of age were measured by how many harsh winters and summers they endured. Their children were named after animals their parents saw or relative to events surrounding their birth. Because life was full of things that they couldn't explain such as death and disease, it was common to assume that it must be the will of the Great Spirit. In this way there was an order of all living things. If he hoped to survive this encounter, he knew he needed to speak within the references the Sioux understood.

He locked a serious gaze at Crazy Horse, desperately trying to look as fierce and determined as he could. "The Great Spirit sent me to help you defeat Yellow Hair in the battle of the Big Horn River. I came to put fear in the white man and strength in the Lakota." As the men listened to Crazy Horse interpret, they began to nod.

He continued, "The Great Spirit wanted Yellow Hair to see that a white man with great power was against him. He wanted fear in the heart of the soldiers. That was the reason I was at the river."

The men seemed to accept the story, and a hush fell over the counsel. Finally one of the elders spoke up. "Ton Ta Tonka, why were you still with the soldiers at the fort?" *The elder had asked a very good question, one that could turn this whole meeting into some blood-colored nightmare and he had asked it in English, which was even more unnerving.*

329

"I..." *careful* he thought, "The Great Spirit has blinded them to who I am. I can live among all people." *Jesus, that was weak* he thought. *But it was the best he could think of. It would be a miracle if he got out of this alive.*

Crazy Horse spoke after a brief silence. "Ton Ta Tonka, I have told the elders what I saw that day. I saw you shoot at the soldiers. They are still confused about why you are staying with the soldiers at the fort."

This was the moment he would either win their trust or suffer the consequences of a lie. He slowly stood up.

"Great elders of the Lakota, I am a white man in appearance. If I am cut, I will bleed. If you shoot me, I will die. I was sent here to live and breathe and suffer this life as we all suffer. Crazy Horse has seen me in battle. He has also seen the Great Spirit take me away. The Great Spirit has also sent me to live with the white man. I do not know the reason. But you should know, I am a brother to the Lakota. I have used my powerful weapon to help the Lakota defeat Yellow Hair. I am a friend of the Lakota."

Several of the men, including Crazy Horse spoke quietly as Taylor slowly sat down. *It was his best shot. Hopefully it would save his life.*

Crazy Horse spoke. "Ton Ta Tonka, the elders want to know when the Great Spirit will take you away again."

"I don't control that," replied Taylor. "When I go and when I leave is never my choice. Whatever happens to me is at the will of the Great Spirit. I am but dust in the wind." *He couldn't help himself on that one. He knew the group "Kansas" wouldn't be around for another hundred years or so.*

Crazy Horse and the elders spoke at length before he finally stood to address Taylor. "Ton Ta Tonka, would you want to stay with the Lakota or go back to the white man's fort?"

Great, just great, thought Taylor. *Now what?*

****

Dillon had been working on the message all morning. Carving his note into the handle of the fiberglass shovel handle had been far more difficult than he thought it would be. Satisfied with the result, he handed the shovel to Coleman who had been watching him intently from across the room. "Tell me what you think, John. Can you read it?"

"Dillon here in Deer Lodge, Nov 16, 1898. Ania dead. Found moving Vortex to send this through. Tell my family. Dillon."

"You think this will work?" questioned Coleman, handing the shovel back.

"Well, John, I have to try. Now I need the blacksmith to turn this shovel part into a spear."

Coleman pushed himself out of his chair "All right, let's go build a spear."

331

Dillon knew that his attempt to send a message was a billon to one shot, but even with those odds against him, he had to try.

Walking in the early afternoon chill, he knew that if he ever got back to his reality, he would be returning a changed man. Gone would be the superfluous trappings of modern life. Things he had held so dear before would no longer be the driving force behind his life. Material possessions he had worked so hard to get would have little to no value for him anymore.

He had learned to simplify things, learned to live on the hard edges, become the man he had so long repressed. He now had a heightened sense for danger, a perception for the visceral. His reflexes were sharper, his vision was better, and his coordination was more precise. He was sleeping sound, eating less, and was noticing a clarity of thought he had never experienced before. In the last month and a half he was a changed man.

As they walked by the window of Miller's store, he caught his reflection. The image brought him up short. He now had a heavy black beard and long hair that nearly touched his collar. He stared at the face in the glass, startled by the man that stared back. There was something different in the eyes now showing through.

Coleman turned back to Dillon when he recognized he had stopped. "You all right?" he asked, looking in the window. "Something we need to pick up?"

"No, I'm fine. Just haven't had a good look at myself in a while, that's all."

Coleman lit his pipe. "Everybody changes, my friend, some for the better, some for the worse."

Old man Miller suddenly appeared on the inside of the window, his permanent scowl and general sour disposition clearly marked on his face. He gave the two a mean squint and then disappeared back into the store. "That is a prime example there, Dillon. That one has definitely changed for the worst."

Dillon laughed, shoving his hands deep in his coat pockets. "C'mon, I'm about to freeze. Let's go find that Blacksmith."

A mile from town, a small heard of mule deer looked up from the scrub grass in unison as a strange refraction of light and sound danced along the ridgeline. The low hum drew their attention and then on a silent command, they bounded away. The anomaly held its form a moment longer and then disappeared in the muted sunlight. The laws of cosmic attraction were still in place.

Chapter 23

Greg slowly turned the gain up on the meter, trying to stay within the prescribed limits. "Ed, check these readings out. I'm having real trouble trying to dial in a baseline."

Baker took a quick look at the data and back to his laptop. "Just a second. I need to see where the breakdown is occurring. We should be pulling a lot more wattage than this." This was the first time Baker had used the refined Thorium in any of his work. He was amazed at how Taylor had used the natural substance as an energy source, a radiation shield, and a marking beacon for the process.

Thorium, a grey, white, silvery substance similar in appearance to mercury, had been discovered in the late 1820's and was currently being studied by all the major players in the world as a cheap, relatively stable energy source as opposed to uranium. He knew that the French were now experimenting using Thorium as a nuclear fuel in place of Uranium in several reactors.

Baker adjusted the power fluctuation levels. "Okay, Greg, check it now. You should have a fairly steady baseline now. Mark it at five, five and a half."

Greg checked the data again. "All right, it's holding. I think you got it."

Kelly walked over, sitting down in one of the lab chairs next to Baker's workstation. They had been up since six, eaten a quick lunch, and were now setting up three of the four array panels in the center of the expansive building.

"Well, Ed, what do you think?" questioned Kelly, taking off his safety glasses. "Is this going to work?"

Baker sat back in his chair. "According to the data I'm getting, we should be able to run a few full-power diagnostic tests in the next day or so. It's amazing how detailed Taylor's notes are."

Kelly took a sip of the cold coffee he had been nursing since lunch. "And you still think there's no way we can use that...whatever it is, over there in the basement?"

Baker shook his head, giving Kelly a look of concern. "That anomaly is not stable. In fact, I am shocked that it is still contained. That thing could end up killing us all."

"You have any idea what's keeping it there?" Kelly asked, putting his feet up on the table edge.

Baker thought for a moment as Greg walked up and sat down. All three were showing signs of heavy fatigue from the nearly nonstop work. "Yeah, I have a theory why it's still there," replied Ed, checking his laptop again. "I was reading Taylor's lab notes. He was making a crude attempt at refining ore Uranium."

"That's true," announced Greg. "He was using a commercial centrifuge. I saw it. He had it on line just before the explosion."

335

"Well, this little tidbit of information is enough to keep you up tonight. My guess, and mind you it's just a guess, is that the only thing keeping the continuum where it's at and somewhat stable is the residual Uranium ore that's still left near it. Of course that's just a theory."

"You gotta be shitting me, Ed!" replied Greg, more than a little alarmed. "What happens when all the energy is drained from it? I mean it's been a couple weeks now. Then what?"

Baker took his safety glasses off and tossed them on the table. "Hell, I don't know, Greg, total elimination of the world or nothing. I have no idea. This is all new ground for me. If that is what is keeping it here, I'm surprised it's lasted this long."

Kelly was starting to fear for his friend. The pressure was beginning to show in his sharp responses and increasing irritability. Several times he had seen him standing at the pit railing, staring at the anomaly.

"Ed, if you were to guess, how soon could we be up and running?" questioned Kelly.

Baker thought a moment, looking up into the bright indoor stadium lights. "We have at least a week's worth of diagnostic testing and then a few days of fine-tuning after that. I guess about ten days."

Greg leaned forward in his chair. "Okay, guys, now for the million dollar question. What do you think Chalks is going to do once we get his thing up and running?"

Kelly looked over at the Agent, busy on his computer at the far side of the building. "My guess is that he is going to feed us into the array one at a time, just to see if it works."

"Which means, we have to get him first," replied Greg.

"Exactly," replied Kelly. "There is no other way around it."

"That's all well and good, guys," whispered Baker, "but what do we do after we get Chalks. I mean this place is a fortress. You plan on shooting your way out of here?"

Kelly let the question hang for a moment. "I'm working on something. Give me a day or so, and I think I may have a way for us to get out of here."

*****

They had been on the move for an hour by daybreak. Dillon pulled his collar tight against the cold wind that seemed to come from every direction as they rode. Coleman had insisted on coming along, saying four eyes looking for the future was better than two.

As they moved through the cold dawn, the only sound was the heavy thud of hoof beats on frozen ground. As they rode, Dillon let his mind drift on the cherry blend tobacco smoke from Coleman's pipe. He knew he was grasping at straws. The chances of seeing, much less finding the opening or doorway or whatever it was he was looking for, was about as remote as it could be.

Yet, he had a strange feeling that he was doing the right thing. His effort was being measured, calculations were being made, and, in a cosmic sense, trying to find the door home seemed logical, correct.

The first golden rays of cold sunshine spilled over the bluffs, turning the frost on the scrub grass into sparkling diamonds. High above, a Red Tail hawk drifted in a slow arch, looking for a breakfast of field mice or rabbit.

"You need to tell me what we're looking for, Dillon," announced Coleman, adjusting himself in the saddle, the stiff leather creaking under his weight.

Dillon looked over at his friend and smiled. "How the hell do I know what we're looking for, John? You're the one that told me I just had to get out here."

Coleman laughed. "Well, Goddamn, I really didn't think you'd take my advice. I thought you fellas from the future had better sense than to listen to a brush-cutter like me." They were now retracing the trail they had taken the day they found the shovel. It was as good a plan as any.

An hour later Dillon started to recognize the landscape. In fact, to his great surprise, he was able to find the exact spot where the shovel had stood imbedded into the ground, the deep depression still visible.

"Here it is, John. I'll be dammed. We were able to find the spot! Pretty amazing!" He dismounted and knelt down, touching the frost-crusted hole. "Hopefully, whatever brought it here is still out here," he said, scanning the open prairie.

"Tell ya what, Dillon," replied Coleman, stepping down from his horse. "I'm gonna build a fire and heat up some coffee. I think we might be here awhile."

Dillon walked over to his horse and untied the shovel from the saddle ties. The blacksmith's heat and skill had formed the shovel blade into a sharp spear-point, making it a little more aerodynamic and improving its strength.

"That's one hell of a spear you got there," announced Coleman, striking a match to a wad of tinder for the fire. "How do you plan on using it?"

Dillon sat down next to him as the small fire sputtered to life. "Well, I hope that this anomaly has enough internal energy to pull it. I figure it weighs about four pounds. If I can get close enough and throw this hard enough, it might get through."

Coleman smiled. "That's a lot of 'Ifs'. And if someone comes by, how we gonna explain you running around throwing that fancy spear in the air out here in the middle of nowhere?"

Dillon laughed. "You'll think of something, John. I have great confidence in your ability."

By ten o'clock that morning, both men were chilled to the bone after running out of coffee and the meager amount of firewood they brought. They continued to sit by their horses, wrapped in their saddle blankets quietly watching nothing.

"Goddamn, I'm cold, John!" announced Dillon, standing up stamping his feet. "We're not getting anywhere sitting here. Let's head back before we get pneumonia."

Coleman slowly got to his feet. "I won't argue," he replied, throwing the saddle blanket over his horse. "A person could freeze to death looking for the future."

"John!"

"What?"

"Look over there," whispered Dillon.

Coleman turned around. "Where?"

Dillon pointed off to his left and smiled. "About thirty yards off....there was a, a sort of light shimmer."

"Dillon?"

"What?"

"Why the hell are we whispering?"

Dillon laughed. "I have no idea. Wait, there it is again! See it?"

Coleman stepped up beside him, squinting. "I'll be damned. Looks like heat coming off the ground on a hot day. I can hear it too. Sounds like strong wind in a canyon."

Dillon watched the anomaly dance and twist twenty yards away. Its form reminded him of some kind of nearly transparent dust devil.

"What do you think I should do?" questioned Dillon raising the shovel to his shoulder.

"I think you better run over and spear that son-of-a-bitch! That's what we came here for."

Dillon laughed nervously. "You're right, John. You're absolutely right. All right, here I go."

Walking quickly across the uneven ground, he headed straight for the anomaly. This was not going to work, he told himself as he closed the distance. This was not going to work. He was now within ten feet of the anomaly, its deep hum clearly heard.

At five feet away he began to feel a slight but growing sense of nausea and disorientation. He could feel the hair on the back of his neck start to rise as he cocked his arm to throw.

Fighting back the bile and the blurred vision, he threw the spear with everything he had, all the fear, all the pain, and all the emotion he held inside giving energy to his effort. The last thing he saw was the shovel snap sharply skyward. The last thing he felt was the frozen prairie hitting him hard on the side of his face.

****

Testing the waters, Clark drove right up to the Shady Brook checkpoint and presented his FBI credentials at the gate. The soldier in full combat gear, looking as if he could have stepped off the dusty streets of Baghdad, walked up to the side of his car. "This road is closed, sir. You'll have to turn around," he announced looking into the car.

"Morning, soldier. Dave Clark, FBI. I need to get through."

The soldier stepped back. "That's a negative, sir. You are not authorized access. Please turn your car around."

"You do realize that I am an FBI agent and have Federal jurisdiction?"

The soldier stepped back, charging his M-4. "Sir!" he shouted. "I am authorized lethal force in defending this check point. Move your car out of my area, now!"

Clark attempted to open his door to get out but was immediately pushed back into the car as the soldier kicked the door shut, raising his weapon. "Last chance!" he shouted.

"You're making a big mistake, soldier!" shouted Clark.

The soldier snapped the weapon off *safe*. "Would not be the first time, pal. Move your car before you die in the front seat."

Clark put the sedan in reverse and slowly backed up to a spot where he could turn around. He was absolutely sure the soldier would have fired.

A mile and a half down the road he pulled off the highway, trying to think of what his next move should be. It wasn't as if he did not have enough on his plate already with all the cases he had. The two bank robberies in Santé Fe, along with the homicide on the Rez, gave him enough work to fill his schedule for weeks. Yet, being taken off the Shady Brook case bothered him deeply, troubled him for reasons he was still unable to pin down.

Maybe it was the fact that on a basic level he just hated being pushed around. He didn't consider himself a tough guy, but his feelings were a product of his past like everybody else's. He had been a small kid with ears that stuck out making him an easy target for schoolyard bullying and general harassment. He knew it was the kind of crap a lot of kids put up with, but it had marked him early and deep, and he had vowed to never be bullied again.

He started lifting weights in junior high, working out two hours a day to gain fifteen pounds of muscle by his sophomore year. He made the high school football team because of his speed and hitting ability, turning all the hurt and humiliation into pay back for others. He sat in the graduation ceremony on that warm Friday night in June of 1974 and made a decision that changed his life. He spent one last weekend with his girlfriend but on that following Monday morning he told her to find someone else and he enlisted.

He was at Perris Island two days later, Sempi Fi, Airborne, Recon and then on to SOTG. The Marines gave him the structure he needed and the carved-in-stone attitude that he could accomplish just about anything he set his mind to.

343

College, law school, and two failed marriages later he was in Quantico, a thirty-four-year-old rookie FBI Agent. He spent five years in the New York office, hating every minute of it, not for the work, but the place, the traffic, the noise and the sky-high rents all of which pushed him into applying for a transfer as soon as he could. He wanted the open ground and all the scenery that went with it. New Mexico had fit the bill.

No, he was going to find out what was really going on in the sleepy town of Shady Brook. He now considered it a personal challenge.

Chapter 24

It had been two full weeks since Carol Gander had heard from her husband and today she was going to do something about it. She had flown in from Billings the night before and had gone directly from the airport to the condo of a Mister Chris Kelly in Fredericksburg, Virginia. Finding the condo empty, she was now headed back to the airport. She was going to New Mexico.

It wasn't like Greg to not call all this time. Nor was it his style to keep her out of the loop for this long. Weeks earlier, he had told her the whole story about Taylor's lab, the money, and the incredible tale of time travel. All this from a steady, serious-minded, tenured professor, and most importantly, the man she loved. Carol was now deeply worried.

When they last spoke, they had agreed that he would come home the next day or so in an effort to bandage their bleeding marriage and smooth things over with the University of Montana administration concerning his job. There was no way on God's green earth she was just going to walk away from 7 years of marriage without finding out what had happened.

****

Taylor knew if he accepted Crazy Horse's offer to stay with the Sioux, he would be a witness to some heartbreaking events. He knew that in less than a year, Crazy Horse along with all the rest of the Lakota would be imprisoned on reservations. He also knew that in September of that same year, he would be bayoneted to death by a soldier at Fort Robinson, Nebraska, while trying to escape.

The country's collective rage against the Indian for the killing of Custer would be unstoppable. The entire Plains Indian way of life had come to a close at the speed of a rifle bullet even though he had tried with everything he had to stop it. Their way of life was over; mercifully, they didn't know it.

He slowly stood up, praying that he would be able to pull off a successful bluff. "I thank you for the invitation to stay with the Great Lakota but the Great Spirit sent me to live with the Whites, my own kind. I am going to do what the Great Spirit has told me to do." He heard Crazy Horse interpreting his words. "I am sad to leave, but I must go. They will be looking for me, and I do not want them to track me here. You have found peace in this place."

He walked over and picked up the Sixty, expecting to feel a bullet or a blade in the back at any moment. He turned and looked at the seated warriors.

"May I take the horse with me that I came on? I have something to trade for it." He knew he was taking a big chance, but he had to try. He reached into his fatigue pocket retrieving the small thirty-eight pistol. Crazy Horse stood up, staring intently at the gun. Taylor handed it to him "I want you to have this weapon. There are only six bullets in it, but it may help you some day."

Crazy Horse held the weapon up to the light, visibly impressed.

"You do not have to cock it to shoot it," announced Taylor. "Let me show you." Crazy Horse reluctantly handed the weapon back. Taylor motioned with his thumb toward the cylinder release push switch. He opened the weapon, dumping the rounds into his hand and closed the cylinder.

Crazy Horse appeared awe struck by the ease of unloading the pistol. Taylor held the gun barrel up and pulled the trigger twice. *Snap, Snap.* Seeing the effect he was looking for, he opened the cylinder and reloaded the weapon. He handed it back to Crazy Horse. "A trade for the horse."

Crazy Horse nodded. "It is a good trade," he announced solemnly. "Black Elk will take you back to the Whites."

"Thank you, Cha Ho Ah. You are my friend, and I thank you for your help." Knowing that the Plains Indians did not shake hands, he nodded, confirming the transaction. For a few awkward moments, Taylor stood looking at one of most feared Indians in western history, not sure of what he should do next. Crazy Horse nodded towards the tepee entrance. "I will give you two horses for this fine gun, Ton Ta Tonka."

Taylor picked up the ammo can and stepped outside the tent with Black Elk close behind. Moments later a third Indian walked up with two horses and handed the leather reins to Taylor. Neither was saddled. Relieved to be leaving with his life, he wasn't about to ask for more.

An old woman from the gathering crowd handed him a small canteen and a bundle of smoked meat wrapped in a leather hide. He stood with the twenty-pound M-60 slung across his back, having no idea how to mount the horse without stirrups or a saddle to hang on to. Sensing his quandary, Crazy Horse stepped up and shouted a terse command. Immediately, a black leather McClellan cavalry saddle was produced and mounted on one of the horses. A chill ran up Taylor's spine as he noticed the large caliber bullet hole in the back rim. It must have been a terrible wound for the owner and horse alike.

"Stay alive, Ton Ta Tonka. I would like to see you again," replied Crazy Horse as Taylor pulled himself into the saddle, trying to hide his difficulty in the mount.

"You as well, my friend." He nodded to Black Elk who was now mounted beside him. "Lead the way."

Two hours later, they moved out of the narrow gullies and onto the windswept prairie. Taylor found himself preoccupied with how he was going to explain the machine gun and the Indian ponies when he got back to the fort. It should prove to be a very interesting conversation.

****

By six-thirty that evening Carol had already picked up her bag, checked out her rental car, and was headed east on Highway 68 toward Shady Brook. She had no idea how to find Doctor Taylor's house or what she would do once she did.

She checked the rental car GPS, which told her to take "exit 12", nine miles ahead. Brushing back a nervous tear, she rolled the window down, letting the sweet smell of cool desert sage fill the car.

She had been second-guessing herself the entire trip. Why had he stopped communicating? Was he dead? Did the government finally catch up and take him down? Was she putting herself in danger by trying to find out the answers? As she drove, she played the questions over and over in her head, coming to the conclusion that the only thing she could do was keep driving.

She hadn't been sleeping or eating well, worried about the sudden lack of communication from Greg. Her friends all knew Greg and had tried to be reassuring when they talked with her, but last week the walls of strength and resilience came crashing down.

One day someone had asked a simple question about how Greg was doing, and all the turmoil and fear spilled out. Several of her friends had ushered her into the office restroom after finding her sobbing in the hallway. Her boss had given her a week of vacation time and told her she could have more if she needed it. Three hours later she was on a plane to D.C.

Now Carol was driving across the New Mexico desert searching for answers.

Ten minutes later the green and white EXIT 12 sign came into view. She switched on her high beams and was surprised to see that the off-ramp was lined with concrete jersey barriers and blocked by a guarded checkpoint - a military checkpoint. She rolled to a stop as two soldiers approached in full combat gear and weapons, their powerful flashlights blocking her vision.

"Ma'am, this road is closed. You'll have to turn around and leave the area."

She held her hand up to shield her eyes from the light. "I, I'm trying to get to Shady Brook. Is there another road in?"

"No, ma'am, there is no other road. You'll have to turn around and leave. This area is off limits to civilian traffic."

"Why is this way into town off limits? I really do need to get to Shady Brook. My husband may be...."

"Ma'am," interrupted the soldier. "I've already told you there is no civilian traffic allowed into Shady Brook. Now if you do not turn your car around and leave, you will be arrested. Am I making myself clear?"

Carol gripped the wheel until her knuckles went white. "Yes, you are making yourself very clear, sir," she replied in an angry, yet controlled tone. "I am leaving. But rest assured, I will make a complaint. This is outrageous."

"Yes, Ma'am," replied the soldier, stepping away from the car. "That's fine, Ma'am. Now move your car and leave the area."

As she backed out of the lane and turned toward the highway, a heavy, sick feeling in her gut told her that Greg was involved in whatever was going on here. Her husband was in trouble, real trouble, and she knew if she was ever going to sort this out, she needed to find someone that would listen.

It was a long drive back to Albuquerque.

****

Dillon slowly sat up, trying to focus. He could see Coleman kneeling beside him but his voice seemed far away, distorted, as if he were talking under water.

"Dillon, Dillon, are you okay? Goddamn, son, I have never seen anything like that."

351

"Help me stand up," replied Dillon weakly. "What happened?"

"Hell, son, you threw that shovel into that thing and it disappeared. Poof! Just like that. Never seen anything like it. My God, that was something. You sure you're okay? Looks like that thing knocked you out cold."

"Yeah, I'm fine," replied Dillon, picking up his hat. He smiled at Coleman's excitement.

"Well, I'm glad it was entertaining, sure didn't feel very good."

"Oh, it was entertaining all right! Hell, let's go get something else to throw at that thing!"

Dillon laughed. "Yeah, well next time, you go throw something. I don't like getting dirt in my ears."

Coleman patted him on the back. "It's a deal, partner."

They had walked back to their horses, mounted up and started for home as the late afternoon sun began to set. The little warmth left in the day quickly faded. Dillon smiled and pulled his collar tight against the biting wind as Coleman jabbered on about the day and how incredible the experience had been. He had a deep satisfaction he hadn't felt since his arrival, knowing that he was actively doing something to fix his situation.

Little did he know, that in the future those efforts would change everything.

That night as he lay wrapped in exhausted sleep, lulled into deep vivid dreams by the snap of green wood in the stove, the anomaly danced and shimmered to it's own rhythm not far from town. The laws of cosmic attraction were stronger then ever now. It knew where it needed to go.

****

He had only been in the office a few minutes when the phone on his desk began to ring. "Dave Clark."

"Yes, this is Carol Gander. Are you an FBI agent?"

"Yes, ma'am, the receptionist has put you through to the correct office. How can I help you?"

There was a pause on the phone, "Ma'am, are you still there?"

"Yes, I'm sorry. I'm still just trying to figure out what I am going to say. I am very nervous."

"Nothing to be nervous about. How can I help you, Mrs. Gander? It is Mrs. isn't it?"

"Yes, it is, which is why I am calling you. You see, my husband is missing. I, I mean I think he's in trouble."

Clark pulled up his chair and took a sip of the four-dollar cup of coffee purchased down the street on his way in. It was already getting cold. "Ma'am, have you contacted the local police?" he asked, growing tired of the conversation.

"No, sir, I have not. Agent Clark, are you familiar with a town not far from here called Shady Brook?"

353

The name hit him like he had been punched in the chest. "Ah, yes, yes I am. What does your husband have to do with Shady Brook?"

"This is going to sound really strange, but I drove up there last night and could not get past a military check point. I think my husband is being held there."

Clark was scrambling to find a working pen in his desk. "Ah, Ma'am, where are you right now? Are you in town?"

"Yes, I'm staying at the Marriot."

"Great. Mrs. Gander, there is a coffee shop right next to your hotel. It's called the Horizon Café. I would like to meet with you there if I could. Let's say, ah, twenty minutes?"

"That would be fine. What do you look like?"

"Good question. I am six foot tall, have a blond crew cut and I wear glasses. I've been told I'm an ugly version of Drew Carey."

"Okay, twenty minutes."

"Thank you, Mrs. Gander. I'll meet you there."

Twenty minutes later to the second, Clark walked through the doors of the Horizon Café. Carol, who was three booths down by the windows, spotted him immediately. To her surprise, he did resemble Drew Carey though he was thicker in the neck and shoulders, giving him the appearance of a football player. She nodded as he caught her eye and motioned for him to sit.

"Mrs. Gander?" he asked, sitting down across from her.

"Yes, pleased to meet you."

The waitress quickly made her way to their booth and poured him a cup of coffee. "Thank you, Molly," he said to the waitress. He smiled at Carol. "I come here a lot. They know I like coffee."

Carol put her hand over her cup. "No more for me right now, thank you. I'm still working on this."

Clark waited until the waitress left before speaking. "Now, Mrs. Gander, how can I help you?"

"Please, call me Carol."

"Okay, Carol, how can I help? You mentioned that your husband has some kind of connection with Shady Brook?"

"I really don't know where to start. It is an unbelievable story, and I am still in shock that I am telling it to an FBI Agent."

"Best thing to do, Carol, is start from the beginning."

Carol took a deep, nervous breath. "Okay. A month and a half ago, Greg, my husband found something while on a dig on the Custer battlefield in Montana. He found something that was linked to a Dr. Taylor."

Clark took out his small notebook and began to write. "Do you know what it was that your husband found?"

"No, not exactly, but he flew to Shady Brook and met Dr. Taylor."

"How did he connect Dr. Taylor and the town of Shady Brook with what he found?"

"I, I'm not sure, other than the fact that they were able to get together, and they started working together."

"Working together, how?"

Carol looked out the window at the passing traffic and then back to Clark. "This is where it really gets odd. You see, my husband is a tenured Professor at the University of Montana, well-respected in his field and has been his entire career."

Clark could see that she was on the verge of tears. "Take your time, Carol. Just tell me what happened. There is no judgment here."

She used one of the paper napkins to dab her eyes. "Well, he ended up staying at Dr. Taylor's home, laboratory, or whatever it is for two weeks, two weeks with someone he barely knew. Then Greg came home with over thirty thousand dollars and this incredible story that he had been able to go back in time"

Clark looked up from his pad. "Excuse me? Carol, did you say he went back in time?"

"Yes."

"As in time travel?"

"Yes."

Clark sat back in the booth. "Carol, when was the last time you saw Greg?"

"It's been just about a month since I saw him. He came home briefly from Taylor's place with even more money and some thumb drives."

Clark returned to writing on his pad. "How much money?"

Carol let out a heavy sigh. "Over three hundred thousand dollars."

Clark looked up from his pad. "Where did Greg say the money came from?"

"He said it came from selling gold coins Taylor had picked up from the past."

Clark nodded as he continued to make notes. "Okay, do you know what was on the thumb drives?"

She hesitated, looking around the room. "He said they contained Taylor's process and mechanical lab plans for moving through time."

Clark sat back stunned, suddenly connecting the dots between the anomaly he had seen, the extraordinary efforts to seal the town of Shady Brook, and the removal of the rank-and-file law enforcement that had been on the burn site. *Greg Gander and Doctor Bruce Taylor had invented time travel and the Government knew it.*

He came to the jolting realization that whoever was really controlling everything that was going on in Shady Brook would soon be shutting himself and Carol down. For the first time in his career he felt genuine fear. They would be coming for them, and there was nothing he could do about it. He realized that their lives were now measured in hours, maybe minutes.

Chapter 25

As the evening sun began to set on the western horizon, Taylor was suddenly aware that he was riding alone. He had been deep in thought for the last hour and had not even noticed that Black Elk had fallen back and then disappeared altogether. *Just as well*, he thought, adjusting the sling that held the Sixty against his back. *The closer they got to the fort, the more dangerous it was for the Indian, any Indian.* He looked back over the darkening landscape only to see his other pony dutifully following on its tether. Black Elk had melted into the darkness as quiet as smoke.

He finally stopped in that soft muted time between darkness and the afterglow of sunset. Easing himself down from the saddle, he felt the extra weight of the machine gun pinch his back and knees. He had ridden all day and now felt the full weight and pain of being in the saddle that long. He dropped the gun in the grass and with the last of any real strength unsaddled his horse. Now relieved of its load, his horse shook and stamped the turf. The ponies began munching on the tall sweet grass.

Taylor slumped to the ground, letting the warm night air wash over him. *God, he was tired*, he thought, dragging the heavy gun closer, maybe even too tired to eat. He heard a screech owl in the distance and then the soft wind gusting through the tree. As he looked up into the dark purple-blue sky, he told himself that he needed to soak it all in, to breathe it, to taste it, to remember all of this. In reality, this is what he had come for.

Since his divorce, he had worked to find peace by wrapping himself into the safe cocoon of science, only to find that it provided little past the sharp edges of "cause and effect" knowledge and applied logic.

No, he needed to feel this, the thick high grass cooling the sweat on his back and neck, the warm gentle breeze of the closing night that would lull him into exhausted sleep and these precious moments. This moment, this minute, these wonderful stolen seconds of time were worth all the effort. He was here. He was lying safe in the tall grass looking up into the unpolluted western sky of his dreams. Within a minute he was asleep.

****

"So, what's the plan now?" questioned Coleman sipping his coffee. He and Dillon had arrived before the café's first patrons that morning and were now in the middle of their breakfast.

"Well, I thought I might ride out and see if anything came back," replied Dillon buttering his toast.

"You want me to come along? Looks like it's gonna snow."

360

Dillon thought for a moment. "Naw, that's okay, John. I know you have paperwork to do. I won't be long. I just wanna check around a bit. Give me an hour or two."

Coleman sat back lighting his pipe. "Well, Dillon, if you decide to catch a ride home on a rainbow, I'd appreciate it if you'd leave the horse."

Dillon smiled. "I promise, John. I think you've given up enough horses to this endeavor already."

May walked up with the large blue metal coffee pot. "You boys need anything else?"

Coleman tugged gently on her apron. "Just to see that pretty face three times a day."

She blushed and smiled. "You owe me a dollar for breakfast."

"Gosh, May, you know the County pays for me and my Deputy here."

She slapped him gently on the shoulder "I'm charging you personally, John Coleman, because you're a rounder. Now you want more coffee or what?"

Dillon caught sight of something out the café window that took his breath away just as he raised his cup. In the middle of the street, not thirty yards away, danced the shimmer. Its strange distorted glow was unmistakable. Dillon slowly lowered his cup. He nodded to Coleman. "John, look out the window."

Coleman turned in his seat. "I'll be damned," he whispered.

May walked over and looked out the window. "What are you boys looking at?"

Coleman and Dillon were already moving.

"Nothing, May," announced Coleman, following Dillon to the door. "You just stay inside!" he shouted stepping out onto the porch.

Dillon slowly stepped down to the street from the porch.

"Be careful, Dillon," announced Coleman from behind.

As he stepped closer, Dillon could hear the familiar low hum, like the sound of a large electrical transformer.

"I don't know what to do, John!" he shouted over his shoulder.

Coleman eased up beside him, his pipe clenched tight in his teeth. "Well, compadre, I think it's time you got back to that family of yours. You might not get another chance like this."

Dillon looked into the face of his friend. "I don't know what to say. I mean, you saved my life. You gave me a home, you…"

"It's okay, Dillon," interrupted Coleman gripping his shoulder. "You would have done the same for me. We both know you ain't supposed to be here. Go on home or wherever this thing is suppose to send you".

Dillon laughed nervously. "That's what I'm afraid of. It's the 'just ending up' God knows where, maybe nowhere."

362

Coleman thought for a moment smiling. "Well, if you don't try, a year from now you'll be kicking yourself for not taking the chance."

Dillon nodded, his stomach twisted with fear. "You're right. I have to take a chance." He extended his hand. "You take care of yourself. I won't forget ya."

Coleman shook hands. "You too, there cowboy. You've been a hell of a deputy. You leaving will probably save ol Mac Dugan's worthless life."

Dillon looked back at the anomaly. "Okay. Okay. I guess I'm going to do this. Jesus, John, this scares the shit out of me." He looked back at the Café window. May was still standing there watching. He waved, wanting to say something.

"She wouldn't understand, Dillon," announced Coleman. "I'll talk to her later, maybe down by the river."

Dillon laughed. "You do that, my friend. God knows it would be good for you." He shook hands again. "Good-bye, John."

"Good-bye, Deputy. Go on home."

Dillon smiled, took a deep breath, and stepped towards the shimmer. Ten feet away, five feet away, three feet away, the nausea was starting to grow. A foot away he raised his hands in front of his face and took the final step. His vision closed down to mere pinpoints of light as the rushing sound in his ears grew deafening.

His legs could no longer carry his weight, and he felt himself falling. A tremendous blast of frigid air sucked the breath out of his lungs as he tumbled forward. Intense vertigo and a sense that his legs and arms were slowly being pulled out of their sockets hit him. As he tumbled, he fought against the pressure attempting to pull him apart. With his remaining strength he pulled himself into a fetal position, feeling as if he were at the very edge of death.

Just as he was about to let go, give in to the incredible pressure and speed of the jump, he became suddenly aware of a temperature change and a slowing of movement. He relaxed as he felt the pressure ease and then a quick dropping sensation, like that of a rollercoaster rolling off a high arch. He slammed into the soft ground with a thud and tumbled in the tall grass, as if he had stepped out of a moving car. Wherever this was, he had arrived.

****

Baker had been up over an hour now, standing on the side of what was now called "the pit". Looking at the anomaly had become almost a ritual for him first thing in the morning. "Morning, Ed," announced Greg, stepping next to him at the railing. He handed Baker a cup of coffee, noticing that the physicist looked more haggard than normal.

"Morning," replied Baker taking the cup.

"Chalks breaking your balls about running the tests?"

Baker nodded while staring at the anomaly. "Yeah, told him I needed more time." He looked at Greg with worry and fear etched deep in his face. "The process is ready."

"What do you mean 'ready'? I thought we were at least a week out?"

"Nope, I ran two computer simulations this morning and everything checks out. It's ready."

"Do you know what this means?" questioned Greg whispering.

Baker nodded. "Yep, it means our lives are now measured in hours. If we don't do something, we're done."

Greg's head was spinning. Of course he knew they were getting close to completion of the process, but having Baker telling him it was now ready jolted his system. Drastic action would have to be taken and quickly. He and the others were convinced that as soon as Chalks had a working machine at his disposal, everyone connected with the project would simply have an accident or disappear.

"So, what's the plan?" questioned Greg, looking over at Chalks standing at the far side of the facility.

Baker thought for a moment. "Well, I'm not much of a fighter. I'm a scientist. I've been thinking, I need to meet the man who discovered this process. I intend to find Taylor."

"I'm not surprised you would say that, Ed," replied Greg smiling. "I've been thinking the same thing. What do you think Kelly wants to do?"

"I think it's going to be really crowded for our trip," replied Ed.

Greg knew Ed was right. There was no way they could overpower the guards and Chalks. They had to risk an escape.

"What about the process, and how do we get back?" questioned Greg trying to keep his voice down.

Ed handed him a small device about the size of a small cell phone. "Take this. It's an activator. If you're standing in the array and push the button, you will jump in less than a second to the prescribed coordinates."

Greg quickly stuffed the device into the Hazmat suit pouch. "How do we get back?"

"If the machinery is still on and the power-base is still feeding the array, you can activate it from wherever you're at. I've made some modifications to the circuitry."

Greg could see that Chalks was headed in their direction. "What kind of modifications?" he asked quickly.

"When you come back, I have everything preset to deliver you to Barstow, California."

"What? Why the hell Barstow? There's nothing there."

"Exactly," replied Ed as Chalks walked up.

"All right, guys, coffee break is over. Let's get to work. I want those diagnostic tests run today. I want to be up and running by COB Wednesday. That gives you two days. No more bullshit, no more delays. I've been going over the data, and I know you're close if not already there. So let's move."

"Wednesday is too soon," protested Ed. "We can't rush this thing."

Chalks stepped up inches from Baker's face. "Listen up, asshole. You will do what I say, or I declare the process finished and you guys are done. Oh, and by the way, your suits are bugged. I have been listening to all of your devious little schemes about escape and contacting Doctor Taylor. I've decided to be nice and give you a couple of days. Don't waste them."

Baker was stunned. "You've been monitoring our conversations the whole time?"

"Yeah, Ed, I know it's a downer. I have stayed alive all these years by NOT trusting people like you. Now get to work before I change my mind."

Greg was about to say something when Baker suddenly grabbed Chalks in a bear hug from behind. "Grab his feet!" shouted Ed, dragging Chalks backward. Without hesitation Greg quickly scooped up Chalks' thrashing legs.

"Throw him over," grunted Ed. "Throw him over."

With all the strength he could summon, Greg pushed the lower portion of Chalk's body over the top rail. He tumbled through the air, head down, his arms flailing. Greg was stunned at how easy it was. They had been standing right above the anomaly, and Chalks landed on his back perpendicular to the split.

There was no sound, no explosion, just a muted flash of blue light, and he was gone. Greg expected to be shot at any second, but realized after several moments that no one in the immediate area had apparently seen the murder.

Greg, with Baker close behind, was now running towards the array. Alarm bells and flashing emergency lights came to life revealing that the assault had been seen by the control room guard through the many cameras surrounding the area.

Just coming out of the make-shift kitchen, Kelly saw Greg and Ed in their blue Hazmat suits running clumsily in his direction. Heavily armed guards were now pouring into the building as Greg reached Kelly. "Chalks is dead!" he shouted breathlessly. "C'mon, we're leaving!" He nearly jerked Kelly off his feet as they stumbled toward the array.

Greg turned back as he reached the array center and saw that Baker was walking backwards with one of the control devices held high over his head. "Nobody move!" he shouted. "Anybody attempts to stop me, I push the button and everybody here can watch the pilgrims come ashore."

Shouts of "Hold your fire!" and "Check your fire!" could be heard throughout the large building. As Ed stepped next to Greg, Kelly could see hundreds of tiny red laser lights moving across their bodies. At any second he expected to be shot to pieces.

"What happened?" he shouted over the alarm buzzers. They were now in a tight huddle with Ed holding the device above his head.

"Goddamn it! Somebody tell me what the hell is going on!" he shouted inches from Greg's ear just as Ed turned toward him smiling, dropping his arm as he pushed the button.

****

Dillon lay on his side, trying to catch his breath as the sound of crickets and other sounds of the night slowly replaced the roar of rushing wind. With effort, he got to his knees as his vision cleared, allowing him to focus on his surroundings. It was warm, maybe eighty degrees, and he was kneeling by a moving body of water, a river. He could smell the water, the damp earth and weeds.

He slowly stood and looked into the clear night sky, trying to get his bearings. Looking north, he found the North Star, and to his surprise, a large campfire burning on a hilltop on the other side of the river a good two hundred yards away.

He took off his heavy buffalo coat and did a quick check of his personnel possessions. The pistol was still secured in its holster, and his badge was still pinned to his shirt. He had lost his hat. He checked his pockets and discovered that he still had his billfold and the two extra ammunition magazines. After experiencing the violence of the fall through time, he counted himself lucky to have what he did.

Exhausted from the jump and knowing that you don't walk up on someone's campfire in the middle of the night, he decided to find a place to get some rest until sunrise. With the warm weather and his heavy buffalo coat, he knew he could get some decent sleep.

Walking through the dark, he was surprised at how smooth and flat the ground was, almost like it was already a campsite. The thought made him freeze in mid-step. He strained to hear any sign, any sound that would tell him that others were near. In the distance, coming from the direction of the campfire, he was sure he heard the sound of men talking and then it was gone.

He took several more steps and stumbled over a row of rocks into a wide pit of ash, a long dead cooking pit. He got to his feet and quickly drew his pistol, more confused than ever about what he had walked into. It appeared to be a large campsite but the darkness made it hard to judge. As if the universe heard his need, a full moon slipped from behind the clouds, revealing a sight that made his blood freeze. As far as he could see by the light of the moon were countless rock-lined cooking-pits.

The massive abandoned camp carried the feeling and vibration of life. He walked quietly through the camp, now noticing tall teepee lodge poles standing silently against the night sky, the skins removed, leaving the skeleton frames behind. Even in the muted light, he could see that the abandoned village went on for miles. The spirit of the thousands of people who had lived here hung heavy in the warm air.

He slowly moved further and stopped to see a dead horse at his feet. Even in the half-light of the moon he could see the gaping bullet hole wound just above the eye. As he stood slowly taking in his surroundings, something in his memory was trying to push through, trying to tell him what this was. He took several more steps, suddenly realizing the truth.

"Bighorn," he whispered out loud. He was on the Big Horn River in the Indian camp, at the origin of the counterattack on Custer. He crouched down, pistol at the ready, not sure what he should do next.

A sudden sound from his left made him look hard in that direction. It was a chirping, a high-pitched sound, yet a controlled whistle. Adrenalin shot through his body as he suddenly realized that he was hearing a signal. He stood, turning to run. *Thwack!* The blow to his forehead lifted him off his feet and into unconsciousness before he hit the ground.

Three dark shapes materialized out of the gloom from the tall weeds by the river. They stood over the body talking quietly. One of the shapes knelt down and wiped the blood from the face. In the moonlight, blood looks black. The shape stood up and mumbled, "White man." A second shape leaned close. "I'll be damned."

Chapter 26

"Mister, you awake?"

Kelly was having trouble figuring out where the voice was coming from.

"Mister, you sick?"

Again the voice came through, far away, odd, yet familiar. Slowly his vision cleared, and the face of a young boy came into focus. "What, who are....."

"I been watching you, Mister," interrupted the boy. "How come you in that ditch? You sick?"

Kelly raised himself up on his elbow. "No, I'm not sick. Who? Where is this place?"

"This is Texas. You ain't no vagrant are ya? My pop says we ain't got no use for vagrants. Pop says vagrants are no count, and we run em off. You a vagrant?"

Kelly slowly sat up, trying to comprehend what he was seeing. "No, I'm not a vagrant. Who are you?"

The boy looked to be about ten or eleven though it was hard to tell. His face was deeply freckled and sunburned. He wore a faded blue bib overall that appeared to be at least an inch too short exposing bare feet covered in grey dirt past the ankle.

"My name is William J. Hacker," he said proudly. "But everybody calls me Whizzer."

Kelly painfully stood up, just as a strong bout of nausea rolled across his stomach. With his hands on his knees, he retched, almost hitting the boy's feet.

"God almighty! You must be a drunkard. Pop says we ain't got no use for them neither."

Kelly stood up feeling slightly better. The bright sunlight and heavy heat told him that wherever he was, it was summer.

He brushed the dust off his pants, fighting back a second round of motion sickness. Finally getting a good look at his surroundings, he could see he had been lying in a shallow ditch beside a dusty dirt road in the middle of nowhere.

For as far as the eye could see, brown fields of knee-high wheat swayed gently in the hot breeze. A blistering sun hammered onto his neck and back as he stepped into the middle of the dirt road. The boy followed, his bare feet kicking up tiny dust devils. "Where you from, Mister? How'd you get out here anyway?"

Kelly took off his heavy sweatshirt, still trying to figure out where he had landed, alarmed that neither Greg nor Baker were anywhere in sight. "Ah, where did you say this is?"

The boy seemed surprised by the question. "Are you simple or somethin, Mister?"

"No, I'm not simple."

The boy pointed down the road to a group of buildings barely visible in the heat shimmer. "Over there is Waxahachie. Pop says ain't nothin in that town but no accounts and Oklahoma dirt."

374

Kelly tied his sweatshirt around his waist, trying to figure out which way he should go. "What's in that direction?" he asked, pointing over the boy's shoulder.

"My house is that way, half mile, maybe."

"Whizzer, that's what they call you?"

"Yep, everybody calls me that because I used to have the TB, made this funny sound when I'd cough and talk. I use'ta have it when I was jus'ta spud. I don't have the TB no more."

Kelly looked at the boy closely. "You had TB, Whizzer?"

"Yep, killed ma two years ago and my little sister, Beth, last summer. Pa says it's in the Oklahoma dust. Says Oklahoma is no count."

"Well, I'll tell you what, Whizzer. I think I'm going to head into town. Where are you headed?"

"Headen back home," replied the boy pointing down the road. "Pa gave me a nickel to get a loaf of bread from ol man Chulick's store. Haf ta get back."

Not really wanting to know the answer, Kelly asked the question. "Whizzer, what year is this? What's the date?"

The boy thought for a moment. "August 17, I believe, nineteen and thirty three."

Kelly shook his head in disbelief, looking towards town. "Unbelievable," he mumbled, "absolutely unbelievable.

375

****

Ray Branson slowly walked to the railing and peered into the hole where the anomaly lay. "I think it's getting smaller, possibly collapsing!" shouted one of the scientists to Branson, over the deep roar. "I don't think it's safe to be standing here. At this rate of decline, the anomaly should be closed within hours, maybe even a day." Branson nodded and motioned for the small group of scientists to move back and follow him.

Branson had been on the scene within an hour of Chalks' "assisted" disappearance over the rail by Baker and Gander. He was now the Kingdom lead on the operation, his mandate - to complete the job Chalks had started. It was obvious to Branson that Chalks' carelessness had caused his death. He had underestimated the men in his charge and failed to properly control the people and the mission. It was a stupid mistake that he would not repeat.

As the small group of physicists and scientists gathered around him, Branson stepped out of the blue Hazmat suit and handed it to his second in command, a shaved-head, no-nonsense, retired Marine gunnery sergeant, who carried an air of lethal hostility that put everyone in attendance on edge.

"All right, listen up, guys," announced Branson adjusting his tie. "Nobody goes near the pit. It appears that it's shutting itself down. Monitor the decline with CCTV only. We are standing as close as I want anyone to get to it. Is that understood?"

One of the men in the group spoke up. "Sir, how are we going to take our readings if we have to stand this far away?"

Branson gave the man a flat stare. "What did I just say?"

"I heard what you said, but how...?"

Branson stepped closer to the man. "No, I don't think you heard me at all. What I said is that nobody goes near the pit!" he shouted in the man's face. "That incudes YOU. Now does anyone else need a Goddamned clarification on what I just said? Anyone?" The men shook their heads. "Okay, now that we all understand each other, this is the way I want this done. Everything, and I mean everything, is to be dismantled, boxed, labeled, and prepped for shipment out of here within twelve hours." He stepped back, allowing his aide to move into the group.

"Mister Taggard is now going to hand out material shipping instructions for all of you to follow. Everything you wear or have brought here will be boxed and shipped. That includes cell phones, computers, wristwatches, clothing, everything. You will be leaving here in a paper suit. Is that understood?"

Branson scanned the faces of the men, recognizing complete compliance.

"All right, special trucks will be arriving in about three hours to load all of the material you box up. That means you are already behind schedule. I suggest you all get moving."

The men stood for a moment until Taggard started shouting. "Goddamn it, let's go, people! There is way too much shit to get done and very little time to do it in. Start packing!"

Outside, twenty cement trucks along with a small army of cleared government construction workers were getting ready to dismantle the huge metal structure, and pour massive amounts of nuclear grade concrete over the entire site. By sunrise, this entire block of New Mexico landscape would be a smooth barren parking lot, a parking lot where no one would ever park a car.

The odd looking area would be labeled a hazardous dumpsite and would never be put on the EPA clean up schedule. Never. As far as the United States Government was concerned, this small patch of New Mexico simply would not exist. They would hide the secret in plain sight, wrapping it up in so much government red tape that it would take a century to unravel.

By nine o'clock that night, most of the building had been taken down and all of the trucks loaded. Branson flipped through the pages of inventory and handed the clipboard to Taggard. "All right, start moving people out of here. I want this place to be a ghost town by morning."

Taggard nodded. "Yes, sir."

Branson had read and discussed the elimination order for all the primaries and peripheral people involved with Jonah, but after lengthy discussion, a new direction had been chosen. Plausible denial and standard government subterfuge would be the new course of action.

As Branson had advised, they didn't have to eliminate everyone; just a few high profile shot callers would get the message out. To Branson, it was the best kind of government response - the fear and control of the masses at the hard-edged example and expense of a few - perfect and all very neat. The real gears that ran the world would keep spinning.

****

"Look, he's coming around. Goddamn it, Virgil, why'd you hit him so hard?"

Dillon tried to focus on the face behind the voice. "Who, what's going on?" he gently touched the wound on his forehead. "Jesus," he whispered.

"Yeah, I'm real sorry about that, Mister. I thought you was one of them Indians. I don't take no chances with them bastards. Didn't mean to thump ya so hard; didn't know you was a white man."

Dillon's eyes finally focused, and he was surprised to see that he was lying beside a large campfire, ringed by at least twenty cavalry soldiers and several Indians. One of the men knelt down and slowly helped him to his feet. "Like Virgil said, Sheriff, they didn't know you were a white man down there in the dark."

Dillon suddenly realized that he was still wearing his badge. He reached for his holster and found it empty. "Ah, I was carrying a pistol. Has anybody seen it?" he asked, rubbing the back of his neck. He felt like he had been hit by a car.

"Oh, yes, sir, Sheriff," replied the young soldier stepping forward. "Here it is. That's one fine gun you have there, Sheriff. Never seen one like it."

Dillon took the pistol from the man and put it in his holster. "Thank you, Captain," he replied, noticing the rank on the young soldier's uniform. "Ah, if you don't mind me asking, why are you here?"

"We were just about to ask you the same thing, Sheriff. We're part of the burial detail for General Custer and his men. Been here two days now."

Dillon nodded, looking at the faces of the young men standing around the campfire. It was hard to tell through the heavy beards and moustaches, but he guessed they were all around late twenties to early thirties.

"So, this is the Little Bighorn Battlefield?"

"Yes, sir. The river is over there," replied the Captain. "My men were down there getting water when they ran across you. Sheriff, if you don't mind me asking, what are you doing here?"

"Ah, I ah," he was trying to pick his words carefully. "Been tracking a man by the name of Taylor. You haven't run across anybody by that name, have ya?"

The Captain gave him a strange look. "Ah, Sheriff, is there some kind or reward for this man Taylor?"

Dillon wasn't sure what to say, but took a chance. "Yes, yes, there is a reward."

"Well, Sheriff, you might be in luck. I came across a man the day of the battle, said his name was Doctor Taylor. Didn't have a horse, supplies or anything. Strangest fellow I've ever met."

Dillon was stunned. "You have got to be shitting me," he replied before he could stop the words.

Immediately the crowd of men broke into laughter. "Well, Sheriff," replied the Captain smiling. "I've never heard that expression, but I'm telling you the God's honest truth. We took him back to Fort Kehoe couple weeks ago."

Dillon's head was spinning. "How far away is that from here?"

"Bout a four day ride. Say, is this Taylor fellow dangerous? We just thought he was some crazy drifter."

Dillon was still having trouble digesting the fact that Taylor was here. "Yeah, he's dangerous, all right, probably the most dangerous man I have ever known."

"What's he wanted for, Sheriff?" questioned one of the men from the group.

"Murder," replied Dillon looking at the man.

"Who was it he killed?" asked the Captain.

Dillon thought for a moment as some of the green wood in the large campfire popped and snapped. "Me, he killed me."

381

Chapter 27

Clark sat in his car at the Shady Brook exit in utter disbelief.

"This is incredible," he said driving off the ramp and onto the surface street. "There is nothing here. They have moved everything."

Carol twisted in her seat. "There was a military check point right over there. That's where I was stopped. Even the concrete barriers are gone. How in the world could they have moved everything that fast?"

Clark had picked her up at her motel that morning fully expecting to be turned away at the Shady Brook exit on their way to Taylor's lot. For Clark, the sudden, unexplained normalcy of the area was emotionally jarring.

Still trying to comprehend what they were seeing, Clark turned down Holston Street where just three days earlier he had stood beside the ash-filled hole where Doctor Taylor's house had burned.

Now, anchored in the middle of the residential street was an eight-foot high chain link fence with a large red and yellow sign that read:

Hazardous!

US Government property

No trespassing under Title 18 US Code

The fence surrounded an area at least sixty yards across and a hundred yards deep - in the center, a massive, smooth-as-glass, concrete slab and nothing else. Fifteen-foot high permanent light stands that held high-density halogen lights and large CCTV cameras were located at each corner of the slab.

Clark stepped out of his car, stunned at the bareness of the block. Every house on both sides of the street had been taken out, right down to the dirt. There was nothing left that would have told anyone passing by that this had once been a normal middle class neighborhood. It was absolutely surreal.

"What do we do now?" questioned Carol stepping up beside him. "My husband is missing, and this place has something to do with it. I just know it!"

Clark could see that she was just barely hanging on. "Carol, I swear that we are going to get to the bottom of this. I know what I saw that day when I was here, and it wasn't a concrete slab with a fence around it."

"I just cannot believe this," she said, wiping a tear from her eye. "I mean, my God, Greg is a respected teacher. He has friends and coworkers. What am I going to tell them? What am I going to say to his parents?"

Before Clark could answer, a car drove up behind his. "You folks need to leave the area," announced the man walking up. "This is government property, and you're trespassing."

Clark pulled out his FBI credential. "FBI. I'm not trespassing. We'll be gone in a minute."

The man walked up pulling out his own credentials, "Tomlinson, Homeland security. You'll have to leave now."

Clark leaned in close to the man's face. "Back off, Tomlinson, or I'll have you arrested for interfering with a Federal Agent."

Tomlinson smiled without humor. "You know, Clark, I am really going to enjoy this."

"How do you know my name?"

Tomlinson stepped back and without saying a word drew a huge pistol. Before Clark could draw the 9mm sig he always carried, Tomlinson fired twice, *(Phat Phat)* both sedative darts striking him in the neck and face. With all the strength he had left, Clark drew his weapon and attempted to shoot, only to be kicked in the groin and slammed to the ground.

The drug effects had been incredibly fast and effective. He blanked into unconsciousness in seconds. Stunned by the suddenness of the attack, Carol turned to run and was immediately shot with two darts to the back. Her last conscious thought was that one of her shoes was falling off.

Seconds later a large white, unmarked van pulled up. Both Carol and Clark were zipped-tied at their ankles and wrists and quickly placed in heavy black body bags, before being loaded into the van and driven away. The entire procedure took less than a minute.

The only witnesses to the drama were several large desert buzzards that had been circling high overhead. A cool wind gusted up from the shallow valley, erasing even the tire tracks.

Fate and powerful men in high places had decided that nothing would be left to chance, nothing.

****

He had been staring at the body for an hour, trying to figure out what to do and where to go. After coming to, he had peeled off his blue Hazmat suit. The jump from the lab had been harsh, violent. He had been able to hold on to Baker during most of the transport but, at the last moment, he lost his grip.

They had slammed into the ground as if they had stepped out of a car going sixty miles an hour. Baker had been thrown into a large rusted rolling hay rake, impaling him from his throat to his thigh.

Greg had landed in the tall weeds along the road and except for road rash and bruises had fared well. He now stood over the body of the physicist, trying to figure out how to get him off the forks. The blood from the horrific wounds had pooled in the bottom of his Hazmat suit, making his body look huge in death.

With great effort he gently pulled Baker off the thirty-inch tangs, doing all he could to not cause any more physical damage. He was finally able to lay him on his back. Thick blood oozed out onto the ground from his sleeve as Greg unzipped his blue plastic suit.

He desperately hoped Baker had held on to the activation device during the jump; it would be his only way home. Repulsed by having to search through Baker's blood-soaked clothing, he was relieved to find the device in one of his pants pockets along with a set of keys and his wallet.

As a hot gust of wind blew dust in his eyes and the bright sun pounded down, he wiped the blood off the plastic, trying to think of what he should do next. He knew he was on the edge of a wheat field but could only guess that he was somewhere in the South, Oklahoma, maybe Texas.

He stepped onto the dusty dirt road, trying to see any landmarks or sign posts that could tell him "where" he was, or more importantly "when". Looking north through the heat shimmer of the afternoon, he could just make out the uneven outline of rooftops and buildings, maybe three miles away.

To the south lay nothing but endless fields and this single-lane dirt road. The open expanse was incredible, a fact that only deepened the irony that Baker was killed by hitting a fixed object in all this openness.

Greg remembered that Taylor had worried about falling into things when they first met. Looking at Baker's destroyed body proved the point. Determined not to spend anymore time here, wherever "here" was, he crouched down in the middle of the road, gave Baker one last look, and pushed the button.

Nothing happened. Panic flashed through his body as he pushed it again and again and then a fourth time. Desperate, he stood up with tears streaming down his face and pushed the button with both thumbs until his knuckles went white. Still nothing happened, no bright flash, no movement, nothing. The device did not work.

Emotionally shattered, he stumbled off the road and sat down beside Baker's body. Heavy, overwhelming despair washed over him as he tried to think of what he should do next. He thought about Carol and what she must be going through. He thought about his parents and his job at the university and everything else he had left behind. He was a fool for pursuing this, he thought. This is what it had come to, lost in an unknown time, sitting beside a dead man.

In the distance, he heard the odd yet familiar sound of an engine coming closer. He quickly stood up, grabbed Baker's collar, and dragged the body deeper into the weeds. There was no way he would be able to explain Baker's death to anyone coming by. He kicked the Hazmat suit into the ditch and stepped out into the road. The engine noise was coming from a black Model T pickup truck that was getting closer.

His clothes were still relatively clean, having been under the suit when he hit the ground. He quickly wiped the dried blood off his hands and tried to look as normal as possible as the truck pulled up and stopped in a thick cloud of dust. Two men, both well into their sixties, sat in the truck. "You need a lift there, young fella?" questioned the driver, waving the dust away that had billowed in from the stop.

"Ah, yes, sir, I sure do. Sir, could you tell me what town that is up there?"

The man looked genuinely surprised by the question. "Well, that's Waxahachie."

"Waxahachie, Texas?"

"Well, son, I doubt there's another. You need a ride into town or are you want'n to get fried in this sun?"

Greg smiled. "I'll take the ride if it's okay with you."

"Hop in the back," replied the passenger. "Ain't no more room up here."

Greg walked around to the back of the truck and hopped into the wooden bed. He spotted a large wooden box filled with empty fruit jars that rattled and clinked together as the truck moved down the bumpy road. Most of the jars were wrapped in what appeared to be old yellowed newspaper. He reached over and pulled out a page that announced the sale of livestock and farming supplies. What suddenly made his heart skip a beat was the date on the top of the page. May 15, 1933. "My God," he whispered, trying to comprehend the staggering implications of his new reality.

A half-mile away, Kelly heard the sound of a vehicle coming up the road. He had been walking at least an hour, and the hot sun and relentless heat were now starting to take a toll. Hopeful that he might be offered a ride, he stuck his thumb out, striking the traditional hitchhiker pose.

As he walked backwards, he could see a black Model T pickup come into view, followed by a heavy dust trail. He had no idea that cosmic attraction was still in effect at that moment.

The cosmos was still following its own mysterious path.

****

For Dillon, it had been a gruesome day. The burial detail had fanned out across the rolling hills of the battle site, still finding the badly decomposing remains of their fallen comrades. Dillon had offered to help, becoming a witness to the ferocity of the fighting.

Many of the Sioux and soldiers alike suffered horrendous, close quarter wounds from large caliber weapons, dying almost instantly from the impact. For three days now they had been locating, burying, and marking the graves where the men had fallen. The simple white crosses dotted the sunbaked hills for miles.

On a late afternoon of the third day, Captain Weir sat down next to Dillon by the wagon filled with tools and the remaining crosses. "I want to thank you, Sheriff, for giving us a hand with this. You didn't have to do it."

Dillon handed his canteen to the officer. "It was an honor, Captain. Thank you for giving me the chance to help."

"You know, Sheriff, I have to tell you, there's something about the way you talk and just your manner that's a whole lot like Mister Taylor. No offense."

Dillon smiled. "You're very perceptive, Captain. In reality, Taylor and I are from the same place."

Weir had been gracious in allowing him to stay; his protection and sharing of food had literally been a lifesaver. The soldiers did not have much as far as provisions, but what they did have was eagerly shared. It was a humbling experience to have men, who already lived on the hard edges of life, trying to make your own existence livable.

Weir lit a small pipe, an endeavor that seemed odd for such a young man. "And where would that be, Sheriff?"

Dillon thought for a moment. "Omaha, Nebraska. Both of us are from Omaha. We went to school together."

Weir blew a smoke ring before responding. "Well, Sheriff, I've been to Omaha but I never met anyone like you and Mister Taylor," he winked. "I guess we all have our secrets."

Dillon laughed. "I guess so, Captain. I guess so."

Three hours later, the detail had packed, saddled the horses and were on their way back to Fort Kehoe. Weir seemed content for the moment to not ask any more questions concerning Dillon's arrival, his lack of provisions, or what he was really doing in Indian country alone. Though not asked, he knew there would be a time when the young captain would want some real answers, answers that would tip the scales of all credibility and logic. Dillon was dreading that conversation.

****

He had seen the ocean before, many times. He had seen it off the coast of Ireland where the water, a deep azure blue, changed to a pale green as it broke on shore. He had seen it off the coast of Maui, where a warm, deep turquoise beckoned the spirit and calmed the mind. This scene was different.

He was sitting on a cold, wind-swept cliff high above a turbulent sea, unlike any ocean he had ever seen before, with no idea of where he was or how long he had been unconscious. A light, frigid rain began to fall, making small pop, pop sounds on his Hazmat suit as the waves continued to crash on the rocks below.

391

A heavy gust of wind welled up from the water carrying the familiar smell of sea salt and brine. He shivered from the temperature drop, wrapping himself tighter in the suit, while trying to clear his mind. Suddenly, a voice coming from behind him jolted him out of his misery. "What kind of fur is that?"

He turned to see a man dressed from head to toe in thick animal-hide clothing and a fur hat holding a cap-and-ball buffalo gun.

"Ah, hello," replied Chalks weakly. "Who are you?"

Cautiously, the man stepped forward, keeping his rifle at the ready. "You speak English?"

"Yes, I do. Who are you?"

The man lowered his rifle. "Well, I'll be dammed!" shouted the man loudly. "Another white man, way out here!"

Chalks stood up, still not sure if his new acquaintance was friendly. "I see you speak English also, and your name is?"

The man smiled and stepped closer, extending his hand. "God al-mighty," he replied loudly. "I'm sorry. Just haven't heard so much of the King's English spoken in a long time. Name's Smith, Jedediah Smith." He shook hands with an iron grip. "What's your name, friend?"

"Chalks, Jason Chalks."

"Well, that's a proper name, by God. Say, if you don't mind me asking, Mister Chalks, what's that you're wearing? Never seen a pelt nor cloth like it."

"It's a Hazmat suit. Did you say your name was Jedediah Smith, like the famous trapper?"

Smith laughed. "Well I'll tell you, Mister Chalks, I'm not sure how famous I am, but my name is Smith and I do trap to keep beans in the belly. Say, you don't look so good there, Mister?"

"What year is this? And, and, where am I?" questioned Chalks, working hard to control the rising panic.

Smith seemed confused by the question. "Well, not too sure of the year," he replied, scratching his beard. "But right down there is the cold Pacific Ocean, and the rocky ground you're standing on – Oregon."

"Oregon," whispered Chalks.

"Yep, been trap'n up past the Snake River for a couple years now. And I have to tell, sir, you're the first white man I have seen this far west. How the hell you get here?..."

"The year, Goddamnit! What's the year?" shouted Chalks above the wind and rain.

Smith stepped back raising his rifle. "No need to be shout'n, Mister. In fact, if you keep carrying on like that, we may get some company that neither one of us really wants."

Chalks raised both his hands. "I'm sorry. I didn't mean to shout. Just, please, tell me the year."

Smith lowered his rifle, thinking, "If I reckollek, it's 1830, maybe 31, hard to keep track this far out. Why is that so important?"

393

Chalks slumped to the ground as if punched in the chest. "1830," he mumbled. "Jesus Christ!"

Smith looked up into the rain. "Well, not sure if He's still here, but the Devil is alive and well in these parts, Mister Chalks, and unless you want to meet him up close, we need to get off this ridge." He reached down and helped Chalks to his feet.

A low peel of thunder rolled across the landscape as Chalks slowly followed his new guide through the rain soaked woods. Smith already knew what Chalks would soon find out - that their presence had not gone unnoticed. Men with deadly intent were following not far behind.

For Chalks, being with Jed Smith in the 1830's would soon be the least of his problems.

Chapter 28

To anyone not knowing the reality of the situation, you would have thought the two men riding in the back of the old Model T pickup truck were long lost brothers who had suddenly and unexpectedly found each other. As the truck bounced and weaved down the dusty dirt road, Greg told Kelly how Baker had been killed, and that, after trying it many times, he knew the device did not work.

"Well, you have any idea why the return device doesn't work?" questioned Greg, trying to rub some of the blowing dust out of his eyes.

"My guess is that they turned the power off on the other end after we blasted out of there," replied Kelly. "I have a feeling that this may be home for awhile."

Greg suspected the same thing but had kept his suspicions to himself. Now, hearing his own fears verbalized made him incredibly sad. He looked at Kelly through the dust. "You know what year this is?"

Kelly shook his head. "No, but I have an idea."

Greg handed him the newspaper page. "Date's at the top. You think we did the right thing?"

Kelly handed the paper back and smiled. "You did the only thing you could have done, Greg. We were headed to a federal prison somewhere or to a grave. It was just a matter of time with Chalks."

"I still can't believe I helped Baker throw that son-of-a-bitch over the rail. I, I just got caught up in the moment."

Kelly punched him on the shoulder, grinning. The blowing dust had stained his front teeth dirt brown. "C'mon, snap out of it. What's done is done. Let's get our heads straight and try and figure out how we are going to get by in 1933. Where in Texas are we anyway?"

Greg coughed up a throat full of dust stained phlegm and spit. "The driver said the town up ahead is Waxahachie."

Kelly had a shocked look on his face. "You're shitting me! My grandfather was from Waxahachie, Texas. He was born and raised there."

Greg was stunned. "What does that mean?"

"What happens if we see him? I mean, what happens to you? Hell, what happens to the universe?" He was starting to babble.

The truck suddenly came to a stop. "End of the road, fellas!" shouted the driver from the cab. "The town is just up there."

Greg and Kelly jumped down from the truck bed and walked up to the driver's door. "Thank you for the ride, sir," announced Greg, extending his hand. "Would have been a long walk."

"Well, no problem, young man. These are hard times. No reason to add to it. Okay, I gotta git. The wife is gonna send the dogs out after me soon. You boys get out of this sun." He shook hands with Kelly through the window before grinding the truck into gear. Just before pulling away, he looked over at Greg and smiled. "Pardon my saying so, but you boys look a bit haggard."

"Yes, sir," replied Greg. "It's been a long day."

"Well, if you don't find what you're looking for in town, I can always use a hand... out at my place. My ranch is the other direction. Can't pay much but the beef is good."

"Thank you, sir," replied Greg. "We might just take you up on that."

"All right then. My place is easy to find. Just ask anybody where the "Circle K" spread is, and they'll point you in the right direction." He smiled, tipping his sweat-stained hat and then drove away.

Greg turned away from the billowing dust from the truck, his mind still reeling from the idea that Kelly had a relative from the area. As the dust cleared, he looked over at Kelly who appeared to be in some kind of catatonic shock. "Hey, what's wrong? You okay?"

He looked at Greg with astonishment. "The Circle K ranch belonged to my family for years. My dad always talked about it when I was a kid."

Greg was stunned. "So, what are you saying?"

Kelly was on the verge of tears. "What I'm saying is that I just shook hands with my Grandfather."
397

****

He had slept well past sunrise, awakening to find his horse's nose inches away from his face, blowing short bursts of hot wind on his cheek and nickering softly. Evidently, the horses were ready to go and were wondering why he wasn't.

Taylor sat up letting a new peace wash over him. He had been sleeping on the ground for weeks and awakening fresh after riding his horse all day and eating over a campfire each night. He had provisions, two good horses that seemed to moderately enjoy his company, and he was in the land of his dreams. The fresh air, the Montana land, and the crystal clear mountain waters were feeding his soul. He realized that life really could not get much better.

He was not the man he had been when he first hit the bank of the Little Big Horn River almost a month ago. He was changing, hearing things he hadn't heard before, picking up scents in the wind that had gone unnoticed in the past. He was using muscles he hadn't before and was feeling stronger with each passing day. Most of all, he was falling in love. He was falling in love with the land and the peace of the past.

As he saddled his horse, he tried to remember a time when he felt more at ease. He couldn't recall ever feeling this aware of himself and his place in the world around him.

Taylor looked down at the Sixty. Only days ago he would have relished the opportunity to carry the weapon into the fort. He would have used it to convince the doubters of his message. But in his growing wisdom, he knew that doing this could have a devastating effect on the future. His appearance had been disruptive enough. Bringing an automatic weapon to a group of people at this point in time could have unimaginable consequences.

He knew he had only one course of action.

He knew Black Elk could not be far behind. Crazy Horse had given him firm instructions to make sure the white man made it back to the fort in one piece. Sensing the opportunity to seal the image of the weapon's power, he set upon one last task before returning to the fort.

He hobbled the horses and tied them securely to the tree. He opened the ammunition can and took out the two hundred-round belts. Walking a distance away from the horses, he lifted the feed tray on the weapon and snapped it shut after loading the ammunition. Putting the sling over his shoulder, he made his way to a small rise in the ground fifty yards to his left, a perfect platform to ensure his visibility. He took the weapon off "safe" and pulled the charging handle to the rear. With all the dramatic flare he could muster, he let out a blood-curdling scream and began to fire. *Bam, bam, bam,*...more screaming ....*bam, bam, bam, bam.* He let the gun run on full auto, a series of brilliant red tracers tearing through the morning sky. The heavy gun bucked against his waist as he blasted a spray of heavy divots of dark earth twenty-yards away.

399

Taylor welcomed the physical release of energy and recognized true liberation as the last of the ammunition cleared the gun. He quickly bent down and reloaded the last hundred-round belt, breaking off five rounds from the end. Tossing them over his shoulder, he began firing and screaming at the top of his lungs. As the last round cleared, he whipped the sling off his back in a dramatic gesture and threw the gun to the ground.

Taylor walked away smiling, knowing that Black Elk would find the weapon and the unexpended ammo. He recognized the power of the image he had created as he fired the weapon before going in to be with the white men – unprotected and unafraid. It would confirm the vision reported at the Battle of the Little Big Horn. He already knew that the gun would be kept and protected, that the myth of Ton Ta Tonka would be secure.

Taylor pulled himself into the saddle. He would take his time riding back to the fort. He wanted to savor the morning and clear his mind for the tasks and challenges that lay ahead.

The rolling wide-open range unfolded to the horizon topped by an expansive blue sky. The beauty brought tears to his eyes. He rode to the sounds of the rhythmic creak of his saddle and the muted methodical thud of Indian pony hoof-beats on the grassy ground. He was home.

****

"You do understand that we have to perfect this process."

"Doctor Crase, I want you to know that this project has the highest priority within the United States Government. All assets are at your disposal."

Crase eased back in his chair, studying the three army officers and lone civilian seated on the other side of his desk. "So I have everyone's full cooperation? Full control?"

"Full control," replied the General. "And since the lab will be at Wright Patterson, a controlled-access facility, you can rest assured that security will not be a problem."

"Ah, Doctor Crase," questioned Branson, "do you still believe that it's imperative that we get the people back that have gone through the time continuum?"

"Absolutely," replied Crase. "The longer these people are allowed to roam free through regressive time, the more chances they have to create a catastrophic event that could literally end life as we know it. We have to get them back as fast as we can."

Branson took the file he had been carrying and laid it on the scientist's desk. "This is the team that is going after these people. Their names and backgrounds are listed. They should be ready to go in about a week. The new lab is almost ready."

Crase scanned the list. "I don't recognize anyone here. Aren't they from the scientific community? Who are these people?"

Branson sat back in his chair taking a deep breath, knowing full well that a battle was about to ensue. "They're soldiers, Doctor, the best in the world. They will track these people down and eliminate the threat."

Crase was stunned. "Eliminate? Are you insane? These people have been through an incredible experience. This is history making, no pun intended. They have to be studied, interviewed. My God, don't you understand the scientific value alone for bringing these people back?"

"Well, Doctor, those are all really admirable ideas from a scientific viewpoint. But the people who are calling the shots on this thing see this adventure a bit differently. This discovery equals power, and the folks who are writing the checks for this intend to keep that power. So we will all live and work under the mandate they set."

"I don't know if I can work that way, Mister Branson," replied Crase.

Branson smiled without humor. "Let me tell you what, Professor, if you like your fancy office and the grant money for your fine work in your little world here at MIT, you will see the wisdom in cooperating with me and these fine dedicated officers here. It really is not up for debate. My rules. My game. Are we clear on that?"

"That sounds like a barely concealed threat, Mister Branson."

"Not concealed at all, Mister Crase. You're one of the sharpest guys in the world concerning this subject. If you want to miss the opportunity to work on this, it's your call. But we work my way or not at all."

"And, if I refuse these conditions."

Branson locked an icy stare on Crase. "I would not be sitting in this chair if I did not have the juice to back up what I say, Doc. You want to be a hardass; that's something I understand. Because of the importance of this project, I would not hesitate to make a phone call to protect it. You could end up in a federal prison being the girlfriend of the worst sex offender I could find. You want to test me?"

"Well, ah I, ah..."

"That's what I thought, Professor," interrupted Branson, getting up from his chair. He extended his hand across the desk. "I appreciate your cooperation." The other officers stood up as Branson pulled on his overcoat. "Okay," he announced, smiling, "we have a plane to catch."

Outside, in the busy streets and shops, from Kendall Square down to the waterfront on Memorial Drive, people moved through their day, wrapped in the normalcy of urban life all confident that forces greater than themselves would keep the clocks running and events in their lives consistent with logic and fairness.

A million personal dramas of everyday life played out in private and public, the participants totally unaware of what was being planned. The power of the universe and all of its fragile wonder would soon be in the hands of a few.

It would be interesting to see if God was paying attention…

Part Three

Zero Trace

Chapter 29

Taylor had arrived at the fort in the late afternoon drawing only mild interest from the soldiers and Indian scouts that lived in the sprawling compound. A layer of alkali dust covered clothing, horses, weapons and tents giving everything a dusty white color. The combination of the ankle high dust, the relentless Montana summer heat, and the insistent horsefly infestation gave life a very raw edge.

As Taylor walked through the fort's makeshift front gate leading the two Indian ponies, he had received only a nod and a halfhearted wave from the duty soldier sitting in a chair tipped back against a fence post. The soldier appeared either too hot or too bored for conversation or inspection as Taylor passed by.

He walked up to the camp mess tent and tied off his horses hoping the cook had something in the pot. A week earlier he had befriended the man and had been fed leftovers after the normal mess hours. "You can eat when I feed the scouts if you don't mind eat'n with them bastards," he had announced.

Taylor stepped inside the tent just as General Miles's aide was stepping out. "Ah, Mister Taylor, great to see you again," the officer greeted, shaking his hand. "What happened to you? We were quite worried when you disappeared."

Taylor sat down on one of the mess's long benches. "Well, Captain, I can assure you it's been a very interesting week. I did not leave the fort on my own accord."

The young officer sat down. "I'm not following you. What happened?"

"Just after I talked to you and the General that morning down by the river, I was "persuaded" at gun point to leave with an Indian."

The officer looked stunned. "My God, man, how is it that you're still alive?"

Taylor smiled. "I'll make you a deal, Captain. If the General still wants to talk to me, I will tell you both the whole amazing story. I think you would find it interesting."

The officer smiled. "All right, Mister Taylor, I'm headed over to the General now, and I will let him know you're back with the living. Looking forward to hearing that story of yours." The officer excused himself and left the tent.

Taylor nodded to the heavyset cook, who was wearing his customary filthy apron. "I see you're back!" he shouted from the far side of the room. Thought you'd been scalped."

Taylor smiled, trying to imagine all the rumors floating around the fort about his disappearance. "Nope, still got it all," he replied, patting the top of his head.

The cook grunted a response and then pointed to a small barrel by the stove. "Got some new hard-tack in yesterday. It's in that barrel yonder. At least I think there's some left."

Taylor walked over, opened the lid and took out three large crackers. "Thank you. First thing I've eaten all day. I, ah.. didn't catch your name."

407

The cook wiped his hands on his apron. "My name? My name is *mud* if the First Sergeant finds out I've given you food between meals. You need to git till supper."

Taylor nodded and stuffed the rock-hard biscuits in his pockets. "Oh, okay. I understand. Thanks again." Stepping out of the mess tent and into the hot afternoon sun, Taylor noticed that two Indian scouts he had not seen at the fort before were looking closely at his horses tethered to the rail.

He stepped down from the porch. "Hello," he announced, untying the reins from the post. "Something I can do for you, gentlemen?"

One of the Indians gave him a confused look while patting the haunches of one of the horses. "These are Lakota horses. How did you get them?" he asked stepping closer.

Taylor untied the second horse. "Crazy Horse gave them to me, two days ago." He saw no reason to lie to the men. In fact, when he thought about it, he was quite proud of the fact that he had been given the horses by one of the most feared Indians in history. He was now beyond caring what people thought about what he said.

The scout leveled a hard stare. "Why would Crazy Horse give them to you?"

For some reason the Indian's demeanor and barely concealed mocking tone hit Taylor wrong. In fact it really brought up his anger. He stepped close to the scout, not bothering to hide his hostility.

"Crazy Horse gave those horses to me himself. We were together at the battle. Ask around from some of your friends. They will tell you about me. I am Ton Ta Tonka. If you ever question my honor again, I will kill you. Understand?"

In his entire life he had never threatened anyone. He had never been in a real fight. Hell, he hadn't even played contact sports in school. Now here he was, squaring off with two Crow Indian scouts who had probably lost track of the number of men they had killed in their lives.

"Ton Ta Tonka," whispered the scout, his face and stare softening. He turned to the other Indian who looked like he was either about to cry or run. *"Ton Ta Tonka,"* he announced, gesturing to Taylor.

The other scout nodded numbly and raised his hand in a quick greeting. *"Ton Ta Tonka,"* he repeated softly. Evidently Taylor's exploits had spread further than he thought. He collected the reins from both horses, nodded to the scouts, and walked away. He had never performed a better exit. *Ton Ta Tonka* indeed.

****

409

Hearing a steel door slam shut and feeling the heavy pinch of the handcuffs behind his back were the first two physical sensations Clark had as he awoke sitting in the restraint chair. He had no idea how long he had been unconscious. His last ragged memory was the brief altercation in Taylor's neighborhood. As he tried to clear his vision, he realized that he was wearing a hood. He was having difficulty breathing due to the pressure of wide restraints across his chest and legs. He suddenly could sense the presence of people in the room.

"Who's there? What's going on? I'm a Federal Agent! I demand to know what's going on!" he shouted, pulling against his restraints.

"We know who you are, Agent Clark," replied a voice calmly. "And you're in no position to demand anything."

"Take this Goddammed hood off so I can see who I'm talking to."

A sharp heavy blow to the left side of his face jolted his head back making him see stars.

"Mister Clark, you will not speak until I ask you a question. Do you understand?"

"Hit me again you son of a..." shouted Clark only to be suddenly rocked by another punch to his face.

"Mister Clark, we can do this all day if you wish, but all I need you to do is nod your head that you understand."

Clark nodded, tasting his own blood.

"Very good, Mister Clark. You appear to be a fast learner. Now, your education can begin. Have you ever heard of *Regressive interrogations*, Mister Clark?"

Clark nodded *yes*.

"Very good. Well, just to refresh your memory, they were first used during the Iraq war to extract valuable information from Iraqi prisoners. We found out that the techniques were marginally successful at information gathering but an important side benefit the process produced was a pathological aversion to the subject being discussed. In other words, the prisoners developed an incredible emotional response to any subject that was the focus of the interrogation - really something to see.

"Why are you doing this?" Another stunning blow to his face. He was now swallowing a small yet steady stream of blood.

"Ah, you see there, I did not ask you a question. Every time you forget this you will be reminded, understand?"

Clark nodded yes.

"Very good, Mister Clark. Now last week you were at a residence where something unusual happened. Correct?"

Clark nodded.

"Very good. Now, I am going to give you a few word associations followed by some rather unpleasant sensations, that frankly, you will really have no control over. I do apologize in advance, but it's either this or we take you to some very remote part of the country and shoot you through the forehead. Nod that you understand."

Clark could feel the panic start to rise as he strained against the restraints. "You son-of-a-bit….." A sharp blow to his stomach chopped the words and the breath right out of him.

"Mister Clark, you're really making this a lot harder than it has to be. Now, here is the first set of words. They will be given three at a time at which point a stimulus will be administered. Now this stimulus can come at the beginning of the words, in the middle, or at the end. And again, I do apologize in advance for what you're about to go through.

Clark could feel his shoes and socks being removed and what felt like a large wet sponge being fastened around his neck. He felt metal wires wrapped tightly around his big toes.

"The first words are: Anomaly, Continuum and Quantum." A half second later a powerful jolt of electricity blasted through his body, creating a jaw-locking spasm in every muscle. The pain was incredible.

"Now, for the second set. Again I apologize for the pain: Linear, Hyperspace, Elements." Clark was still gasping for breath when the second jolt snapped his head back into the plastic seat. Throughout his life he had suffered injuries, from broken legs to a dislocated shoulder in the Marine Corps, but nothing compared to this searing, all-encompassing, full-body agony.

By the fifth set of words his bowels had released, and he drifted on the edge of unconsciousness. Later that afternoon, he didn't feel the restraints removed and the thorough medical exam that was conducted.

After he was cleaned and zipped into a clean jumpsuit, he was put back in the chair and the lessons began again. Three doors down from Clark's cell, Carol Gander was going through the same process. She was only scheduled for three days of reeducation. Unfortunately, Clark would be given five. Nothing would be left to chance.

****

They had been riding four days and arrived at the fort just before dark. Dillon had been allowed to ride in the supply wagon, a four-day body beating by every rut, prairie-dog hole, and sagebrush hump the Montana landscape could dish out. When the wagon creaked to a stop in front of the mess tent, he stepped down, vowing that he would never ride in a wagon again.

"They probably have some coffee and biscuits inside," announced Captain Weir, dusting the alkali off his uniform with his hat as he walked up. "Quite a ride."

413

"Yes it was," replied Dillon. "So, this is Fort Kehoe?"

Weir looked around, the fatigue etched deep in his face. "Such as it is, though that's not the official name of this place. Captain Kehoe was a friend of mine. He was a very well-liked officer." Dillon could see the sadness in the young officer's face. He obviously had been deeply affected by the death of his friend. "Anyway, I think there's an extra cot in the stable, Sheriff. The Quartermaster over there in that tent will give you a blanket."

"Captain, I want to thank you for your hospitality and help getting me here," he said shaking hands. "You probably saved my life."

Weir smiled. "Well, it was my pleasure, Sheriff. I hope you get your man. Do you need me to send some troopers with you to help round him up?"

"No, it's fine, Captain. I can handle Taylor myself. He won't be violent, I assure you."

"All right then, if you're settled. This fort isn't that big. If he is still here, I'm sure you'll run across him. If you'll excuse me, Sheriff, I need to check in with my Major. I will probably see you at breakfast."

"Thank you, Captain. Goodnight."

Fatigued to the bone from the four-day trip, Dillon decided to try and get something to eat before sleeping. He stepped into the large, dimly lantern-lit mess tent and was surprised to see the place full of dust-coated soldiers. The mess stewards were cleaning up from the evening feed in a flurry of activity in stark contrast to the obviously exhausted group of troopers finishing up the last of their meals and coffee.

As he moved through the group on his way to the coffee pots and stacked biscuits, Dillon felt at ease that he at least looked similar to the rest of the men in his presence. His clothes, from his boots to his shirt, were of the period. He was just as dusty and dirty as the rest. His full beard and collar length hair made him blend right in. The only noticeable difference was his height, which was a good two to three inches taller than any man in the tent.

He picked a reasonably clean mug, filled his cup, picked up several of the fist-size hard-tack biscuits from the stack and made his way to one of the far tables near the back entrance. The heat in the tent added to the heaviness he felt as he slowly sat, feeling every mile he had traveled from the battlefield. He could not remember when he had been so tired.

He had been careful to keep his shirt un-tucked, concealing the pistol he wore on his belt; the last thing he wanted was a curious discussion about his firearm. The only thing he really wanted right now was a place to lie down and sleep.

He finished his coffee, ate one of the biscuits, and stuffed the second one in his pocket for breakfast. He wasn't sure if he would be allowed to eat with the troops in the morning. Stepping outside the tent, he was struck by the coolness of the evening air compared to the stifling, unmoving air inside the canvas and wood mess hall. As he began to walk back to the wagon to pick up his buffalo coat, he noticed something familiar about the man walking towards the mess tent.

As the individual got closer, Dillon was stunned to see that the man, though heavily bearded and wearing almost shoulder length hair, was dressed in modern style woodland print camouflaged fatigues.

Taylor looked up as he was within arm's length of the man who was staring at him intently. "Good evening," he nodded passing by.

Dillon caught him by the arm. "Doctor Taylor, it's me, Agent Dillon."

Taylor slowly turned, astonished. "My God," he whispered. "My God."

****

"So what do we do now?" questioned Greg. They had walked into town still in awe of the fact that they were really in 1933. Greg could not shake the thought that this was a movie set. He caught his reflection in the store window as they walked by, something he couldn't see in a dream, giving credibility to the fact that it was all real - tangible.

It was now late afternoon, and the Texas sun was casting long shadows on the street and the dusty facades of the buildings. Men were starting to head home from work, school was out, and wives were at home getting ready for the evening meal. Life, in all its wonderful routine, was happening now.

Kelly sat down on the small bench in front of the Rexall Drug Store, wiping the sweat away. "Jesus, it's hot here."

Greg sat down beside him pulling his wallet out. "Check your money. Let's see what we've got."

On the walk into town the men had avoided the subject of Baker's death. It was still too fresh, and for Kelly it was just too painful to talk about. Baker had been a good friend, and the thought that he was really dead was inconceivable. Everything he heard, touched, smelled or felt had a dreamlike quality to it - an odd sensation that everything being said or seen was about a half second off.

Kelly took out his wallet. "I just thought of something."

"What's that?" asked Greg, going through his own wallet, the sweat from his face dripping onto his hands.

"None of the money we are carrying is going to pass for real currency here. If I remember my American History, President Roosevelt took the country off the Gold Standard this year. They changed the look of the money."

417

"What else do we know about nineteen thirty-three and this area? Oh, and by the way, I have forty-seven dollars," announced Greg.

"Ah, let's see," replied Kelly. "Hitler's coming to power in Germany. Roosevelt is the President. The country is in a major depression. Bonnie and Clyde are raising hell around here. The area... oh, the movie "Places in the Heart" with Sally Field was shot here."

Greg looked at Kelly with genuine surprise. "That's it? That's all you know about nineteen thirty-three?"

"Okay. What do you know about nineteen thirty-three?"

"A hell of a lot more than that! Geez, you engineering majors live in a very small world."

"All right," replied Kelly, counting out his money. "You tell me what you know about nineteen thirty-three. And I have one hundred and seventeen dollars by the way."

"Okay, Wiley Post is the first guy to fly solo around the world. You're right about the depression; the unemployment rate is 25 percent. Alcatraz becomes a Federal penitentiary, and prohibition ends this year, December, I think. Oh yeah, they also made marijuana use illegal this year."

"To be honest with you, Greg, that's not a whole lot more than I know."

Greg smiled, watching a Model-T car along with an assortment of trucks roll through with a steady rhythm. He found it fascinating that he could hear the drivers and passengers talking to each other as they drove by. There were no boom boxes, no urban thump of woofers or tweeters, just the sound of six cylinder internal combustion engines and conversation. Even though it was a relatively busy street, the urban roar of any modern day metropolitan center was totally absent. This was his second trip into the past, and both times he had been keenly aware of this difference - the lack of assaultive noise pollution.

"Well, what I do know is that we are going to need food and shelter until we get a plan of action."

Kelly nodded. "You're right. We need to worry about when someone finds Ed's body."

"Jesus, I forgot about that," replied Greg suddenly alarmed. "What the hell were we thinking? I mean this town is not that big – what - maybe eight to ten thousand people? When they find the body, the police are going to see how he's dressed, and people are going to start noticing we kind of look like him. It's just a matter of time, maybe only hours, before somebody starts connecting the dots. We're screwed."

Kelly thought for a moment. "Maybe not. Let's find a place to lay low till dark. We need to find out when the next freight train goes through."

"You're kidding?"

"If you have a better idea, my friend, I'm all ears."

419

"Why don't we head out to your grandfather's place? You already shook hands with the guy, and the world didn't end."

Kelly shook his head. "No, I don't want to risk any of my family, past or present, with this. My dad is only about eight or nine now. It's just too risky. You understand, don't you?"

Kelly was right, thought Greg. If the two met, a thousand things could change the path of the young Kelly's life. A word, an idea, any small thing could have a negative effect on the entire Kelly lineage. Avoidance was the right move.

"Okay," replied Greg. "I can see the railroad tracks over there. It's my guess the freight station isn't far. I think I know what you're planning."

Chapter 30

It had been over two months since Dillon had seen Taylor for that brief time in his lab. He remembered a disheveled, slightly overweight, bookish type. The man standing before him now was at least twenty pounds lighter with long, almost shoulder-length hair and a full beard. The difference in appearance was striking.

Taylor stepped closer. "You're, you're one of the agents that came to the lab, you're...." Before he could finish, he was struck by a solid punch to the left side of his face that lifted him off his feet. It felt as if he had been struck by lightning. Dazed and trying to sit up, he felt a second stunning punch to his mouth that instantly split his lip and slammed him flat on his back. Dillon was now standing over him gripping the front of his shirt, shouting.

"You son-of-a-bitch, I'm going to blow your Goddamn brains out! You piece of shit! You have any idea what you have put me through? Do Ya?" Dillon slammed Taylor back on the ground, jamming his foot into Taylor's chest and drawing his pistol.

"Hold it right there!" came a shout from behind Dillon. "Put the gun down, Sheriff." Dillon heard the clicking of several weapons. "There will be no executions in this camp, Sheriff." Captain Weir stepped up close. "Put the gun down, Sheriff. We can do this another way."

Dillon took a deep, ragged breath and stepped back holstering his pistol. He nodded to the officer, suddenly aware that a large group of soldiers were now quietly standing close by watching.

He took another step back raising his hands. "I'm sorry. I'm sorry. I lost control."

Weir helped Taylor to his feet. "You all right?"

Taylor nodded and spit blood into the dust. "I'm fine, I'm fine."

"Sheriff, I assume this is your Mister Taylor. We don't have a stockade here, but I can put him in irons if you desire."

Dillon thought for a moment. "No, that's fine, Captain. That won't be necessary. I can handle it from here. Thank you."

"Very well, Sheriff. I'm sure my Major is going to want to see you both in the morning. Are you sure we're not going to find Mister Taylor dead before then?"

Dillon smiled, still catching his breath. "No, Captain, I'm fine really. He is in no more danger from me. I promise you."

"All right then. I'll collect you after breakfast. The rest of you men break it up. Show's over. Go on. Go on with your duties," commanded Weir.

The soldiers slowly dispersed as a low distant peel of thunder rumbled in the distance. Dillon walked over to Taylor, embarrassed by his lack of control. "I ah, I'm sorry. It's...been a rough couple of months. I ah..."

"It's okay, really. I understand. You have to believe that I did not want this to happen to you. I really didn't," he pleaded, spitting more blood.

"At this point, I really don't know what to think." Dillon could see how genuinely contrite Taylor was, making him feel worse by the minute for assaulting him.

"Why do they keep calling you Sheriff?" questioned Taylor, touching his lip gingerly.

Dillon smiled. "Let's go sit down somewhere." He pointed towards the stable. "I've got quite an interesting story to tell you."

****

The four men that had been chosen were all in their middle thirties and at the peak of their physical strength and endurance. All four had been in the Military Special Operations community having served multiple tours in Iraq and Afghanistan. They had been selected from a group of over five hundred Tier-One operators. None of the men were married or had any other strong family attachments that might get in the way of mission success.

Two of the men were from SEAL Team Six. The other two were Army SOCOM out of Fort Bragg. They had been in seclusion at the Farm in northern Virginia for two weeks now training for the jump. Ross Centrez of the CIA Training and Operations sector stood near the firing range table pointing out the firearms that were going to be used in the mission.

"Guys, these are two of the weapons you will be carrying when you are transported. You have four days to become experts with their use. This is the Colt Forty-five, circa 1873, single action revolver. It has a 7.5-inch barrel and fires a 255-grain bullet at around 900 feet per second. It will ruin your day if you get hit with this thing."

"This one is the Springfield 45-55 caliber, breach block-loading carbine. This was standard Army issue throughout the late 1800's. It weighs about nine pounds and has a maximum effective range of 600 yards although I would not rely on my ability to hit a man-sized target at that range with this rifle. In addition to these weapons, some of you will be issued the 1911 Colt semi-automatic pistol. It looks like it was made in 1911, but it has been heavily modified internally with titanium springs, match grade barrel, guide rods, etc."

"As I said, these particular weapons look exactly like the originals but have had metal and site upgrades along with trigger and action jobs. In addition, you will be shooting modern match-grade ammunition. That will make quite a difference in accuracy and reliability. Any questions so far?"

One of the men spoke up. "Why are we using this weaponry? Doesn't it reduce our tactical ability to engage?"

"I'll take that one," announced Branson from the back of the room. He had been involved with every phase of the operation, from closing down Shady Brook to team selection and training, and was adamant about keeping complete control. Even though it was unspoken, he knew his head was on the block with this one.

"If one of you is killed, or God forbid, loses a weapon and then it's found in that time reality, it will not create the disruption that a modern firearm would. You folks will be dressed in period clothing, given currency that is appropriate for the time, and will have a general understanding of the culture and nuances of the period. As we have already discussed at length, we should be able to put you within a few meters of the target. Take your shot, make sure with a second, do your photo and DNA checks and then Evac. Nothing fancy. You don't talk to the locals. You are to have NO, and I repeat NO interaction with the population whatsoever.

This is a deep cover operation to the extreme, guys. I cannot stress enough how important it is that you stay exactly within the mission parameters. Any deviation from the mandates could have catastrophic results to you, your family, and possibly the world if violated. Everyone understand?"

"Yes, sir," replied one of the soldiers. "We all know how important this is. We won't let you down."

"Good," replied Branson turning to leave. "You men will be transported in pairs and will be heading down range in five days. Get ready, gentlemen. This will be the mission of a lifetime."

****

"I have to tell you, man, I am so hungry. When was the last time we ate anyway?" Greg tossed a rock at the trash pile.

425

Greg and Kelly were sitting by a small stream near the railroad tracks. They had moved into a dusty stand of cottonwood trees at dusk hoping to avoid any unwanted attention.

"I think it's been at least eight hours," replied Kelly. "The train is still about an hour off - if it's on time".

"You ever jumped a freight train before?"

Kelly smiled at the memory. "Yeah, I did, once, when I was in college. It's harder than it looks."

"What's hard about it?"

Kelly thought for a moment. "Well, the car ladder rungs are higher than they look, and the train is always moving faster then you think. You've gotta really haul ass to catch it."

The sound of heavy footfalls crunching on gravel could be heard coming down the tracks. Kelly looked up as three men appeared out of the gloom. Kelly nodded as the men stopped. "Evening fellas."

The men formed a small semi circle. "This ain't a social, call pecker-woods. Empty your pockets," announced one of the men.

Kelly stood up. "Hey, listen, guys, we don't want any trouble."

"Too late, shit-for-brains. Do as you're told or I'm gonna cut you from asshole to elbow."

Greg quickly got to his feet. "Hey cool it, guys. We're not bothering anybody. Why don't you just move on down the tracks?"

The dark shape wheezed a drunken laugh. "Listen, boy, I ain't gonna tell you again. Empty them pockets. Now!" he shouted.

Suddenly, Kelly dove into the nearest man, knocking him off his feet with a driving tackle. Greg could count on one hand the number of times in his life he had been in an actual fistfight, but now, spurred on by a massive surge of adrenalin, he found himself rushing at the nearest shadow, swinging and kicking with all his strength.

His fist made contact with the man's neck, slamming him to the gravel with a thud. The third man dove into Greg knocking him off his feet. They both tumbled into the weeds by the stream.

Greg punched, gouged and fought to stay on top of the man as they wrestled in the dark. The man's body odor and heavy whisky breath filled the air as Greg rained down blow after blow. He pounded him long after the man had stopped fighting, releasing every bit of pent up rage, fear and sadness that had filled him.

"That's enough!" shouted Kelly, pulling him off the man. "It's over."

Breathless, Greg fell back into the weeds, still not sure of what had just happened. Kelly knelt beside him in the dark. "Hey, buddy, it's okay, it's okay. They're down. You got em."

Greg struggled to stand but found his legs too weak to support him. "Jesus, what the hell is wrong with me?" he gasped rolling onto his back.

Kelly stepped up the short incline to the tracks to check the other intruder. The only sound was the chirp of crickets in the dark. "Shit," he whispered in the gloom.

Greg got to his feet. "What's the matter?"

"This guy isn't breathing. I think he's dead."

Greg struggled up the incline still shaking and knelt down next to Kelly. "What happened?"

"Looks like he hit the back of his head on the rail when I took him down," replied Kelly. "Are you hurt? You get stabbed or anything?"

Greg wiped the sweat out of his eyes. "No, No I'm good. You sure he's dead?"

"Yeah, he's dead. There's brain matter on the ground. Looks like the rail split his head wide open." He stood up and walked over to the man Greg had been fighting.

Exhausted, Greg sat back on the gravel. "Good God, we're changing things every minute. There's no telling what this destroys in the future."

"Yeah," Kelly agreed from the dark. "I have some more bad news. I don't think this guy is breathing either."

Before Greg could answer, he heard a freight train whistle in the distance. "We got to get out of here, Greg."

"What about these guys?" asked Greg getting to his feet.

Kelly was already moving down the track. "C'mon, the woods are full of guys. We gotta move!"

Stumbling through the gloom, Greg was suddenly aware of dark shapes moving and running through the brush the same direction.

"C'mon! We gotta catch that train before it picks up speed!" shouted Kelly from the darkness. Greg was now running full-out, desperately trying to keep his footing in the loose gravel.

The whistle sounded again, this time much closer. There were now at least twenty men moving through the dark, many carrying knap sacks and bedrolls.

The train was now in sight, picking up speed. An air of desperation filled the air as the train thundered closer. Greg caught up with Kelly, and they stepped off to the side of the tracks as the engine rolled by. "Run!" shouted Kelly. "Catch the first car." Sprinting across the gravel, Greg could see the metal rungs of the boxcar ladder.

Kelly was right, the train was moving much faster than it looked and the first rung was at least shoulder height. With his last bit of strength, he jumped and caught the second rung. Hanging by his arms for what seemed like an eternity, he was finally able to pull his feet up to stand on the ladder.

"C'mon up!" shouted Kelly from atop the car. "We made it."

Greg crawled up the last three rungs and was helped to the roof, totally spent. "Jesus, that was a bitch," he gasped.

Kelly sat down beside him, their legs hanging over the side. The night air heated by the train's huff of smoke only added to the perspiration that had soaked through the men's shirts. The train sounded a long mournful wail. "God, what a night!" he whispered, looking up into the sky. "What a night!"

As he watched the muted amber lights of Waxahachie fade in the distance, Greg knew that out there in the dark, people were living lives. They were dreaming, planning, and putting everything they had into just being alive.

He was here, breathing in the air of 1933, covered in the grime, dust and blood of his new reality. He had never been more tired, hungry or exhilarated than he was at this moment. As he lay back watching the stars, he let the heavy, steady thump of the train movement roll him into a deep state of relaxation. The adrenalin of the fight and the run to catch the train was wearing off, leaving behind the hard memory and a stark realization of what a man will do to survive.

The Greg Gander he was this morning was not the same Greg Gander he was tonight. A minute later he was asleep.

Chapter 31

That is an incredible story," replied Taylor. "And you say you just walked into the anomaly and ended up here?"

They had talked through the night, Dillon describing Deer Lodge and his deadly run-in with the Dugans and Taylor relating his futile attempts to change the course of history at the Little Big Horn.

"Yep, and I have to tell you, it was a pretty hair-raising experience. How's your lip?" questioned Dillon as he knelt down by the water. They had ended up at the river just as the sun rose. Several other soldiers were cleaning up near by.

Taylor gently dabbed the wound as he looked at his reflection in the water. "Looks worse than it is. You know, you took a big chance walking into the anomaly like that. It was a million to one shot that you'd end up here."

"I know, but I had to take a chance. I miss my family, Doc. I just want to get home."

"And you said you threw a shovel into the anomaly?"

"Sure did. Thought I could send a message. Pretty foolish, huh?"

Taylor smiled. "Not foolish at all, Dillon. I can only imagine how much you miss your family."

Even though it was only early morning, the temperature was already in the eighties. Dillon sat down on the river rock and pulled his boots off. He slid his feet into the cool water to soak. "There's something else I wanted to ask you?"

Taylor sat down beside him. "What's on your mind?"

Dillon thought for a moment, trying to put the dramatic emotional changes he had been going through into words.

"Ah, I really don't know where to start. It's just that, since I've been here, I have noticed some real changes on how I react to things and people in general."

"I've noticed," snickered Taylor, dabbing his lip with the wet cloth.

"Yeah, I know. That's kind of what I'm getting to. In three months time I have killed four men. I was never even in a fistfight before all of this. I don't know what that change means."

"I've noticed the emotional differences in myself as well. My aggression levels are way up. I've also noticed physical changes - dramatic weight loss, accelerated hair growth, things like that. Pretty amazing actually."

Dillon nodded. "I guess you could say that. My question is: If we ever get back, will this emotional state continue?"

Before Taylor could answer, Captain Weir stepped down the riverbank to where the men were sitting. "Morning, Sheriff, Mister Taylor. General Miles wants to see both of you."

"Morning, Captain," replied Dillon. "You going to be able to attend the meeting?"

Weir smiled. "Wouldn't miss it. Gotta feeling there's more to you two fellas than meets the eye. C'mon, the General's waiting."

****

Branson was impressed by how well the procurement people had done in providing authentic clothing to the men who now stood milling around the lab. The first two prepared to jump were dressed as if they had just stepped out of the 1870's.

Each had been armed and had been given currency of the period. They were each carrying the small return device activator along with a tiny digital camera and blood sample kit. Over the last four days the men had spent hours at the range becoming extremely proficient with the weapons they were to use. Branson sat down next to Crase, the lead scientist in the laboratory. "Are the coordinates still valid?" he asked, checking the computer screen.

Crase adjusted his glasses and then punched in more data before answering. "Well, according to the resonance pattern, I would say they are holding. You do understand that we are breaking new ground here."

Branson sat back in his chair. "I understand perfectly, Professor Crase. Everything we do here now is breaking new ground. Are you having second thoughts about your abilities to make this operation a success?"

Crase shook his head, not willing to start sparring with Branson. In his mind the intelligence officer was overly confrontational, seeming to look for a fight at every turn. Over the last week there had been several heated arguments concerning time lines and procedures. Crase had had a first hand look at how volatile Branson could be.

"No, I just want everyone to be aware of the fact that this is extremely dangerous and that we cannot be overly cautious."

"You let me worry about the dangers, Professor. You just make sure this project works. That should be your main focus."

It was a snarky comment and one that hit Crase wrong. "You know, Mister Branson, I have been doing this kind of high-end work for many years, and I don't like the tone that seems to be getting increasingly hostile. This is the greatest discovery ever made and extraordinary precautions need to be taken. I just don't want us to lose sight of that."

Branson locked a hard stare on Crase. "You know, Professor, when we talked the first time at MIT, I thought I made myself clear as to who was responsible for all the decisions that were going to be made here. Did I not?"

"What you did was threaten my life."

Branson leaned in close. "I'm only going to say this one more time, Crase. Just do your job and make this happen. You need to look around this room. Take a good look. Right now, there are ten other scientists in here just like you. I have my pick of the litter. If you become an obstacle or an impediment to this project, your life will change and not for the better. Do we understand each other?"

Crase nodded weakly, shaken by the exchange. "Yes, yes, I understand."

"Good," replied Branson standing. "I want the first team to jump within the hour. Get it done, Professor."

****

General Miles along with two of his aides were already seated just outside the command tent as Taylor, Dillon, and Captain Weir walked up. A gust of wind blew in, moving the tent flaps like flags. When it cleared, the General stood up, brushing the alkali from his sleeves. "This infernal dust, it's enough to drive one insane. Good morning, Mister Taylor, Sheriff. Have a seat. I think we have some things to discuss."

Taylor pulled up one of the camp chairs as did the others. Taylor could sense that the General was in no mood for small talk. This meeting had all the trappings of a formal inquiry.

"Mister Taylor," announced the General, "I had no idea that you are a wanted man. Would you care to explain yourself?"

Taylor had been somewhat amused when Dillon informed him that he had told Captain Weir that he was wanted. Now, the accusatory tone in General Miles voice was downright unnerving.

"Ah, General, I'm not really wanted, per say. I really think we need to get some context as to what is really going on here."

"Really?" replied the General. "Then how do you explain the Sheriff's statements that you are wanted out of Omaha, Nebraska? I would be very careful with my words if I were you, sir."

Dillon could see where this was going and spoke up. "General, I think there has been a misunderstanding. Doctor Taylor is not from, well, I don't know how to put this without sounding crazy, but he is not from this time....and neither am I."

The General shook his head, his expression flat. "Gentlemen, if I do not get some believable answers to my questions, I can assure you that the consequences will be severe. In these territories, I am authorized to hang malcontents at my discretion."

Before Dillon could answer, a sudden blast of icy wind struck him in the back, a sensation he instantly recognized. He turned just in time to see a blinding bright light, followed by a figure of a man tumbling upside down in the air. The man slammed into the dirt with a thud, knocking Weir off his feet in a cloud of Alkali dust.

General Miles was now on his feet, moving backwards, as his aides instantly drew their revolvers. Dillon sat transfixed, watching the intruder through the dust rolling onto his side and then onto his knees.

The man dressed in period clothing and holding a large handgun quickly wiped the dust from his eyes and focused his stare on Dillon. "Are you Agent Dillon Conroy or Bruce Taylor?" he shouted, still on his knees. Even though he was a good twenty feet away, Dillon could see the silver grey bullets in the pistol's cylinder pointed in his direction.

Dillon stumbled backward trying to get out of his chair and draw his weapon as several thunderous gunshots went off from several directions close by. The attacker's head was instantly blown apart as three, forty-five caliber rounds crashed in. The lifeless body pirouetted over backwards landing in a tangle of legs and arms.

"Jesus Christ!" shouted Taylor, still trying to comprehend what he had just witnessed.

Dillon, with weapon now drawn, slowly walked up to the corpse, stunned by the ferocity and speed of the shooting. The General's aides walked beside him, their own weapons cocked and at the ready. "You okay, Sheriff?" asked one of the officers, kicking the foot of the body. Dillon was jolted by the sound as the officer fired another round into the chest of the dead man. "Goddamn," he announced. "Ain't ever seen the like! That son-of-a-bitch just jumped right out of the sky."

Dillon, aware of armed soldiers moving all around him, stared at the body as Taylor walked up.

437

"He was going to shoot you, Dillon," announced Taylor, still in shock. "I, I can't believe how fast they reacted. That was incredible."

Dillon cautiously knelt down over the corpse. He slowly went through the man's pockets, found a small leather-bound case, and handed it to Taylor. He then noticed the thin dark green 550-parachute cord around the man's neck. With trembling hands, he gently pulled the cord out of the man's bloody shirt, discovering something that literally made his heart skip a beat. On the end was a small white plastic box, a box no bigger then a cell phone.

Taylor knelt down beside him. "My God, is that what I think it is?" he whispered. Dillon handed him the device and picked up the dead man's pistol. "He wasn't sent here to take us home, Doc. He was sent here to kill us."

General Miles walked up, visibly shaken. "I ah, I am not sure what I just witnessed. But I am now more inclined to believe that you two men are involved with something extraordinary. I cannot risk the men in my charge so I request that you leave this compound this afternoon."

Taylor nodded. "I understand, General."

"I'm glad you do, Mister Taylor, because I certainly do not. Captain Weir, see to it that these men have enough provisions for a week and then escort them out of the compound. Is that clear?"

"Yes, sir" replied Weir dusting off his uniform. "Sir, what about the body?"

Miles took a deep breath. "Get a burial detail together, Captain." He turned to Dillon, his anger clearly visible, "That will be the end of my courtesies, Sheriff. Do we have an understanding?"

"Yes, sir. We'll be leaving right away."

The General walked away, followed by his aides, still shaken by what he had seen.

"Captain, I'm really sorry for all this. It's just that… it's very hard to explain," announced Taylor.

"Well, Mister Taylor, I think the General has pretty much done all the explaining that needs to be done. We need to do as he says. I think there's a limit to his patience."

An hour later Dillon and Taylor were mounted up and heading out of Fort Kehoe. Both men knew that the situation had now changed. Whoever was currently in charge of the *process* had decided that anyone not under their control was a risk, a liability that needed to be dealt with. Even more troubling, if they had sent one assassin, they were capable of sending more. Next time, they would not have the protection of experienced soldiers who were used to taking quick lethal action. Next time, it would be different, much different.

****

By sunrise, the train had stopped in the grimy spur yard on the north side of Dallas. Here, in this massive train yard, the Texas line met the Union Pacific run, a twenty-three-hundred mile steel highway that stretched all the way to Los Angeles.

Once in the yard, Greg and Kelly had managed to avoid the Railroad Agents, uniformed armed thugs who worked for the railroad, whose sole purpose was to keep people from riding the freight trains by any means necessary. They were a tough, no-quarter bunch that was rumored to deliver a vicious beating at the slightest provocation. Many a man on his quest for work had been discovered in the yard and beaten nearly to death.

Later that morning, as Greg and Kelly made their way through the massive switchyard, they spotted the west-bound, 50-car Union Pacific Limited coming onto the main spur from the terminal loaded with coal and cotton and moving less then five miles an hour. The decision to go west seemed to be made. Picking fruit in the warm California sun was a lot better than freezing to death during an east coast winter.

For Greg, taking this train was like going home. He had done his undergrad work at Stanford and had made his home and met Carol in Montana, all three significant life changing moments happening west of Texas.

For Kelly, leaving Texas was bittersweet. He had family, real family back in Waxahachie. He knew, like Greg, he simply could not risk meeting any of his relatives, and California was just about as far away as he could get.

Waiting for their chance to catch the freight train, they had positioned themselves on a low-water refueling bridge that spanned the main line. Knowing that it would be incredibly dangerous jumping a freight train in the daylight, Greg and Kelly had been lying down out of sight for hours as rail agents walked by below throughout the day.

A hundred yards away, the westbound freight slowly rolled and thumped its way in their direction. Greg tried to ignore the hollow pain in his stomach from the lack of food as he lay feeling the growing vibration through the steel of the approaching train. It had been over a day and a half since they had eaten anything. Kelly, who was on his belly facing him, looked up and smiled. "Hell of an adventure, huh?"

"How far a drop do you think it is to the top of the car?" questioned Greg nervously.

Kelly tried looking through the board cracks to the track below. "Can't tell from here, but I would guess about three to four feet. Shouldn't be too much of a drop."

Greg looked down between the cracks, smelling the grease and soot of the thick wood planks. The smell of the hot metal and creosote of the train yard, the way the gravel felt under his feet, the voices of men doing their jobs at a distance were all signs of a transcendent life. These things that he felt, smelled, and touched were not present for his benefit or entertainment. They were happening and existing because they were real. These things would be taking place whether he was here or not. Life, in all it's wonderful routine, continued on its own time.

The engine was now passing under the bridge, its sound deafening from where they lay. Kelly tapped Greg on the arm. "Let's go!" he shouted, getting to his knees. He stood up and then quickly hopped over the rail, landing squarely on top of the boxcar three feet below. Greg did the same landing several yards down on the same car. They both lay facing each other, pleasantly surprised at how easy the effort had been. The train was now picking up speed and within minutes was moving at least thirty-five to forty miles-per-hour. Greg sat up, letting the warm breeze blow through his hair. Kelly crawled on his hands and knees to where Greg was sitting. "Next stop – California, my friend!" he shouted above the noise.

Greg smiled. "How long do you think this trip will take?"

Kelly positioned himself beside him. "I would guess about a week. Depends on how many places we have to stop. I think we're going to be dodging Railroad Agents the whole way."

Content to let the subject of thuggish Railroad Agents die, Greg decided to just sit in the warm sun and let the rhythmic rocking of the train drain the fear and fatigue away, at least for a few hours. He was hungry, thirsty and filthy, yet oddly, he felt at peace about where he was and what he was doing. Traveling felt right. Not that he was running away but that he was heading to a place he needed to be.

Greg didn't consider himself a religious man, but over the last thirty-six hours he had whispered more silent prayers then he had his entire life. He realized that faith in a higher power was all he had. He drew comfort from the belief that a benevolent God was watching over all of this, cheering him on - smoothing the way. It may have been naive, but it was a solid emotional ledge to stand on.

The adventure had stripped him of his title, his possessions, and the identity he had lived for years. In modern reality, he was a man of letters and achievement. He owned things that insulated him from the harshness of life. He had a home, clean sheets, food in the pantry and two cars parked in his garage. He owned ten pairs of shoes, carried credit cards that gave him the freedom to always buy, eat and travel whatever and wherever he wanted. Now, at this moment, at this time, he was just another down-on-his-luck dustbowl survivor with dirt under his fingernails sitting on top of a boxcar headed west.

As Greg watched the sundried countryside roll by, he knew he had been given a great gift - the gift of self-discovery, a chance to see what kind of man he really was, a test of the spirit and body. He had changed.

In the coming days, Greg would feel the very full weight and emotional cost of that change. Fate was playing its part - the cosmic wheels of circumstance were turning.

443

Chapter 32

"Okay, Mister Chalks, I think we're gonna have to fight our way out of this." Smith knelt down in the small clearing loading his rifle. They had been running through the thick woods and rain for an hour. "We don't have much time. Here." Smith handed Chalks a flintlock pistol. "I figure there's about four, maybe five. She's already primed. You just got to cock it."

Chalks peeled off his Hazmat suit. "Are these the people chasing us? Why are they doing this? What's going on?"

Smith reached up and pulled Chalks down to his knees. "Listen, Mister, these are Ojibwa raiders, and they're gonna be rid'in in on us any minute. Keep your head down and shoot low." Smith smiled, extending his hand. "Been nice meeting you, sir. I'll see ya on the other side if this gets thick."

Instinctively, Chalks pulled his Glock nineteen from his holster, handing back the Flintlock. "I don't need this."

The first shot buzzed by Chalk's ear, the war painted attacker materializing out of the thick underbrush twenty yards away. To Chalks, a veteran of extensive close quarter combat and countless hours of range and kill-house shooting, engaging multiple assailants was well within his ability.

He crouched and fired two quick rounds center mass, dropping the raider where he stood. From his left, three more attackers burst from the underbrush on a dead run. Smith fired his rifle, knocking one of the men off his feet ten yards away. Chalks stood his ground and fired four shoots in quick succession, killing the remaining two, their bodies spinning to the wet ground. As Smith was still reloading his rifle, Chalks calmly walked over to the freshly dead and fired a bullet into each of their heads. He did a quick reload and then holstered his pistol, consciously slowing his breathing and the adrenalin now blasting through his system. He had reacted as he was trained - simple, yet deadly mechanics -nothing more.

Smith stood totally stunned by what he had just seen. "Good God almighty!" he shouted walking up to Chalks. "That was the damnedest thing I ever seen. You got three of them bucks, and I only shot once. I never saw the like!"

He walked past Chalks while drawing a large skinning knife from his belt. "Let me take care of this and then you need to let me see that fancy gun of yours." As if he had done it a thousand times, he bent down to each man, grabbed the topknot and, with almost surgical precision, sliced the hair and top layer of skin off the head.

He tucked the bloody scalps into a small leather bag he wore on his belt. "Them Hudson Bay folks pay hard coin for Ojibwa hair," he announced, wiping his knife and bloody hands on his leather leggings. "Fella once told me that Europe is wall-papered with Indian hairpieces. Can't see the draw myself, but if them Dutchmen are pay'n, I'll damn sure take-em."

As the rain began to fall with renewed intensity, Smith walked up and handed Chalks the bag. "You pick the three you want out of there. It's only right, since you were the one that sent these devils where they belong."

Chalks handed the bag back repulsed by what he was touching. "Naw, that's all right. You keep em. I'm not much for that kind of thing. Here, go ahead, take them all."

"Much obliged, Jason, mighty Christian of ya." Smith took the bag. "We better keep moving. This ruckus is bound to get someone's attention although watching you fight gives me a whole lot less to worry about."

Chalks picked up his Hazmat suit and rolled it into a manageable ball. "Jedediah, is there some place we can get out of this rain? I'm about to freeze to death," he asked, trying to control his shivers.

The trapper smiled and pointed. "We're heading east to the river. Gotta canoe hid down in the brambles about a mile from here. If we don't get tangled up with anymore of them malcontents, we should be to my dug-out by dark."

Chalks nodded, the rain dripping off his chin. "Sounds good. Lead the way before I drown." Smith laughed and then set off on a blistering pace through the woods.

To Chalks, it felt good to be moving. He always had felt better when he was involved in something physical. It allowed him to clear his mind and focus on whatever problem he was facing. As he trotted close behind Smith, it was staggering to think that he was actually in the 1830's. *Why here, why now?* Catching his second wind, he jumped over a large log, ducked under a canopy of rain soaked tree limbs, amazed at how fast and nimble Smith moved through the thick woods - effortless and as quiet as smoke.

Chalks thought back to his Ranger days at Fort Stewart, Georgia, runnin and gunnin with the 1st/75th Ranger Battalion as a young E-6 a lifetime ago - the *Carter years*, a bad time for the country and even worse for the military. There had been no mission, no direction. Vietnam was over, the dead and walking wounded had been brought home, and the bloody Middle East conflicts were not even on the horizon.

The only thing the newly formed Ranger battalion did was run field-training exercises, (FTXs) against the 82nd Airborne Division in and around Fort Bragg during miserable four and five day war games with rifle-fouling blanks and artillery simulators. It had been a lot of sleeping in the rain and freezing at night for no other reason than "to keep the troops occupied".

He had breezed through Basic, AIT, Airborne and Ranger school, always in the top five percent. Three months later he landed a much sought after slot in Sniper school at Benning, which he aced as top shooter of his graduating class. Jump Master, Path Finder training soon followed, along with JOTC in Panama, which gave him a lot of hard core patches on his fatigue shirt but left him without the one thing he really wanted – combat – the knowledge of what it was really like to go to war.

He was planning to leave the service after his second enlistment, tired of all the senseless road marches and peacetime Army crap that was the norm. With no family to go home to (whatever that meant), the future looked bleak. The idea of heading back to the San Joaquin Valley, finding a factory job, and then living out the rest of his life in quiet desperation had terrified him.

Salvation had come in a chance meeting at the annual Quantico FBI shooting competition in Virginia. The Army and Marines always sent their best for this yearly event. Chalks had been chosen to represent the newly formed Ranger Battalion. By the end of the competition, Chalks had shot a "Possible" – a perfect score of 300, a feat only accomplished three times in the fifteen-year history of the competition. Just before heading back to Stewart, he was approached by a "Recruiter" who gave him the opportunity of a lifetime. Come to work for the CIA, the dark side, and he would get all the real world trigger time he could handle.

For Chalks it had been a perfect fit. Five months later he was discharged and picked up a one-way ticket to the Farm. He had weapons training, explosives training, close quarter combat that became so automatic that he could do them in his sleep. He had escape and evasion training or more commonly called SERE school -everything that would make him the precision instrument for killing that he was now. Nine years of dark side, wet work from Columbia to the Balkans gave him the credentials he needed to catch the eye of the Kingdom. He was their rising star, and now as far as they were concerned, he was dead.

Chalks saw the river come into view as he followed Smith on a trot through the last stand of trees and underbrush. The rain had stopped, leaving him soaked to the skin. "Over here!" shouted Smith, dragging a canoe from the river reeds. "Grab one of them paddles. We're losing the light."

They pushed off and after several deep strokes felt the strong current pull them into the middle of the river. Even though he was chilled to the bone, Chalks felt an unexpected calm wash over him as the brilliant green landscape silently glided by on both sides of the river.

To the west, just off the horizon, golden shafts of sunlight beamed from the cloud cover, coloring the treetops and the water a reddish golden light. As Chalks moved the paddle through the crystal clear waters, he thought to himself, if he was truly lost in the deep folds of time, there were worst places to be-much worse. For the first time that day, he smiled. "Amazing," he whispered.

****

The first thing he noticed was the smell of the sheets, that commercial yet familiar clean smell of institutional washing products. The room itself appeared to be a standard hospital recovery room, a muted seascape painting hanging on pastel colored walls, a single metal chair positioned beside the bed.

Clark had no idea how long he had been unconscious. The last bout of interrogation had been brutal; the electric shocks had been non-stop, along with the water treatment and carefully controlled word association drills. The last thing he remembered, just before his world went black, was the pain of an injection in his neck.

For five days he had been kept in a small concrete cell, the temperature set at a very uncomfortable 50 degrees. He had been wet all the time, dressed only in a set of black military fatigues without shoes or socks. Every eight to ten hours of the day or night he had been pulled from his cell, wrestled into restraints, and tortured and interrogated. Now, after five days of hell, he was lying comfortably in a hospital gown under clean sheets, having no memory of how he got there.

Thirsty, he rolled his tongue across his teeth, suddenly feeling the small, stiff thread of stitches in his upper lip. He had received medical treatment and had no recollection of being treated.

An older man, one Clark had never seen before, entered the room wearing a stethoscope around his neck. He sat down in the chair and started writing on his clipboard, "How are you feeling, Agent Clark?" he asked, not looking up as he wrote.

450

Clark pulled himself up on one elbow, "Who are you?"

The man reached for Clark's wrist, checking his pulse. "I am Doctor Smith, and I'm the one who is in charge of your care."

Clark laid back. "Is this some test, some trick?"

Smith smiled. "No trick, no test," he replied writing down more notes. "I'll check on you later. Make sure you eat." He left the room just as quickly as he had come, leaving behind more questions than answers.

Moments later, a different man came into the room. He was younger, dressed in a dark suit and tie. He nodded, "Good morning, Agent." Instantly, a bolt of fear shot through Clark as he recognized the voice of his interrogator. The man pulled up the chair and sat down. "Are you comfortable? Have you eaten breakfast yet?"

Clark was shocked by the man's nonchalant manner. "What's going on? Is this some kind of trick?"

The man smiled. "This is no trick. Anyway, our time together is finished. I am sure we have gotten our point across."

"And what point is that?"

"Well, let's see. How do you feel when I bring up the word *Anomaly*?"

Instantly Clark felt a twinge of panic and nausea roll through his body.

The man patted Clark on the arm. "Ah, very good, Agent. I can see by your reactions that our time together was well spent. I think you now understand that what you encountered in Shady Brook is something we do not, and I repeat, do not want investigated. Do you understand?"

Clark nodded, fighting back the urge to vomit.

"Good, you also need to be aware of the fact that everything that was accomplished with you this week was implemented with your organization's approval."

"What does that mean?" whispered Clark.

"What that means, Agent, is that the FBI wants the same thing we want - your total cooperation in this matter. You will be kept here for a few days to rest and recuperate, and then you will be released to continue your career and your life, forgetting about all this nasty business."

"What about Carol Gander?"

"Oh, she's fine. I'm getting ready to go see her now. She should be discharged today and back home in Montana tomorrow."

"Did she go through what..what I did?" questioned Clark.

The man smiled, "Of course. She only had to go through three days but she made it. She is now on the same page as everyone else."

"What about her husband?"

"You mean Greg Gander?" The instant he said the name Clark felt panic and a gripping tightness in his chest.

"Now, see, you've gone and stirred yourself up again," announced the man softly. "You have to remember that certain people and certain subjects are going to cause you great distress. You need to avoid these things, do you understand?"

Clark nodded, fighting back the tears. They were not tears of sadness or remorse but tears of rage at not being able to control his emotions. They had done something to him, something that had reached the dark places of his heart.

"When can I leave here?"

The man stood up to go. "In a few days. You lost a bit of weight, and we need your lip to heal before you're discharged. For now, all you need to do is eat, rest and heal up. Then you can have your life back."

Clark slowly sat up. "Can I ask you a question?"

"Sure."

"Is this normal? I mean, is this your job?" questioned Clark. There was no malice in his tone, only curiosity.

The man thought for a moment. "I think what you're really asking is - are you the first person to go through what you have been subjected to. Am I correct?"

"Yes, that's what I am asking."

453

"Well, what I can tell you, Agent Clark, is that the kind of treatment you received is done every day and has been for well over forty years. You need to look at this last week as a great gift. Your superiors felt that you were worth keeping alive. The alternative was a quick death. So you see, this really was your lucky week."

Clark was stunned by the man's admission. "So you're saying this is something that is normal and has been going on for a long time?"

The man smiled. "Absolutely. As a matter of fact, we have a member of the NSA that starts his five day "correction" around noon today."

"Jesus," whispered Clark, trying to absorb the information.

"Well, He really doesn't have much to do with this kind of business. But I do want you to remember two things. First, you will be watched very carefully from now on. Secondly, if we have any problems with your behavior, you will be eliminated. You would never see it coming. This was your only stay-out-of-the-grave card, and it's been played. Are we clear?"

Clark nodded before he could stop it. "Yes, it's clear."

"Very good, Mister Clark. Oh look, your breakfast is here. Smells wonderful."

Chapter 33

Just as Dillon and Taylor were about to leave the fort, Captain Weir approached. "Fellas, I have to say your company was anything but boring."

"Thank you for the saddle," Dillon stated, indicating the saddle on Taylor's mount.

"I felt you should have it for all your help with the burial detail." He reached to shake hands with Dillon. "Sheriff, I hope you find whatever you're looking for."

"Captain, it's been my honor to meet you. I can't thank you enough for your help. Oh, tell Virgil, no hard feelings," he said pointing to the wound on his forehead. "I know he was feeling bad about that."

Weir laughed. "I'll be sure and let him know." He extended his hand to Taylor. "Mister Taylor, I wish you well."

"Thank you, sir. It's been my pleasure." Taylor hesitated and added, "Captain, in the future, you are remembered as a brave and loyal officer. I think you must already be aware of the impression you are having on history."

"I do my best." He handed Taylor a small leather bag. "Dillon told me you have a special interest in General Custer. We salvaged a few things from the battlefield. I want you to have these." He dropped two buttons into his palm. "These came from the General's shirt."

455

Taylor didn't know what to say. "I ,I can't take these."

Weir stepped closer to Taylor's horse. "No, Mister Taylor, I really want you to have them. I don't know why, but I think you are more deeply involved with the General and how he met his end than anybody here."

Taylor tucked the pouch into his shirt pocket. "I will treasure them, Captain."

Weir smiled. "Well, I think it's time you gentlemen started your journey. We don't want to upset the General anymore than he already has been."

Taylor thought for a moment, looking over at Dillon and then Weir. "You know, Captain, you could come with us."

Weir grinned. "It's a tempting offer, Mister Taylor, but I really don't think I'd fit in the future."

Taylor laughed. "So, you're a believer now?"

"Well, I'm not really sure what I believe. But I have seen some things that I cannot explain. As someone with a rather practical viewpoint of the world, I recognize that maybe there are things out there that I just don't need to know."

"Fair enough, Captain," replied Taylor nudging his horse forward. "Fair enough."

As they rode out of the fort, Taylor fell into a deep melancholy. Sometimes it was hard to know the future.

"You okay, Doc? Thought you would be happy about the very real possibility they we can get back to where we belong."

"I am very happy about that," replied Taylor. "It's just that I know what's in store for the Captain."

"What, what happens?"

Taylor adjusted his seat in the saddle. "Well, for starters, he'll die in less then six months. That's' why I asked him if he wanted to go with us."

"I was wondering why you did that. What happens? How does he die?"

"Well, history records that he suffers from something like Post Traumatic Stress Syndrome following the battle. He starts drinking and dies before the end of the year."

"My God," whispered Dillon. "What do you think would have happened if he had agreed to come with us? Would it have saved him? Wouldn't that change the future?"

"To answer your question, I'm seeing a pattern," he sighed. "Despite my best, if not clumsy efforts, I have been unable to change the course of things. I doubt that however persuasive our argument, the good Captain wouldn't have stayed right where he is."

"That's pretty amazing," replied Dillon. "How is it that things are still happening the way they did despite all of the things we have done that should have changed them?"

Taylor had been thinking about this ever since his first jump. "I really don't have an answer. But I know *this* is real. The sky is blue. The dusty ground we are now riding over is solid, and I'm sweating through my shirt from the heat. We just talked with someone who is written about in history books. So *this* is as real as our reality."

They rode in silence, each man deep in thought, putting distance between the fort and their future.

Dillon turned in his saddle. "Well, how far away do you want to be from the compound before we try to activate the jump?"

Taylor thought for a moment, overwhelmed by the thought. "I really think we need to get a few more miles away and then make camp. I think we need to come up with a strategy concerning the return."

"I agree," replied Dillon. "I think we need to sit down and really plan how we want to do this. It looks like our situation has gotten a lot more complicated."

"Complicated, you could say that."

****

Crase slowly scrolled through the electron scan checking for any carbon-based molecular residue that would indicate that a person had passed through the continuum. "I don't understand. I am still getting the same readings as we had when we sent him through, but nothing is coming up about his return."

"How can we be sure he went through?" Branson asked, checking the data himself.

Crase put on the reading glasses he kept on a chain around his neck. "If you look here on this spectral graph, you'll see the natural energy flux that is being put out from the process." He punched in the hard-drive playback of the jump. "Now, if you look carefully, you can see the variance change when our man goes through. It is really quite remarkable."

Branson leaned close to the screen. "So those tiny blue lines indicate that a human being went through the continuum?"

"That's correct, and what's really fascinating about Doctor Taylor's process is that we can now see that carbon-based life, particularly humans, resonate a measurable energy signature, a signature that is compatible with a particular environment."

Branson sat back in his chair. "I'm not sure I'm following you."

"Well, what we are beginning to see is that people in this current reality emit a certain frequency, if you will, that is in harmony with the current environment. It's measurable, and it is a constant. What we see on the energy fields from hyperspace, which is essentially the past, is a different set of baseline energy readings."

"Okay, I think I'm following."

"When a different entity is introduced into the hyperspace continuum, a different energy signature is picked up, and it can be seen on this graph here. In a nutshell, we are seeing that we resonate and match the energy environment that we live in. We are in harmony with our current space."

459

Branson nodded. "Okay, I think I'm on the same page. So what you're saying is that this current time, our time, has a certain energy level, a level that is in harmony with living things that are currently on the planet. In the past the levels were different.. Is that what you're saying?"

"Correct. Doctor Taylor figured out a way to measure and quantify the difference. It is a stunning discovery."

"So what does that mean as far as the process?" questioned Branson.

"It means that as long as we monitor the relevant energy readings of hyperspace, we can see when a carbon-based life-form, a human being, is introduced into that reality. It's like looking at a heat signature on an infrared camera. The energy readings will look completely different than the surrounding area. This is how we are able to put our people within meters of our target."

"Incredible."

"Which is why I think we have a problem," replied Crase taking off his glasses.

"What's the problem?"

As of about two hours ago, we are not picking up anymore readings from our guy who went through."

"What does that mean?"

"It means that he is not putting out any life resonance energy. Most likely he is dead."

Branson thought for a moment. "Okay, here is what I want done. Complete the scan on the same area and send in the second team member."

"You do realize that we may be sending these men into certain death."

"I understand perfectly, Professor. I can send people down range all day. Finish the scan. Find out where the targets are, and get our man in the pipe. What about Gander, Baker and Kelly?"

Crase checked his laptop. "Ah, according to the presets, we have a pretty close calculation that they landed somewhere in the 1930's. It's extraordinary when you think about it."

"Have you been able to run down a location?"

"Not yet. We have been putting all of our efforts into the Doctor Taylor jump."

Branson sighed deeply. The fatigue was starting to set in. "All right, send the second team member after Taylor, and then shift everything to finding Gander and the others. I want this wrapped up as soon as possible."

****

By nightfall, it was cool enough outside to be uncomfortable riding on the top of the boxcar. "Let's get inside," shouted Kelly pointing down.

Greg nodded and slowly started crawling on his hands and knees to the ladder rung near the backside of the car. Kelly, feeling a lot more confident with his footing, walked over to the ladder and disappeared over the side.

461

Negotiating the ladder in the dark was one thing. Carefully climbing around the side and jumping into the open doorway was another far more difficult matter. After several hair-raising minutes, they were both able to climb down and jump into the empty car. Greg was surprised at how much warmer it was inside. "Man, it's dark in here," announced Kelly. "I can't see a thing."

"At least it's warmer than outside," Greg said, noticing that the floor was slick with packing straw. As his eyes began to adjust he could see that the car was empty except for large mounds of hay blown into the corners. "Looks like a good spot over there." Greg kicked a large pile of the straw. "I think this is my bed for the night."

Kelly shuffled a second large pile together. "This is mine. Hopefully, there aren't too many bugs in this stuff."

As Greg settled into the straw, he felt the small square plastic return device in his back pocket. It was strange how he had forgotten about it during the day. "Hey, you think I should try the button again?" he asked.

Greg could hear Kelly moving around in his straw pile. "Well, if you do, make sure I'm within arm's reach. I don't want to get left behind. Besides, what makes you think they have turned the process back on?"

"Well, if they did, it should work. It's just a shot."

Kelly thought for a moment, trying to ignore the hunger pangs that were getting worse by the hour. "Hey Greg, what do you think all this means?"

462

"I'm not sure I'm following you."

"Well, I guess what I'm trying to say is, do you think we are supposed to be doing this...you know on a spiritual level?"

Greg was surprised by the question. He had never even thought about the morality of it all. "Ah, gosh, I really never thought about it in that way. You're talking about God and all that, right?"

"Ed got himself killed doing this," replied Kelly softly, "and I'm the one that brought him into this. It's my fault."

"C'mon man, that's not true. Ed wanted to do this just as bad as we did. It's terrible what happened, but it wasn't your fault."

"I still can't believe he's dead."

After an awkward pause, Greg spoke. "How far do you think we've come?" he asked wanting to change the subject. This had been the first time Kelly had brought up the death of his friend, and Greg could hear the heavy grief in his voice.

Kelly cleared his throat, grateful for the darkness of the car. "Well, let's do the math. This train has been moving around forty-five to fifty miles-per-hour for the last eight hours or so. I'd say we've come at least three hundred and fifty to four hundred miles, maybe a bit more."

"So, I would guess we are still in Texas."

"That would be a good guess. Listen, Greg, I really don't think I can go another day without food. If you think it might work, I am all for pushing the button. I really am."

Greg rolled the device around in his hand. "You mean that? You want to try it now? Ed said he had it programmed to take us to Barstow."

In the grey black darkness of the car Greg could see Kelly brushing back his straw pile and getting to his feet. "C'mon brother," he announced extending his hand. "Let's see if we can go home. Barstow sounds pretty good right now."

He pulled Greg to his feet and then held the grip with both hands. "Push that son-of-a-bitch. Let's go."

Two cars back Jake Hall wrapped his blanket tight around his shoulders, trying to keep the cool wind from making him anymore miserable than he already was. From his seat atop the car, he had watched as the two men climbed off the roof and disappeared below. He had been riding freights for a year now and had seen many a man fall off the roof trying to climb down. It was just too dangerous, if not downright crazy, to climb around on a moving train, and those two fools had done it in the dark.

Just as he was about to nod off, he saw a brilliant flash of blue light that lit up the dark landscape on both sides of the boxcar the two had dropped into. The flash only lasted a second, leaving Hall to believe someone had started a fire. *Great,* he thought, *if there was a fire the railroad bulls would be all over it and this long quiet ride to the coast would stop.* Through the darkness he continued to watch for any further signs of fire coming from the car. He sniffed the night air and, not smelling any smoke, began to relax. Whatever had happened down there was none of his business; he had other things to worry about.

****

Crase happened to be sitting at his monitor when the power drain hit, a drain so large that it actually dimmed the lights in the building.

"Good God, what was that?" shouted one of the scientists from the other side of the lab. "Something just buried all the needles."

Branson, who had been on the phone in one of the other offices when the power failure hit, was now running down the hall on his way to the lab. He quickly card-swiped the doors and rushed inside. "What was that? What just happened?"

Crase was furiously typing on his laptop. "Ah, guys, I think we have a problem," he announced still typing.

Branson stepped beside him, "What's going on?"

"Well, from the looks of it, our system was accessed."

465

"Accessed? How? By who?"

Crase looked up. "No idea. But whoever did it, initiated a jump."

"How is that possible? We haven't sent our second guy yet?"

"I didn't say it came from here. I said the system was accessed. Whoever did it made the jump from somewhere else. The return device signal was a bit different then the one we sent with the soldier."

"How is it different?"

Crase checked his computer, "I believe it was engineered at the Shady Brook facility. The pulse resonance is the same they were using there."

"That's got to be the Baker group. Can you tell me where they came through?"

Crase accessed the data on the computer. "Ah, just a second. Okay, here it is -1933. I'm checking the latitude / longitude coordinates now. If these are correct, the flash came from west Texas. God, this process is amazing! Taylor is a genius!"

Branson had always been skeptical of the loyalty of the scientists currently working on the project. They talked about the *Taylor process* with an odd kind of reverence. From past experience, he knew a hint of hero worship could end up negatively affecting the entire operation. That was something that would not be allowed to happen, not on his watch.

"Keep your accolades to yourself, Doc, and get me a Goddamn location where they landed," Branson angrily announced. "This is where you all really start earning your money."

Crase typed in additional data. "I, ah, I'm not sure, but it looks like the west side of the United States, maybe California, maybe Oregon. I, I can't be sure."

Branson was already punching numbers on his phone. "Get me a tighter location, Crase. I want these guys picked up within the hour." He walked away from the table. "Yes, this is Branson. Get a team in the air headed to the west coast right now. I'll send you the coordinates within the hour." He closed his phone. *This was just too easy,* he thought. Although he had to admit he admired the balls of Baker and his group for trying to come back so soon, he had to make sure they were eliminated. *Too bad - he would have liked to hear their stories - too bad indeed.*

Chapter 34

They finally pulled up to the small wooden dock after a solid three-hour trip downriver. Jason had never seen a night so dark. He was chilled to the bone as they walked up the steep slippery riverbank and into the even darker woods. "Slow down, Smith," he hissed. "I can't see a damn thing." The trapper had disappeared in the gloom. Jason stopped, trying to hear any movement, slowly drawing his weapon.

Suddenly, the night was illuminated by the bright orange glow of a torch up ahead. "Up here!" shouted Smith, holding the torch high. "We made it."

Jason could now make out a narrow, well-used path as he followed Smith through the woods. They climbed a short but steep hill, stopping in front of what appeared to be a large thick, wooden door, the kind you would see on an old ship. Set flush into the hillside, it was nearly impossible to notice if you didn't know where to look.

"C'mon in," announced Smith, opening the door wide. "It ain't much, but it's dry."

Smith led the way into a large room which looked like it had been carved out of solid rock. The ceiling was at least twelve to fifteen feet high and the room at least as wide.

Smith stuck the lit torch into a small metal hook on the wall and then closed and bolted the door behind them. "Here, take one of these," he said, handing Jason a candle from a group of candles sitting along the stone floor. "Can't have you break a leg after we've come this far."

"What is this place?" asked Jason touching the candle to the torch.

Smith lit another candle and started walking further into the cave. "From what I've picked up from the locals, there are supposed to be some abandoned Spanish gold mines in these parts. I found this one about a year ago and made it my home," he answered, his voice echoing throughout the hall.

"How far does this go?" Jason held his candle high, amazed by the massive space. The floor was as smooth as glass.

"Not much further," replied Smith turning a slight corner and then walking down several steps.

Smith stopped and began lighting candles along the walls of an even larger room. Jason was stunned by what he saw. The room was at least fifty feet across and fifty feet wide. Several large bear and deerskin rugs covered a flat and level floor. The smell of smoked meat and dried apples filled the air. Log benches sat next to a large fire pit ringed with stones in the center of the room, the pit's embers glowing orange-red in the muted light.

Jason held his candle high, trying to gauge the ceiling height. "How do you keep from smoking yourself out of here with the fire pit?" he asked, still unable to see the true height of the ceiling.

469

Smith tossed a handful of kindling into the pit. "The room has a natural draw through the ceiling. There's splits in the rock that work just like a proper chimney. It's God's own handy work."

Jason was surprised at the warmth of the cave and how comfortable he felt sitting on one of the fur-covered log benches near the cooking pit. The kindling quickly caught fire, bathing the entire room in a soft yellow light.

"Here," announced Smith, handing Jason a plate of dried meat and a large metal mug. "Not the finest fare you'll find, but it's passable. I made the Elderberry wine myself."

He sat down on the other side of the fire and began to eat. Jason sniffed the meat before tasting it. "What kind of game is this?" he asked, taking a small bite.

Smith took a long drink from his mug before answering. "Elk," he replied wiping his mouth with the back of his hand.

Jason was pleasantly surprised at the meat's taste and suddenly realized how hungry he was. He took a sip of the cold wine and found it to be strong but excellent. As he ate, he began to feel the warmth ease back into his body, allowing the aches and fatigue of the log paddle trip to settle in between his shoulder blades.

Tossing the bones from his meal into the fire, Smith got up from his seat and dropped a larger log into the pit. "That will keep the heat up in here most of the night. I have a pallet where I sleep. There's a pretty good pile of Elk hides over there. You're more than welcome to make a bed for yourself."

Jason finished the last of the sweet tasting wine and set his cup on the bench. "Jedediah, I want to thank you for taking me in. You probably saved my life."

Smith laughed. "Well, sir, I doubt that. From what I saw today I would say it was the other way around. I'm much obliged for your help." He lay down close to the fire as the dried wood snapped and popped. "If you don't mind, my friend, I am played out. I don't think I'd be much good at conversation tonight, so I will bid you a goodnight."

"Goodnight, Jedediah." He quietly pulled off his shoes and wet socks and set them on the rocks by the fire. Smith was already snoring as he walked over the cool stone floor to the stack of hides. Expecting to find a heavy gamey smell of dried skin and coarse hair, he was again pleasantly surprised. He made a makeshift bed of the soft hides and lay down pulling one of the heavy furs over him. As he watched the fire shadows on the ceiling, the tension of the day gradually seeped from his body. Within minutes exhaustion dropped him into a deep sleep, a fitting end to an incredible day.

****

The impact onto the hard desert ground was just as violent and rough as it was landing in Texas, if not worse. Greg had tried to hold onto Kelly as they ripped through the darkness only to be separated just before impact. Greg slammed onto his back and tumbled down a shallow ravine. Kelly fell into a huge stand of yucca bushes and then onto the hard-packed desert ground. Both men lay in the dark thirty-feet apart, trying to catch their breath and fighting the nausea of the jump.

"Jesus Christ," moaned Greg slowly moving to his knees.

Kelly rolled over and retched.

"Hey, pard, you all right?" asked Greg getting to his feet.

"Yeah, yeah, I'm fine. Just got the wind knocked out of me." He pushed to his knees. "God, that was a bitch." He looked around trying to clear the cobwebs. "Do you see anything that looks like Barstow?"

Greg walked over and helped Kelly to his feet. "Yeah, I do. Check it out."

Kelly turned around, brushing the sand from his face. "I'll be damned." He started laughing as Greg bent over with the dry heaves, having nothing in his stomach to vomit.

Less that a mile away, in the dark, on the far side of a busy highway, stood the golden arches of a McDonald's.

Greg stood up laughing with relief. "Can you believe Baker! Having the entire freaking universe to pick for a landing, and he picks a McDonald's in Barstow, California?"

They stood in the dark and laughed like fools, both realizing how wonderful it felt to be alive and back. Finally collecting themselves, they wearily started walking.

"What time do you think it is?" asked Greg. The question hit Kelly as outrageously funny. He stopped and bent over in laughter.

"What the hell is so funny?"

Kelly waved him off, trying to catch his breath. "I don't know, Pard. It's just the way you said it."

In the dim light he looked into Greg's slightly confused, disheveled, and dirt-streaked face and burst out laughing again.

This time Greg began laughing but really didn't know why.

"Oh, my God," announced Kelly finally wiping the tears away. "I haven't laughed like that in years."

They continued walking through the dark, still chuckling at the irony of it all.

They crossed the highway and walked into the brightly lit restaurant. Greg caught his reflection in the store's window and, for the first time in days, saw just how dirty they both looked. His face was covered in black soot, apparently from the train yard. His light blue, long-sleeved shirt, now filthy, was torn at the elbows along with both knees of his pants. He looked like he had been crawling around in the desert for days. "Geez," he mumbled looking at his reflection. "I look like a homeless guy."

Kelly tapped him on the arm smiling. "C'mon, tough guy, let's eat. I'm buying."

*****

"You know what I have to do, don't you?" asked Taylor examining the return device they had taken off the assassin.

473

Dillon tossed a log onto the campfire. "I have an idea."

"We have to destroy the process. The attack by that killer has pretty much solidified for me that this was a bad idea and, it needs to be stopped. The human race is not ready for this discovery. I have done the world a great injustice."

"Listen, Doc, I think you're being way too hard on yourself. There's not a person alive that wouldn't want the ability to travel in time."

Taylor thought for a moment, gazing into the fire. " I thought I was accomplishing something," he said softly. "Now I realize that all I did was cause harm."

Dillon prodded the fire with a long stick. "I'm going to make a confession to you, Doc. These last two months have been the most incredible time of my life, and I mean that in a good way. I have learned things about myself that I would have never known if this hadn't happened. Honestly, I would not trade a minute of it for anything. I really wouldn't."

"Well, because it all has really gotten so far out of control, I am going to have to shut it down."

"How can you do that from here? Don't you have to be in the lab?"

Taylor suddenly stood. "My God, I have been so stupid!" He started to pace.

Alarmed by Taylor's sudden shift in mood, Dillon stood looking around. "What's the matter? What's going on?"

"Don't you see? I've been trying to figure out how the assassin was able to find us, to, you know, to be literally dropped in our lap. I've been thinking about it all day."

"I'm not following, Doc."

Taylor tossed the return device to Dillon. "They've been able to fine-tune the resonance in the process and are using that device as a sort of amplifier to hit the spot where they want to go."

"So this is actually a beacon, like a flare?"

Taylor walked back and forth in deep concentration. "The Government must have some of the best people in the world working on this."

"Hey listen, Doc. Are you saying this thing is still putting out a signal, a signal that can be tracked?"

Taylor nodded. "That's exactly what I am saying. I'm surprised another assassin hasn't shown up already."

"So what do we do? Don't we need the device to get home?"

Taylor sat down. "If we use the device, it will take us back to wherever this guy came from, to the people who want us dead."

The idea of another assassin showing up was a jarring thought. "Okay, so what do we do?"

"Toss me that device," replied Taylor. "If I can see what they changed inside, maybe I can modify it."

Dillon tossed the device, feeling very uneasy about Taylor taking it apart in the middle of nowhere, a device that was possibly their only way back.

Taylor carefully snapped the cover off the device and examined the complicated electronics inside under the light of the fire.

"Wow, this is very interesting," he whispered looking closer at the instrument. "They've changed the polarity receptors and put a larger chip in the relay board. Amazing!"

"So what do you think?" asked Dillon cautiously.

Taylor looked up. "This is some really fine work, real craftsmanship, amazing."

"You think you can do anything with it?"

"Well, without tools, it's highly unlikely. But I have an idea that you're probably not going to like," replied Taylor.

"Okay, what's your idea?"

"If we initiate this device, it will probably take us to the new lab, and we will end up in the hands of the very people we want to avoid."

"Agreed," replied Dillon tossing a stick in the fire.

"What I suggest is that, no pun intended by the way, is that we buy ourselves some time."

"How, and how much time?"

Taylor put the cover back on the device.

"C'mon, Doc, tell me your idea. How much time?"

"Maybe a year, maybe more," replied Taylor flatly.

Dillon was stunned. "A year? You have to be kidding? Doc, I want to get back to my family, and you're holding the pathway home."

Taylor stood up and tossed the device back to Dillon. "If you want to leave, then you have my blessing. But you will be returning to certain death. The people who are now running things have decided that you and I are a grave liability and have to be eliminated. You will be dead within hours after you jump."

As much as Dillon wanted to believe otherwise, he knew Taylor was right. They were marked men. "Okay, what's your plan?"

"I have to shut the process down. I'm thinking we need to send something back that does that."

"What could we send back?" questioned Dillon, already suspecting the answer.

"An explosive device, something powerful enough to destroy the lab and the process."

Dillon stirred the fire with a stick, thinking about what Taylor has just proposed. "Won't that also destroy people?"

"Absolutely, probably take the entire building down."

"So, we're talking about killing people, maybe a lot of people? You really think this is the right call, Doc? I mean self-preservation is one thing. Mass murder is another."

"In my estimation, if we don't do something like this, the opportunity for massive abuse of the process could cost millions of lives. I now realize that no one should have the ability to change the past. Inevitably someone could, and that changes the future."

Again, Dillon knew Taylor was right. It was already evident that the government was pushing a very dangerous, if not lethal agenda, and would not stop until every loose end was eliminated. This had turned from an incredible life-changing adventure to a fight for survival. The assassin that showed up had been dressed and armed with period equipment and clothing, a clear attempt to blend in with the population for the sole purpose of hunting down and killing both Taylor and himself.

A message needed to be sent. And if he was honest with himself, the idea of a total stranger being sent to kill him pissed him off, right down to his socks.

"What do you have in mind?" Dillon asked. "Can you make something out of the limited resources we have here?"

"Taylor thought for a moment. "Actually I think I can. I can use a variation of the Sprengal explosive."

"What's the Sprengal Explosive?"

"It's a combination of potassium chlorate and a nitro aromatic. It's fairly simple really, basically a mixture of bleach crystals, kerosene, and pulverized salt."

Dillon shook his head. "I didn't do well in chemistry, Doc. Why don't you just give me the crib notes on what you want to build."

"Okay, Herman Sprengal invented a process to help with a faster, safer detonation in explosive rates in the late 1800s. His vast expertise in chemistry helped develop an explosive called Rackarock, a really effective mixture of nitrobenzene and potassium chlorate."

"You think we can find that stuff here?"

Taylor looked into the evening darkness as fire flies flitted in and out of the tall prairie grass. "Miles City is about a mile away. I know there has to be a hardware store in town. We can pick up what we need there. The only problem we have is how to pay for it."

Dillon smiled. "Got it covered, Doc." He patted his pocket. "Still got my Sheriff wages from Deer Lodge."

"So you really were an employee of the city." Taylor smiled.

"You better believe it. And I earned every penny," Dillon said, looking deep into the fire.

Chapter 35

Clark pulled on his coat and nodded to the two men who were standing by the door watching him dress. "I need my gun," he announced tossing the hospital gown on the bed. After a full week in the room healing up from his harrowing five-days of *training,* he was leaving without a mark on him.

"You'll get your weapon when we get outside," replied the guard. "Let's go." He opened the door of the infirmary, motioning for Clark to follow. Without further conversation, Clark followed the man down the long hallway and out into the early morning sunshine. It had been two weeks since he had seen the sky. Clark saw his interrogator leaning on the side of his car in the small parking lot.

"Good morning, Agent" he announced cheerfully as Clark walked up. "You look well." He pulled Clark's duty weapon and holster from his overcoat pocket. "I believe this is yours."

Clark took the weapon. "So, I am free to leave. I'm done?"

The interrogator smiled. "Of course. You have your life back, Mister Clark. Go out and save the world."

Clark thought for a moment, trying to get a handle on the moment. The man that had caused him an incredible amount of prolonged pain and fear was now standing three feet away talking to him like they were old friends.

Clark fought the urge to take his pistol and blow the man's brains out right there in the parking lot.

As if reading his thoughts, the interrogator stepped closer. "It's normal for you to be angry, Mister Clark, but you have to remember that this was done for your benefit. We could have just as easily ended your life."

"So, that's the message. Play ball or disappear. Is that what you people are all about?"

"Well, that's part of it. You see, Agent, you needed to see that we really do have control of the big picture. Something that is as important as the *Anomaly* simply cannot be left to amateurs."

The second Clark heard the word, a bolt of fear shot through his body. The sensation literally made him take a step back.

The interrogator smiled. "As you can see, Agent, our time together was well spent. You are reacting correctly to the word stimulation."

Clark took a deep breath, trying to calm down. "Where's Mrs. Gander?"

The interrogator checked his watch. "Oh that's right. You didn't know. She was released several days ago. She is cooking herself breakfast in her home in Missoula about this time."

The interrogator handed him the car keys. "Very nice lady. Sorry you two didn't get a chance to say your goodbyes."

Clark walked around to the driver's side door. "Let me tell you something. On a professional level I get it. You programmed my silence, my cooperation, and I get it. On a personal level, if I ever see you again, I'm going to beat on you 'til I get tired. You understand me?"

The interrogator laughed. "Very good, Mister Clark. I like your fighting spirit. But as a way of saying goodbye, if you ever do see me again, it will be because of your behavior. I can assure you our meeting would be short and very unpleasant. Goodbye, Agent Clark. We'll be watching your career."

"Remember what I said, you son-of-a-bitch," replied Clark, getting in behind the wheel and slamming the door.

As he dropped the car in drive, the interrogator tapped on the passenger side window and smiled while giving the thumbs up. Clark shook his head and then drove out of the parking lot without looking back. Tears of rage and humiliation fell freely as he drove. They had broken him, tore him right down to the core, leaving zero trace of injury on the outside but total devastation within. It was a long drive back to Albuquerque.

****

After Kelly and Greg had eaten almost everything on the McDonald's menu that night, they had walked to the large trucker way-station market that sold everything from truck parts to belt buckles. They had used the opportunity to shower and pick up clean clothing. Even though it felt wonderful to be free, the mood was colored with an unspoken dread. Both the men knew that time was short, that teams of hitters were probably already enroute to their location.

Considering they hadn't slept in twenty-four hours, both felt oddly alert as they walked across the expansive truck parking lot of the Barstow station in the morning's early hours.

"Well, you got any ideas?" questioned Greg. "It's just a matter of time before the feds track us down."

Kelly sipped his coffee thinking. "We need to find a place to lay low until we can figure out what to do next. We recognize now that the device is probably acting as a beacon."

Greg nodded. "I agree. Think we should get rid of it?"

"Yeah, I do," replied Kelly. He looked over at the group of trucks parked side by side in the lot. "Let's find one headed east, put the device on it, and let 'em chase it all the way across country."

"Makes it look like we are hitchhiking," replied Greg smiling. "C'mon, the sooner we get rid of this thing the better."

It took a half-hour of walking around and talking to truckers in the lot until they found a truck that fit the bill. Under the ruse of asking for a ride to the coast, they finally found the perfect candidate, a cantankerous older guy who not only told them he was headed to New York and didn't take riders but to "Get the hell out of the lot or he would call the cops."

As they walked away, Greg slipped the device into a small opening in the channel iron holding the spare tire rack under the truck.

Several minutes later they watched the big eighteen-wheeler pull out of the lot and head for the highway. "Okay, we're invisible for the moment," announced Kelly.

"Yeah, but the minute we use a credit card or make a cell phone call, they have us pinpointed," replied Greg, drinking the last bit of coffee.

Kelly thought for a moment. "I have a crazy idea."

Greg laughed. "Can't get any crazier then it's gotten already. Let's hear it."

"How much money have we got left?"

Greg checked his wallet. "Ah, after buying this fancy new T-shirt along with the cost of the shower, soap and towel rental at the truck stop - sixteen dollars."

Kelly checked his wallet. "I've got about a hundred and twenty. If we cannot use credit, we can move and survive just using cash."

"Hate to tell you this, friend, but a hundred and forty bucks isn't going to get us too far."

484

Kelly smiled. "Yeah, but it just might get us to DC and my apartment."

Greg suddenly remembered. "Jesus! I forgot all about the three hundred thousand I brought with me from Montana. It's in the bottom of that spare bedroom closet under all those boxes of shoes."

"I say we head east," replied Kelly, "get to my place, pick up the cash, and head to someplace with palm trees and sandy beaches, someplace like Bora Bora, until we can sort things out."

Greg nodded. "I have to figure out a way to get a hold of Carol. She must be going crazy by now."

Kelly shook his head. "I have to disagree with you on that one, Pard. You can bet that your phone is tapped with probably the latest in tracing gear, and that would put them on us in minutes."

"So what do you suggest, Chris? She is my wife. I can only imagine what she has been going through."

"Listen, Greg, I know this has been bad for you, but right now we don't have any leverage on this. You helped kill a Federal agent so you have to know that your home in Montana is locked down tight. They knew if you ever got back to this reality it would be the first place you would go."

Greg was quiet, hating the thought of not contacting Carol. She had always been there when he needed her. Her support all through his career had been unwavering. Now, when she needed him the most, he would be staying away. The unfairness of it all brought tears of frustration, tears he quickly wiped away. "Goddamn, I hate this." He took a deep breath. "Okay, what do we do now?"

Kelly patted him on the shoulder. "C'mon, Pard, let's get to the bus station. We have a long ride to Virginia."

****

"You really think we will be able to find what we need in town?" asked Dillon tightening the cinch on his saddle.

Taylor tossed the saddle blanket over his mount. They had been up just after sunrise and were now breaking camp. "I think we should be able to get everything we need." He pulled himself into the saddle and adjusted the holster and pistol he had taken off the assassin. He looked over at Dillon, nudging the horse in the flanks. "Starting to feel like a real cowboy. All I need is a hat."

Dillon smiled, remembering what Sheriff Coleman had said about people in this reality not wanting to be *cowboys*.

As they rode, a warm summer breeze carrying the wild smell of prairie sage pushed against their backs.

"Gonna be a hot one today," announced Dillon looking up into the bright blue morning sky. "I have to admit it is beautiful here.""

486

"What would you do if you had to stay?" questioned Taylor looking straight ahead. "Would that be so bad?"

Dillon thought for a moment. "That's kind of an odd question, Bruce. You know something I don't."

Taylor smiled. "No, it's just that I have found a peace here that I never really had in our time, our reality. Haven't you felt just a little bit of that peace?"

Dillon knew exactly what Taylor was talking about. The feeling had started about the second week in Deer Lodge and had been growing in its intensity right up to the second he left. "Yes I do, Bruce. I actually considered staying in Deer Lodge."

Taylor adjusted himself in the saddle. "How is it that we could leave everything we hold important and vital, come here with nothing, and feel totally content?"

"I know what you mean about contentment. In Deer Lodge I was living out of a one-room shack behind the jail, and it was wonderful. I had nothing but the clothes on my back, a few blankets, and a dry roof, and I was content." It was the first time he had verbalized his feelings to anyone since the jump.

"You miss your family?" questioned Taylor, watching a jack rabbit suddenly running through the tall grass.

"Terribly, but somehow I know they are doing okay. It's the strangest feeling, Bruce, but I know my wife has accepted the fact that I'm dead, and she is holding things together."

"Sounds like a very strong woman."

Dillon smiled. "Yes, she is, one of the reasons I love her so much. You know, Bruce, you never told me about your wife."

Taylor let the question hang for a moment, not sure what to say. He didn't like talking about his ex-wife. He considered her leaving as a major failure in his life. "Well, not proud of it, but my wife left me years ago. It was my own fault."

To Dillon, it was a declarative statement, said with the kind of pain and conviction that generally made other men uncomfortable. For the rest of the short ride into town both men kept their thoughts, each knowing the heavy price that had been paid for being there. For now, for the moment, it was enough to be quiet and let the peacefulness of a Montana July morning do all the talking.

The town of Miles City lay just on the other side of the Tongue River. It had a wide central street and a population of nearly twelve-hundred fulltime residents, a respectable number for a hard-edged cow town in the late 1870's. Taylor spotted the red and white hardware sign on the left side of the street. "Over there," he pointed. "We should be able to get what we need."

It was only nine o'clock in the morning, and already horsemen and wagons loaded with tarp-covered goods were moving up and down the street. Dillon and Taylor tied their horses at the small rail in front of the shop and stepped inside. An older man wearing a wooden peg-leg thumped his way from the back of the dimly lit store.

"Morning, gentlemen, what can I do for you?" he asked, his deep Irish accent unmistakable.

"Morning, sir," replied Taylor. "We need to pick up a few things. Would you happen to have any bleach and maybe some rock salt?"

The man quickly spun around on the peg, "Aye we have. How much do you need?"

Taylor thought for a moment. "Ah, I'm going to need about five gallons of bleach and about twenty pounds of rock salt. You wouldn't have any blasting supplies would you, like fuse, maybe even dynamite?"

The store clerk looked back at Taylor. "If you don't mind me saying, you don't look like miners to me."

"We're just getting started," replied Dillon.

The clerk turned back to the shelves that were stacked high with canned goods and bottles. "Don't have that much bleach, only about a gallon, but I have a full tally of rock salt." He started handing Taylor several cans. "As far as the dynamite, I only have a small supply. The Army gets most of the stuff. I don't have any fuses."

Taylor started stacking the supplies on the counter. "I'm also going to need some kerosene and as much cotton bunting as you have."

After everything was stacked on the counter, the clerk took a small pencil from behind his ear and began adding up the cost.

"Now you're welcome to check my numbers, but all this comes to twelve dollars and fifty cents."

"That will be fine," replied Taylor. " I also need a large rat trap, something with a spring snap on it."

The clerk shot him a suspicious look. "Mighty particular how you catch your rat? Poison is cheaper."

Taylor smiled. "No, I prefer the traps if you please."

The clerk wrote down another sum. "That will come to thirteen dollars even." Taylor nodded to Dillon who quickly took out the small bag of coins.

"I ah, also need a barrel," announced Taylor, "something like that cracker barrel over there by the window. How much is one like that?"

The clerk squinted across the room. "That will be two dollars more." Dillon dropped the coins on the counter.

The old man scooped the money up. "There's another barrel out back. You know, this is a strange list of items. Do you mind telling me what you are going to do?"

Taylor thought a moment. "We are going to build a device to send back through the space-time continuum, in order to shut down a process that is allowing assassins to come into this reality for the sole purpose of trying to kill us."

The clerk stared open mouthed. "You know, all you had to say was *that is none of your business.* You don't need to be cheeky."

Dillon shook his head while gathering up the items. "Thank you for you help, sir. We'll be going now."

An hour later they had rented a small shack for three dollars on the edge of town. With the last of their money they acquired a washtub, matches, varnish, rope, and some two-day-old bread.

Taylor rolled the barrel inside, while Dillon lit a fire out back. "Now tell me again, what we are supposed to boil?" questioned Dillon, adding more wood to the fire.

Taylor poured the bleach into the large tub. "We need to boil this down until it crystallizes. Once we do that, we can start soaking the cotton in kerosene."

"What's the dynamite for if we are making all of this?"

Taylor pulled off the gun belt and his fatigue shirt. 'The dynamite is the internal kicker charge. The chemicals will amplify the explosion by about three times.

"Will it be enough to destroy or disable the machinery on the other end?"

Taylor nodded while adjusting the tub over the fire. "Absolutely, this will be more of a concussion device as opposed to a shrapnel producing explosive. It will definitely get their attention."

"What else do you need me to do?" asked Dillon.

Taylor picked up the rope they had bought. "If you would, untwist the weave in this down to one strand. This will be our fuse. I'm going to soak it in kerosene and the chemical- gunpowder compound, let it dry, then seal it in a thick layer of varnish. That will make it waterproof and windproof. We can also make a blasting cap out of one of the Forty-Four caliber bullet casings on my belt."

Dillon took the rope, amazed and moderately disconcerted at how knowledgeable Taylor was with the subject of making homemade explosives. "How long a fuse do you need?"

Taylor thought for a moment. "Fuse length is determined by burn rate. We make a foot long section, light it and then time it. That will give us the burn rate. I was making the jump through the continuum in less then twenty seconds using the designator in the past."

"So this is going to be a very short fuse?" questioned Dillon.

Taylor smiled. "Are you volunteering to light it?"

"Bruce, I plan on being a block away from this thing when you push the button."

Taylor laughed. "Piece of cake, Deputy. This will be a magnificent device."

Dillon cut off a three-foot section of rope. "Well, won't be a piece of cake for the guys on the other side."

Taylor thought for a moment staring at the now boiling bleach in the tub. "Isn't it amazing the wonderfully terrible things people will do for self-preservation," he said softly.

Dillon nodded. "Yes it is, Doc. Yes it is. God, forgive us."

Chapter 36

"I want the second hunter sent in now," announced Branson.

Crase adjusted the phase resonator. "Having trouble picking up the signal from the first one we sent. In fact, it's disappeared altogether. You still want to risk a second jump?"

Branson leaned back in his chair. "Not even a debatable question. Get him ready, Professor."

Crase nodded. "What about the second group, the ones that made the jump back to this time? I'm getting a strong signal from that device."

Crase checked his watch. "Stay in your lane, Crase. You just get the other hunter ready to make the jump. Now that the second group is in this time, my guys will round them up."

His cell phone buzzed, shutting off any further conversation. "Yes, sir," he announced as he left his chair and began walking out of the lab. He was now getting a call from his supervisor nearly every thirty minutes.

"Yes, sir, things are under control. We should have most of the players in custody within the hour. Everybody has been accounted for, and we are taking care of them as we speak."

At that very moment, Crase saw the energy surge light up the computer screen, the base-line graph spiking nearly off the scale.

"Branson, you need to see this!" he shouted staring at the screen. "Something is coming back. We've been activated."

Branson heard his name and as he turned back to the room caught a fleeting glimpse of a large object suddenly tumbling down the center of the expansive lab. Shocked by the speed and size of the object, he froze in the doorway as the large barrel smashed through delicate electronic circuits and array panels.

"What the hell is...?" A thunderclap explosion cut him off in mid-sentence, blasting him off his feet in a shower of broken glass, flames, and room debris.

Crase had watched in horror as the barrel came tumbling through the array, exploding with a horrific blast near the middle of the room. The overpressure had been tremendous, enough to send him flying through the air and into the sidewall of the room.

Dazed, he fought for consciousness as the emergency fire sprinklers suddenly came on. With heaviness of a dull pain in his lower back and head, he got to his feet and surveyed the destruction all around him. The multimillion-dollar laboratory had been destroyed, leaving its injured occupants stumbling in the wreckage.

On the far side of the lab, Branson painfully rolled onto his side, confused as to why he could not see out of his right eye or move his legs. He touched his face and through his good eye was stunned to see his fingers covered in blood. The last thing he heard as he slipped into unconsciousness was the cell phone in his pocket ringing and a far off voice asking him if he was all right. He didn't have the strength to answer, letting the oddly comforting darkness roll him under.

****

"Well, do you think it worked?" Dillon asked from the back porch.

Taylor dropped the thin rope used to activate the rattrap that triggered the activation button of the device. "I think so. The barrel is gone." He stood up, dusting the knees of his pants. "There really is only one way to find out. We need to push the button again and see if it opens the door."

Dillon slowly walked over to the device that was lying on the ground. "Hey Bruce, I think we have a problem."

Taylor watched as Dillon handed him the device that was now in two pieces.

"Rat trap not only hit the button, it snapped it right in two."

Taylor examined the broken device. "Well, we'll never really know what happened on the other end then," he replied, stuffing the pieces into his pocket.

Dillon shook his head. "So, I guess we're stuck here? I mean, damn Bruce, what do we do now?"

Taylor walked over and picked up his gun belt and shirt. "I think we need to start heading east. We'll try to get to New York, Chicago maybe. Not sure how much time this bought us. If they have duplicated the process once, they can do it again, probably a lot faster than the first time."

Dillon thought for a moment. "You know, if we can get to a rail-head, we can sell the horses for train tickets."

"Good a plan as any," replied Taylor. "You know, if it's any consolation, I feel terrible about what we had to do."

Dillon followed him out front to the tethered horses. "I don't think we really had much of a choice, Doc. This has turned into something that's going to run its own course. We made a move. History will be the judge if we made the right one or not." He pulled himself into the saddle, feeling as if he was leaving the scene of a crime.

As they slowly rode out of town, both men knew they had crossed a line. They had set a course that would have very real consequences. Even though they didn't talk about it, they both realized that whoever was on the receiving end of the explosive was probably dead and no amount of verbal justification would change that.

A hot dusty wind followed them down the street and into the expansive prairie. Dillon rode in a quiet funk, keeping his eyes slightly out of focus, staring at the back of his horse's head. He tried to remember what his wife looked like and was disturbed that he couldn't recall her face.

497

"This is getting a lot harder than I thought it would be," announced Taylor.

"Tell me about it," replied Dillon. "I'm still having a hard time processing everything that's happened to me since I've been here." He was just about to make a second point when out of the corner of his eye he caught sight of something that made his heart skip a beat. "Doc, hold up," he whispered, reining his horse to a stop.

"What, what's wrong?"

Dillon pointed off to his left. "Can you see that?"

Taylor stood in the stirrups, squinting in the bright sunshine. "My God, is that what I think it is?"

Dillon slowly slipped from his horse. "You bet your ass, Doc. That's a one-way ticket out of here."

Forty yards away, the anomaly shimmered in the early afternoon sunlight. Instantly, Taylor realized that sending the barrel through had opened the continuum a little more. The natural order was still doing what it needed to do; it would heal itself. The only thing required of men - to pay attention, sometimes a very tall order.

****

Greg leaned his seat back as far as it would go, trying to get as comfortable as possible. Their bus had just pulled out of Flagstaff, still headed east.

"You know, Greg, we need to talk about Baker."

Greg sighed deeply, the last gruesome image of the physicist immediately coming to mind. "Yeah, I know. Did you know his folks?"

"No, never met them. I knew his ex-wife - sweet gal."

Greg had never really gone through Baker's wallet the entire time he had been carrying it around. He pulled it out of his pocket and handed it to Kelly.

"Here, maybe we should check and see if we have any kind of address for his folks."

Kelly took the wallet and started going through it. "Well, we have some more money. Let's see, forty, fifty, sixty, seventy-eight dollars, some pictures, a couple of credit cards, gym membership card." He pulled back a small bit of lining. "Ah, you're not going to believe this, my friend."

Greg turned back from the window and saw that Kelly was holding up the three thumb drives.

Greg was stunned. "Do you, do you think those are the drives?"

Kelly nodded. "I don't think they could be anything else. Now what?"

"I have no idea, Chris. Those things draw bad news like a magnet. We hang on to them - we're dead. We get rid of them - we lose any bargaining power in the future."

Kelly thought for a moment. "Okay, next stop we find a place to hide this stuff. I don't want to get caught with it."

Greg checked the bus-route map. "Grand Junction is the next town. We can get off and check the place out." Greg took the thumb drives. "How we going to put the genie back in the bottle?"

Kelly handed the wallet back to him. "Not possible now, brother. I don't think things will ever be the same. When Taylor did what he did, it changed the world as we know it."

Greg stuck the drives back in the wallet. "You know, it really is incredible the power we're holding right now. There has to be a way of turning this to our advantage."

Kelly leaned back in his chair. "I'm all ears, Greg. I really don't think the world is big enough to hide something like this. A couple hundred thousand dollars isn't enough money to live on the rest of our lives; it just buys us a little time."

Greg nodded as an idea came to mind. "You know, I just had a thought."

"Hit me. We need a good idea about now."

"Well, instead of running, why don't we do a preemptive move?"

"I'm listening."

"Why keep this a secret? Maybe we should tell every newspaper and television network we know of about this. I think, right now, we should have as many eyes on us as possible."

Kelly thought for a moment. "Okay, I'm in. Where do we start without sounding like *Bill and Ted's Excellent Adventure?*"

"Let's get to a phone at the next stop," replied Greg. "I figure the New York Times, Fox News and CNN are good places to start. Ready to be famous?"

Kelly laughed. "If it gets me off this bus, then I'm ready."

By six-thirty that evening they had arrived in Grand Junction. They walked through the seedier side of town in the growing darkness, passing several Grand Junction police units without incident. The palpable tension of moving around in public made Greg feel as if he were carrying a sign that everyone could see.

Crossing the street past the main bus terminal, Kelly elbowed Greg. "Let's eat; that Denny's up ahead doesn't look too bad. Should be a pay phone in there too."

They took a booth near the back of the room, letting the normalcy of the place wash over them. There was something comforting about the smell of the grill and fresh brewed coffee that always made Greg feel better. It reminded him of time spent with his dad in the local Missoula coffee shop. His father had suffered a fairly severe heart attack and could no longer live alone. Carol and he had moved him up from Ohio to take care of him and did so for two years. On lunch breaks, Greg would meet the old man at the coffee shop near the school, and they would talk about better days, neither realizing that they were living them at the time.

Greg ordered his dinner and handed the menu back to the young waitress. "Chris, I'm gonna hit the head and try and wash some of this grime off."

"Go for it," replied Kelly. "I'll go when you get back; look's funny two dudes going to the bathroom at the same time."

501

Greg laughed and slid out of the booth. If he hadn't been so tired he would have noticed the two men who came in and sat down at the counter and then the other two who followed a minute later. All were in their middle to late thirties and carried the aura of hard-edged physical fitness and barely-controlled aggression, a mannerism that professional rugby players and cage fighters wear like a badge. Short hair, subdued color, 511 clothing, and cross training shoes - the standard "nom de guerre" of operators - hitters.

Things were about to change.

****

"So what you're saying is that the anomaly that's here now is unstable?"

"That's correct," replied Taylor. They had made camp early having seen the anomaly close by. "There is no telling where you would end up if you jumped into that thing. In fact, it's a miracle you ended up here with me in this reality."

"So you don't think we should take a chance? Maybe it's an open door to our time, you know, back where we sent the barrel."

Taylor thought for a moment. "Well, maybe. What I am beginning to believe is that when a jump is made, it leaves a path in the continuum, much like walking through a field of tall grass. Amazing!"

"Bruce, why do we keep ending up in the eighteen hundreds? I mean when I jumped in at Deer Lodge, I ended up here. Why not 1700 or 1600?"

"The only thing I can think of is that the original process was programmed for the 1800's - clear up to 1901. I think it's still following that set of protocols. Without any way to test the theory, that would be my best guess."

Dillon poked at the small fire trying to put his feelings into words. "You never asked me why I took the chance with the anomaly in Deer Lodge."

"I guess I thought you were missing your family - totally understandable."

"Well, I guess that's part of it. I also did it because I am afraid of the changes."

"What changes are we talking about?" asked Taylor, already knowing where the conversation was going. Anyone who went through the continuum was changed by the experience. He was aware of the deep-seated emotional changes a man went through, having experienced them for himself. No matter how hard they tried to fit in, to blend with the environment and population, something nearly imperceptible was off. People they met could sense it, oddly aware that something was wrong with the encounter.

"I think I know what you mean. I've noticed the changes in myself."

"I don't think I can wait a year before I try to go home, Doc. I really don't."

Taylor nodded. "I understand. You do realize that because of the instability of the anomaly, there's a better than even chance it will not take you back to our time."

503

A warm gust of wind blew through the small camp, kicking up dust. "I understand. But what I mean by changes, Bruce, is that I am slowly turning into a different kind of man. I am really afraid that if I stay here another year, I will completely lose the person I was, and that scares me. Christ, I can't believe the things I've done already."

"So what do you want to do?"

Dillon looked up into the night sky and back to the fire. "If I can find the anomaly tomorrow, I'm gonna jump. I have to try and get home, Bruce. I really need to try."

Taylor knew it was pointless to try and persuade him to stay. He knew Dillon had gone through tremendous trauma since his arrival in this reality. The physical and emotional toll was now visible. He missed his family, and that was all the justification a man needed for any action, no matter how dangerous.

"I am going to miss you, Dillon, but I fully understand your actions. If I had something to go back to, I would probably join you."

Dillon smiled sadly. "You know, Bruce, it's a big universe out there. There's a lot of room for second chances."

"Maybe in this reality, but not in ours. No, what I have in my head about how to do this would keep me in a prison cell till I died. My second chance is here. It's all I have left."

"Gonna change the world, Bruce?"

Taylor tossed a small handful of wood on the fire. "No, going to live the time I have left in peace."

"You have a plan?"

"Well, like I said, I'm going to head east, maybe start a small lab somewhere, kind of coax the scientific world a short distance forward, nothing too big, nothing drastic."

Dillon sat back listening as the night sounds closed in around them. "I have to tell you, there's something about this night sky. If I get back, it will be one of the things I miss most."

A coyote yelped in the distance. Night on the prairie was alive with creatures and drama rarely seen in the daylight. The screech owl, the kangaroo mouse, and the coyote all danced in their own natural rhythms in the clear moonlight, oblivious to the men huddled around the small camp fire or the other dark shapes who were at this moment creeping closer through the darkness.

Drama indeed.

Chapter 37

Returning from the bathroom, Greg was stunned to see the two men sitting with Kelly in the booth. For a fleeting second he thought about bolting for the door. A strong hand from behind suddenly forced him into the seat beside Kelly. The older man of the two, now sitting in the booth across from them, spoke up.
"Relax, gentlemen. Everybody just play it cool. Nobody wants to die in a Denny's."

"Listen, dude, we don't want any troub..."

"Hey, listen, Kelly," interrupted the man, "haven't you noticed that I have not given you any trouble? I really don't want to hear anything you have to say. If we wanted you dead, it would have happened an hour ago."

"So, So what is this? Are we under arrest or what?" Greg asked, confused. The two men in the booth and the others he now noticed sitting at the counter had the look of people you just did not mess with.

The obvious team leader spoke up. "Listen, tell me the truth. Did you two fellas really travel back in time?" he asked with a slight smile. "I mean did you, really?"

Greg had no idea where this conversation was headed. "Ah, yeah we did."

"1933 to be exact," added Kelly.

The man nodded, still smiling, "What did the folks back there think about them fancy T-shirts you're wearing?"

"We bought these at a truck stop in Barstow when we got back," replied Greg.

The man laughed. "Yeah, we know. We saw you buy them. See? We could have taken you out anytime. Pretty good trick about putting the return device in that east-bound truck." He pulled the device out of his shirt pocket and laid it on the table. "Like I said, fellas, we could have brought you down hard anytime."

"Then why didn't you? We just rode a Goddamned bus all the way to Colorado. What the hell is going on?" Kelly asked, getting angrier by the second.

"Yeah, we know," replied the man smiling. "Thought the ride would mellow you both out a bit. Okay, here's the drill, guys, we are all going to get up from this table and walk out those doors, get into those two black Suburban's out there by the curb, got it?"

"Look," replied Greg, "you want to shoot us? Go ahead. Do it here. We are not going to make it easy for you."

The team leader shook his head. "Listen, Gander, lighten up. Nobody is going to shoot anyone. For a smart guy, you sure don't listen very well. We could have shot you yesterday. You both have a plane to catch, and it's our job to get you on it. Now are we clear?"

507

Thirty minutes later, they pulled onto the nearly vacant private terminal at the Grand Junction Airport. A single individual met them at the door of the empty lobby. "This way, gentlemen," the man announced, opening the large glass door and ushering them in.

Greg and Kelly followed him across the room and out the back door to the landing ramp. All four of the men who had picked them up at the restaurant quietly followed close behind. The team leader had said nothing on the ride over, only speaking into his radio occasionally.

A Gulfstream Four, it's engines running and the loading stairs down, waited on the tarmac. Their guide stood at the bottom of the stairs and motioned for them. "This way, guys. Watch your step." Tentatively climbing the stairs, Greg couldn't shake the feeling that he was walking up the stairs to the gallows.

As he ducked inside the brightly lit cabin, he noticed that the interior had been set up like a conference room. Most of the seats had been removed, leaving a large table and several seats along the walls. A lone individual, a man who appeared to be in his middle sixties, was seated at the far end of the table smoking a cigarette.

"Come in, gentlemen. Have a seat," he announced. "We will be leaving right away. My name is Daniel Ross. I think you know why you're here."

Greg took a seat along the wall next to Kelly. "Where are we going?"

The man slid several forms across the table. "Before I get to that, I need you fellas to look those papers over and then sign them."

"What are they?" questioned Greg.

The man lit another cigarette before answering. Greg couldn't get over seeing the man smoking on the airplane. In all his years of flying he had never seen it done.

"This looks like a standard Government Non-disclosure Agreement to me," announced Kelly.

"That's exactly what it is," replied Ross sitting back in his seat. "And the second form is a Secrecy Oath statement."

"You gotta be shitting me," replied Kelly. "All of the crap we have been through, and it comes down to this, a stupid 2390 form?"

The man leaned forward, flicking the cigarette ash on the floor. "You don't sign it - you'll leave the plane in a body bag. It's your choice. Trust me when I say you're getting out of this very easy."

"What is it with you guys?" asked Greg. "Why all the threats? All you people do is bully and throw your weight around. We have not broken any law. We have been involved with time travel for God's sake. We're scientists who have no political axe to grind. I am sick and tired of this bullshit intimidation routine from you people."

Ross leaned back in his chair smiling slightly. "Are you done? Great speech, by the way. For starters, Mister Gander, I saw you help murder a Federal agent. I think that would constitute some kind of involvement or action by the Government. What do you think?"

"I, ah , I ..."

"That's what I thought," replied Ross. "How's your indignation now? So, you see, this whole time travel thing, well, quite frankly, has gotten way out of hand, so much so, that the most powerful and influential country in the world is willing to cut a deal with you two."

"A deal? What kind of deal?" asked Kelly.

Ross took a deep drag off the smoke and then exhaled a lung full. "A conditional deal. For starters, I need to know where Professor Baker is."

Greg looked over at Kelly who nodded. "Tell him."

"He's dead," replied Greg sadly. "He was killed on the jump into 1933."

"What happened?" questioned Ross, leaning forward in his chair.

"Well, when you move through the continuum, you're moving at a really high velocity by the time you land in the next reality. You hit the ground hard. As I said, Professor Baker and myself were transported to a hay field in Waxahachie Texas in 1933. I landed beside a dirt road and Professor Baker landed on a large hay rake."

"Hay rake? What kind of rake are we talking about?"

510

"The kind you pull behind a horse," replied Kelly. "Killed him instantly."

Ross shook his head. "Jesus, talk about the luck. You have any proof that Baker is dead besides your word?"

Greg thought for a moment then tossed Baker's wallet on the table. "That's his billfold. I took it off his body. That's the only proof I have."

Kelly shot Greg a quick look of panic, which he ignored. "I can assure you, Mister Ross, that Professor Baker is dead. He died a very quick and brutal death."

Ross examined the wallet closely, pulling out the driver's license and credit cards.

"So this is it. This is all you have?" he asked suspiciously.

"That's all I have. Baker is dead."

"Okay," sighed Ross, dropping the wallet into a plastic bag. "I need you to tell me who sent the exploding barrel back into the lab?"

Confused, Greg looked at Kelly and back to Ross. "We don't know anything about an exploding barrel."

"You guy's didn't build the device and send it back to the lab? It destroyed the facility. Several people were severely injured."

Kelly shook his head, genuinely confused, "Wasn't us."

511

Ross lit another cigarette. "If it wasn't you, why do you think Doctor Taylor would do something like that?"

Greg thought for a moment. "Well, it's just a guess, but if he felt threatened, he might be capable of it."

"Why would someone like Doctor Taylor feel threatened, Ross?" asked Kelly. "The only way Taylor would do something like that was if his life or the lives of others were in imminent danger."

Ross leveled an icy stare. "It's classified, Mister Kelly. Just remember that I am the one asking questions, okay? Are we clear on that?"

"Yes, we're clear," Kelly answered, realizing he had said way too much.

Ross kept the awkward pause, regaining total control of the conversation. "My next question, and either one of you can answer it. Does Doctor Taylor intend on launching any more attacks into this reality?"

Greg was dumb-founded by the line of questions. Whatever chain of events had led up to today had the government extremely rattled.

"I'm not sure what you're looking for," replied Greg, "but if Taylor did something like send a bomb back from wherever he is, he probably had a very good reason. The man is not a loose canon."

"So you're saying you have had no contact with Taylor?"

"None at all. I'm guessing now, but I believe Taylor jumped to the 1870's," replied Kelly. "We landed in 1933 and have had no contact whatsoever."

512

"Are we under arrest?" Greg asked.

"No, you're being detained," replied Ross quickly. "Two of my predecessors have either been killed or severely injured dealing with this case. That is not going to happen on my watch. As to where we are going now? We are heading back to Albuquerque to a medical facility to have both of you checked out. You will have a few days of physiological tests and medical reviews, and then you will be done."

"Neither one of us is sick," replied Kelly.

"Well that may or may not be the case. Doctors want to see if there are any internal effects related to time travel, and since you two are the only living people who have done it, this is where we are headed."

"Then what?" questioned Greg. "Chalks was always talking about Federal prison. Is that still on the table?"

Ross smiled. "Well, that depends on you, Mister Gander. Currently you are considered a National Security risk. Your status as free men or not depends on how our little meeting goes."

Ross took a file from his briefcase. "Now Mister Gander, let's start with you. First of all, your wife Carol has been looking for you. She even went as far as going to Shady Brook and Mister Kelly's apartment searching for answers. She contacted a FBI agent out of Albuquerque, who also became interested in your disappearance."

"You're talking about my case in the past tense. What happened? Is she all right?" asked Greg, more than a little uneasy.

Ross kept his eyes on the file. "She is now. She, along with, ah, let's see, an Agent Clark, were taken to one of our assessment centers for a week. Both came through it all right and were sent home."

Suddenly flush with anger Greg got out of his seat. "Okay, you son-of-a-bitch, what did you do? I swear to God, if you hurt her..."

"Sit down, Mister Gander, everything that she went through is directly on you. You told her about Doctor Taylor and his work with time travel. It was you who left his career and home to follow Doctor Taylor. If anything, you should be thanking me for saving her life. My superiors were more than willing to put a bullet in her head as well as anyone else even remotely connected to you. Count yourself lucky."

Greg slowly sat down. "What is this assessment center?"

Ross closed the file. "Not that I owe you an explanation, but the facility you're asking about is a place we send people who need to be reprogrammed about certain information they know - information we do not want given out to the general public."

"Jesus, you people," replied Greg, just loud enough to be heard.

"That's right, Mister Gander, we are "The" people. The ones who make the hard decisions that no one else has the stones to make. Do you think some gutless President has the balls to keep things on track? Or a do nothing Congress, or any of the other totally worthless supposed *shot callers* in DC? No, Mister Gander, it's men like Jason Chalks, who you helped kill, and Tug Branson, who lost an eye and probably the use of his legs. Those are the men keeping the lid on the garbage can. So you keep your judgment and bull-shit indignation to yourself. You got that? Because if you still want to push it, I will throw your sorry ass out of this airplane so fast it will make your head spin."

For a second Kelly thought Ross was going to start throwing blows, he was so angry. Seething with barely controlled rage, he slowly sat down and opened the same file. "Now, here is the way you're going to play this thing," he said, quickly lighting a fifth cigarette.

Ross took a deep breath. "Okay, you will not, I repeat, will not talk to anyone about your time travel - no media of any kind - nothing. If we see that you have violated our agreement, we will ruin you - IRS, DOJ the works, no threat, but an absolute promise. As far as your job goes, we have made some calls to the main players at the University and your job is secure. Your absence has been explained."

"Explained? How?" asked Greg stunned.

515

"Don't worry about it. Correct pressure has been applied where it was needed, and you're back on their payroll. Trust me when I say the United States Government can throw a tremendous amount of weight around when it needs to. Just go back and do your job. Try keeping your mouth shut. Grow old with that pretty wife of yours."

He closed the file and took a second one from the brief case. "Okay, Kelly, the same goes for you. You're already in the Federal system, so it was a whole lot easier talking and convincing your superiors to have you back. Your job and life are waiting for you when you get back to DC."

Kelly shifted in his chair. "Ah, thanks anyway, but I am not going back to the job. I'm done with Federal Service."

Surprised, Ross looked up from the file. "What are you going to do for a living?"

"Well, I have a degree in engineering. Maybe, I'll get a job building bridges or something. I want out of the city. I might head west."

Ross took another deep drag on his cigarette, keeping a steady gaze on Kelly. "All right, you do that. Keep your nose clean and your mouth shut, and you will live a long, happy life."

"That's my intention."

There was a long awkward pause in the conversation as Ross went back and carefully read several more pages in the file. Finally, he looked up from his reading. "Also, you both need to know that you will have periodical surveillance and record checks, credit, local criminal record, stuff like that."

"How long will that go on?" questioned Greg.

Ross closed the file. "Until you're dead," he replied with a smile. "You will be on our radar for the rest of your lives. You guys really didn't think you would be getting out of this untouched, did you?"

Ten minutes later, the plane made a slow high bank to the left setting up the final approach into Albuquerque.

Maybe, just maybe it was all over, thought Greg feeling his stomach rise and fall as the jet corrected itself for landing. *And then again maybe things were just getting started.* He shifted in his seat, hoping that the three thumb drives he had stuck in his underwear back at the Grand Junction Denny's didn't fall out on the floor. Ross could say what he wanted, but this was far from over as far as Greg was concerned. He looked over at Kelly and winked. No, this was far from over.

Down below, through the soft early evening haze, the city streetlights were just now coming on, their orange-red glow growing brighter by the minute. Life on a Tuesday evening was now in full swing. Most of the Sandia commuters were either home or well on their way. They had no way of knowing that the men in the small government jet that was now on final approach into the airport held such a powerful secret, a cosmic key to a puzzle that had intrigued Man since time began.

As Greg stared out the window watching the desert slowly rise to meet the plane, he thought about what kind of man he was before he met Taylor, and more importantly, the kind of man he had become. It had been as much an emotional journey as it was physical.

He now understood just how addictive going through the continuum really was. He understood Taylor when he said that traveling back through time had become an obsession, something he just had to do. And no matter what threats and persuasions Ross or anybody else threw his way, he was going back. He had to go back; the temptation was just too great.

Chapter 38

It was well past ten o'clock at night when she got the call. Checking her cell phone by her bed, she immediately recognized the 505 area code of New Mexico. Seeing the number made her heart skip a beat as she punched in the receive button. "Yes?"

"Mrs. Carol Gander, please." She didn't recognize the male voice.

"Yes, that's me. Who is calling, please?"

Mrs. Gander, my name is Daniel Ross. I am calling about your husband, Greg Gander."

Standing beside the bed she felt her knees go weak. She slowly sat down, trying to control her breathing. "Yes, what about him?"

"Mrs. Gander, I'm calling to let you know that he is safe and is currently being medically evaluated at a facility here in New Mexico."

"Oh, my God, is he all right? Is he injured? I can catch the first flight out tomo..."

"Mrs. Gander," interrupted Ross, "he is at a classified facility, which means you will not be allowed access. Greg will be here for about a week, and then he will be flown to Missoula. I can assure you that he is fine and is looking forward to getting home."

Carol's head was spinning. "Ah, can I talk to him on the phone? Can he call me?"

"No, Ma'am, there is no communication allowed while he is at the facility. But as I said, he is fine and will be released in five days."

"Where was he found? How did you get him to New Mexico? I have some questions that…"

"Mrs. Gander, I have no further information. Greg will be released in five days and will be able to contact you then. Goodnight, Ma'am. Sorry for the late hour call."

The line went dead leaving her stunned. She quickly punched the return call button and received the operator message that the number she was trying to call had been disconnected. She tried again as tears of joy and confusion streamed down her face. Frustrated, she slammed the phone down on the nightstand. She then tried punching in the number on her phone on the nightstand. Again the same disconnect message played. Just as she was about to hang up, a voice came on that sent an icy chill down her spine.

"Hello, Carol. Please stop trying to call the number back. You will not get through." It was the overly calm monotone voice of her interrogator. "Hello Carol, I know you're there; I can hear your breathing."

"I, I ah, I"

"Relax, Carol, and breathe. You're fine. Greg is fine. I just need you to accept the good news and be patient for a few days. Can you do that, Carol?"

"I, yes I can do that."

"Very good, Carol. Now you do remember our agreement don't you?"

"Yes, I remember."

"Good, now I am going to say something to you that is going to make you feel very tense and possibly ill, all right? But when you hang up and go to sleep, you will feel better. Do you understand?"

She was gripping the phone hard enough to turn her knuckles white. I, ah, understand."

"Okay, Carol, when Greg comes home next week, there will be no talk about the anomaly, continuums, or time travel. Is that clear?"

The words hit her like punches, making her physically recoil. She felt as if she were about to vomit. "I, I understand."

"Very good, Carol. Now please go to bed. You will feel better in the morning."

The line went dead, leaving her deeply shaken. Still in her housecoat, she slowly rolled into her covers, trying to push the memory of her time with the interrogator as far away as she could. By midnight, the shaking had stopped, and she was asleep, resting in the pleasant knowledge that Greg was coming home and fearfully cognizant, even in sleep, that she was being watched. It would be a long night filled with hope and fear.

****

521

The first shot went high, just above Dillon's head. He was already moving when the second shot went into the campfire, sending a spray of orange and red embers into the sky. Dillon, now scrambling through the tall grass, caught sight of one of the attackers running full out in his direction - the man no more than a silhouette, backlit by the fire. He dropped to his knees and fired two quick rounds into the shape that was now nearly on top of him. The attacker staggered forward with a groan, falling dead at Dillon's feet.

A heavy boom to his left from Taylor's pistol filled the night and then only the sound of men fighting. Dillon turned to run toward them but was clipped by a jarring tackle and slammed to the ground where he struggled against a hand holding his throat in a choking grip. Just as the assailant raised a short-handled axe, Dillon jammed the barrel of his pistol into the man's side and fired twice.

Rolling onto his feet, Dillon could still hear the struggle somewhere in the dark and then the sounds of horses galloping away from the camp.

"Taylor!" he shouted. "Where are you, Taylor?"

Frantically, he began searching the ground in a growing dread of finding his friend's body. Finding only the two dead assailants, he realized Taylor was gone – vanished.

Exhausted by the fight, Dillon slumped down beside the dying fire. Still holding his pistol, he dropped the magazine and loaded a full one, a now automatic motion.

The sounds of a screech owl hunting in the darkness could be heard in the distance as a warm gust of late summer night wind rustled through the grass. Dillon was struck by how surreal the difference was between the fight for survival just minutes earlier and the peaceful, quiet setting that had descended upon the camp.

He had now been involved with the killing of six men. *That had to be some kind of record for time-traveling serial-killers,* he thought, laying back looking up into the stars. Odd he thought, he didn't even care to check to see who the attackers were, was repulsed at the idea of looking at another person's body that he had a hand in killing.

He realized he was at an emotional crossroads. Taylor was gone –kidnapped. Both horses were gone, and that meant he would have to follow on foot. He had fired four more rounds, depleting his ammunition supplies by another third. He wouldn't make much of a rescue party if there were heavy numbers on the other side.

He let the question of Taylor's rescue roll through his head, unsure of what he should do. Soon rationalizations for not going after him began to float to the surface. What did he really owe the man? Taylor had brought this on himself and had no family to go back to, had even verbalized it earlier that day when they had spotted the anomaly. Why attempt rescue for someone who wanted to stay where he was?

On the other hand, Dillon had a family to get back to, reason in itself not to try and find him. Why should he put himself at risk, following armed, mounted men on foot – through rough country? Surely the odds were deeply against him.

He sat up, knowing full well what he had to do. He had just given himself half a dozen reasons why it was a bad idea for him to go after Taylor, They were good reasons, valid reasons, objections to action that would hold up under the heaviest of scrutiny. He went over them one last time as he packed up his meager possessions, stripped the bodies of weapons and ammunition, and headed off into the dark.

Following the horse trail through the tall grass in the light of the moon was easy. He just hoped Taylor was still alive when he found him. The son-of-a-bitch would owe him big for this.

****

It had been three days since Jason had arrived in his present reality. Jedediah had been gracious with his time, teaching him about the dangers and benefits of the surroundings. If he had a strong desire to know how and where Jason had come from, he had kept the inquiries to himself.

They spent the days checking trap lines, with Jedediah, the teacher, and Jason, the clueless student. For all his ability as a soldier and survivalist in armed combat, he had no idea how to trap, skin, or otherwise survive in the 1830's environment.

Jedediah had given him an elk skin that he used as a waterproof shawl of sorts, making the cool winds of the Oregon coast a little more bearable. Jason's clothes had been able to dry in the clearing weather.

By the evening of the fourth day on the river, Jason had no illusions of rescue. His body had been rebelling from the lack of sugar and caffeine he normally consumed in large amounts. A dull headache had plagued him for days, making physical effort and general conversation arduous. His diet now consisted totally of smoked meat, salmon from the river, wild onions and turnips.

"So, Jason, you never really told me how you got all the way out in these parts?" questioned Jedediah, hauling a full beaver trap into the canoe while Jason in the back of the canoe worked to keep it steady against the current.

"I don't think you would believe me if I did because I find it hard to believe myself."

"Well, I've heard many a tall tale from men who couldn't shoot half as good as you can. So give it a shot," Jedediah encouraged.

Jason shivered as the cold wind blew across the river, the afternoon sun temporarily hidden behind a group of fast-moving clouds. "Jedediah, you're real, aren't you?"

The trapper pulled the beaver out of the trap. "Not sure what you mean there, Jason."

Jason struggled for the words. "I mean, you're living a life; you're alive. This place is real - the wind, the rain, the cold. It's all real? I don't see or understand how this is all possible."

Jedediah smiled picking up the other oar. "It took you four days of killin malcontents, sleeping in a cave, and runnin a trap line to think that none of this is real?"

"No, that's not what I'm trying to say, Jed. What I'm trying to understand is how can I be here now, involved in your life. I'm having a hard time getting my head around this whole thing."

Jedediah shook his head laughing. "Lord, you do have some entertaining expressions, I'll give you that. But I'm still foggy on what you're trying to say."

Jason started paddling, guiding the canoe into the heavy, slow moving current. Even though he was surrounded by quiet tranquility, he became aware of a growing sense of fear, a vulnerability that he had never experienced before. In his own reality, he could afford to be reckless with his body. If you sprained an ankle playing racket ball, you got an x-ray, took some Tylenol, and healed up. If you got the flu, you just took your medication and waited to get well. But in this time, the rawness and dangers of life were everywhere. A broken leg could be a death sentence. A simple cut from an axe could turn septic and kill a man in a matter of weeks. No doctors, no antiseptics, no medicine - nothing of the physical safety net modern man took for granted was here.

"Jed, I'm going to tell you where I'm from," he announced over the sound of the wind. "I'm from the future – 2013. Jed, you hear me?"

Jedediah turned slightly from his position at the front of the boat. "I hear ya. 2013 huh?"

"That's right. I was dropped into an open space time continuum in New Mexico and ended up here."

Jedediah stopped paddling, his focus straight ahead on the far bank. "Ah, hold that thought, Jason. I think we got company."

Up ahead, a hundred yards downriver, three canoes slowly came into view, each holding at least three men.

"Not sure," replied Jedediah pulling his rifle out of the deerskin scabbard. "Maybe Chippewa. Looks like a hunting party."

"Are we going to have to fight our way out of this?" questioned Jason pulling his pistol and checking the magazine. This was the last thing he wanted to do. There were at least ten men headed their way, and the odds of taking them all without getting injured or killed were remote at best.

"Can we outrun them?" asked Jason, feeling the fear start to rise in his gut.

Jedediah kept his eyes on the men while pointing to the shore. "Just pull to the right, close to the bank - give 'em a wide berth. Maybe they'll just go on by."

Jason corrected their course, keeping a close eye on the men. They were now less then a hundred yards apart and to Jason's relief were not making any movements in their direction.

Jedediah was now paddling a slow but steady stroke, his rifle resting across his knees. Several minutes later the boats were directly across from each other, thirty yards apart. As they passed, Jedediah nodded to the men and waved. The gesture was returned by several of the men as the boats silently glided by.

Jedediah was now digging deep with his oar. "Don't know them fellas; not sure what they're up to. Probably best we get some water between us."

After twenty minutes of hard paddling Jason estimated they were a good two and a half to three miles away from the hunting party. Jedediah turned around in the canoe, looking up into the late afternoon sun. "Now, what's this about you being from the future? First time I've heard of something like that."

Jason pulled up his oar, letting the boat drift in the current. After weighing the positives and the negatives, he had reconsidered his decision to tell Jedediah about who he really was and had decided it just was not worth it. The confusion and possible history-altering scenarios it might bring up were not worth his confession.

"Ah, I was just having some fun. I jumped ship a half a mile off the coast. Damned near drowned getting to shore."

Jedediah nodded as he pondered the explanation. "Well, that makes some sense. What ship did you get off of? I know a few of them Dutch trading boys."

Jason thought for a moment. "Ah, I'd just as soon not say there, Jed. Some things a man just can't be proud of if you don't mind?" He was hoping the ruse would work, not wanting to dig himself too deep in a lie. Jed had been good to him, probably saved his life, and telling him an elaborate lie just seemed wrong.

As the sun dropped lower in the western sky they continued to move downstream talking about pelts, traps, and trading with the Dutch and French.

By early evening they had reached the site of their landing, and to Jason's surprise, he was looking forward to the warm fire they would build in the cave and the salmon they had caught for dinner. It had been a long, cold day but one that had been filled with excitement and learning. As he trudged up the bank in the dark carrying the string of fish, he could see how a man could fall in love with the simplicity of this life. There were no rules to follow, only those that related to survival. No man-made restrictions on where a person could go or what he could say or think – no ridiculous political correctness, no dignity-stealing government over-reach so prevalent in modern society. A man could be truly free here, free to make choices that either kept him alive or killed him quickly. It was natural selection with a hard, very sharp edge.

As they lit the torches in the cave's hallway and bolted the massive wooden door, Jason realized the feeling of unease had passed, and he was feeling oddly settled in this reality. He could do this; he could make it work for as long as he needed. If he got sick, he would get better or die. If he were injured, he would heal. But if not, he would trust and attribute the outcome to God, fate, or just plain bad luck.

By the time the cooking fire had been lit, he had pushed away any remnant of fear, letting it ride on the wispy smoke of the campfire. Sitting back against the fur-covered log, watching the embers dance in the fire, and eating the fresh salmon, he told himself that if this was the way it was going to be for the rest of his life, it could be worse - a lot worse.

A thick heavy rain began to fall that did nothing to the odd glimmer of light that danced and shimmered just below the ridgeline, a mile from the cave.

The cosmic order always corrected itself. Always.

Chapter 39

It had been a real piece of luck. A few precious moments stolen upon his arrival had been enough for him to hide the thumb drives. Knowing full well that all of their clothing and footwear would be searched and scanned, he had hidden them in a tiny hole he created in the mattress. There they had remained securely hidden for two days now.

Greg and Kelly had been put through a full battery of medical tests including blood analysis, mental acuity tests, EKGs, hand and eye coordination drills, and endless one on one interviews with physiologists and neurologists. By the end of the third day, Greg was convinced that the people testing him could not possibly learn any more about him than they knew right now. Just before five that afternoon, they escorted him to yet another psychologist. Kelly had left for the same testing in mid-morning and had still not returned, giving Greg the idea that this was going to be a marathon session.

"Have a seat, Mister Gander," the examiner greeted as Greg entered the room. "I have been going over your test results. I've looked at some of your answers to the questionnaires, and I detect a bit of sarcasm if not measurable hostility to what we are trying to do here."

"What are you trying to do here, Doc?"

The doctor didn't look up but made notes on his tablet.

"Greg, we are trying to see if the experience you have had has had any measurable effect on your mental and physical state."

"So, I gather you *don't* think there would be a measurable effect on my physical and mental status from being threatened with prison, being held without charges, and being forced to undergo days of medical testing?"

The man looked up and removed his glasses, a contrived gesture done to convey sincerity but all it did for Greg was piss him off. "Greg, I'm not sure where all the hostility is coming from. We are only evaluating your response to the extraordinary experience you had."

Greg sat back in his chair. "Then why don't you talk *to me* instead of talking *at me* like I am some kind of lab rat?"

"Is that how you really feel about what we are doing here, Greg?"

Greg had had enough of the passive aggressive bullshit. "Okay, that's it… enough with the third-rate psychology crap… and stop calling me by my first name. You don't know me and I don't know you. I've never seen you before in my life and you want me to sit here and open a vein. It's not going to happen, pal. So go ahead and take your notes and list me as hostile and aggressive because at this stage of the game, I really don't give a shit."

The man thought for a moment and then put his pen and notebook on the desk. "You're right. You're absolutely correct. You have every right to be angry. If I were in your situation, I would be just as ticked off about the last several days as you are."

Greg shrugged. "Okay, so what? Does your moment of clarity get me out of here any faster?"

"No, it does not."

"So, what's the point, Doc? You have pretty much made up your mind about me, and no matter what I say from this point on, that opinion is not going to change, correct?"

"That's not necessarily true. If it brings you any comfort, your friend, Mister Kelly, is reacting the same way. In fact, his hostility is a great deal higher than yours."

"Good, looks like I have some catching up to do."

The man smiled, leaning back in his chair. "Okay, Mister Gander, let's start over, all right? Look at it this way, the sooner I fill out this form providing a decent physiological workup, the sooner you get out of here. How's that for a deal? No one wants to hurt you here, Greg. We're just extremely interested. That's all. You really are a pioneer."

Greg thought for a moment, realizing that the man was right about at least one thing - the sooner he got with the program, the sooner he went home.

"All right, Doc, ask your question. I want to get the hell out of here and get home to my wife. I've put her through enough."

****

Dillon sat in the high grass watching the sun come up in the east. He had followed the trail by the light of the moon all night. Now exhausted, he rested. The wind carried the smell of a cooking fire, a good indication that he was close to whoever had taken Taylor. And then again, he had no way of knowing if Taylor was even still alive. He shook off the early morning chill and slowly got to his feet. While good for traveling on horseback, the knee-high boots he wore were terrible for walking on uneven prairie. Limping across the top of the hill he suddenly caught sight of white smoke coming from the campfire, a good hundred yards below the hilltop.

He slowly dropped down to his belly and crawled through the grass to a better vantage point. Counting at least four men and six horses, he realized the extra horses must be Taylor's and his own. The men standing around the smoky fire were Indians, of which tribe Dillon had no idea. Their voices and laughter carried easily on the morning breeze. To Dillon it seemed odd since two of their members had been shot dead the night before.

He was crawling closer when suddenly something hard and cold was pressed against his temple. To his utter astonishment he found himself looking down the barrel of a rifle held by an Indian lying within arm's reach. He had literally crawled beside the man without seeing him. He braced for the bullet that was soon to follow but was amazed when the Indian held a finger to his lip, giving the universally recognized sign for silence.

Dillon nodded and was stunned to see at least ten other Indians lying nearby in the tall grass. The Indian with the rifle lowered his weapon and whispered *"Ton Ta Tonka"*, pointing down to the camp.

Dillon shook his head, not understanding the words. The Indian whispered the words again as a confused - concerned look crossed his face, obviously surprised that Dillon did not know what he was talking about. Suddenly recognizing the advantage of working in conjunction with the men, Dillon tentatively nodded, and copied the words *"Ton Ta Tonka"*, pointing toward the camp.

Nodding and smiling in pleased agreement, the Indian whispered a nearly silent command to the men lying in the grass. Faster than he thought humanly possible, the men suddenly jumped to their feet in unison and started running down the hill.

Spurred by adrenaline, Dillon jumped to his feet and ran after the Indians who were now firing rifles and pistols as they quickly closed on the camp. The four men seated around the campfire were cut down by a hail of bullets without returning fire, caught completely off guard by the sudden attack. Dillon closed on the scene, amazed at how fast it was all over. The assaulters were already cutting off genitals and hairpieces as Dillon began to approach the dead; evidently grisly trophies were being taken. As Dillon quickly scanned the now bloody camp, looking for any sign of Taylor, he spotted a large buffalo hide lying at the edge of the encampment. Pulling the hide back, he found a battered and bruised body of someone resembling Taylor. Both of the man's eyes were swollen shut, and a nasty deep wound split the man's lip from the top of his nose to his chin, evidence of a terrible beating. Dillon quickly sat him up. "Bruce, it's me. C'mon, buddy, hang in there. I'm here. You're safe; we got ya."

Slowly, Taylor appeared to come around. "What happened, wher..."

Dillon kept him from trying to stand. "Whoa, hang on, Bruce. Just sit tight. Looks like they beat on you pretty good. Just stay still and we'll try and clean you up a bit."

One of the Indians that had been part of the attack knelt down, handing Dillon a canteen of water. "*Ton Ta Tonka,*" he announced pointing at Taylor.

Dillon nodded as Taylor quickly gulped down the water. "Why does he keep saying *Ton Ta Tonka*?"

Taylor poured the rest of the water over his head. "That's the name the Sioux gave me. I am *Ton Ta Tonka,*" replied Taylor slowly getting to his feet. He took a second canteen and poured it over his head, trying to wash the blood off his face and hair. "Crazy Horse gave me that name himself the day he saw me activate the return device and vanish from the little Big Horn battlefield."

Dillon looked around. The Indians were still gathering up the possessions of the dead. "I assume that these guys have been keeping an eye on you, and when they saw this bunch attacking us, they came to the rescue."

Taylor shook the water from his head and spit. "That would be a safe bet." He looked over to the tethered horses. "That one over there is Black Elk, Crazy Horse's number two guy, the Dog Soldier who took me from the fort to meet the chiefs."

Dillon nudged one of the now mutilated bodies with his boot. "Who do you think these guys were?"

Taylor wiped more water from his eyes, studying the corpse. "Not sure, maybe a Pawnee raiding party."

"Well, whoever they were sure didn't set well with this group," replied Dillon, still a little uneasy about the Indians who were now beginning to saddle the horses.

"What now? Do we thank these guys or what?"

Now on horseback, Black Elk rode up, leading Taylor's mount to him. *"Ton Ta Tonka"* he announced loudly. "Mishta ,oyo ,simta moya," he said, motioning to Taylor's readied mount.

"You have any idea what he just said?" asked Dillon, holstering his weapon.

Taylor thought for a moment, taking the reins of the horse. "Yeah I do. He wants me to go with him."

"Jesus, Bruce, you're not serious. I mean, how is that going to help you?"

"Well, I really don't think I have much of a choice on this one. I think they feel they need to keep me safe, and going with them is the only way they can do it."

"Then I'm going with you," replied Dillon, looking to the other Indians who stood watching the exchange.

With the help of several of the Indians, Taylor slowly pulled himself into the saddle. "I don't think you have been invited, my friend. Besides you have somewhere else to go," he said pointing off to his left. Less than fifty yards away, the anomaly danced and shimmered in the morning sunlight.

"I'll be damned," whispered Dillon, awestruck by the sight. He looked up to Taylor. "I can't leave you behind. It doesn't feel right. How do I know you will be safe?"

Taylor smiled. "I'll tell you what. You want to help make me into a legend? That will keep me safe."

"If it helps keep you alive, I'll do anything. Tell me what to do."

538

"I'm going to start reciting a poem. As I do, you start walking towards the anomaly. When you get close, I'll shout. Then you jump. Your disappearance should just about solidify my ethereal status. What do you think?"

Dillon laughed. "I think that's about the craziest thing I have ever heard. They will probably make you chief after watching you make me disappear. You take care of yourself, Bruce." He shook hands. "Been one hell of a ride, huh?"

"That it has been, my friend. I'm sorry I got you involved. You didn't deserve to get rolled up in this," replied Taylor.

Dillon smiled. "Hell, Doc, I got a chance to see and live in the 1870's. Wouldn't have missed it for the world."

Dillon nodded a good-bye and turned towards the anomaly. Taylor broke into a very loud rendition of *Tennyson's Charge of the Light Brigade.*

"Half a league, half a league, half a league onward. All in the valley of Death rode the six hundred!" shouted Taylor standing in the stirrups. His dramatic oration had started to shake-up the Indians who now stood watching him wide eyed.

"Forward the light Brigade, charge for the guns, into the valley of Death rode the six hundred." Taylor began waving his arms and shouting as loud as he could, startling the Sioux even more.

Less than twenty feet away from the anomaly, Dillon could hear the now familiar hum of energy.

"Canon to right of them, canon to the left of them!" screamed Taylor in full performance form. "Canon to the front, into the valley of Death rode the six hundred." Dillon turned to face Taylor and shouted as loud as he could, "Farewell, Ton Ta Tonka."

"Be gone!" shouted Taylor, clapping his hands three times.

Dillon smiled, fell back into the anomaly, and vanished.

The Sioux stood frozen, transfixed by the spectacle. Taylor slowly sat back in the saddle, looked to the sky, and shouted "Ton Ta Tonka!"

When Taylor shouted, Black Elk was so spooked he nearly fell from the saddle. The other Dog soldiers began to wail, shout, and fire their rifles in the air. In the eyes of the Sioux, Taylor had just become a God.

****

It had only taken the new crew three days to get the lab up and running. Daniel Ross, the new head of the project, stood in the middle of the repaired lab, watching the scientists do whatever it was that they had to do to get the process up to speed.

The FBI team had conducted the forensics on the device and debris, discovering that the device was probably not intended to be a casualty-producing bomb. No shrapnel such as nails, rocks, or shards of glass were found. In fact, the barrel had been filled with dried horse manure and straw. The blasting cap had been crudely crafted from a forty-four-caliber shell casing that detonated a single stick of dynamite via a homemade fuse. The FBI lead had concluded that if Taylor could make such a device, he could have easily made one much more deadly. The pervasive thought among the team was that the device appeared to be a warning shot across the bow, as opposed to an overt act of war.

Crase had been allowed to stay with the project and was now helping set up the new array panels near the center of the room. He had been pleasantly surprised at the new project manager's tone and with the generally calmer demeanor surrounding the project.

Ross answered his cell phone on the second ring. "This is Ross. That's correct. Go ahead and discharge both Gander and Kelly - plane tickets home - the standard exit package. I don't think that will be necessary. We've already had a *come to Jesus* meeting. Either one of them start going sideways, they know we will be on them like a bad smell."

Crase walked up just as the conversation ended. "Mister Ross, everything is up and running now. Do you have a specific operational task ordered?"

Ross thought for a moment, wishing smoking was allowed in the lab. "Tell you what, Doc. I'm going to step outside a minute, make a few calls, and then we will get started. All right?"

Crase nodded. "Very good, whenever you're ready."

A split second later, the tremendously loud sound of rushing wind filled the lab followed by a blinding white light. Sure that another barrel was coming through, Crase dove to the floor. Ross staggered back as he caught a glimpse of the shape in the light. A man tumbled out of the glare and onto the smooth white-painted concrete lab floor.

Dillon rolled to his feet, weapon in hand, and grabbed the only person within reach. He jerked Crase to his feet, holding his pistol to his temple.

"Drop the gun, asshole, or I scatter this guy's brains all over the room!" Dillon shouted as he spotted a thin man wearing a dark suit running in his direction holding a pistol.

A man dressed in western clothing came running into the lab from the far door carrying the same big colt revolver the assassin had been carrying and took up a shooting stance beside the man in the dark suit. "I can drop him, sir!" he shouted cocking the hammer on the big colt. Dillon was looking down the barrel of a canon.

"No!" shouted Ross. "It's 0kay. Put your guns down."

The SEAL kept his position. "Sir, I can take him."

"That's an order, Sailor. Put your weapon down!" shouted Ross.

The SEAL slowly lowered his pistol. "Yes, sir."

Dillon stood as steady as he was able, doing everything he could to fight the nausea. "Who the hell are you people? Are you the same sons-of-a-bitches who sent a killer through to hit Taylor and me?" he shouted, swallowing back the first wave.

Ross held up his hands while kicking his pistol away that he had laid on the floor. "Nobody here wants to hurt you, Mister Conroy," he announced stepping closer.

"Really?" replied Dillon nearly vomiting a second time. "So we are all friends now? Is that it?"

Ross lowered his hands. "Like I said, nobody here wants to hurt you."

Dillon could not hold it any longer and spewed vomit like someone opened a fire hose. Ross, Crase, and even the SEAL jumped backwards trying to avoid the yellow goo. Dillon went down to his knees, sending another gush onto the floor.

Ross and the other men held their positions. "Jesus, are you all right?" questioned Ross, looking as if he were about to puke himself.

Crase stood against the far wall, shaking the vomit out of his hair, thinking that it might have been better to be shot.

Dillon smiled, wiping his mouth with his gun hand. "Never better," he slid his pistol across the floor, making sure it went through the vomit. "Do what you got to do. I give up."

Chapter 40

"And you need to sign both of these forms and this release form." The agent slid the papers and pen across the desk. During the past five days, Greg and Kelly had been separated. Now they sat side by side in one of the complex's main offices. "The US Attorney will be here in a minute to give you guys some information." Greg and Kelly signed the forms and handed them back to the man.

The agent collected the forms. "Thank you, gentleman. Sit tight. I know you have planes to catch. We'll get you out of here on time."

He left the room, locking the door behind him.

"Do you still have the drives?" whispered Kelly, leaning close.

Greg put his finger to his lip and nodded as a much younger man walked into the office carrying a briefcase and a stack of papers. He sat down and immediately opened his case.

"Morning, gentlemen, my name is Woodall from the US Attorney's office in Washington. I am here to provide you with the final disposition of your case."

"Our case?" questioned Kelly. "Are we being prosecuted for something?"

The attorney closed his case. "Not officially. Due to the extremely sensitive nature of this case, there will be no formal charges. However…Mister Gander, you are an accessory to the murder of a Federal Agent. There is video tape evidence that clearly shows your participation in the event."

Greg nodded. "I understand, and I take full responsibility for my actions."

"Mister Gander, the United States Government, in its infinite wisdom, has decided that since you were not the main perpetrator in this assault and due to the highly sensitive circumstances surrounding the event, there will be no charges filed. This was against my recommendation. However that was the decision."

"I really am willing to take responsibility for my actions," replied Greg.

The attorney snapped his briefcase shut. Mister Gander, I couldn't care less about your willingness to take responsibility. I am only here as a messenger to tell you that my office will not be filing charges. If I were you, I would keep any confessions of atonement to myself. Now, here are several forms that I need you to sign, and then you can be on your way.

With a look of total disdain he slid the papers across the desk and left the room as quickly as he had come in. The previous agent entered, passing him in the doorway. He closed the door behind him and took his seat.

"All right, guys. Here are your plane tickets. The car out front will take you to the airport."

"So that's it? We can leave, just like that?" asked Kelly.

The agent pushed the tickets across the table. "Just like that. Both of you are lucky to be walking out of here."

"What's that suppose to mean?" asked Greg.

The agent sat back in his chair. "It means you got lucky, and if I were you, I wouldn't push that luck. Oh, by the way, we know about the thumb drives you've been hiding in your mattress. We erased them the first day you were here. The ones you have in your pocket, Mister Gander, are blank."

"So now what?" questioned Kelly.

The agent pushed his chair back, gathering the signed paper work. "Now, you both get out of my office and enjoy your deal from the Government. I assure you, gentlemen, it is highly unusual."

Kelly leaned across the table, just before leaving. "Hey, you never told us your name...or who you worked for in the government."

The man leveled a cold, angry gaze. "I work for a group that you want nothing to do with, tough guy. You're punching way over your weight class on this. Just so you know, Chalks was a friend of mine. You still want to push the issue?"

Greg tapped Kelly on the arm. "C'mon, Chris. Let's get out of here."

The agent held Kelly's stare. "That's good advice, Kelly. I'd take it if I were you."

Kelly nodded. "Okay, all right. We're gone."

They left the room, stepping out into the brightly lit hallway. "Jesus, Chris, that guy looked like he was ready to take your head off. I wouldn't provoke these people if I were you," announced Greg stepping out the front doors.

"Well, I just didn't want these guys thinking I was afraid of them. Kind of dumb I know, but I hate being bullied." They both slid into the back seat of the car.

Greg shook his head. "I just want to get out of here without any more hassles."

Kelly smiled, putting on his sunglasses. "Honestly, Greg, I think the hassles have just begun." Greg turned back to the window, watching the early morning commuters moving by on the highway. It was a beautiful New Mexico day with temperatures in the middle fifties.

In the back of his mind, Greg knew that there was no way they were walking away from this untouched. No, the Feds had a plan. But for the moment, he would take this chance to enjoy the freedom and the time with Carol. He had a lot of explaining to do. He just hoped she would listen.

****

Ross reread the last paragraph in the AAR, (After Action Report) on Stone Gate, wondering if the course of action originally taken had been correct. He allowed himself a certain level of introspection, was keeping his trepidation and concern in check with regard to senior level decisions. He was a rule follower - a team player, an important characteristic that had caught the eye of heavyweights in the Intel world. It was their power that could really promote and shepherd his career.

Ross had quickly moved up the ranks within the FBI but twenty-three years later had gone as far as he could in the organization. Until last night, that is, when he was called to a private meeting, and the Director appointed him the man in charge of what was now being called the "Process".

Time travel had been accomplished but was now the most closely guarded secret in the world. Maintaining that secret had become his mandate.

The last paragraph of the Stone Gate document read:

"Any living survivor of time travel, along with everyone remotely associated with the survivor, must be eliminated, due to possible information compromise."

The highly classified report further stated:

"The general population of the United States is not emotionally equipped to handle the idea of viable time travel. Exposure of information related to viable time travel could be catastrophic to the social fabric of the general population of the country."

Ross was now the final authority on whether or not to implement the written directive. Many times in the past he had been involved in sanctions - 'government speak' for killing/ elimination/ discreet counseling. It had been going on for years, and he had grown tired of it. Having convinced the powers that be that this new approach would be better in dealing with the issue, his viewpoint was still unproven ground. The hard truth was that there were three men alive today who had traveled back in time, and the government of the United States was "trusting" these men with that secret.

Maybe it was his age or the tremendous emotional weight of all that executive action that made him advocate for a different way of dealing with these people. Over the years he had seen a dramatic shift in the decision makers leaning more heavily on direct sanction as opposed to reeducation and monitoring. The wars in Iraq and Afghanistan had buried the needle when it came to Government sanctioned killing. The deadly machine had been revved to the max and allowed to run with no one manning the cut-off switch. In the early days of both wars, if you got on the wrong side of a "Target Package", you were dead in twelve hours.

Sitting back in his chair, Ross lit a cigarette and let the memories of those blood-colored days working out of the Perfume Palace near Baghdad rush back. He had been working as liaison with the DOD and had been in a direct chain of command link with the SOCOM community. Translated, he had had a large group of meat eaters at his disposal, and he had used them. Bomb makers, paymasters, trainers and basic street corner bad guys with a rusty AK and half a magazine, all went down in swift bloody and final action. And it had all been directed from his second floor office at camp Liberty.

It was on his second rotation that he had begun to feel a tug in his gut whenever he handed over a new dossier on some new target. The hit list had just kept on getting longer and the charges and accusations more vague. Third person Intel had now been good enough to warrant heavy action. Ross had been convinced that half the bastards on the kill list had nothing to do with organized terrorism,but had been the victims of personal vendettas and corruption beefs. And the boys in the digitals had been more than willing to punch a ticket because everybody wanted to know what it was like to kill someone.

He had kept his epiphany to himself, slowly cutting down on the kill orders and instead opting for confinement. He served three tours in Iraq and one in Afghanistan, and when the boys in the back room had decided he had had enough blood on his hands, he was promoted out of the zone and put in charge of Domestic operations - state side. The move up the food chain had not come a moment too soon. Three more days, hell, three more minutes of that job and he would have resigned, tossed his CAC card and keys on the desk, and walked.

This is why he had lobbied so hard to keep the three men and their families alive. He just did not have the stomach for the heavy action anymore. Way too many ghosts were rattling their chains around his living room at night.

He tossed the folders on his desk telling himself that he was doing the right thing. Gander, Kelly and Dillon Conroy would stay alive along with their families as long as they kept their end of the bargain. If the trust was broken, then all bets were off and the full wrath of the Kingdom would descend. If that really did happen, Ross knew he might as well pencil his name onto the list. No one would be spared, not even him.

****

Dillon barely recognized the face in the mirror. The heavy beard and long hair gave him the look of some lonely desert prophet. He moved around his room freely, a room with a large bed, a full-size bathroom, and a flat screen TV with hundreds of channels. The mag lock on the door though gave evidence that his room was admittedly a very plush cell.

They had taken his clothes, leaving him in a hospital gown and slippers, and had allowed him to keep his beard and long hair. They had promised him that he would be released after a five-day evaluation. Not having confidence in that promise, he found himself either pacing the large room or staring out the window. The view from his window felt alien to him now. The cars, streetlights, and all the rest of the modern day trappings were in stark contrast to the uncrowded vistas, open skies and fenceless prairies. The life he had had before this grand adventure was still out there, the sameness of it just three floors down, and all it did was make him sad. For months all he had thought about was getting home. Now that he was back, he longed for the life he had just left behind. His feelings and perception of himself and his purpose had dramatically shifted. Looking out into the early afternoon sunshine, he was startled to recognize just how profound that change had been.

Too much had happened to him to allow him to fit in the present time. He knew he would have little patience for the petty complaints of people involved in more shallow difficulties in this time. He had killed six men in violent confrontations and had connected with the simple struggles of living in a time when life and death were a breath apart. Each time he had been involved with a struggle at that line between life and death, he had felt a deeper shift. His love for his wife felt like it had been in another lifetime. Something else, something that transcended a person-to-person emotional connection, had taken over his heart, and he wasn't going to fight it. He had made a decision to come back and now realized he would do everything in his power to leave. He did not belong here anymore.

A knock on the door interrupted his deep thoughts. "Are you up?" Ross stepped into the room.

"Been up," replied Dillon turning to sit in a chair.

Ross sat on the edge of the bed. "Well, I see you've decided to keep the beard. Looks good on you."

"Kind of got used to it. So, what's the plan? What am I doing today?"

"More tests - a shit-load of psychological exams. Couple more days and you will be released. I know your wife will be glad to see you."

"Have you called her yet?" Dillon asked.

"No, I was going to do that this morning. You do realize that you have been listed as dead? I think she has received the life insurance already."

Dillon shifted in his chair. "Ah, that's what I wanted to talk to you about. Let her keep thinking I'm dead."

"I don't understand. You don't want to tell your wife that you're back?"

"No, I don't. sir, I honestly don't think I belong here anymore."

"And why is that? What happened to you out there?"

"In addition to you guys trying to kill us? A lot. That brings up the next subject. How come I am still alive when just a few days ago an assassin showed up in Montana trying his best to shoot me and Taylor."

Ross looked confused. "Did you say a few days ago?"

"Yes, Why?"

"How long do you think you have been gone?"

Dillon thought for a moment. "I don't know, a month, maybe two."

Ross shook his head. "You've been gone just under a year."

Stunned, Dillon spoke. "Ah, what, a year? But it only felt like a short time. I, I don't understand."

Ross smiled "Neither do we, Dillon. That's why you're here. The top people in this field, the doctors, the psychologists, they are all here trying to figure these things out."

Dillon thought for a moment, stroking his beard. Some things were starting to make sense - the seemingly fast hair growth, the quick physical healing, and the soundness of sleep. "All right, I get it, but why the change on the government side? Why am I still alive?"

"Change in management. There have been several different managers over the last year, and now I've been put in charge of this project. I've convinced the shot-callers that we should try something different."

"Okay, then you're the guy I need to talk to."

"By the way, what happened to the man that was sent back to your location?" Ross asked.

"The army killed him. He landed right in the middle of General Miles Camp, ready to start shooting. The soldiers killed him before he could get a shot off, thank God."

"You really want to go back?"

"Yes, Deer Lodge 1890, late September to be exact."

"You're serious?"

"Serious as eye cancer, Ross. When I told you I don't belong here anymore, I meant it. I've changed. Can't explain it but it's true. You have to send me back."

Ross shook his head. "I really doubt Higher is going to allow you to go back. This is a full-blown, hardline government project now with extremely narrow guidelines on access and control. There is a list a mile long of researchers, scientists, and historians who have signed up for this thing, and I don't think you qualify."

Agitated, Dillon got up from his chair. "Jesus, Ross, who is more qualified to go than someone who has already done it? I tell you, this thing has changed my life dramatically. I feel no connection with *here* anymore - none."

A knock on the door interrupted the conversation. A nurse stepped in carrying a small tray of vials. "Ah, I can come back later," she announced, sensing the men were involved in a serious conversation.

"No, that's fine," replied Ross. "I was just leaving." He nodded to Dillon as he turned to leave. "We'll talk more about this later." He closed the door behind him.

****

Kelly stepped out of the government car parked in front of his condo complex, still not believing that they had been released so easily. He fully expected to be picked back up at any moment. He and Greg had said their good-byes in Albuquerque with a mixture of sadness and relief. Walking up the stairs to his condo, Kelly couldn't shake the feeling that he was destined to see Greg again. He unlocked the door and reached to turn on the lights, but nothing happened.

He looked down to see that he was standing on a pile of mail that had been pushed through the mailslot. He shuffled through and found several power company bills and shut-off notices. He checked the date on the most recent notice – it was over 2 months from the time he made the jump. Stunned by the revelation of the amount of time that had passed, he walked into the dark spare bedroom. Inside the closet, he fumbled around for the large black canvas gym bag. He returned to the living room and dumped the contents onto the kitchen table. *It was all there, well over a quarter million dollars.* Stacking the money back in the bag, he stopped short as he picked up a small plastic baggy, inside - the three thumb-drives. Bruce or Greg had made another copy of the process? Did Greg know? Was this the reason Greg did not go crazy when the FBI agent told them that they had found and erased the drives?

An hour later he had separated the mail into two piles - those he needed to keep and those he didn't. He burned those he didn't in the small fireplace. He packed up a few of the clothes he wanted to take, passport, and a laptop, and stepped out into the late afternoon chill. Leaving the keys in the lock, he started for the parking lot and spotted a cab.

"Where to?" asked the driver as Kelly slid into the back seat.

"Dulles airport. I am not in a hurry. Take your time." As he watched the passing traffic, he was surprised how little regret he felt at leaving this place - a place he had considered home. Everything was still as he had left it - people driving and people talking on phones, people working, people wrapped into the lives they led at ever-increasing speeds.

Watching the living go by, Kelly thought of his options. He had never been to Istanbul - never had the time or the money to go. Now he had an abundance of both. Yes, that would be a good move. Besides Israel wasn't too far away, and they had a first class scientific community. It might be a good place to make some new friends.

The cab merged into traffic. Five minutes later Kelly nodded off to sleep. He hadn't been this relaxed in months, well, maybe years.

The black sedan easily blended in with the rest of the commuters in the heavy traffic. It stayed exactly two car-lengths behind the taxi. Inside, serious-minded young men kept a close watch on the car ahead.

People never change, only circumstances.

Chapter 41

Carol met Greg in the baggage claim area, fully expecting to see the man she had not seen in over a year. He stood watching for his bag, seeming deep in thought when she tapped him on his shoulder. After a surprised second of recognition, he hugged her, lifting her off her feet, and kissed her.

He slowly let her slide down until her feet touched the ground and brushed away the silent tears running down her cheek. "I know," he whispered in her ear pulling her close. " I know all about it. You don't have to say a word, baby."

Ten minutes later they were walking through the parking lot on the way to her car, hand in hand. "You want to drive?" she asked smiling.

Greg tossed his bag in the back seat. "No, sweetheart. Take us home. You're in charge."

A young soldier dressed in fatigues sat on one of the outside airport benches and watched as the small blue Toyota pulled out of the airport lot and onto the highway ramp.

He picked up his duffel bag filled with foam rubber for effect and slid into the back seat of the van that had just pulled up to the curb.

"Blue Toyota," he announced to the uniformed driver. "Traffic is light, so you should not have a hard time keeping them in sight."

****

Ross had been in the main floor office all morning going over the new protocol and procedures recently developed by the three research scientists who now sat across from him.

"I'm thinking about putting one of the original jumpers back into rotation," he announced, looking up from the paper work.

"You think that's wise?" questioned one of the men. "Who knows what kind of impact he's already had on the project, much less what he might change if he goes back."

Ross sat back in his chair and lit a much-needed cigarette. "You know, I've heard that argument before, but I am beginning to think that it really does not make that much difference. I mean look at the record. Dillon Conroy was involved in the homicides of six men, all from the 1800's. Those men were killed, taken out of the gene pool, and you know what happened to this reality? Nothing."

The researchers stirred in their chairs, clearly uncomfortable with the assertion. "With all due respect," replied one of the men, "we really don't know the effect yet of that. There's too much we don't know about this field to risk sending back a tourist. It's just too dangerous for everyone."

Ross blew a smoke ring in the air before answering. "There are *many* things to consider. I have copies of this man's pre-employment psych evals taken at the NNSA. Compared to what he took two days ago, the only thing that's the same is his name. He left here almost a year ago as one kind of person and returned completely different. I think we need to think about what kind of responsibility we have to the folks who get caught up in this process."

"Sir," one of the scientists began, "we really do not know yet the long term or even the short term effects of time travel on anything. I think it's extremely dangerous and, quite frankly, reckless."

Ross nodded. "I understand your concerns, and I assure you I have considered them and I have made my decision. Get him ready. He goes back tomorrow."

****

Later that afternoon as Ross sat alone in his office, he recognized that he would have to justify his decision to send Dillon back. His superiors would not appreciate an emotional need on his part to rectify a wrong, not even close. The men he would meet that evening were hard line gatekeepers, the real tough guys in the shadow world, the ones that truly "ran the world".

Ross had just begun to hear about the new plans - some major time travel expeditions with the intent to change history for one purpose or another. They were considering everything - from affecting the Civil War to killing Hitler in WWII, all things that would have an incredible effect on the history and future of Mankind. If these types of plans were allowed to develop, then nothing was out of bounds in Ross's mind. Where would this ability meet reason? Just because you had the ability to change the world didn't mean you had the right to do it.

By the time he boarded the government jet to DC that evening, he had made up his mind. If there really was a benevolent God, he hoped He would understand.

****

Jason awoke having slept harder last night than he ever had. The combination of smoked meat, salmon, and elderberry wine had tasted amazing and had seemed to hammer him flat for a good eight hours.

Rubbing the sleep from his eyes, he sat up and discovered Jedediah already up and packing rifle and gear. "Morning, Jason," he announced in his normal cheerful voice. "I have something I want to talk to you about."

Jason rolled out of the makeshift bed and slowly stood, stretching out the soreness. "What's that?"

Smith handed Jason a rifle and a leather bag of caps and shot. "I've been thinking. It just ain't Christian to have a man running around these parts without a rifle. I have an extra, and I'd like you to take it."

563

Jason took the gun, surprised by its weight. "Ah, Jed, I can't take this. It's yours."

Smith waved him off. "No, I ain't going to argue with ya. I know you're a damn fine shot with that fancy pistol of yours, but when we get downriver, you might be needing something with a little more range on it."

Jason pulled the rifle to his shoulder and snapped the hammer. "Thank you, Jed. I will treasure it. What did you say about downriver?"

Smith sat down on one of the fire pit logs. "That's the second thing I wanted to talk to you about. You see, I have business to attend to in Ohio and, well, I was wondering if you wanted to go along?"

Jason smiled, "Where at in Ohio?"

"Cincinnati."

"Cincinnati, Ohio, no shit?"

Smith laughed. "Not sure about the shit part, friend, but yes, Cincinnati. You know the place?"

Jason pulled on his shirt. "Hell yes, been there many times. Used to fly through there on my wa...." He caught himself too late.

Smith was now watching him closely. "What do you mean you used to fly there? I had no idea you had that kind of talent," he asked with a sideways grin.

"Well, ah, what I meant was that I've gone through there before and the time just flew by." *That was really weak*, he thought.

Smith thought for a moment. "Well, I'm glad to see you're up for the trip," he announced slapping his knees. "I figure we leave as soon as we can, like to get to the trading post before dark."

Jason slipped the cap and powder strap over his shoulder. "Let's go. I'm ready."

Jason liked the way his new rifle felt in his hands as he stepped into the early morning chill. The cool, crisp breeze carried the heavy scent of pine and river water. He recognized that he was feeling more comfortable with his surroundings by the day as he turned onto the now familiar path to the small dock. The sun began to come out just as they finished loading the heavy bundle of pelts, large Elk hides, and food provisions for the trip.

Within minutes of pushing off for their forty-mile paddle down stream, Jason had worked up enough heat and body sweat to take off his fur cape and jacket. The heavily laden canoe glided easily through the water, the strong current driving the boat at a constant speed. Once they made it into the main channel, they sat back, making only small paddle corrections, letting the current do the work.

For Jason, the physical effort felt wonderful. He was using muscles he hadn't used in years. Not even in the army did his body react to the challenges of physical labor as it did now. Senses of smell, taste, and touch had never been more acute.

As he scanned the bank, he caught sight of something to their far left that instantly ran a chill down his back. He couldn't get the words of warning out fast enough. In the blink of an eye, the wonderful peaceful morning on the river turned into sudden terror. A volley of shot from three Indians thundered from the bank, the first ball hitting him in the left shoulder, spinning him out of the canoe and into the fifty-degree water.

The mind-numbing cold sucked the air out of his lungs as he struggled to keep his head above water. He could feel the heavy current tugging at his boots trying to drown him. As he fought through the searing pain and the pull of the river, he saw the now empty canoe drifting on the surface. Smith had vanished.

Another ball whizzed by his ear, smacking the water just behind his head. Fighting desperately to stay afloat, he could see the Indians on the bank shooting and running parallel to his position. The ambushers ran, loaded, and fired in a smooth deadly dance as he continued to flounder.

With a bend in the river coming up fast, the current mercifully pushed him away from his attackers. Just as he was about to go under for what he was sure would be the last time, his feet hit solid rock allowing him to stumble towards the weed-choked bank. Another ball hissed by, blowing a thick divot out of the muddy earth as he scrambled up the bank and tumbled into the tall weeds. As two more balls zipped past, he dropped low, crawling into the woods as whoops and shouts echoed from the far bank. He couldn't believe he was still alive.

Drawing his pistol, he checked his mag, making sure the weapon was clear of water and debris. With survival adrenaline pumping through his veins he rolled to his feet and sprinted deep into the woods. As he ran, he could hear the shouts of pursuit. The men crashing through the bush were closing fast. He dove over a large log and then came up over the top, his weapon at the ready.

Less than ten yards away, an Indian on pounding legs was almost on him as he fired two rounds. The attacker's momentum carried him over the log and into a heap on the other side just as another Indian fired his rifle, the shot blowing a fist sized piece of bark out of the log next to Jason's elbow.

Jason fired two more times, missing the attacker completely. The Indian dropped his rifle and with a blood-curdling scream rushed his position with a short axe raised high.

Jason had just enough time to take a breath before firing three more times, dropping the attacker in midstride. The pain in his left shoulder was now beginning to cramp, slowly paralyzing his entire left side. A third attacker crashed through the woods with an axe in each hand and dove in the direction of Jason's head. Jason ducked, firing four rounds into the man's body as he passed him. The lifeless form tumbled dead into the weeds.

Breathless and in shock, Jason pulled the last full magazine from his belt and loaded the weapon. Barely able to move his left side, he painfully got to his feet. With labored effort he stumbled deeper into the woods, not knowing if there were more in pursuit, the only sound - his own ragged breathing.

567

He could only walk, his left arm hanging loosely at his side. A strange coldness that had nothing to do with the weather started to roll from his thighs to his stomach, making it hard to keep his balance. He was losing blood, a steady trail running off the tips of his fingers. His vision began to narrow. Faces of people he knew flashed through his mind's eye. The sounds of laughter and voices turned him around several times as he staggered through the brush. He began to struggle for his breath and dropped his pistol, not having the strength to hold it any longer. In a small clearing, he swayed gently with his face turned up toward the brilliant blue sky. He fought the urge to lie down, instinctively knowing that he would never get up again if he did. He spit a throaty wad of blood-laced phlegm as a strange humming sound off to his right pushed through the fog of dying. He stumbled forward reaching to steady himself on a nearby tree. The hum became louder as he forced his legs to move. "One more step," he gasped. "One more. C'mon Ranger. Let's go." Nausea became overpowering, the hum nearly deafening as he took a last halting step and fell.

****

Crase was pleased with the control they had developed over the power fluctuations that had plagued the 2nd lab's set-up of the Process. They were now able to slow the modulation from the small yield reactor making the coordinate identification tremendously more efficient. It was truly amazing how fast adjunct information was being gathered and incorporated into the Process.

Crase had just poured his third cup of coffee that morning when a power spike alarm sounded throughout the lab. He dropped his cup into the sink and started running from the small kitchen, knowing the alarm only meant one thing - that something had activated the continuum and was coming through.

He pushed through the doors of the laboratory just as the repaired arrays lit up with a brilliant, million-candle power flash of bluish white light. A tremendous blast of frigid air filled the room as the body of a man flopped out of the light and onto the floor like a lifeless doll.

Shocked by the man's bloody appearance, Crase and several other scientists slowly crept closer to the body. He knelt to search for the man's pulse as several others were already running out the doors shouting for a doctor.

Crase recoiled in recognition when the delirious man moaned and turned his head toward him. It was the face of Jason Chalks, bloody, bruised, and back from the dead.

****

It had been two days since Greg had arrived home, neither speaking of their separate ordeals. The university had called the day before informing him that his classes were scheduled as usual and that they were looking forward to seeing him again. The conversation had been a stilted surreal affair with lots of awkward pauses and contrived friendliness. Someone with real power had put the yips into the shot callers about his return, and they were welcoming him back in the fold of western academia.

As the sun began to set, he sat on his tiny back porch nursing a rum and coke, trying to put some kind of understandable logic to the events of the last several months. Carol was sitting on the couch in the living room in her customary pink bathrobe and fuzzy slippers, concentrating on paper work from her office.

On the surface, things appeared to be normal. They started to drop into their normal routines, sharing meals and light conversation, making love as they always had, showering together and drifting to sleep in the same bed. But they were still not talking about the feelings and impressions of the time they lost together. Though he hadn't found a mark on her body, Greg knew that the woman he loved had been injured severely. In the unguarded moments, he could see the trauma in her eyes. It broke off a piece of his heart every time he did.

Carol seemed just as resolved to maintain her countenance as he was. He had his job back and they were together, and for now that was enough. Just as she was about to walk out onto the back porch, the doorbell rang. Looking through the window she noticed the FED-X truck in the driveway. She answered the door, pulling her robe tight. "Hello?"

"Yes, ma'am, I need a signature for a delivery to Greg Gander."

"I'm his wife. Will that work?"

"Yes, Ma'am, that will be fine. Just sign right there on the X." He handed her a large thick envelope, thanked her, and quickly trotted back to his truck.

Carol read the address and name on the return label and a chill ran up her spine. It was from Chris Kelly in Virginia. The overnight package had the heft and look of something of great importance. She took a deep breath, slowly calming herself down. She walked back through the living room and out onto the porch, dropping the package on Greg's lap. "It's from Kelly," she announced, crossing her arms. She stood trembling under her robe, fighting the urge to cry. Greg looked at the package and then into her eyes. "It's okay, sweetheart. Nothing else is going to bother us. I promise."

For some reason the comment made her angry. "Don't make promises you can't keep," she replied, brushing back a single tear. "I want this to be over, Greg."

He pulled her close. "It's okay, Babe. We're going to be all right." He picked up the envelope. It's your call. Say the word and I'll throw this in the trash."

She lifted her chin and looked into his eyes. "No, I am not going to run from this. Open it."

Greg had an idea of what was in the envelope the minute he saw it. If he were honest with himself, the verbal resolve to be totally done with Taylor's work was just that - verbal. In his heart he was still very interested in discovering more about the Process and all that it entailed.

He opened the envelope, dumping the contents onto the small patio table. Two large bricks of hundred dollar bills and a small plastic baggy containing three thumb-drives spilled out.

Carol pulled away, groaning with pain. Unable to control the tears anymore, she walked back into the house. She could feel the walls caving in, and there wasn't a thing she could do about it. This was far from over.

Chapter 42

Ross had calculated the risk, measured the outcome, and knew that what he was planning to do was the right course of action. His review of what had happened to the men who had gone through the continuum was a mixed bag of tragedy and triumph. Four men had died, one had been severely injured, and all who had survived had been emotionally changed, possibly forever.

It was a small sample of action and consequence, but to Ross it was enough evidence to not let the project continue. There were some things in life that just did not need to be meddled with; time travel was one of them. He knew his actions would be the end of his career and probably his life. But in the deepest part of a badly battered soul he knew the lives of millions depended on a reasoned decision. The potential abuse of the power held by any individual, group, or government was too risky. Taking the responsibility of the past and the future was a power no one had the right to own or manipulate. Sitting in the G4, headed back to Wright Patterson with a decision made, he began to make a plan.

He decided that the only weapon strong enough to destroy the Process was the Titan virus, a monster of a computer virus that had been discovered and confiscated from the Soviet Union in spring of 2013. The virus had been literally designed and launched by a twenty-three-year-old computer hacker who lived in the basement of his mother's house in Estonia.

Before it had been stopped, it caused the Soviet Union stock market to drop 200 points, eradicated the financial records of sixteen million Internet users, and put a sizable dent in the firewalls of half of the Fortune Five Hundred companies in the United States.

After the local counterpart of the Soviet GRU caught the kid, none of his relatives ever saw him again. Rumor had it, he had been taken to the nearest open landfill in handcuffs, dropped in a hole, and a bulldozer used to bury him alive - a hard-edged warning for any other hackers out there who wanted to do the same. It had been classic Soviet street justice. When Ross had asked the lead Estonian investigator why the case had not been allowed to go to trial, the Agent gave him a flat stare and said the case was too complicated for the judges to understand so they had taken care of the problem. As Ross had taken the discs containing the virus program, he thanked his lucky stars he hadn't been born in Estonia.

By the time his plane touched down that evening, he had affirmed in his mind that he would first send Dillon back as he had requested. It would be the second to the last act against his superiors, superiors who were at that very moment deeply involved in plans to change the world.

As he stepped down the plane's short loading deck onto the tarmac, he placed a call. "Crase, Ross here. I want you to collect Dillon from the hospital. Yes, that's right. They'll take care of all that. You just get him to the lab. I'll meet you there in about an hour. Okay, I'll see you then."

He slid into the back seat of the government Lincoln. "Driver, take me by my quarters. I need to pick something up," he commanded from the back seat.

"Yes, sir."

A light rain had been falling all that day, and by the time Ross reached his townhouse, the sky had turned even darker. The air was charged, the ozone heavy in the evening air. It looked like the worst part of the storm was still to come.

As he walked up the stairs, he didn't notice the Lincoln pulling away from the curb behind him. He was focused on the task at hand, going over in his head the steps needed to send Dillon back before destroying the project with the Titan virus. Stepping inside the darkened apartment, he was surprised when the light switch failed. He stepped back onto the landing of the apartment, noticing that the porch light to his and the adjoining two units were also dark. Chalking it up to a building-wide power outage, he turned on his cell phone and used the small light to navigate through the apartment. The files he needed were kept in a large safe secured in the master bedroom closet. Walking through the bedroom door, he knew instantly that something was terribly wrong. Just before impact, he recognized that he was standing on a large thick sheet of clear plastic.

A neck-snapping jolt from the rear slammed him to the floor as the suppressed 45-caliber slug tore through his brain and out his right eye. He never felt the last two rounds that took the entire left side of his head off. The assassin along with two other men quickly wrapped the body and taped it into a manageable bundle. They went about their grisly work in quiet precision, each man attending to the task. The reduced velocity slugs were dug out of the wall along with the two in the floor. The holes were patched and spackled, the room straightened, and the body removed. The safe was then cleaned out along with all the clothing and suitcases that had been stacked in the closet. To any investigator that might come looking for a Mister Ross, the man had simply vanished into thin air. No body - no evidence - no case.

Crase answered the phone on the second ring as he sat in his own car across the street from the townhouse. He had watched as the body of his former boss had been loaded into the dark green van just before they drove away.

"Yes, I'm here. They just left."

"Very good, Mister Crase. As you have witnessed, our organization deals harshly with people who do not cooperate."

Crase did not recognize the man's voice on the phone. "Yes, I see that."

"On the other hand, we assure you that we reward people who are loyal to the organization. I want to personally thank you for helping us in this endeavor. You are now in control of the project. You have, as I assume you will continue, provided a great service to your country.

Crase drew a deep breath, trying to contain his relief and excitement. "Thank you very much, sir. I am honored by this opportunity."

"We are aware that you have some pressing financial concerns, and we want to assure you that you will be well compensated for your efforts, Professor Crase. Please stay focused on keeping the Project up and running. We will be moving quickly in the coming weeks, and we need everything working smoothly – without distraction."

"Yes, sir, I understand completely. Sir, my last instructions from Ross were to pick up Conroy from the hospital and deliver him to the lab. What are your instructions concerning Mister Conroy?"

"Mister Conroy will be released from the hospital tomorrow and will be sent back home to his wife and family," replied the voice. "He is no longer your concern."

Crase could hear the hostile edge in the man's voice and was not about to push any issue that would provoke the organization. He had seen first hand the result of such provocation. He now understood why he had been instructed to drive to Ross's townhouse, stay in his vehicle and not make contact. They wanted him to see what happens to people who try and leave the herd.

577

"I understand, sir. I want to again thank…"

"That will be all for tonight, Professor," interrupted the voice. "We will be in contact. Good night."

The line went dead, leaving Crase suddenly feeling that he had just made a grave mistake. If he stepped out of line with his new taskmasters, it would not be an annoying embarrassing letter of dismissal. He had just made a deal with the devil, and now he would have to live with it. He slowly drove away fighting the urge to throw up. A deal with the devil indeed.

****

The next morning Dillon walked down the steps of the hospital as instructed by the guard. He had eaten the served breakfast, been examined by the doctor, given some non-descript street clothes and been instructed to wait outside on the curb. He now stood looking up into the early morning sunlight, still not sure what the day would hold.

The skies had cleared, and the temperature was in the low sixties as a yellow cab pulled up. "You Conroy?" shouted the driver rolling down his window.

Dillon leaned into the window. "Who's asking?"

"Well, if you're Conroy, I'm your ride to the airport."

"I didn't call a cab."

"Listen, Mister, if you don't want a ride, that's fine with me. The fare is already paid for. If you want to walk, it's up to you. But the airport is a good ten miles away."

578

Dillon thought for a minute before sliding into the back seat of the cab. "Okay, let's go."

The driver turned and handed him an envelope. "I'm supposed to give you this."

Dillon took the package. Inside was a first class ticket to his home in Virginia, a rental car reservation, and five thousand dollars in cash. He unfolded the handwritten note, already sensing what it was going to say.

"Mister Conroy, your request for "Travel" has been denied. We suggest that you return home and join your family. Your employer will be contacted and will reinstate you in your former position. You will have back pay added to your next check. The cash is for expenses. We will expect no further contact." The note was unsigned.

He read the letter several more times trying to see if he had missed something concerning the Government's position. They were washing their hands with everyone involved - plausible denial was the new normal. As far as they were concerned, he needed to go back to his life and forget about the whole affair.

As he looked out onto the early morning traffic his mind drifted off to the wind-swept buttes and the wide-open spaces of Montana. He thought about how free he felt riding along side Coleman on the big grey. The smell of sage and old leather haunted his memory. He ached for the chance to see those open spaces, devoid of freeways, cars and people. After experiencing periods of peace *in the past*, the radio in the cab seemed to be playing at a deafening level, the turbaned driver nodding to the irritating beat of Indian music.

"Hey!" Dillon shouted from the back seat, "You wanna turn that down?"

The driver looked in the rear view mirror. "You don't like Indian music?"

"No, I don't. It's too loud."

The man turned the music down, mumbling something under his breath.

"You say something?" Dillon asked, feeling that familiar flame start to burn.

The driver looked in the rear view mirror, open hostility bright in his eyes. "Americans are not very tolerant."

Dillon leaned up close to the dirty plexi-glass partition. "Hey!" he shouted. "Just pull over and let me out. I'll walk."

The driver aggressively pulled to the side of the road and slid to a stop. "Fine by me. You can walk the next three miles to the airport."

Dillon stepped out of the car on the driver's side and moved up close to the open driver's window. "Hey, asshole," he replied only inches from the man's face, "I ever see you again I'm going to kick all the teeth out of your rag-head face." The man tried to put the car in gear and drive off. Dillon quickly reached in and snatched the keys from the ignition.

"You can't do that you bastard!" the man screamed, frantically reaching for the keys.

Before walking away, Dillon threw the keys as far as he could into the woods. "Looks like we're both walking, dipshit."

He smiled as he listened to the driver scream and holler as he walked away. This kind of behavior was probably going to be his new normal, and if people in this reality didn't accept him for the man he was now, then too bad. The world would just have to deal with it. As John Coleman always said, "No one lives forever. But as long as you're breathing, cover the ground you walk on." He had never really understood what John was trying to say with that phrase just after his gunfight with the Dugans. Now it seemed to fit.

Good thing he wasn't armed today, he thought thumbing a ride, a semi now hissing to a stop. "Where you headed?" shouted the bearded driver. Dillon thought for a moment. Everything had changed for him. There was no way he could go back to his old life, his old reality. He no longer fit the emotional mold of the man he had been. He stepped up onto the running board of the truck. "I'm headed west, trying to get to Deer Lodge, Montana. How far you going?"

The driver smiled, showing a silver front tooth. "Well, climb on in. I'm headed to Bismarck. That will get you in the neighborhood."

As the truck slowly merged into the early morning traffic, Dillon looked into the truck's side mirror and smiled. The taxi cab driver was still on his hands and knees searching the weeds for his car keys, screeching and wailing about the injustice of it all.

The truck driver reached over and punched a CD into the truck stereo, the heavy, familiar guitar riff from the Rolling Stones *Satisfaction* ripped through the cab. "I like the oldies!" shouted the driver smiling. Dillon laughed. It was a fitting song for the way he felt.

He had no real idea where he was going and no set plan on what he would do once he got there. All he really wanted now was time to think and decompress from the last few months. He had money in his pocket, and he was out of the rain. What more could a man want? New normal indeed.

****

After doing some extensive in-depth research, Greg had been able to contact the leader of the Lakota Sioux tribal council out of Pine Ridge. He had been able to speak with one of the elders, John American Horse, an eighty-five-year-old native Lakota Sioux tribe member who had lived his entire life on the hardscrabble edges of the reservation. After several lengthy phone calls, American Horse had finally agreed to meet with him.

It had been three weeks since the money and the thumb drives had arrived at his door, and Carol was still showing signs of trauma and distress whenever their conversations wandered into the area of Taylor, the money or the thumb drives. At her insistence, he had to remove all evidence from their home.

He had told her the night before that he was headed out of town on school-related business, a lie he felt bad about telling. She initially appeared to give him the benefit of the doubt but pounded another nail into the coffin of their floundering marriage when she told him that *if he wanted to go to South Dakota on "Business" then that was fine with her. As far as she was concerned, he could stay there.* Something valuable had been lost between them and there was nothing either one of them could do to bring it back. Greg had no way of knowing she was planning to be gone by the end of the month.

He was a solid hour early for their meeting at the Black Sheep Coffee Shop in Sioux Falls the following day. American Horse assured him that he wouldn't be hard to spot. He would be the only Indian warrior in the place. An hour later, almost to the minute, Greg watched as a small, elderly man who carried himself with an air of pride, followed by two Indians in their mid twenties, pushed open the large glass doors of the coffee shop and stepped inside. The old man wore a straw cowboy hat, crisp white shirt buttoned at the neck secured by a large agate stone bolo tie and moved with the ease of a much younger man. They spotted Greg from across the room immediately. Greg slid out of the booth as the group approached. He extended his hand. "Mister American Horse, it's a pleasure to meet you. Thank you for coming."

The old man shook hands firmly, his deep-set eyes sizing Greg up. "They have very good pie here," he announced solemnly looking around the room. "We should have some."

Greg smiled, pointing him to a seat. "That's a good idea," he replied. He nodded to the two younger men, neither of whom attempted to shake hands but took seats at a nearby table in a stony silence.

"They are my helpers," announced the old man slowly sliding into the booth. "They don't talk much and really don't care for whites."

Greg cleared his throat, shaking off the awkwardness of the meeting. "Sorry to hear that," he replied as he took his seat.

The old man took a long drink of the ice water the waitress had set in front of him. "You have nothing to be sorry about. I am the one who has to put up with their rudeness," he smiled. "What would you like to talk about, Mister Gander? Unlike them, I enjoy talking to the whites."

Greg laughed and took a small notebook out of his coat pocket. "Well, thank you, sir. It's an honor to talk to you. As I said in our last conversation, I am interested in the Ton Ta Tonka ritual and ceremony, the one that's held every year not too far from here." The young waitress with a mouth full of braces stepped up with her pad at the ready. "You gentlemen ready to order?"

"Ah yes" replied Greg. "My friend here says you have great pie, so we would like to have some. What kind do you have?"

The waitress tapped the side of her cheek with the pencil as she started a rapid-fire list of available choices: "Apple, Blackberry, Strawberry, Blueberry, Boysenberry, Raspberry, Lemon, my favorite - Chocolate, Peach, and Key lime, which is to die for."

"Your choice, sir." Greg nodded to the older gentleman. "And whatever those two would like is on me." Greg looked to the two seated nearby.

The girl looked over at the two younger men who were sitting quietly at the other table. "I like your hair," she announced to the men, referring to the shoulder length braids they both wore. She turned back to Greg. "I'd just die to have hair that long," she gushed smiling.

585

"That can be arranged," replied the old man, solemnly taking another drink of water. "I will take strawberry."

Greg had to fight the laughter as he watched the waitress completely miss the inference of the old man's comeback. "Okay, strawberry for you. And what would you like?" she asked Greg while looking over his shoulder at the two younger men.

"Ah, I'll take apple," he replied. She wrote down the order and without looking back, practically skipped to the young men's table.

The old man looked up from his glass and nodded. "We call that kind of girl in our language, Con, chuck aw hela ta nwah."

'What does that mean?" Greg asked.

The old man smiled. "Roughly translated, it means good in the blanket, empty in the head. I had a wife like that many years ago. It was the best time of my life."

"I'll have to write that down," replied Greg laughing.

The old man winked. "There are some things that all men have in common."

Greg was pleasantly surprised by the old man's candor and dry humor. In his past contacts with Native Americans he had found them somewhat stoic, quiet in demeanor and speech. American Horse was the polar opposite - lively, perceptive and bitingly funny.

"Sir, as we talked about on the phone, I'm very interested in the Ton Ta Tonka ritual and ceremony."

The old man thought for a moment. "Why are you so interested in Ton Ta Tonka?"

Greg flipped through several pages in his note pad. "As a teacher and researcher I am very interested in Native American studies. I have actually spent most of my life in this field."

The old man fixed Greg with a steady stare. "And what have you learned after all those years of education?"

Greg could sense that the old Indian was measuring him. He obviously wasn't going to give up what he knew about the ceremony in idle conversation.

"Well, I've learned that a great injustice was committed against the Native American Pop...."

"Please," he interrupted waving his hand. "All white people think they have to apologize for being strong and powerful."

Surprised, Greg looked up from his pad. "You don't think the western migration of the whites pushed you off your lands?"

The old man smiled. "Of course they did. And treaties were broken and many were killed. But as far as an injustice goes, I disagree."

Greg was genuinely surprised by the comment. "I'm not sure I am following your train of thought."

American Horse took another long drink of water before answering. "Many years ago, when my father was a young man, the Lakota were at war with the Pawnee and the Crow people. They were known to kill each other on sight. My father fought many battles using the weapons invented by the white man. The Lakota were the first to get the Henry and Winchester rifles, and many Pawnee and Crow were killed with them." The old man looked over at the two younger Indians and then back at Greg. "If the situation was reversed and the whites were living on the prairie and the Lakota invented the Henry and the Winchester, they would have been used to take possession of the land from the white man."

"I thought the American Indian was basically a peaceful group who only took from the land what they needed to survive?"

The old man smiled. "Then you did not learn much after all those years of study. The Indians have been fighting with other Indians since the beginning of time. There were wars over hunting grounds, water, females, grazing rights, horses."

"So you don't think the white man has taken advantage and suppressed the Indian?"

The old man nodded slowly. "Of course they have, and if the Lakota had that power, they would have done the same thing. It is the nature of all things. The strongest elk in the herd gets to mate with the females. The strongest wolf in the pack is the leader. The strongest trees survive the fire. It has always been this way."

Greg shook his head. "I've never heard a Native American put things that way."

"My father told me once that he would be the happiest man on earth if he could kill all the Crow and Pawnee. Does that sound like a peaceful man to you, Mister Gander?" The old man smiled wide. "I have surprised you?"

Greg laughed. "Yes, sir, you have. It's a very interesting point of view."

The old man nodded to the waitress as she delivered his pie. "The Lakota are still angry at the whites for all the broken promises, but we are more angry at ourselves for letting it happen. Many will not admit it, but we should have fought harder."

Greg studied the old man's face. A life of experience and hardship had been burned deep into every line. "You think that kind of prolonged struggle would have changed the outcome?"

The old man looked up from his pie. "No, but it would have made us feel better about ourselves."

Greg did not know what else to say. Platitudes and apologies for the plight of the American Indian didn't seem appropriate at the moment. He wasn't sure if American Horse's views were wide spread among the Lakota, but he had said them with such conviction that it was clear they were solid in his mind. Maybe that was all that needed to be said.

They finished their pie in silence as the early afternoon lunch crowd started to filter into the café. After his second cup of coffee was poured, the old man spoke up. "Ton Ta Tonka was a warrior sent to the Lakota by the Great Spirit to help fight yellow hair at the Big Horn River."

Greg started writing, not wanting to miss a word of the old man's narrative. "Why did the Sioux call him Ton Ta Tonka?"

"In our language, *Ton Ta Tonka* means 'rushing wind'. It's the sound they heard when the warrior first appeared and disappeared." One of the younger Indians got up from his table and leaned in close to American Horse whispering something. The old man nodded and then motioned for the man to sit back down. "I have to leave. I have a doctor's appointment."

Greg looked up from his notes. "Ah, okay, is there another time we can get together? I really would like to know more about this."

The old man slowly slid out of the booth, straightened his hat, and adjusted his tie while giving Greg a very strange, penetrating look. "I know who you are, Greg Gander," he announced softly.

Confused, Greg shook his head, not sure where the old man was going. "Ah, okay, I ah…"

"You are the Greg Gander that was spoken of by Ton Ta Tonka. According to the legends, he said that someday a Greg Gander would be asking about him. This is why I have agreed to meet with you. You are Greg Gander. It is MY honor to be here."

He reached into his pocket and pulled out a very old-looking small sheet of leather that had been rolled up and tied with a section of horsehair twine. With great care he set it on the table. "That's for you," he announced softly. It's been with my people for over a hundred years."

Greg looked at the old man and then at the two other men who were now standing, staring at him intently. Carefully he untied the string and unfolded the sheet of leather, his head spinning with the possibilities. Printed neatly in red, in what appeared to be a hand written note, was a paragraph of words in English.

September 29,1876. To Greg Gander, I am well and am currently the guest of the Great Lakota somewhere in the Big Horn Mountains of Montana. When you read this I will be long gone, having spent my last days on this earth in blissful happiness among a brave and wonderful people. My adventure has been great and I would not have changed a thing. Hopefully you will look back on your days with joy as well.

Thank you for your friendship, Greg. May time be kind to you as it has been for me. You have all my faith,

Ton Ta Tonka.

Greg sat in stunned silence, reading the note a second time. Taylor had reached out from the past and communicated an astonishing message. The old man nodded while touching Greg's shoulder.

'The ceremony is in three days, Greg Gander. You are invited."

Chapter 43

Greg was on his way back to his hotel from dinner. It had been two days since his meeting with American Horse. He had called home several times, but evidently Carol had stopped answering the phone. He had left six or seven messages, none of which had been returned. It was nearly seven o'clock at night when he pulled into the Days Inn parking lot.

The place was full. He walked through the lobby in deep concentration without noticing the two young men sitting in the small waiting room. If he had been more observant he would have noticed that even though they wore civilian clothing, they carried themselves differently. He would have recognized the military demeanor of those he had dealt with before.

He opened the door with the plastic card and stepped inside. He instantly jumped in shock as he saw the man sitting in the high backed chair on the far side of the room. "Jesus Christ!" he shouted, backing out the door as strong hands from behind pushed him back into the middle of the room.

"Sit down, Greg," the man commanded.

Greg was stunned. "You're dead. I mean, how did you get back? We..."

"Yeah, I know," interrupted Chalks, motioning for Greg to sit down. "I thought you might be surprised. It was one hell of an adventure. You guys dropped me right in the middle of the 1830's with no food, no shelter, nothing but wilderness and a whole lot of Indians that wanted my head on a stick."

Greg slowly sat on the edge of the bed, scarcely believing his eyes. "I am truly sorry for throwing you over the rail that day. I feel bad…"

"Let it go, Greg," interrupted Chalks holding up his left arm. From his shoulder to his wrist, an intricate chrome and black plastic device covered his arm. "I got a little souvenir from the trip. Gives me about three times the strength I used to have in this arm. Course, without it, I can't pick up a paper clip. Pretty cool huh?"

Greg had no idea what Chalks was getting to or if he would still be alive in the next ten minutes. "I, ah, I'm sorry you were injured. Like I said, I really feel bad about the whole thing."

Chalks got out of his chair and walked over to the small black refrigerator. "I see you have a few beers in here. Mind if I have one?"

"Not at all."

Chalks took out one of the bottles, popped the top off and took a long slow drink, emptying half the bottle. "Ahhh, that's good stuff, Greg. You have good taste."

"You didn't come here to drink my beer," replied Greg, feeling the fear starting to grow.

593

With his bottle in hand, Chalks sat back down with a sigh. "No, Greg, I did not come here to drink your beer. I did talk to your wife Carol yesterday though. She's a beautiful woman by the way."

"Is she all right? She hasn't been answering the phone."

Chalks drained the rest of the beer from the bottle and tossed the empty on the bed. "She's fine, Greg. She told me where to find you. Oh yeah, got some bad news on the home front, buddy. Looks like she's packing up her stuff - getting ready to hit the wind would be my guess."

"Get to the point, Chalks. If you're here to kill me, just do it. I'm tired of the games."

Chalks smiled. "I'm not here to kill you, Greg. If I were, you would already be dead. No, I'm just here on a courtesy call. You see the program is in full swing, and everything is about to change. I just wanted to let you know that."

"What do you mean - about to change?"

Chalks shook his head. "Past, present, future, hell, we now have the ability to be God. We can raise the dead, kill millions, mold the world anyway the shot-callers see fit. Pretty amazing stuff, Greg."

"So what happens to me?"

Chalks looked over at the two agents who were standing by the door. "Nothing happens. We are now in the plausible denial business, Greg. We don't have to kill you to keep you quiet. We can control the time before you were even born." He stood up and took another beer out of the refrigerator. "You have a good time at your ceremony tomorrow. Should be fun with all them old Indians."

"You know about the meeting? How did you find out I was invited?"

Chalks held up another bottle. "This one is for the road. You should know by now that we have a pretty good surveillance team." He leaned close to Greg's face. "The only reason you're still alive, pal, is that I asked the heavies to keep you alive."

Greg could see that Chalks was barley under control. "Why, what's the point of all the intimidation?"

Chalks tossed the open bottle over his shoulder. "Because you and that son-of-a-bitch Baker tried to kill me and because I want you to worry for the rest of your life that I may just go back to when your parents started to date and shoot them both through the head." He nodded to the men to open the door. Just before leaving the room, he turned and held up the damaged arm. "I figure I owe you, tough guy. Fair is fair."

Greg watched the men leave, closing the door behind them. It felt as if all the air in the room had been sucked out as the door clicked shut.

He sat staring at the door a good five minutes, trying to get his head around the fact that Chalks had survived being dropped into the continuum and had somehow returned. It was a strange, disconcerting feeling to know he now had a mortal enemy in the world, an enemy just waiting for the chance for revenge.

He lay back on the bed, taking stock of all that had happened since the day he had met Taylor. He had experienced time travel and had some incredible memories. It had cost him his marriage and possibly his job. He had beaten a man to death with his bare hands and had been there when Baker had been killed. Now a shadow government agency run by some crippled assassin who wanted him dead had him under twenty-four-seven surveillance.

Exhausted by the stress, he kicked off his shoes. Unable to relax, he decided that he would try to get through to Carol one more time tomorrow. He would make it easy for her to leave if she really wanted to. He owed her that. He had caused all of this to happen and would tell her so. It wouldn't change her mind, but it would be the right thing to do.

Earlier that day he had been ecstatic about being invited to the Ton Ta Tonka ceremony. Now, after seeing that Chalks was back and very much alive, all the joy and excitement about being invited to the sacred ceremony had been replaced by fear and uncertainty. He asked himself what he would gain by going. How would being there improve his life or provide any tangible insight as to why all this had happened. He drifted off to sleep, his dreams filled with swirling images of unfamiliar faces and distorted whispers in the dark.

****

It was nine-thirty when he pulled into the Custer Battlefield National Park parking lot. He had slept fitfully the night before at the hotel, chalking it up to a bad pizza he had for dinner. The four-grad students should be showing up anytime now, having rented a second car. They had been to the battlefield several times, but this was the first time they would be allowed to dig in a part of the park that had only been briefly examined in 2009.

Needing to kill some time before everyone started showing up, he punched in the numbers on his cell phone, hoping to catch his wife before she headed out to work. "Hey, sweetie. It's me. You headed out the door?" He could hear her car radio playing in the background.

"Yep, headed to work now. Traffic isn't too bad. How was your night?"

"Fine," he lied, not wanting to make her worry that he wasn't taking care of himself. They had been married seven years, and he had never been happier. He loved his job at the university where he had met Carol. She had been an administrative aid, and their meeting had resulted in a whirlwind courtship and marriage four months later. "Look, Babe, gotta go. Just wanted to say good morning and tell you I hope you have a great day."

"All right, love you. Call me when you get out of the field." The line went dead just as he noticed a green government pickup pulling up beside his car. The man looked over in Greg's direction and waved before getting out of the truck.

597

Greg met him on the sidewalk in front of the building. "You been here long?" he asked.

"No, just pulled in. My students should be here any minute. You know, you look very familiar. Have we met someplace?" The familiarity of the man was overwhelming.

The man extended his right hand. "I am Jason, Jason Chalks. Pleased to meet you."

As Chalks reached awkwardly with his right to shake hands, Greg noticed that Chalks wore a complicated looking prostatic on his left arm. Chalks noticed the curious look.

"Had a hunting accident some time ago. I'm part six million dollar man now. Anyway, I'll be your point of contact for your dig. I'm the BLM supervisor for the park and the artifacts. C'mon, let's go inside and get the plot maps for your site."

As Greg followed him into the building, he had the strangest sense of deja vu. In fact, he was sure he had met the man before. He just couldn't remember where or when. He had experienced this feeling in the past but never this intense.

They walked into the expansive hall and through a set of large doors to the administrative offices.

Entering a small, cluttered office, Chalks snapped on the light and moved in behind his desk that was stacked with papers and folders. "Just moved in here last week. Still unpacking. Sorry for the mess. Have a seat."

Greg pulled up a folding metal chair from the corner of the room. "So where were you stationed before you came here?"

Chalks sat down behind his desk with a sigh. "Well, I worked out of the DC headquarters for five years."

"You miss the big city?"

"Not much. Don't miss the traffic and the high cost of living. Anyway when this post became available, I put in for it and got it. I like the landscape. The people are great out here."

"You know, I hope this doesn't sound strange, but I am almost sure we have met before. I just can't shake the feeling."

Chalks sat back in his chair leveling a steady gaze. "Maybe we passed in an airport or something. Hell, we might have met in a past life or something."

Although it was a strange comment, it oddly seemed to have a pronounced color of truth to it. "Maybe," he replied, suddenly feeling uncomfortable with the slant of the conversation. "Ah, you said you have some grid maps."

Chalks nodded, "Yep, sure do." He rifled through the stacks of papers on his desk finally coming up with the folder. "Here you go," he announced, handing the file over. "The areas marked in blue are the areas you and your team can dig in. We will have a couple of our folks out there with you while you are on site. They won't get in your way; they just have to be there by law."

Greg checked the map, "Looks good. I'll get my kids ready to go. With your permission we'll go ahead and drive over there."

As he was about to leave, Chalks spoke up. "Hey, Greg."

"Yes?"

"I was just wondering how you slept last night?"

"Excuse me, ah, that's kind of an odd question."

Chalks moved out from behind the desk and leaned close. "We changed everything."

The hair on the back of Greg's neck was now standing straight out. "I, I don't know what you're talking about."

Chalks held the awkward pause, staring at him intently. "How's Carol this time around?"

Greg felt as if he were about to pass out. "I, I, how do you know my wife? Who are you anyway?"

Chalks smiled without humor. "You have yourself a good dig here, Professor." He brushed past in the doorway. "Like I said, we could have known each other in another life. Have a good day there, Greg. I'll be seeing you." He made a gun sign with his fingers, dropping his thumb as if shooting. He turned and walked away, leaving Greg standing alone in the hallway.

"Hey!" shouted Greg feeling sick. "Who are you? Who are you? He ran down the hallway and out through the doors to the main exhibit hall. He could already see Chalk's pickup leaving the parking lot through the large glass windows at the front of the building.

He ran out onto the sidewalk shouting, "Hey, stop! Who the hell are you? Stop!" He trotted out into the empty parking lot as the truck drove out of sight.

"Sir, can I help you? Are you okay?" Greg turned to the voice and saw an armed park ranger wearing the customary round ranger hat walking toward him. "Sir, do you need some kind of assistance?"

Greg pointed down the road. "Did you see that BLM truck that was just here?"

The Ranger stepped closer, his hand on his holstered weapon. "No, sir, I didn't. Is there something I can help you with?"

Greg looked around the parking lot and then back to the Ranger. "Ah, well, do you know all the staff who work here?"

"Yes, sir, been here five years."

"Do you know a BLM guy by the name of Jason Chalks?"

The officer frowned thinking. "No, Nobody from BLM is on staff here. Are you sure that's the correct name?"

Greg felt as if he were about to pass out. "Ah, I guess I'm mistaken. I'm okay. I think I'll go sit down for a bit."

"You do that, sir. If you need any assistance, just flag me down. I'm the Ranger supervisor here." The officer turned and started walking away.

"Officer," he called after the man, "you are aware that my team and I are conducting a dig here this week?"

The Ranger opened the door of his patrol unit and slid inside. He looked over at Greg and tipped his hat slightly. "You have a good day, Professor Gander. Try not to get too much sun."

Greg's heart felt as if it were about to pound out of his chest. "How do you know my name? I didn't tell you my name!" he shouted.

The officer smiled as he started the car. He backed out of the parking spot and slowly drove along Greg's standing position. "Well, Professor, like you were told, we changed everything. Maybe you'll get it right this time." He pointed his finger in the same way as Chalks had done while dropping his thumb and winking. "Take care, Greg. Watch out for that pretty wife of yours." He drove away, leaving Greg in stunned silence. High overhead a red tail hawk circled the rolling landscape, looking for field mice and rabbits. He had been riding the thermals all morning. Instinctively the bird had stayed clear of the odd shimmer of light that now seemed to dance and weave it's way in and around the grass-covered hills and coolies. It moved to it's own rhythm, danced to a music only it could hear.

Off to the east, a thick, warm wind blew in, kicking up the alkali in a large swirling dust devil. It slowly plowed along the hilltops pulling itself into a tight white column of dust a hundred feet high. The land of the Lakota, the Pawnee, and the Crow would always have the magic. The power of the greasy grass and the brown water river would never die. Only the men who tried to control it would be turned to dust. It would always be that way.

THE END

ABOUT THE AUTHOR

William Clark is a retired international security consultant, working in many of the most interesting places of the world, including Kosovo, Trinidad, Nigeria, Iraq, and Congo.

Bill has long held a fascination in the Battle of the Little Big Horn and made multiple trips to the area in research. He wrote many books in his earlier years including *AN HONORABLE ENDEAVOR,* and *DRAGOONS/ SOUND OF SABERS* but saved this novel for his retirement. Like a good wine, he allowed the characters to develop over a long period of time.

Bill lives in Coloma, Michigan, a small town close to Lake Michigan, with his wife and dogs. He enjoys sculpting and writing.

ACKNOWLEGEMENTS

Special acknowledgement is made to Linda Clark and Terri Clark. Their support and editing/formatting talents have been invaluable.

Made in the USA
Columbia, SC
01 April 2021